Perfidious Albion

by the same author

Idiopathy

Perfidious Albion

SAM BYERS

FABER & FABER

First published in 2018
by Faber & Faber Limited
Bloomsbury House
74–77 Great Russell Street
London WC1B 3DA

Typeset by Faber & Faber Limited
Printed and bound in the UK by CPI Group (UK) Ltd, Croydon CRO 4YY

A CIP record for this book
is available from the British Library

ISBN 978–0–571–33629–6

 Supported using public funding by

**ARTS COUNCIL
ENGLAND**

FSC
www.fsc.org
MIX
Paper from
responsible sources
FSC® C020471

2 4 6 8 10 9 7 5 3 1

Do not forget that ideas are also weapons.

— Subcomandante Marcos

0000

I think . . .' said Robert, touching the tip of his forefinger momentarily to his lips and frowning down at the floor. 'I think I just reached a point where I was like, if it's not *now*, then I'm not *interested*. You know?'

Jacques DeCoverley, to whom Robert was speaking, absorbed this statement like a particularly complex scent he had just detected on the air, angling his head and eyes slightly upwards and flaring his nostrils in appreciation. He had a way of manufacturing a reflective smile, as if he'd been ambushed by yet another sadness or paradox it remained his nobly silent burden to shoulder.

'Who wants to write something that's already yesterday?' he said, arching a copious eyebrow and peeling away a lock of tightly curled hair that had adhered to the patina of sweat on his forehead.

Jess watched them – their little dance, their little chess match of self-consciousness – feeling screened-off, remote.

'But then . . .' said Robert. 'What *isn't* yesterday these days?'

The smile slithered back across DeCoverley's lips as he took a moment to ponder just how much was yesterday right now.

'Indeed,' he said, taking a ruminative sip of his Negroni and slicking a finger across his glossy brow. 'These are post-present times.'

Jess, standing slightly behind DeCoverley's elbow and out of his sightline, tried to catch Robert's eye so she could make a face. It struck her that once, in a different time of their lives, he would already have been looking, attendant to her expression. Indeed, they had met at a function not dissimilar to this one. Then, as

3

some man she could no longer name, inflated by the imagined importance of his own opinions, had not once but three times interrupted her, Robert had cut across him, angling his shoulder to communicate the man's irrelevance, and said, with a conspiratorial glint in his eye, *But what do you think . . . Jess, isn't it?* Now, his need to let her know he was listening had dwindled. When he did glance her way, it was fleeting, awkward, and seemed to suggest her mockery was misjudged.

She looked down at her drink. When she raised her gaze again, DeCoverley had slid an arm round Robert's shoulders, and was leading him away.

'You know,' Jess heard DeCoverley say as they left, 'we love what you're doing at the moment, Robert. This stuff about the estate. So vital. So *now*.'

A bandoned, yet unwilling to appear so, Jess circled. The room, it seemed, was full of men triangulating. They used directions to establish a base of conversation, as if how they'd arrived communicated something about who they were. Somewhere off to her left, someone was saying, 'We came the back way. B-Three-One-Four and get off at Cockwell. Saves you the argy-bargy at the double roundabout.' To her right, someone was saying, 'I've said it before and I'll say it again: until they make it dual carriageway I'd rather stick pins in my eyes.'

It was an atavistic conversation. Once, the sharing of routes had allowed a gently competitive comparison of cunning. Now, it masked a drabber reality. None of these men had made any decisions about their travel at all. Instead, they had simply punched a postcode into their Sat-Nav. Their active involvement was no longer needed, yet somehow the pride remained.

The work of locating themselves complete, the business of defining themselves could begin. Loaded with coders who'd flocked to staff the tech park and artsy North London refugees fleeing the cash-haemorrhage of the city, Edmundsbury increasingly existed in the collapsed distinction between creativity and commerce, and so was awash with people determinedly codifying their output.

'Well obviously my work is very much about challenging dominant discourses of ability and success and what constitutes quote unquote *good* art, so I work almost exclusively in crayon.'

'I just felt I wanted to comment overtly on the artistic scene and creative praxis in general via a medium that was both performative and organic, so I've been working with a variety of types of mud and various different walls and just seeing if I can, by literally *throwing* the mud at the wall . . .'

Across the room, Jacques DeCoverley had kettled a gaggle of single women into a corner and was holding forth on the radical opportunities for situationist protest afforded by sex in a lay-by. Beside him, Robert nodded and laughed on cue.

DeCoverley was a blow-in from the city, recently resettled and now flushed with the glow of post-London life. In terms of aspiration, leaving London was the new moving to London. You slogged it out, made a name for yourself, then decamped to the sticks and devoted yourself to trashing city life on Twitter while roaming the fields in pursuit of your tweedy ideals. For a long time, DeCoverley had described himself as a street philosopher. Unlike the usual use of the term, this had nothing to do with his non-academic outsider status. Instead, it referred to the fact that his work was literally about streets. He'd done a whole book on pavements (*Under The Beach: The Pavement!*): their cultural history, their, as he liked to put it, physically marginal yet psychogeographically central status. His follow-up, an oral history of pedestrianisation called *No Cars Go*, had proved rather less successful. Now that he was almost certainly no longer able to maintain the illusion of highly paid success in London, he was reinventing himself as a deep-thinking rural gentleman for the twenty-first century, wearing wellington boots indoors and waxing lyrical about a 'lost' England comprised entirely of hedgerows and loam.

Of course, DeCoverley couldn't just quit the city and be quiet. He had to dress up his departure as a statement. Having laboured in interviews to make the case that something 'authentic' was emerging from parts of England he genuinely seemed to think had not existed before he started wandering about in them, he was now under pressure to ensure reality aligned with his descriptions. Hence his parties, which he referred to as 'salons', and to which he invited everyone he could think of – local, Londoner, and other – in a bid to establish something of which he could reasonably describe himself as the centre.

Deeply cynical though Jess might have been about DeCoverley's artful manipulation of his own surroundings and status, she had to admit these little soirées had grown in notability since the first one a few months ago. Tonight, DeCoverley had outdone himself on the buzz front by securing the attendance of several members of Rogue Statement, an anonymous collective of theorist poseurs who Jess and her friend Deepa referred to as the Theory Dudes. Their stated aim was, as they put it, to decode the encoded fascism of everyday life. Their first groundbreaking and extraordinarily well-received polemic had been a ferocious exposé of the fascism of iced buns. After that, it was egg-white omelettes. Soon they were finding fascism everywhere: in sofas, marathons, dog shows, vinyl flooring, socks.

'Look,' one of the Theory Dudes had told her earlier that evening, when she'd asked him why he seemingly felt more responsibility to decry the fascism of falafel wraps and justified margins than he did the street-level violence and creeping intimidation that was an increasingly common feature of what some were already calling the New England, 'violence is upsetting. It's emotive. But it's just a *symptom*, yeah?'

Maybe it was, Jess thought, but so were so many other things, and yet still the question of what they were symptoms *of* remained unanswered.

'But anyway,' Jess heard Robert saying as she dallied at the bar, 'enough about me. How goes it with you, DeCoverley?'

'Oh, you know,' said DeCoverley, '*desperately* trying to work but *constantly* torn away by other requests. I'm rapidly coming to the conclusion that the best thing I could do for my career right now would be to write something wildly unsuccessful. I *pine* for obscurity. Don't you?'

'Constantly,' said Robert.

'The trouble is, I just can't do it. It's a curse, being this tapped in to the culture. I'm just *out there* all the time, like a dowsing rod. *Quivering.*'

He squinted, momentarily pained by his own significance.

'I guess that's what we sign up for,' said Robert, using his slowest, most sincere nod, reserved exclusively, Jess knew, for his hastiest, least sincere statements.

'That's one way of looking at it,' said DeCoverley, 'but for me personally there was never any choice.'

'You mean, because you're not qualified for anything else?' said Jess innocently, breezing by and unable to bite her tongue.

'Ah,' said DeCoverley to Robert, 'here's your lovely girlfriend. No, I meant because I have nothing but philosophy coursing through my veins. Because I cannot *but* be anything other than I am.'

'Exactly,' said Robert, narrowing his eyes at Jess before clumsily adjusting the subject. 'Do we know if Byron is coming?'

'Stroud?' DeCoverley beamed at being asked, then savoured the fact that he was in the know enough to be able to answer. 'Couldn't make it, sadly.'

Byron Stroud was currently the man you needed to know if you wanted to give the impression of knowing the right people. His rise through the opinion-sphere, occasioned largely by the fact that he wrote almost exclusively about the opinion-sphere and so produced articles that were both fallen upon and fawned over by their subjects, had been rapid. This being the age of the over-exposed personality,

reclusive tendencies were invariably interpreted as either artistic statements or shrewd attempts at personal branding, so the fact that Stroud
had thus far declined all invitations only added to his aura. No-one
went quite so far as to claim to have met him, but they all, when talking about him, affected an air of first-name familiarity that suggested
they *might* have met him. It was a social signifier to which Robert had
become particularly sensitive, meaning he would now, Jess thought,
be trying to work out exactly what DeCoverley meant by Stroud not
being able to make it. Had DeCoverley *heard* from Stroud? Had he
heard from someone else who had heard from Stroud? Or had everyone, like Robert, emailed Stroud and received nothing in response?

'Couldn't?' said Robert. 'Or didn't want to?'

'Oh,' said DeCoverley vaguely, 'I'm not sure Byron would even
acknowledge that demarcation.'

Jess popped to the toilet to tweet. Back in the room, an assort-
ment of indistinct men – bearded and earnest and flushed with
credentials – talked at her or for her, but never quite to her.

'Of course,' she heard someone say, 'it's getting to the point where
marriage is the last truly radical act.'

This was a recurrent theme. At every party a new last radical act.
Faced with a future so rapid in its occurrence and uncertain in its
shape, people clung to familiarity. Fearful of appearing retrograde,
they refashioned their nostalgia as subversion. Home ownership
was the last truly radical act. Monogamy was the last truly radical
act. Parenting was the last truly radical act. *Not wanting it all* was
the last truly radical act. Everything else, it seemed, was dead.

'I mean, time was when people actually had conversations.
Remember that?' someone brayed at Jess through a mouthful of
bar snacks.

'Exactly right,' said his wingman. 'Conversation's dead.'

She found Deepa in her habitual darkened corner, idly stirring a drink with her straw and wearing an expression that suggested she was amusing herself in ways that couldn't safely be shared.

'Oh thank God,' said Deepa. 'I was starting to think I might have to mingle.'

'I've mingled,' said Jess. 'Upshot is: don't mingle.'

They leaned side by side against the wall, Jess enjoying the brief coolness of the faux wood panelling before the heat of her back rendered it as sweaty as everything else.

'Saw you dallying with the Theory Dudes,' said Deepa, tilting her chin towards the huddle of serious young men in the middle of the room. 'Still working on a cure for fascism?'

'I literally overheard one of them talking about fascist molecules,' said Jess.

'Robert seems to be enjoying himself.'

'Nice that you no longer even pretend to like my partner.'

'He's got enough people pretending to like him,' said Deepa. 'Why get in the way?'

Jess laughed. They swapped drinks without saying anything. It was something they did. In restaurants they ate each other's food.

'I feel like we haven't run people down enough,' said Jess, taking out her phone. 'We're shirking our responsibilities.'

Deepa eyed Jess's phone. 'Someone's breaking their own rules,' she said.

'I have location disabled.'

Deepa sipped Jess's drink and looked out across the party.

'Riddle me this,' she said as Jess hit send, then locked and pocketed her phone. 'If you start enjoying something you used to only find interesting, is it still interesting?'

'You're saying enjoyment erases interest?'

'I'm saying that saying you're interested in something can be a pretty good way of masking the fact that you're enjoying it, and

9

that enjoying it too much calls into question the extent to which you're merely interested in it.'

'Oh come on. You don't enjoy your work?'

'Not so much that it stops being work.'

'Is that what's bothering you? You think my work's too enjoyable?'

'I think your work might no longer be work.'

They watched as, across the room, Jacques DeCoverley checked his phone, swore under his breath, then pasted his smile back on for a passing twenty-something.

'OK,' said Deepa. 'I can see how that might be kind of satisfying.'

By midnight, the evening was losing pace. The energy of these things was always front-ended. People arrived with opinions they wanted to disgorge. Once they'd done so, they succumbed to a collective petite mort. Jess prided herself on never going over to Robert and letting it be known she was ready to leave. The dependency of such moments unsettled her.

He joined her just as she was about to hold forth to Lionel Groves, a tall, greying man with jaw-length hair and a rough beard about whom everyone seemed determined to use the word *rugged*. After a progressively unsuccessful intellectual career based entirely on scathingly dismantling the work of his peers, Groves had reinvented himself as an *international man of feeling*. His most recent book was an alphabetically arranged series of micro-essays on things that made him cry. Having 'done' tears he was now 'doing' laughter, and had published a series of 'provocations' about the importance of humour in the face of oppression and good grace in the face of injustice. His Twitter feed was a carefully curated gallery of nauseating bromides like, *It's not always what we feel that's important; it's the very fact that we feel at all.* Dumbstruck by his own capacity for emotion, he spoke at all times as if he were the first man on earth to experience a feeling. Apparently affirming this delusion, people huddled round him at parties and used him as a litmus test for what they should be feeling themselves. It was, Jess thought, the age of beatified masculine emotion. Everywhere you looked, men were sweeping up awards for feeling things.

'Of course, Palestine is such a *sad* situation,' he was saying. 'Don't you think? I find it hard even to watch on television now because it just makes me so *sad*.'

'What about the environment?' someone said. 'Does that make you angry?'

'Fearful,' said Groves. 'And sad, of course. But laughter does give one such *hope*, I find.'

'How do you feel about how you feel?' said Jess. 'When you feel sad, do you also feel a little bit proud?'

He turned to her slowly. He had a way of smiling in the face of hostility that Jess found enraging.

'Well hello,' he said. 'You're Robert Townsend's girlfriend, aren't you?'

She looked at Groves – his practised sadness, his calibrated roughness – and felt only a familiar, disenchanted rage of the sort that Groves would almost certainly have advised her to laugh off.

She sucked in air, primed for a withering response, only to be interrupted.

'I'm Robert,' said Robert, leaning across Jess and shaking Groves's hand. 'I see you've met my girlfriend.'

'Adorable,' said Groves. 'Such energy.'

'Misplaced at times but never anything other than well meant,' said Robert, placing a hand on Jess's back and shooting her a quick sideways glance. She thought again of that moment they'd met, the tingling thrill of his canny, collaborative attention. Now she was the one being managed, the speaker to whom he pointedly turned his shoulder.

She toyed, briefly, with the idea of some kind of retort. She was not averse to public conflict. Indeed, there were times when she wondered if, as their ability to constructively argue in private declined, public friction might be one of their last shared sources of heat. But her energy, like that of the room, had evaporated.

'Pity not to see Byron here,' said Groves.

'Ah yes,' said Robert. 'He couldn't make it, unfortunately.'

'Couldn't?' said Groves. 'Or wouldn't?'

'Well,' said Robert, 'is that a demarcation Byron would even recognise?'

'Quite so,' said Groves, slightly icily.

Robert turned to Jess, rubbed her shoulder awkwardly. 'How are you bearing up, hon?' he said. 'Can you *stand* another half an hour or are you itching to get away?'

His attentiveness, she felt, was bait for the attention of others. She was about to say she wasn't in a rush, despite being desperate to go, so that he'd have to make more of a show of wanting to leave, despite wanting to stay, when somewhere behind her, on the other side of the room, she became aware of movement. She saw Robert's eyes slide sideways from hers, his gaze move over her shoulder to whatever it was that was happening. She heard someone say, 'Thank you, thank you, great to see so many of you here,' and turned to see a small, pale man making his way to the front of the room clutching a sheaf of papers.

It wasn't an entirely unusual occurrence. The relentless social and professional injunction to self-publicise meant the general public had to be perpetually alert to the possibility of what had come to be called guerrilla readings. Once, well-meaning literary evenings had offered a safe and trusting environment in which writers could indulge their oratory urges, but public charity had proved finite. Now, traumatically released back into the care of the community, a generation of authors hooked on the salon's spotlight were forced to forage for attention where they could.

People began to boo.

'Oh for fuck's sake,' said Robert. 'Seriously. Enough of this shit now.'

'Get off,' someone called.

The man found a patch of space towards the front of the room. There was, Jess thought, something amiss with his face. The more she looked, the less certain she became that it even *was* a him. The clothes read male, as did the hair and the voice, but the features were decidedly androgynous.

'May third,' said the man. 'Twelve seventeen a.m. WWW dot teen sluts dot com. Who am I?'

He was wearing a white shirt, cream chinos, and a loosely knotted paisley tie. As Jess watched him speak, the issues with his face became more apparent. His cheeks and lips moved in a manner at odds with the words he was making. His forehead remained motionless, as did the skin around his eyes.

'May seventh,' he went on. 'Eleven thirty-six p.m. WWW dot balls deep in burkha dot com. Who am I?'

Tolerance for these unsolicited readings had reached rock bottom. People turned hostile quickly, shouting for the man to leave. Someone asked him who he was, as if his ultimate crime was to be unknown.

'May thirteenth,' he shouted. 'Nine oh seven a.m. Email. *Dearest. I have to be quick. She'll be home soon . . .* Who am I?'

Jess felt men to her left and right moving towards the reader, flanking him. Others followed. Someone said, 'That's enough,' and someone else said, 'Not here and not tonight.' The would-be reader tried to raise his voice, stepped back to avoid those who were now reaching out towards him. Someone had a hold of his shirt. He shouted, 'Let go of me,' several times, and lashed out slightly hopelessly at his nearest attacker before being knocked to the floor. Then he was up off the floor, transported doorwards by his legs and arms. In his fist was a sheaf of flyers: A5, sparsely printed, black and white. Writhing in the grip of his restrainers, he tossed the flyers upwards in a fluttering cloud. As they landed, Jess could read what was printed in the centre of the otherwise blank page.

What Don't You Want To Share?
First Disruption. The Square. Friday. 8pm.
WWW.WEAREYOURFACE.COM

As he passed, Jess was able to see his face, and what was wrong with it became clear. When he blinked, his eyelids were set back, recessed. He seemed to have two sets of lips, one behind the other. His face wasn't his face at all, she realised, but an eerily life-like rubber mask covering the whole of his head. Even his hair was synthetic.

'What don't you want to share?' he called. As he was carried round the corner, out of sight, he said it again, louder. '*What don't you want to share?*'

An awkward silence followed: the sound of mass drink-sipping and throat-clearing, a moment of collective and individual readjustment.

'What *was* that?' someone said.

There were shrugs.

'Welcome,' someone else said, 'to the post-meaning world.'

The man beside him nodded sagely.

'Meaning's dead,' he said.

———

'I mean, was it some kind of art thing? Some kind of satire?'

They drove home through the warm dark of early summer, Jess at the wheel, the party receding behind them like a drained wave.

'He was wearing . . . What was he wearing?' continued Robert. 'Some kind of mask?'

'But a mask that looked like a face.' Jess gave a little shudder. 'Creepy.'

'Whose face? Was it a famous face?'

'Not one I've ever seen.'

'Because I could understand it, maybe, if it was a famous face.'

'Maybe he's famous underneath the mask.'

'Maybe,' said Robert, 'it was Byron bloody Stroud.'

Outside, the East Anglian flatland unfolded blankly, smears of hedgerow streaking the space between car and field. How long had they been here, away from the city? Jess was still disoriented by the unbroken blackness. She cracked the window, tilted her face to the sped-up air that entered.

'Please don't smoke in the car, Jess.'

'Do I look like I'm smoking?'

'You look like you're thinking about smoking.'

Ahead, as they rounded a bend, the sulphurous glow of The Arbor split the dark, its hot white security lights throwing spark-like reflections off the tensile fencing and angled glass. Over the gate, the name of the multinational tech company that had made its home here was gently spotlit in determined sans-serif: *Green*. In places, thick trees obscured the shattered light, giving it the appearance of either stars or pin-pricked, glowing data points.

'We've become one of those plate-glass couples,' she said.

'Meaning what?'

'Meaning people see right through us.'

'I take it you didn't particularly enjoy the thing,' said Robert.

'When do I ever?'

'What are we going to do? Stay home?'

'Those are our choices? Go to something we don't like or stay home?'

'Effectively, yes.'

'And they say romance is dead.'

'Everything's dead.'

'That is such bullshit. That's exactly why I hate these things. You just come away spouting the same posturing nihilistic claptrap as everyone else.'

They pulled into the driveway in silence. Once, Jess would have experienced these lapses in dialogue with a hair-shirt discomfort.

She would, many times, have ended up saying something conciliatory simply for the sake of saying something. But she'd come to realise this was merely playing into Robert's hands. His conversation was like his affection: he used it to get what he wanted, and when that didn't work he weaponised its withdrawal.

She locked the front door behind them and wandered through to the kitchen for a drink of water, letting the tap run for a few seconds before filling a glass. Her Robert-sense alerted her to his presence behind her. Even without looking at him she could picture his posture: slightly hunched, hands in his pockets. They each knew their post-tension choreography. He became tentative, uncertain. She was more poised, waiting for him to ease things.

She was still sipping the water when she detected the inevitable creep of his hand, holding her, pulling her towards him.

'I hate it when we argue,' he said into her ear.

'Me too,' she said, patting his hand but not turning round.

'Sorry for being a prick,' he said. She could feel his smile against her flesh: placatory, slightly dismissive. He wanted, she knew, for her to turn around, kiss him, tell him he wasn't a prick. Instead, she carried on looking ahead, turning the now-empty glass in her hand.

'It's fine,' she said.

He drew a breath and held it. She waited for his response. She felt as if she could hear him thinking, weighing potential retorts.

'Love you,' he said.

It was as close as they got, these days, to an argument. A sharp word or gesture; a careful, fearful retreat.

'Love you too,' she said.

0001

'You're nobody until somebody hates you, Robert. And now someone really hates you, I think it's fair to say you're finally really somebody, no?'

'But *why* does she hate me? What have I done?'

Robert's morning had begun, after the usual ritual of coffee and a quick scroll through the bile-filled comments under his latest piece, with a pep talk from Silas.

'You're ruffling feathers,' said Blandford. 'You're writing about what's *real*. Of course people are going to hate you.'

As he was saying *real*, Silas had leaned enthusiastically close to his webcam, causing his face – self-consciously unshaven and set into a rictus of gurning enthusiasm – to loom so impossibly large on Robert's computer screen that Robert was forced to minimise the window to a small square in the corner.

'Right.'

'It's like those fish. You know, the ones that are so massive they're covered in smaller, crapper fish.'

'Sucker fish.'

'Sucker fish. Yeah. This Julia whatever she's called, she's a sucker fish.'

'Then shouldn't she be more sycophantic? Like, to follow your analogy through, shouldn't she be sucking up to me?'

'No-one sucks up any more. It backfires. If she sucks up to you, someone's going to start hating on her for sucking up to you, and you know what? That someone is probably going to get attention for it.

So better to get in there early with some pre-emptive hatred and get credit for that. Anyway, hatred equals hate-clicks, so, you know, win.'

'But I don't want hate-clicks. I want people to like what I'm doing.'

'Like, dislike,' said Silas. 'What's the difference?'

Robert took a moment to process the fine line this question walked between inadvertent profundity and total vapidity – the exact fine line, of course, that Silas's website – *The Command Line* – had staked its success on exploiting.

He scrolled below the line for perhaps the fifth or sixth time this morning. Julia Benjamin – 'JuBenja' – had commented at her usual length and wild pitch, bemoaning 'not so much what Townsend stands for as what his ideals so conveniently obscure: his baffled, ageing technophobia; his dewy-eyed romanticisation of a rose-tinted working class; and his determination, through all the usual smug, tub-thumping, sub-Hitchens, mansplainer posturing, to make himself the heart and focus of every cause. Townsend doesn't care about the people of the Larchwood, he cares about the extent to which he's *seen* to care about the people of the Larchwood, and so his every self-congratulatory intervention reads less like the *cri de coeur* he so clearly wants it to be and more like the shameless exercise in self-promotion and personal glorification it really is.'

'It's a bloodbath, Silas.'

'Well, let it get bloody, that's my motto. She's half-responsible for making this thing the thing that it is.'

'What do you mean she's half-responsible?'

'She's pulling traffic. People are now clicking on your articles and scrolling straight to the comments section to see what she's written.'

Robert sank back in his chair as this profoundly depressing piece of news took up residence along the sciatic nerve of his psyche.

'Anyway,' Silas said. 'Moving on. About this estate.'

'The Larchwood,' said Robert, trying to ignore the fact that Silas had moved on without agreeing to do anything about the fact that Robert's reputation, talent, and manhood were being daily dragged through the mud. The way Silas referred to the Larchwood only as *the estate* bothered him. As if the fact of it being an estate was all you needed to know.

'People are loving this estate, Robert. They're loving its plight. All this . . . What's the word you use?'

'Decanting.'

'Decanting. Right. This estate has become an emblem. Of what, who knows, but it's up there. It's like the bat signal. You've put this estate up there in the sky and everyone's looking and everyone's feeling like it means something. Yeah?'

'Well, I hope so,' said Robert.

'But here's the thing: it's kind of capital-J journalism, you know?'

Robert paused, briefly thrown by the fact that Silas had somehow managed to deploy this phrase as a criticism.

'Well I am a journalist,' he said.

'Right,' said Silas. 'Sure. I mean, absolutely. It's just that, this is *The Command Line*, you know?'

'Meaning what?'

'Meaning, what's our angle? We can't just go out there and take everyone else's angle, Rob. The existing angle, the obvious angle, is really no angle at all. Do you see what I'm saying?'

'People are being forced out of their homes so a private corporation can erect some kind of mega-complex. That's the angle, Silas.'

'Right, and that's great. I mean, it's not great, obviously. But it's great you're so . . . right-on about it. And, hey, gentrification, right? People are loving gentrification right now. All the gentrifiers are guilt-reading pieces about gentrification like it's going out of fashion, which, conveniently, it isn't. So market-wise you're like completely dead on. But what I'm saying is: decanting, social housing, mega-corporation, all of that, great. But is it edgy, Rob? Is it *now*?'

'I've actually been congratulated on just how now it is, Silas.'

'But could it be more now? That's what I'm thinking.'

What, Robert wondered, could be more now than now?

'Well it's *happening* now.'

'But we could take so much more of a now angle, don't you think?'

'Meaning what?'

'Meaning all this technology stuff. This, what do you call it?'

'Ubiquitous technology.'

'Ubiquitous technology. Right. The whole point of this new project is that it's going to be some kind of networked solution, right? What I'm saying is, hang on, that's kind of cool. Couldn't we do more with that?'

Robert took a long, steadying breath.

'We've had this conversation, Silas. I'm not writing some trendy fucking tech piece, OK? I'm writing about *people*. This estate, this story, this whole thing, it's about *people*. People are being kicked out of their homes. People are being lied to. People are being intimidated. Are you telling me people don't want to read about—'

'They want to read about things that are cool, funny, or evil. That's the holy trinity.'

'Have you read the proposals, Silas? We're talking a stratified tenancy model here. We're talking separate entrances for different tiers of residents. We're looking at a network in which people can accrue *community points* by logging in and offering their services. It's a *game*, Silas. If you're telling me that segregating a community according to income and property value and then *gamifying* what little social mobility they have left isn't evil, then I don't even really know what evil is any more, to be honest.'

'I would say that it's more *sad* than evil, Rob.'

'I'm sorry, Silas, but you can't just boil everything down to—'

'We're very much in the boiling down business, Rob. Boiling down is like totally what we do.'

'I'm not dumbing this down for a bunch of children, Silas. This is about lives. This is about—'

'Alright, alright. Jesus. Don't give me the speech again. Let's change tack. What if we zoom in, make it more relatable?'

'You're saying: personalise it.'

'I'm saying: less *massive thing that is happening*, more *tiny person that it's happening to.*'

'Like, find someone who embodies what's happening and—'

'Exactly.'

Robert nodded, already coming round to the idea.

'Alright,' he said. 'I'll find someone.'

'Great.'

'And meanwhile, you'll try and do something about this Julia—'

'Glad we had this chat, Rob.'

———————

Darkin awoke to pain, so numbness was his first priority. After turning back the covers, he would pause, perched on the edge of the bed, as life and all the agony that came with it flowed downwards to his feet. Then he would stand and feel it spread, feel himself weaken before it. There was a moment, always, when he swayed, when the floor loomed closer and sparks lit the gloom of his vision. Sometimes, he'd sit back down, cowed. Other times, he would simply fall – straight forwards, face to the floor.

If he didn't fall he walked. It was a tense stand-off between warring bodily factions. Feet and legs were all for holding back, but his stinging bladder waited for no man. Two or three mornings a week he wouldn't make it. For so much of his life there had been a familiarity to what he produced. His shit had smelled like his own shit, his piss like his own piss. He knew his sweat, the intimate taste of his breath. Now, his urine was foreign to him, his saliva unpalatable. He caught wafts of himself as he moved and felt distanced from the man that made them.

Around him, Darkin's flat had begun its own battle with time's effects. Multiple varieties of damp had made brazen incursions:

some pushing upwards from below, some creeping inwards and downwards from the upper edges. A species of mushroom had colonised the corners. Silverfish had overrun the kitchen. Rodents scrabbled audibly behind the skirting boards.

This interior decay was matched by its exterior equivalent. Darkin had lived here long enough to remember the Larchwood Estate's aspirational beginnings. He'd had his suspicions even then, of course, but behind the lofty ideals the plans had seemed convincing. Now everything had slid, and what few neighbours Darkin could name had been pushed out by Downton – the estate's new owner – whose plans for the Larchwood seemed to depend on it being empty.

His mission to the bathroom completed, Darkin would make a cup of tea with which to wash down his tablets, light a cigarette, set his kitchen timer to mark the appropriate interval until his next tightly rationed smoke, and settle down with his newspaper of choice, *The Record*, at which point he would be reminded that the decay he saw and felt in his body, his flat, and the estate outside was merely the closest observable evidence that everything, without exception, was going to shit.

From the pages of *The Record*, a near-dystopian vision of England emerged. The country was overrun, under threat, increasingly incapable. Hordes of immigrants massed at its borders. Its infrastructure frayed at the seams. Basic morality was eroding at an alarming rate, worn down by tolerance, permissiveness, turpitude. Darkin found this both terrifying and reassuring. Like any long-standing *Record* reader, he read not to have his fears assuaged, but to have them confirmed.

If you believed *The Record*, there was no such thing as an honest politician, only a succession of swindling careerists clinging to the Westminster bubble. Every so often, *The Record* would proclaim one, lone politician to be different – so different, in fact, that they were barely a politician at all. This time around, that man was Hugo Bennington, vocal rising member of England Always, a once-ridiculed but determinedly plucky party making a surprising noise in parts of the country, such as Edmundsbury, hitherto ignored by the self-serving shitshow of London-centric political wheeler-dealing. That *The Record* had decided to endorse Bennington so unequivocally was, even to Darkin, little surprise. Bennington had written a column for *The Record* for a number of years, and still did so. That Darkin was particularly enamoured with Bennington despite a long period of profound political disinterest was also little surprise. Not only was Bennington Darkin's favourite columnist, he was also, as Bennington himself so often reminded everyone, a local lad, born and bred. There was no beating around the bush with Bennington, no political correctness or fashionable concession. He called it like he saw it, and did so in a language you didn't need a master's degree in bullshit to understand.

This morning, Bennington was on good form. His last column had been about Muslims. This one was about equality.

Let's begin, dear reader, with a quick test. Answer me honestly.

Equality: is it a good or a bad thing?

Easy, right? I bet you had to think for all of half a second before you were able to answer me with absolute certainty. Why, equality's a good thing, Hugo! And I agree. Of course equality's a good thing.

But what if I put the question another way? What if I asked you instead: Is there such a thing as too much equality?

In this country, housing is scarcer than it has ever been, yet immigration continues to rise. Unemployment among working Britons still isn't coming down fast enough, yet time and again we hear that companies must have quotas to ensure that for every white Englishman they employ they must also hire three foreigners, two women, and at least one homosexual. Doesn't matter who's more qualified for the job. Equality says you have to hire 'equally'.

Anyone who reads this column knows how strongly I believe

in tolerance, just as I believe in fairness. It's only right that we should try to share what we have with those who have less. But what we have in Britain now is a society that asks those who work to share their earnings with those who scrounge; those who have grown up here to share their hard-fought space with those who have just arrived; and those who deserve their place to share it with those who merely envy it. This is the real cost of equality run riot: a Britain in which there is nothing left to share.

It was rousing stuff. Darkin only had to look around him to see the proof of Hugo's point. What *was* there left to share? Simply because he couldn't see the people who'd profited from his loss, didn't mean they weren't out there, creeping closer, eyeing what little Darkin had left.

A knock at the door startled him. They were probably, he thought grimly, already here.

———————

Deepa's office was just along the corridor from Jess's, but it was effectively a different world. Jess's workspace was bare, almost anonymous; Deepa's teemed with her preoccupations. Photos covered the entire wall beside the door and had crept across to consume much of the space around the window. Above her desk, the pictures were three or four deep, curling at the edges and pulling away from their pins. Huge-breasted, sad-eyed twenty-somethings beckoned the viewer towards their chat and cam sites; naked couples assumed by-the-numbers positions in a series of spartan bedrooms; late-middle-aged women in retrograde lingerie promised, in lurid fonts, that they were just around the corner and desperate to fuck.

The visuals were at odds with the audio. Online for around eighteen hours a day, then struggling to sleep for two, then asleep for perhaps three before battling to wake for the hour that remained, Deepa had developed a range of coping strategies for her digital burnout, one of which was a growing addiction to the accidental ASMR of pre-modern artisanal activity. As Jess sipped her coffee and tried to avoid the gaze of the massed, anonymous women on the walls, and Deepa scrunched her unshod toes into the carpet (another wind-down technique), Deepa's computer speakers emitted the continuous and arrhythmic sound of chisel on stone. Deepa claimed these hour-long, unwavering streams of analogue endeavour relaxed her, and her collection appeared to be vast. During other visits, Jess had been subjected to thirty solid minutes of someone turning the pages of a book, or what seemed like an infinite loop of someone patiently sanding some wood.

'So he was, what?' said Deepa, staring at her feet as they gripped the carpet. 'He was reading web addresses.'

'And times and dates.'

'Like an internet history.'

'But with finer detail. There was part of what sounded like an email.'

Deepa said nothing. She was still looking at her feet. Deepa's attention was a complex and often conflicted thing. In much the same way as she never had fewer than ten browser tabs open, she rarely had fewer than four possible loci of focus and thought either. Jess had long ago given up trying to get her full attention and now accepted that Deepa was usually listening, even when she appeared to have no real awareness that Jess was there.

'It was the mask though,' said Jess.

'I liked the mask,' said Deepa vaguely.

'It didn't creep you out?'

Deepa shrugged, then raised her naked foot to Jess's face and wiggled her unvarnished toes.

'Do these look normal to you?'

'These what? You mean your toes?'

'My toes, but more specifically my toe *nails*.'

'They look . . . I mean, what do non-normal toenails look like?'

Deepa put her foot back on the floor and turned to her computer.

'Deepa, no,' said Jess. 'I don't need to see—'

But it was too late. Deepa had already image-searched *abnormal toenails* and now Jess was being confronted with a gallery of ingrown, fungal, cancerous, and untrimmed, talon-like toenails.

'Deepa, for fuck's *sake*. No. OK? Your toenails do not look like any of those toenails.'

'You don't think they're kind of . . . thin? Or papery?'

Deepa's extraordinary capacity for digital information came with a range of side effects. The sleeplessness was probably the major symptom, but in the last few months hypochondria had been playing rapid catch-up. She had *Web MD* bookmarked. Every itch and ache was cross-referenced. In the past fortnight alone, she'd diagnosed herself with three new ailments.

'I was talking about the mask, Deepa.'

Jess had learned, through trial and error, the complex rhythm of acknowledgement and disregard Deepa required. She became irritated when ignored, but if you followed her distractions too far, the wormhole could prove bafflingly deep.

'It was . . . I wouldn't say blurred,' said Deepa, her toes now momentarily forgotten but the search results still sadly tiled behind her, 'but indistinct somehow.'

'Maybe a mask made from a poor-quality image?' said Jess, nodding towards the photographs over Deepa's desk.

But Deepa was done with the mask idea. Instead, she'd picked up one of the flyers left behind by the man at the party.

'*What don't you want to share?*' she read. 'Maybe a blackmail thing?'

'I'm going to be very seriously fucked off if this turns out to be some kind of PR stunt,' said Jess.

'It probably will,' said Deepa. 'Everything does.'

Jess's brief nod in the direction of Deepa's collaged image-library had now distracted her. She found the effect of all these layered stares unnerving – a visual white noise that was hard to ignore.

'How's this going?' she said.

'It's endless,' said Deepa. 'I've abandoned all definitions of progress.'

Deepa's research was into what she called Digital Figurants – images of anonymous women long detached from their owners and now folded into the scenery and libidinal economy of the web – either used, siren-like, to lure lonely, late-night browsers onto the rocks of malware-heavy porn sites, or fashioned via 4chan into their own kind of currency; grouped into multi-gig archives and afforded value through erotic exchange. Her project was one of re-identification. She found these women, named them, and allowed them to talk. In doing so, she argued, something personal, something human, was reclaimed from the web's imagistic swamp. It was both an opposite and complementary angle to that taken by Jess. For Deepa, the dislocation of image from identity was traumatic, abusive. For Jess, the deliberate creation of an identity gleefully unhinged from both the body and the personality that created it was liberating, rebellious. The point at which they met was exactly the space that other theorists contested: the blurry interstice between the real and the virtual, the online world and its unplugged counterpart.

Deepa typed the web address from the flyer into her browser. The words WE ARE YOUR FACE filled the screen. Behind them, what appeared to be random images flickered at high speed: screen grabs of porn; time codes; an email inbox; snatches of forum chat. The effect was strobe-like, disorienting.

'Hmm,' she said. 'Suspiciously intriguing.'

Jess nodded wearily. It was something they often talked about: the uncanny, almost wizardly brilliance of viral marketing; the creeping feeling that only something boring could be relied upon to be serious.

Deepa was still peering at the website.

'I don't get all this public stuff,' she said. 'Why bother getting everyone in one place? If you're doing something that's genuinely underground or outsider, why risk being caught or identified? Seems kind of long-winded and resource-heavy to me.'

'Bringing us back to something corporate.'

They watched the screen quietly for a few seconds. Bits of breast; an erect cock; a credit card receipt; emails redacted with thick black lines.

'People are sniffing around,' said Deepa.

'Around this?'

'Around you.'

'Well, no-one knows anything except you,' said Jess.

'Precisely the problem,' said Deepa. 'It's starting to raise eyebrows.'

Jess nodded. 'Point taken. I'll come up with something.'

Deepa flopped back in her chair and placed her feet on her desk, where Jess, whose brain had not yet expunged the worm of doubt deposited there by Deepa, now stared at them, wondering if indeed the toenails were normal.

'I say this as your friend and colleague . . .' Deepa said.

'Oh God, you only ever say that when you're about to say something I don't want to hear.'

'I'm worried, that's all.'

'What's the worst that can happen?'

Deepa replied with a simple look. Jess laughed. She put her coffee cup down and stood up.

'OK,' she said. 'On that note.'

Deepa nodded at the computer screen. 'I'll have a little play with this if I get time,' she said. 'One of us should probably look into it anyway.'

Jess's office was three doors down from Deepa's, along a fiercely bright, frosted-glass corridor that ran along the front of the private research institute in which they worked. After the softer light of Deepa's room, the glare was slightly unnerving.

Jess's workspace contained almost nothing: a computer, a notebook, a shelf displaying only the most obvious and expected texts. The few clues to Jess's life and work wore their good taste as a disguise: three Cindy Sherman self-portraits along the back wall, a Japanese Noh mask over the desk.

She looked at the mask, noting the resonances it conjured in her psyche: the flat, sad gazes of the anonymous women in Deepa's office; the woozy, rubbery blankness of the man at the party.

We are your face, she thought. *What don't you want to share?*

She threw a few essentials into her bag, shut down her computer, and stepped out into the hallway, locking her office door behind her.

Jess wasn't sure when the architectural love affair with glass was going to come to an end but whenever it was it wouldn't be soon enough. As politics and commerce had become murkier, so the buildings in which vital transactions took place had become ever more resplendently clear, as if recognising that in the flattened homogeneity of the present all actions, both benign and malicious, now looked the same: a squint at a screen, a series of keystrokes, the choreography of global espionage now no different to the micro-ritual of online shopping.

Cocooned in her car, cigarette lit, window down, she turned the key in the ignition and backed with excessive assertion out of her parking space. At the barrier, she had to use her swipe card to exit. This, Jess thought, was the cognitive dissonance of working at a research facility so heavily funded by a corporate monolith like Green. On one level, there was more intellectual freedom than at any of the country's failing, intellectually incapacitated universities. She didn't have to teach, for one, and although there was an expectation that she publish at least occasionally, there was none of the driving pressure to justify her work or make it profitable. As a result she could, when she was deeply immersed in what she was doing, just about convince herself that she was operating independently. But then she would leave her office, and be reminded once again that although her research wasn't always as closely monitored as it could have been, she was arguably more observed than at any other time of her life. This was why so much of her work was done off site: to keep it safe, keep it hers. Because who knew in what ways Green might, one day, decide to follow up on their gift of funding?

Either side of her, the woodland that ringed Edmundsbury's outer edge began to blur, revealing itself not so much as nature but as a glitch in her optical experience of nature – a screen-smear of something once organic. She imagined she was moving not along a road but through fibre-optic cable, distilled to an infra-red essence. She had a fantasy that this was what happened when you died: you became pure data, informational light travelling at reeling speed, not quite free but fast enough to feel so.

Situated almost in the centre of town, Jess's destination – Nodem – had been founded by two self-proclaimed 'techno-bedouins' called Zero and One as a reaction against what they saw as the increasing corporatisation of both the web and the infrastructure on which it depended. As far as Zero and One were concerned, privacy was a life-or-death issue, so much so that they had renounced their names in favour of interchangeable binaries. Hooked up to its own off-grid server, and with not just each individual terminal but also the whole enterprise routed en masse through enough layers of encryption and redirection to send even the most hardened practitioner of online espionage screaming into the distance, Nodem aimed to couple that most antiquated of institutions – the internet café – with that most contemporary of demands – internet access that wasn't monetised, monitored, and morally compromised. It was staffed, on principle, only by Zero and One. No-one had any idea how they were making enough money to stay open. The only people who used the place were the three or four most paranoid people in town.

'Hey,' said either Zero or One as Jess walked in. Zero and One's names were indeterminate: they swapped them in order to maintain their anonymity.

'Why don't you take, er . . .' One (or Zero) gestured with unnecessary specificity towards the corner of the completely empty room. 'Terminal three.'

'Great,' said Jess.

'Brownie? Coffee?'

'Sure,' she said. 'Both.'

Zero/One wiped his hands on his apron, on which was written *I Don't Need GPS to Find My Moral North*, and disappeared through the beaded curtain at the back in search of provisions.

Jess located terminal three and sat down. Nodem was, somewhat incongruously given its supposedly bleeding-edge manifesto of contemporary anonymity, rather homely. Its smell – over-baked brownie; wickedly strong coffee; dust warmed and singed on its journey through multiple CPU heat sinks – was soothingly familiar, its scavenged, mismatched aesthetic strangely charming. The terminals spanned several eras. Keyboards rarely matched screens. Coffee, when it came, would be in a random mug. The brownie would be served on whatever flat-ish device of outmoded data storage happened to be to hand.

She fired up her terminal and opened a browser. Zero and One's custom-built operating system was notoriously precarious. Colours spontaneously switched places, random windows strung with forbidding-looking lines of code erupted at will in little clusters and then vanished. Freezes were common, as were grinding, interminable lags in the browser, no doubt due to every keystroke bouncing from Venezuela to Estonia and back again before triggering anything. At times, you could practically hear the hardware wheezing. But slowness was, as Zero or One would point out to anyone who expressed any irritation at the speed of their browser, the point. It was the very need for immediacy, by now hardwired into every inhabitant of the hyper-developed world, that had led to so many people unthinkingly abandoning privacy and anonymity in the name of convenience and rapidity.

Regardless of whatever ideology of patience lay behind Nodem's programming, being here too long made Jess uncomfortable. There was always, still, at this lingering, imminent moment as the little sand timer spun calmly in the centre of her screen and she waited for access, a complicated pinball game of emotions ricocheting around in her body. Excitement, a sense of daring, fear. Sometimes it was there from the moment she walked in; sometimes it arrived a little later. Then there was guilt, of course, and finally, always coming last no matter in what order the other emotions chose to announce themselves, a sense of grubbiness, almost shame.

While the system took its sweet time, Zero/One wandered over with her coffee and brownie – the coffee in a chipped, dishwasher-bleached mug that looked like it had once carried a picture of Princess Diana, the brownie perched on a scratched CD ROM. Once he had fully retreated, Jess moved her fingers to the keyboard, and turned her attention to the question of who to become first.

Today, there was only one persona at the forefront of Jess's mind, primarily because she happened to know that he was at the forefront of so many other minds. The party last night had been instructive. Somehow, through that peculiar alchemy of virality, one of her creations had become not only noticed, but hyper-noticed – observed, discussed, and in demand. She now found herself in the bizarre situation of standing around at parties listening to people like Robert and DeCoverley pretend they knew someone of whom she categorically knew they had no direct knowledge. *He couldn't make it, sadly,* she remembered them both saying. And what was all that stuff about demarcations he would or wouldn't recognise?

The timer on Jess's screen stopped spinning and the page she was looking for loaded one element at a time. She typed Byron Stroud's username into the email account she'd created for him. Sure enough, there were emails from everyone who'd been at the gathering: DeCoverley, Lionel Groves, one or two of the Theory Dudes, even Robert.

Byron: said DeCoverley's email, in typically presumptuous fashion. *Missed you at the thing last night. Would have been marvellous to have your voice there. We really must meet. A drink soon? JDC.*

My friend, said Lionel Groves's email, already, in the space of two words, cleaving to Groves's house style of self-aggrandising pomposity and gushing, weirdly antiquated sentiment. *Such a shame to find you absent last night. Let us meet soon. Groves.*

Hi Byron, said Robert's email. Was it just because Jess knew him and could hear, even in the simplest of written exchanges, his voice, or did his opening seem characteristically tentative? *I'm not sure if you got my last email, but just in case you didn't I thought I'd drop you a line again to say how nice it would be to meet up sometime. As I said in my previous email (apologies if you got it and are now reading this twice!), I'm such an admirer of your work, and I'd love to pick your brains whenever you have a moment. Like I said before (sorry again if I'm repeating myself), you can read what I've been working on <u>here</u>, <u>here</u>, <u>here</u>, and . . .*

The email was painful, awkward. Jess recoiled from its neediness, its sycophancy, its blunt depiction of a side to Robert that Robert kept from her. But she also, as she was reading it, recoiled from the fact that she was reading it at all. She had not, when she began this project, considered the potential for blurred boundaries. In retrospect, she had been guilty of precisely the dualistic fallacy she abhorred in the thinking of others. Of course, nothing was truly separable from anything else. The private, the public, the personal, the professional. Everything bled.

Even transgression, she thought, logging out of Stroud's email and redirecting her browser towards its next target, had a tendency to slip its moorings. You started out small and things swelled from there. Targets multiplied. Focus blurred.

The comments section of *The Command Line* prompted her for a log-in. Her fingers hovered over the keyboard, just as they always did, as if teasing her with the possibility that today they would change their mind, move on.

But the moment, as it always did, passed. Her fingers tapped out her username, *JuBenja*, and then hit enter.

Darkin had never been much of a one for knocks at the door. In the latter stages of his life, ambivalence had toughened into animosity. While Flo was alive, towards the end of her time with him, a procession of professionals had tromped through the flat delivering news that ranged from not very good to awful. The last knock had been when they'd come to take her off to the home. Two paramedics, two policemen, two social workers. One of them tried to get Darkin to sit on the sofa and have a cup of tea. Darkin was having none of it. Next thing he knew, he was in handcuffs and Flo was being stretchered down to an ambulance.

The knock that rang out through the smoke and fug of Darkin's living room on this particular day was not, it had to be said, particularly polite. It was sharp, insistent, pointedly excessive. He debated not answering it. His head was full of worrisome scenarios, most of which he'd picked up from *The Record*. He pictured himself opening the door a crack, peering round, only for it to be forced back in his face, knocking him to the floor. Men in balaclavas would burst in. Their voices would be Polish or black.

Further clarification, shouted through the door in a kind of stand-off during which Darkin refused to co-operate until he knew who he was speaking to, yielded no reassurance. The man's name was Jones. He worked for Downton. When Darkin opened the door, slightly out of breath after shuffling over with his stick, Jones stepped straight in, looking not at Darkin but at the flat, his lips and nostrils registering his response.

'It can be hard to keep up with a place,' he said.

Jones's suit was deep blue with an oil-on-water shimmer. He

looked long and hard at Darkin's twin sofas before perching himself with some discomfort on the outer lip of the one opposite Darkin's habitual spot.

Darkin didn't say anything. He hadn't liked the man when he'd heard him through the door, and he liked him even less now that he was addressing him in person. He sat down opposite Jones and reached for his fag packet. Kitchen timer be damned, he thought. These were exceptional circumstances.

'I'm afraid I'm going to have to ask you not to smoke, Mr Darkin.'

'It's my flat.'

'But for the moment it's also my place of work.'

Darkin lifted his fingers from the fag packet and picked up what was left of his tea. It was stone cold, but he wanted something to do with his hands.

'What do you want?' he said.

'I could ask you the same question,' said Jones. 'What do you want, Mr Darkin? May I call you Alfred?'

'No. What do you mean what do I want?'

'I mean: what do you want from life? If I could wave a magic wand, what would you ask for?'

'Can you wave a magic wand?'

'You'd be surprised what I can do.'

'I doubt that.'

Mr Jones smiled politely.

'How old are you now, Mr Darkin?'

'Old enough.'

'And your health is none too good, is it?'

'Nothing wrong with me that a few spare parts wouldn't fix.'

'Indeed.' Mr Jones paused. He looked as if he might be about to recline on the sofa but then thought better of it and leaned forward, interlacing his fingers between his knees. 'We take our more senior residents very seriously, you know.'

'Good to hear.'

'Every now and then, we like to pop round and check on our vulnerable adults.'

Darkin had heard the term vulnerable adult before, applied to Flo. Nothing good had come of it.

'I'm not vulnerable,' he said. 'So you don't have to worry.'

'Oh, but you are, Mr Darkin. You're very vulnerable.' Mr Jones looked around pointedly. 'Do you know what I see when I look around here? Hazards. Hundreds of hazards. Trip hazards, fire hazards. Do you think you'd survive a fall, Mr Darkin? In this place, I mean? Because there's so much to knock against on the way down, isn't there? Look at that table. Catch the corner of that and there'd be no helping you.'

'I've survived so far.'

'What I'm saying is, you manage now, but for how long?'

When Darkin didn't answer, Mr Jones pressed on.

'Anyway, like I say, I just wanted to assure you that you're listed on our system. That way, we can respond appropriately if anything happens. Obviously, as one of our owner-occupying tenants who has not signed up to our maintenance programme, you don't rely on us to do your repairs. But as I'm sure you understand, we're still responsible for all sorts of things that your wellbeing might depend on. If your gas or electricity supply was interrupted and you were unable to cook or heat the home, for example, a gentleman as frail as yourself could become ill very quickly. Just the same as if there was a carbon monoxide leak, you'd be far more likely to succumb to the fumes before you could exit the property. It's very important we know these things, Mr Darkin, so we can keep you safe. Of course, if you ever began to feel that a different property would be more suited to your needs, we'd be only too happy to—'

'I'm fine here.'

'Of course you are, Mr Darkin. Of course you are. I'm just saying if—'

'You won't get me out.'

'No-one wants to get you out, Mr Darkin. We just want to help you.'

Darkin nodded. Mr Jones stood up and ran his hands quickly down the buttocks of his suit before giving the palms a quick glance.

'I'll be going,' he said. 'Just remember, we're here if you need us.'

He held out his hand for Darkin to shake. 'Don't get up. I can see myself out.'

Darkin did not initially shake Mr Jones's hand. He didn't want to shake it and didn't see why he should. But Jones didn't let his hand drop. He just held it there, in front of Darkin's face, smiling gently, not moving, until eventually Darkin shook it just to get rid of him. The moment their hands touched, Jones's thin smile both broadened and softened, becoming genuine, toothy.

'No-one holds out forever,' he said. He reached down with his left hand to Darkin's stick, which Darkin had propped between his knees. 'Let me take this for you.'

'No, it's fine.'

'It's no trouble.'

Darkin tried to reach for the stick but Jones had already lifted it away and taken a step back. The moment he was without it, Darkin felt a sudden, sharp panic.

'Pleasure to meet you, Mr Darkin,' said Jones, making for the door. 'I'll leave this right here.'

———

Robert parked his car a little way from the Larchwood and then walked the remaining distance. The estate lacked an obvious entrance. Instead, you found yourself amidst it, the street opening out into a generous but dilapidated square encircled by four- or five-storey blocks of flats.

There were traces, even now, of what the Larchwood was once

supposed to be. It rejected the grey uniformity of earlier, more brutalist efforts. The mid-rises were gently rounded at the corners and asymmetrical in height, lending them an off-kilter appearance. The walkways that ran along the fronts were created from a kind of decking. Plants had once lined the edges and crept up the walls, but the service contract had long since expired and the so-called vertical garden had died, leaving behind denuded stumps and dry, ropey remnants. At some stage, the decision had been taken to paint each door a slightly different shade, giving the whole estate a childlike, playful air. Once, Robert thought, the effect had probably been uplifting, but now, with all the colours thinned and bleached by rain, and much of the woodwork cracked by frost, the diluted palette was insipid, woozy.

Aside from its physical deterioration, what really signalled the Larchwood's grand failure had nothing to do with bricks and mortar and everything to do with atmosphere. The place was almost completely silent. Every visualisation and artist's impression Robert had seen featured children playing while their associated adults stood around the square with cups of tea. But activity had drained from the shared spaces with dismal speed. There was still life here, of course: many flats, despite the purchase orders, the pressure to leave, and the increasing sense of abandonment brought on by the decanting process, were still inhabited, but their occupants existed largely in isolation.

Now, a new vision of togetherness awaited the estate. Downton were hacking community. Not only would it be cohesive, it would also be profitable. Tenants would be able to use the site-specific social network for all the things people claimed had been lost. They could gossip, catch up, ask to borrow some sugar. Critically, though, they could do so *more efficiently*. Why go round all your neighbours asking for some sugar when you could just post a floor-specific request and check the replies?

The implications were not merely social, but practical. Why send out engineers and security specialists when there might very well be expertise and know-how located right there within the building, able to respond immediately? With the Downton system, tenants would be able to list their skills and interests and show themselves as available for certain tasks. Community points accrued by an electrician picking up a few odd jobs in his own building during his off hours could, thanks to Downton's proposed zoning of the development according to tenant profile, be exchanged for perks and rewards ordinarily reserved exclusively for upper-strata tenants, such as limited off-peak use of the promised rooftop garden, or even, ultimately, depending on how the reward-to-return ratio was calibrated, and depending, obviously, on tenants also having the necessary capital to fund the difference in value, a full property upgrade. Social mobility was back, and it had never been more fun.

Robert decided to begin his search for a subject on the first floor and work his way up. That way, if he got lucky early on, he wouldn't have expended unnecessary energy on the climb.

Doorstepping people, it quickly transpired, was not a particularly popular thing to do in a place where every uninvited knock brought yet more dismal news. Not only, one ageing resident informed Robert, leaning on the jamb of her door and never taking her eyes off the walkway that stretched out behind Robert's left shoulder, had Downton already sent their own 'journalist', who under cover of writing a 'local colour' piece had proceeded to skim from people's recollections all kinds of valuable and ultimately unsettling data, they had also gone to great lengths to identify people who'd commented off the record to other reporters so that said individuals could be leaned on all the more forcefully. One man, hollow-faced with drained resolve, half-whispering through his barely ajar door, said that the day after an article appeared in which his name was used beside a comparatively harmless quote about the way in which the transfer of ownership had been handled, a letter had been hand-delivered advising him of a five per cent rent increase. A week after that, his electricity began to fluctuate – the lights flickering and dimming, the fridge clicking into sudden silence before whirring back to life three or four seconds later. It lasted, he said, two or three days, and he still, even though everything was now fully functional and the fault had almost certainly been a coincidence, couldn't entirely shake the notion that the fluctuation had been (and here he paused, leaned closer, hissed the word through the crack in the door) a *message*. When Robert asked him why he was telling him all this if the only likely result was further pressure, the man said he'd signed, and so there was nothing more they could do to him. When Robert asked him how much he'd lost in the deal, the man said he didn't want to talk about it.

At the next door Robert tried, a younger man answered, propped up on crutches, a baby grizzling from a room somewhere behind him, the sound competing with the automatic weapons fire and gratuitous death-howls of what Robert assumed was a violent video game.

'Oh, Downton,' the man said with a grim smile. 'Yeah, they're round all the time. They've got this new thing where they come and *check on you*.' He made quote marks in the air with his fingers, then tilted his head towards his crutches. 'They like to make sure I'm OK.'

'You use those all the time?' said Robert.

'Accident at work. I think I'm a particular irritation for Downton. Disabled, baby in the flat. They need to be a bit more careful than they have been with other people.'

'They've been heavy with people you know?'

'They're not stupid. All the heavy stuff I've seen is when they've got some kind of legal basis. Rent arrears or whatever. Then they really pounce. Otherwise, it's the friendly-but-not-friendly pop-round – you know, the quick chat, the *discussion of your options*.' He laughed wryly, then ran a fingernail up the wall beside him, flaking paint and plaster coming away in a powdery cloud. 'Or maybe they don't come round at all,' he said. 'Maybe they just let you fester.'

'Is anyone organising anything?' said Robert. 'Is there a tenants' group?'

'People are kind of worried about consequences,' said the man. 'But there are ideas floating around.'

'Thanks,' said Robert, unable to think of any more questions.

'What's your name?' said the man.

'I'm sorry?' said Robert, hesitating.

'So I can look for your piece.'

'Townsend,' said Robert, oddly reluctant to reveal his own name despite the fact he was asking people to reveal an awful lot more to him. 'Robert Townsend.'

'I'll google you,' said the man, giving a smile and a wave.

It was all good detail, Robert thought, but it was nothing he, and by extension his readers, didn't already know. He needed not the facts, but the personification of those facts: the one representative individual who could embody the situation.

One level up, the first flat he came to did not bode well. The windows were filthy – streaked with dust, grime, and what looked like half a kebab. A light was on, but the curtains – yellowed and ragged and surely completely ineffectual when it came to keeping out the light, were drawn. He knocked anyway.

For several seconds there was no answer. Then, as Robert was debating knocking again versus walking away, a voice – irritable and already defensive – came from inside the flat.

'Hello?'

'Oh,' said Robert. 'Hello?'

'Who's there?'

'I'm . . . My name's Robert. I'm doing some research in the area and—'

'What sort of research?'

'Just . . . research.'

'If you've come from them, you can keep walking. One of your lot's already been round.'

'What lot?'

'Downton lot.'

'I'm not from . . . Did you say someone's been round?'

'What's it to you?'

'I was just interested to know if someone else has been round, that's all.'

'Never you mind who's been round.'

'OK. Look, I'm sorry I bothered you. I'll—'

'Hang on.'

Robert paused, expecting the door to open. Nothing happened.

'Hello?' said the voice again.

'Hello,' said Robert. 'I . . . Did you tell me to hang on?'

'Yeah.'

'OK . . .' There was another pause. 'Er, hang on for what?'

'I can't get up.'

'What?'

'I can't get up. I need a hand.'

'Are you hurt?'

'No. He moved my sodding stick and now I can't get up.'

Robert tried the door.

'It's locked,' he said.

'I know it's fucking locked, for fuck's sake.'

'Then how am I supposed to help?'

'The window.'

Robert moved over to the filthy, forbidding window and ran his fingers gingerly round the frame.

'There's no way in,' he said.

'Going to have to break it then, aren't you?'

'You want me to break your window?'

'What are you, daft or something?'

'I'm just saying there must be another way. Hasn't someone else got a key? What about the fire brigade? I could call them and ask them to—'

'Don't call anyone,' the voice said urgently. Then, more softly: 'Please. Please don't call anyone. I don't want anyone to know.'

'Alright,' Robert said. 'Don't worry, OK? I'm going to help you, so just . . . You're going to be fine. Alright?'

'Thank you.'

Even as Robert began looking around for something suitably solid and weighty, a perturbing thought was beginning to tickle at the fringes of his mind. His feelings, he noted, were in a state of oscillation: concern on the one hand, but on the other, uncomfortably, excitement.

Outside a neighbouring flat, a small collection of broken furniture lay piled. Picking up a stool, Robert prised off the leg and, after a few trial strikes, used it to break the window.

To say the smell that poured forth was a single smell would have been a gross oversimplification. It was a conglomeration of overlapping, intertwining olfactory experiences. The top note was fag smoke, but under the tar there was something far worse, far more complicated and human. Urine was involved, that was for certain, and also a very specific kind of sweat. Then there was everything Robert could see in the kitchen now that he was peering in: mouldering food, past-it milk, a fermenting, overflowing bin.

Across the dingy living room, through a lingering cloud of smoke, Robert spotted the man he'd been speaking to. He was sitting on one of two sofas, looking across the flat, through the small, open-plan kitchen area, to the window. He was, Robert thought, quite extraordinarily thin. His beard was rough and grey, the moustache stained yellow in one corner. When he smiled a rather off-putting smile, Robert could see that the man's teeth were almost brown.

'I'm Robert.'

'Darkin.'

'Darkin?'

'My last name. It's what people call me.'

'Right.'

'Well, come on then. Hop in that window.'

Robert pulled the window open as far as he could, took a deep breath, held it, and climbed up onto the window ledge. Beneath the window the sink was full of washing-up. Clambering over that, he ended up on the edge of the counter and was able to jump down.

'My stick's in the corner by the door.'

Now that he was inside the flat, surveying the faded carpet and sagging sofa, the near-impenetrable ash cloud and the remains of what appeared to be nothing but sandwiches on the kitchen counter, it struck Robert that it was entirely possible Darkin had never left it, or not for a long time anyway. The place had that over-lived-in feel, a fleshy sense of its own microsystemic life. Everything in here, Robert thought, was positively teeming, but somehow, at the heart of it, was death, creeping in, going about its business.

He saw a walking stick propped by the door, picked it up, and walked over and handed it to Darkin, who neither thanked him nor made any move to stand. Robert felt, without really being able to say why, that he was not expected to leave just yet.

'Can I, er . . . get you anything?' he said.

'Might as well get the kettle on, eh?' said Darkin, lighting up a fag. 'You don't mind if I smoke.'

'Well . . .'

'Wasn't asking.'

'Right.'

'The other bloke made a fuss about it. Now I'm all out of whack.'

'What other bloke?'

'The bloke before you. Said it was his place of work.'

'Is he the one who moved your stick?'

'That's the one.'

'Why did he do that?'

'Because he's a cunt.'

'Was he from Downton?'

'Yeah.'

'And what did he want?'

'To tell me I'm *vulnerable*.'

'And then he moved your stick.'

'Yup.'

'Deliberately.'

'Yup.'

'And you told him you couldn't stand up without it?'

'Not exactly, but he knew.'

Robert turned towards the kitchen and sought out the kettle. He tried to clear some of the limescale by swilling it under the tap a few times but it was a losing battle.

'Where are your teabags?' he called over his shoulder.

'Cupboard above you.'

Darkin's cigarette was not merely generating smoke of its own but somehow reanimating the dormant smoke of fags gone by. Robert found the teabags alongside half a loaf of bread and a jar of jam whose label was so faded and sticky he could no longer make out the brand.

'When was the last time you went shopping?'

'Bloke goes for me.'

There were two mugs in the sink. Gingerly, Robert lifted them out of the carnage by their handles and ran them under the hot tap. There was no sign of a sponge or a cloth so, with some reluctance, he squirted washing-up liquid onto his fingers and swished them around the inside of the mugs before rinsing a teaspoon he found lying on the side.

'Lived here long?' he said.

'Long enough.'

'Always on your own?'

'Not always, no.'

'Wife?'

'Dead.'

'Sorry.'

Robert watched the kettle boil, testing words and phrases in his mind. *Infirm old widower . . . harassed and intimidated . . .*

'You like it here?'

'Not really. No sense moving now though.'

'But you must have liked it when you moved here.'

'It was alright then.'

'It's changed a lot.'

Darkin nodded.

'You probably remember when all of this was fields, right?'

Darkin shot him a look. Robert moved on swiftly.

'Sugar?'

'Three.'

That plus the fags explained the teeth, Robert thought. He found a bag of sugar on the side, its contents clumped and browned like cat litter, and dumped the requisite number of teaspoons in Darkin's cup, already on the lookout for an opportunity to dispose of his own tea without appearing rude. He carried the two mugs over and set them down on the coffee table before perching himself on the sofa opposite Darkin. As the cushions took his weight, they exhaled their grimy history with a wheezing sigh. Robert was already building his piece in his mind. He would, he thought, punctuate it with sparse but tragic detail: the out-of-reach stick; the overflowing ashtray; the fact that Darkin's jumper, now that Robert looked closely, was on inside out.

'No-one gives a shit about people like me,' said Darkin finally. 'That's the truth. We worked. We paid our taxes.' He took an exploratory sip of his tea. 'Like bloody dishwater.'

'When you say *we* . . .' said Robert, subtly recoiling from that casual first-person plural.

'But that's not what gets you ahead, is it?' said Darkin, pointedly ignoring the question.

'What isn't?'

'Working hard. Looking out for yourself. Not asking for anything. Doesn't make a difference if your face doesn't fit.'

'Doesn't fit where?'

48

Darkin leaned forward and looked right down the barrel of Robert's gaze in a manner that quickly caused Robert to discover much of interest in the contents of his tea.

'My face . . . doesn't . . . *fit*,' said Darkin, jabbing the air with his fag-bearing index and middle fingers for emphasis. 'Try and tell me different.'

He sank back against the sofa cushions. 'Don't give me that look,' he said.

'What look?'

'That judgemental look.'

Robert held up his hands in what he hoped was the perfect picture of innocence. 'No judgement here.'

'Pull the other one,' said Darkin. 'You think I don't know that look? Well, here's news for you: I don't give a shit.'

'About what?'

'About what you think.'

'Right,' said Robert, who found the idea of someone not caring what he thought strangely offensive. 'Fine. I'm not asking you to.'

'Then stop looking at me like that.'

'I'm just . . . What do you mean your face doesn't fit? Do you mean—'

'Let me ask you a question,' said Darkin.

'OK.'

'Equality . . .' said Darkin.

Something in Robert's face must have shifted in a way he was unable to mask, because Darkin's shifted in turn.

'Yeah,' said Darkin. 'See? And you don't even know what I'm going to ask yet.'

'What?' said Robert. 'I'm listening.'

'Equality,' said Darkin. 'Good thing or a bad thing?'

'I . . .' Robert faltered, reluctant for some reason to offer a response that might risk Darkin's disapproval.

'Good thing?' he said tentatively.

'Are you asking or telling?' said Darkin. 'It's a simple question.'

'Good thing,' said Robert. 'Obviously.'

'Obviously?'

'Well . . . Yeah. Equality, right? It's a good thing.'

'How much equality?' said Darkin.

'What?'

'How much equality?'

'Well, until everything is equal, I suppose. That's kind of the point of—'

'Equal? Or more than equal?'

'Isn't more than equal the same as, you know, not equal?'

'Say you go for a job, right?'

'Right.'

'And you're qualified for that job.'

'OK.'

'Do you think they'll give it to someone like you?'

'I'd like to think so.'

'Then you're living in a fantasy land.'

'Why?'

'Because they can't give it to you, can they?'

'Because . . .'

'Because they've got to give it to a foreigner. Quotas, isn't it?'

'Well, I don't think—'

'Look around here,' said Darkin.

'OK.'

'These used to be for local people. How many local people you think live here now?'

'Well, hardly anyone lives here now.'

'But who do you think is *going* to live here?'

'Rich people,' said Robert. 'That's the point. They're decanting—'

'Decanting shit. They're making room.'

'Making room for—'

'For all the foreigners.'

'What foreigners?'

'What foreigners. Listen to you. You know how many foreigners come to this country every year?'

'About—'

'Too many, that's how many. And they've got to live somewhere, haven't they? And because of all this bloody equality, instead of just telling them to go away, we say, yeah, sure, come and live here. We'll give you a house, we'll give you benefits. We'll let you move your bloody family over here so you can all talk foreign to each other.'

'But there's no—'

'The cities are full,' said Darkin. 'Been going on for years. Read the papers. Where do you think they're going to go now? Got to go somewhere.'

'But if you look at the statistics . . .'

'Lies,' said Darkin. 'All lies. You can't trust statistics. Who do you think makes all the statistics in the first place?' He shook his head. 'You want to get something out of this country? Change your colour.'

There followed an uncomfortable silence.

'Not that I've got anything against them personally,' said Darkin.

'Of course not,' said Robert.

'I've met some nice ones.'

'Absolutely.'

Distractedly, Robert picked up his tea and drank from it, only to remember the condition in which he'd found the cup. Hastily, surreptitiously, he returned the cup to the table, a bitter, possibly imagined aftertaste arising at the back of his throat. He sucked on his gums, working up his saliva, hoping to wash away or dilute whatever it was he'd just inadvertently consumed.

A strange and uncomfortable side effect of haranguing your partner in secret, Jess had found, was the extent to which you were guiltily sweet to them in person. Before the arrival of Julia Benjamin, the scent of something stagnant had hung around their lives. Now, they were refreshed. At pains to conceal what she did during the day, Jess slipped into a different skin in the evening – a skin Robert, to Jess's increasing discomfort, seemed to like.

'Hey hon,' she said, breezing into the kitchen where Robert was cooking and depositing her laptop bag on a dining chair.

This was another new phenomenon: these moments when she lost the ability to say his name, and so leaned on a term of endearment in order to address him.

'Hey,' he said, turning and smiling. He was at the cooker, something deeply red and strongly spiced simmering on the stovetop in front of him. From the tinny portable speaker on the worktop, a self-consciously relaxed American male droned his way through a podcast.

She leaned in to kiss him. He tasted of chilli and tomato. Her lips came away tingling.

'What's this?' she said, reaching past him and stirring what was in the pot.

'An experiment,' he said. 'Constructed entirely out of what was to hand. You want some wine?'

She sat down at the dining table and rested her feet on a chair.

'Yeah,' she said. 'Half a glass.'

'Staying sharp for the big event?'

'Something like that.'

He put half a glass of red in front of her and then topped up his own from the bottle.

'Any idea what you're expecting?'

She shook her head, shrugged. 'Who knows? Could be anything. Could be bullshit.'

'What does *Deepa* think?'

Deepa, in Robert's pronunciation, was always italicised. He didn't like her, probably because he was aware she didn't like him. Out of a sense of decorum, though, he'd been able to distil his feelings into the simple pointed utterance of her name, thereby avoiding any protracted disagreement. It annoyed Jess, but she accepted the compromise. Sometimes it even amused her.

'*Deepa* thinks it's probably bullshit.'

'Is there anything she doesn't think is bullshit?'

'She's open to persuasion in terms of things being bullshit or not bullshit, but nine times out of ten she decides they're bullshit. To be fair, eight times out of nine she's right.'

He didn't argue. This was the rhythm of living with someone, Jess thought. You knew what each other believed. You could allude and move on. Arguments were a conscious choice.

'For what it's worth,' said Robert, fussing over the sauce, 'I agree with her.'

Jess widened her eyes in faux disbelief, reared her head back a little to emphasise the tease, but smiled while she did it.

'I know, I know,' said Robert, laughing. 'I'm losing my edge.'

She still didn't know what to do with this new-found ease. She enjoyed it, fretted about it, wanted more of it, yet was unable to relax when it occurred. She was operating at multiple levels of reality, she thought. Everyone was, in their own particular way. What was different for her now was that all her levels were transparent, like glass floors in a soaring building. She could look all the way down from her happiness, through the charm and ease that fed it, to the vertiginous lower levels of her guilt.

'How was your day?' she said.

He shook his head, suddenly serious.

'I don't know,' he said. 'Awful, really.'

She put her glass back down on the table and looked up at him with concern, mirroring his tonal shift. 'What happened?'

'Well it got off to a flying start because I had to have a Skype call with Silas, which is always, you know, an exercise in total fucking surreality. I was trying to get him to do something about the comments section. Which he totally won't do, by the way.'

'I told you.'

'I know, but it's driving me mad. Anyway, the point is that Silas has got this thing about *humanising* the estate story. You know, finding a single story that provides a kind of empathetic hook or whatever.'

'Not a terrible idea. Particularly by Silas's standards.'

'No, by Silas's standards it's basically a moment of genius. So I went over to the estate and knocked on doors and asked around and all that. No-one really wanted to talk, as you can imagine.'

'Scared, I assume,' she said, taking another sip of wine.

'Very scared. With good reason. So I was knocking on doors, getting what I could, and I got to this real *scene* of a flat. Stuff smeared on the windows. Dark. And when I knocked on the door, this *guy* called out, saying he was stuck and couldn't get up. He wouldn't let me call anyone, so I ended up breaking his window to help him.'

Robert had stopped attending to whatever he was cooking and was now standing with his back to it while it popped and spat behind him. He was looking not at Jess but slightly past and above her.

'It was this old guy,' he said flatly. 'Stuck on his sofa. Couldn't get up. Said someone had been round and moved his stick. Flat was . . .' He shook his head. 'Filthy. Stank.'

'Jesus. What did you do?'

He shrugged. 'What could I do? Made him a cup of tea. Chatted.'

'Hey,' she said, gesturing to the empty dining chair beside her with her foot, 'come and sit down.' When he did so, she slid off her shoes and rested her legs across his lap. 'So what are you going to do?'

At this, he seemed to snap out of his momentary drift elsewhere. 'Oh, write about it,' he said firmly. 'For sure. It's perfect.'

'People need to know,' said Jess.

'Right.'

He'd begun bouncing his knees slightly, making it difficult for her to rest her legs on them. He took a swig of his wine, his eyes narrowing slightly.

'That'll give her something to think about,' he said, almost, but not quite, to himself.

'Who?'

'Oh . . .' He waved the moment away, his knees still again. 'No-one. That woman.'

'The commenter?'

'Yeah. Julia whatever.'

'Why would it—'

He shook his head, got up, and returned to the cooker.

'I just think if the piece was emotive enough, she'd have a lot of difficulty doing her usual cynical deconstruction in the comments section, that's all. And even if she did, I don't think she'd find it was met with the usual level of appreciation.'

'But that's not a reason to—'

'Of course it's not the reason. I'm just saying that it would be a nice little bonus, that's all.'

He'd put his wine down on the worktop and turned to face her. This was something that happened to them now. The opportunity for an argument would present itself. They would look at each other, weigh up the extent to which they wanted to yield to temptation. Then, usually, they would simply move on, skirting around the booby-trapped moment.

'You're right,' she said. 'Human-interest stories tend to put off the trolls.'

He nodded.

'Anyway,' he said. 'We should eat.'

While they ate, they talked about the day's events on the web, asking each other if they'd seen this or that post, tracked this or that social media shitstorm, or caught a glimpse of whatever eye-rolling thinkpiece headline was currently whipping up derision across right-thinking networks. This being dinner, they selected things about which they could agree. Some digital–analogue distinctions, Jess thought, still applied. Online, the aim was to court controversy. At home, you cherry-picked for accord. Points of reference were not difficult to locate. They had, like everyone they knew, seen broadly the same things, and entertained broadly the same thoughts about the things they'd seen. She'd begun to feel that the unspoken aim of these evening conversations was reassurance. It was their way of telling each other they were still in the same place, still reachable via familiar co-ordinates. They had to tell each other this, she thought, because the place they'd reached was in fact not familiar at all. Territory had shifted beneath them. Their maps had failed to update.

Whatever this was – this non-space of domestic harmony and digital dissent – had begun, as everything now seemed to begin, with an article. Some years back, when her academic career had been more nascent, Jess had published a piece of research on masculine identity within online gaming culture. Roughly a month later, a counter-article appeared, written by an increasingly notorious 'thinker' called Stefan Ziegler, who at the time was building a name for himself as a populist quasi-intellectual adept at dressing up anachronistic opinions in the trendy garbs of big data and repackaging his assumptions as 'unintuitive' thinking. By the time he wrote this particular article, he'd already published numerous thinly veiled troll-pieces masquerading as mathematical insights on, among other things, the bell curve, the statistical improbability of rape as a real-life occurrence, and why game theory could be used to make the case against foreign aid to the developing world. He was, basically, a bigot with sums, and in the self-satisfied geek-bro circles in which he performed his ideas, sums were the going currency.

In this particular piece, Ziegler had put forward the argument that the hyper-masculinised and essentially misogynistic culture of online gaming, far from being a distasteful throwback to a pre-enlightened age, was a perfect example of the way in which super-charged male competition gave rise to a highly productive strain of male co-operation. That this very specific strain of masculine bonding flourished in an environment where male aggression towards women went largely un-policed, Ziegler contended, was strong evidence in favour of the idea that certain workplaces, far from striving towards the kind of messy equality that was, at the time, so much in vogue, should in fact strive towards *less* equality in the name of greater productivity. As was his style, Ziegler had bombarded his readers and editors with data. In doing so, he had not only appropriated Jess's research without crediting it, he had also used it to draw conclusions offensively at odds with her own.

Deeply hip to Ziegler and his ilk's rhetorical strategy of drawing people into an argument and then accusing them of becoming 'emotional', Jess met data with data, publishing a paper in a sympathetic academic outlet clarifying her own work and deconstructing Ziegler's misinterpretation of her findings. Ziegler, in turn, ignored all of Jess's points, stripped out two or three mildly contentious passages from her article, and posted them, shorn of context and padded with foaming interjection, onto his blog, where they were fallen upon by all the raging gamer man-children and men's rights activists who'd read in Ziegler's earlier piece a long-awaited anti-feminist rallying cry. Within twenty-four hours, Jess was subjected to over five hundred tweets threatening her with everything from professional disgrace to rape and death. Someone got hold of her personal email address and posted it on a forum. Her home address and mobile number leaked. Photographs of anonymised men standing on her street or even outside her house were splashed across the web. A wreath was delivered to her door.

In some ways, Jess was prepared for this. She'd always suspected, given her work and gender, that at some point a bunch of feral men were going to go to town on her reputation. She'd seen numerous colleagues go through similar things. What she was less prepared for, however, was Robert, and the way his response to what was happening fell so far short of what she expected and demanded his response should be. For all his rhetorical bluster in his columns, Robert was, like most men who press the language of conflict into the service of intellectual debate, pretty averse to actual confrontation. Given the fairly incontrovertible evidence of what Jess was experiencing, downplaying what was happening was difficult. Instead, he opted for the next most convenient course of action: querying the reasons for its occurrence.

'He could have stolen anyone's work,' was one of his most oft-repeated pronouncements. 'I'm not saying it was OK he ripped off your research but I don't think he ripped off your research because you're a woman. He ripped off your research because it was the research he needed for his piece.'

'Everyone gets hate on the internet,' was another favoured rhetorical position. 'I mean, literally everyone I know who writes online gets some kind of abuse. It's not necessarily gendered.'

Here, Jess would generally point out that she was fairly certain none of Robert's male friends had received emails to their personal address and texts to their supposedly private mobile phone number describing in graphic detail all the things the anonymous sender intended to do to their genitalia. Nor, she assumed, did many of the insults received by these possibly made-up friends refer specifically to their gender as if it were their gender itself that was repellent. In an effort to drive home to Robert exactly what she was being asked to deal with, Jess had taken out her phone in the kitchen and begun reading messages aloud at random.

I've got a crowbar I'm gonna bring round your house and shove up your fucking cunt you fenimist bitch.

Good luck getting raped you ugly fat whore.

Enjoy your last hours alive, cunt.

At this point, to his credit, Robert had visibly paled, then become apologetic, and then, finally, angry on her behalf. So angry, in fact, that he had written about it, in one of his first, and, as it turned out, defining posts for *The Command Line*. Almost as quickly as she had found herself attacked, Jess became the subject of swelling online support. A charity set up to help women experiencing online harassment became aware of the situation and offered to help. They scrubbed Jess's accounts, rebuilt an untraceable life for her, and even, in a move Jess particularly enjoyed, de-anonymised many of her attackers, allowing Jess to send personalised greetings cards to their home addresses, letting them know exactly with whom they were fucking, and what they could expect to happen if the fucking continued. The worker assigned to Jess by the charity was Deepa, who volunteered for them whenever she wasn't at work on her research. When things had died down, Deepa had pointed out the position at the institute and suggested Jess go for it, a move that, conveniently in terms of both physical safety and ongoing solvency, meant leaving London. Little by little, things settled. Jess and Robert settled with them. His career picked up; hers progressed. They were solvent, safe, successful, and, superficially, happy.

But in her quieter, undistracted moments, an anger that had nested and bred began to show itself. At work, or out with friends, or chatting with Robert, she felt largely herself. But at night, as she tried to sleep, or driving the country roads with little in the way of traffic to sustain her attention, Jess would be struck by a rage that reared up from within and then, finding no reasonable outlet, thrashed around inside her, kicking up torn scraps of discarded memory and trampled feelings. Bits of online messages would flash up in front of her eyes. Threats would once again seem imminent. She would picture Ziegler's face, recall passages from his article that still, even with all this time having passed, made her skin hum with fury. She even started seeking out her own fuel, sitting up late into the night, long after Robert was asleep, poring over Ziegler's latest article, or tracking yet another eruption of misogynist harassment online, cranking herself into a pointless, insomniac fury.

Robert began to struggle. His support remained, but his understanding faltered. As far as he was concerned, the event was over. They had handled it, come out on top. It was a time, he seemed to think, in which they ought to be congratulating themselves. Sometimes, he would climb up to the attic where she worked, dressed for bed and upset by her absence, and peer over her shoulder at her online reading. He'd try to soothe her, distract her, charm her away. *Let it go*, he'd say. *It's over, let it go.* And she'd smile and allow herself, on the surface at least, to be calmed. She agreed with Robert, felt reassured by his concern. It was over; she did need to let it go.

It struck her that perhaps what she needed to do in order to let it go was express it, release it somehow, in a way that wouldn't simply set the whole cycle off again. And so, late at night, in a desperate bid for sleep unpunctuated by the rattle and buzz of whatever was trapped inside her, she created a blank Twitter account from which she called Stefan Ziegler a cunt.

She had wanted, quite simply, to know how it felt. As soon as she did it, she knew: it felt complicated. The moment she hit the button to send the tweet, an event was created around which her thoughts and feelings began to orbit. There was an initial thrill; a few sweaty, adrenalised moments, but at the same time, various sub-strata of sensations began to press upwards from beneath her enthusiasm: a sense of shame, a suspicion that she had, in some small way, reduced herself or, worse, *been* reduced by a situation she should have resisted or evaded.

Just as she was considering deleting the tweet, though, Ziegler acted. The difficulty for Jess was that he did not act in any of the ways she had anticipated (a cutting response, a call to his followers to attack, the redeployment of Jess's abuse as further evidence of Ziegler as world-weary victim, etc.). Instead, he simply, without a word, blocked her, thereby rendering Jess's new anonymous Twitter account effectively useless. Online violence, she now saw, was a more sophisticated endeavour than she had initially envisaged.

Over the next day or two, the sense that she had been both attacked by and refused entry to a system that callously wielded aggression with no concession to consequence scratched away like a burrowing animal in her brain. It was as if both anonymity *and* visibility had been denied her. When she attacked Ziegler intellectually, in public, she was threatened. When she hectored him anonymously, nothing happened. As herself, she was too visible to safely function. As an anonymous heckler, she wasn't notable enough to make an impact. Where, she thought, did that leave her? What options were available? If Jess became certain of anything in the days that followed, it was that simply giving up and getting on with some less controversial research was not an option. After that kind of retreat, she thought, her life would be intolerable. She would be intolerable to herself.

The Ziegler experience was harrowing, but informative. She came to think of it as the inverse revelation to that of Dorothy in Oz. Jess had not pulled back the curtain to find a wizened old man operating the controls of a monster; she had swept aside the old man and exposed the vastness of the beast behind him. There would always be Zieglers: self-interested, self-protective men masking their ambition and prejudice behind so-called analysis. It was what supported Ziegler that appalled her: an apparatus of misogyny in which opinion was the greenhouse for aggression, discussion the doorway to harassment.

So the problem became less one of revenge, and more one of statistical proof. A tessellating system of hostility had revealed itself to her; now she needed to unmask it to others. To do this, she needed to drag it from its natural habitat – the world of opinion and rhetoric and flippant, combative dismissal – and into the very space it falsely professed to inhabit: the world of research; the world of cold, hard, verifiable reality.

It would be no good, she thought, doing this as herself. Her name as a researcher was now, thanks to Ziegler, inextricably linked to the worst elements of that which she wanted to research. The only option, it seemed, was to become someone else entirely. Or, to be more specific, not one person, but many: an infiltration team.

She began working on fake CVs – falsified publication histories that would take weeks to unravel. She pitched widely, operating as both men and women. Her fields of interest were broad, carefully calibrated to draw on her talents without overlapping with her actual work. Personalities began to emerge, and with them, opinions. Paradoxes in her own thought became enmities between the minds she had imagined.

As complicated as the maintenance of these separate strands of activity quickly became, Jess's multiple bylines and viewpoints were merely the user interface of what she was piecing together. Behind the personae, behind the ideas and opinions she was imagining, Jess crafted a system of analysis that tracked the repercussions of her rhetorical interventions across the web. Every tweet, every sentence in every thinkpiece, every comment below the line, every shared link, could now, because Jess was in control of so many more variables than the average online user, be tracked and mapped as they made their way along the pathways of thought and response that shaped the web. It was the online equivalent of a barium meal. She fed ideas into the internet's hungry maw, then traced their progress through to its bowels.

Robert, meanwhile, was thriving. His piece on internet misogyny for *The Command Line* had accrued a readership far beyond his usual reach. As a result, he now spoke about inequality with a new-found confidence. He'd written a piece on how men could contribute to challenging misogynist discourse. He built a following on Twitter, and became known for his socially minded interventions and carefully targeted trolling of bigoted celebrities. Soon after they'd moved to Edmundsbury, he'd heard about the plans for the Larchwood, and had claimed the cause as his own.

And of course, Jess loved to see him thrive. Who, she would often ask herself, when she began to doubt the extent to which she welcomed his success, did not love to see their partner thrive?

And who could possibly complain about his credentials? He had, after all, supported her in the most public way possible, and now wrote with what appeared to be genuine passion about issues she admired him for taking on.

But the more adulation Robert attracted, the more she was reminded that in many ways his success had its roots in her harassment. The more she watched Robert confidently making feminist assertions at parties, in print, even at home, in the kitchen, where he increasingly felt comfortable debating with her the finer points of third-wave feminist praxis, the more she found herself reminded of exactly what it had taken to trigger his much-congratulated awakening: her having to read those threats and degrading insults to him, out loud, in their home, visibly distressed, effectively rubbing his face in something he should have recognised from a comfortable distance.

She knew all the ways her discomfort would sound if she described it, and all the ways Robert would respond. It was jealousy, he would think, bitterness. She wasn't happy with how her career had turned out and so was lashing out at his. She was still angry with Ziegler, with the men who had attacked her, and now was shifting that anger onto him, even though he had, quite demonstrably, been there for her when she needed him. He could even provide *citations* for his support. How many people could do that?

She slept less, was more and more taken in by her project. Robert sensed, but couldn't entirely explain or understand, the changes in her. He started to worry. She started to worry about the ways in which he worried. She needed a release. By this point, she had other vectors of expression. Everybody, she told herself as she logged into the comments section of *The Command Line* for the first time, needed a safety valve. Every partner needed things they kept veiled for fear of feeling subsumed.

The justification was simple, but the practice was far more complicated. She had reckoned without Robert's insecurity, which he kept concealed beneath his idealism, his forthrightness. She had failed to calculate the extent to which Julia Benjamin's comments would come to preoccupy him, the ways in which he would start to consider her responses before he even wrote anything. His columns became subtly more strident, his voice a shade more rigid. A sense of opposition emerged, and, to Jess's dismay, revealed itself to be something she needed, a friction that was lacking elsewhere.

Now, daily, whether she was hooked up at Nodem, marshalling the avatars she'd once imagined as troops, or driving home, reflecting on what she'd done, or lying awake at night, peopling the image of her own face with the imagined faces of her creations, Jess felt anything but powerful. She felt, instead, dissipated, fragmented, diluted. Something in her, be it energy or power or basic motivational force, was finite, and she had not doubled it but divided it, again and again, until she felt scattered and disparate and no longer in command of her gathered selves. This, she thought, was what men did to you. No, not every woman in the country had taken quite such drastic measures, but all of them, as far as she could see, used self-division to approximate completeness. You were this woman at work. You were this woman at home. You were this woman in bed. All your energy was expended in compartmentalisation. The power required to be whole was diluted.

She looked up at Robert. He was running his fork across the surface of his plate, scooping up what remained of the sauce. As if sensing her looking at him, he glanced up and smiled.

'We should go,' she said.

He nodded. 'I'm ready,' he said.

———

In the post-tech park era people half-jokingly referred to as Edmundsbury 2.0, change was abundant. Touting for planning permission in a town not yet consenting to their arrival, Green had trumpeted their own efficiency, and played up the changes they could effect. Sweeteners had been offered and accepted: new cabling, a town-wide private network, increased download speeds, heightened security. Convenience and modernity had won out over suspicion. Now, though, discomfort had crept back in. The aftermath of some intangible shift was in the air. It was something people talked about at odd hours: in the early morning after a night of drinking, at the end of a particularly reflective meal as the bill was being settled. The word *uncanny* was bandied around a lot. Visible change was no longer the issue. The unease stemmed from the unseen, from the near-invisible yet perfectly measurable changes Edmundsbury's environment had undergone. Keen to invest in schemes that might not have brought any financial return but which promised to accrue ideological interest, Green had offered to help the town meet its goal of becoming more environmentally sound. The project was heavily publicised, but the details were not. How many people in Edmundsbury were therefore conscious of the fact that the illumination emitted from their once-familiar street lights had shifted ever so slightly along the spectrum? Was anyone aware, as Jess was, that the direction of this shift was, to a fractional but nonetheless important degree, closer to full-spectrum daylight, meaning that, almost undetectably, anyone out walking after dark was subject to a micro-alteration of their circadian state?

Even when changes were digital, the effect, Jess knew, could be physical. Complaints about traffic had increased by almost two hundred per cent. Local opinion held that the arrival of the tech park had led to the arrival of more people, which had led in turn to greater congestion on the roads – an assumption that clearly had at least some basis in reality. But plotted on a graph, the increase in internet speeds and the increase in traffic complaints could practically be overlaid onto each other. People's collective capacity for patience had decreased in inverse proportion to their expectation of immediacy.

As she and Robert walked towards the town centre, Jess considered the way in which all of these individually small and almost unnoticeable changes in experience added up to a seismic shift in consciousness. Around her, perfectly unaware people traversed pools of altered light, their senses tuned to new pitches of speed and immediacy. Perhaps, she thought, their heart rates were infinitesimally accelerated, their pupils micro-dilated, their breathing a quarter of a respiration faster and shallower. Perhaps all these adaptations, in what they saw and how they saw it, added up to something irreversible, evolutionary. Or perhaps the creeping change responsible for Edmundsbury's collective, semi-conscious unease was nothing more than the digital mimicry of an organic inevitability. Progress was always present; it was only its speed that changed: from faster than light down to glacial, imperceptible to vertigo-inducing. Nothing was ever stable; nothing was ever at rest.

And this was just the physical, the tangible. In the world of feelings and perceptions, drift was endemic. Look at Robert, she thought, walking with his hand in hers. Once, such a statement would have seemed excessive, unnecessary. Now, there was something vital about it, as if it was their own little resistance to time's effects, their gloss on the countercurrents beneath and around them.

They had turned out of their suburban street and were now walking along the main road that led into the town centre. Half of Edmundsbury, it seemed, had made it out for the show. The atmosphere was both edgy and excited. Nervous chatter filled the streets.

Edmundsbury's so-called historic but now blandly small-town centre, a short walk from Jess and Robert's terraced house, was in many ways the epicentre of the peripheral changes that orbited it. Once home to a fruit and livestock market, it was now fenced in by coffee chains and panini outlets. No-one went into town to shop any more. They went there to drink coffee and eat – a vague café culture which at least seemed focused on the idea that a town's ethos should centre more on the gathering together of people than the availability of purchasable goods. But when you scratched the surface, things were effectively the same: a culture of expenditure, a town-life predicated on the separation of people from their money.

The sight of the town square filled with people gave rise to the sensation that whatever was happening was, in some as yet uncategorised way, significant. Regular boundaries and uses of public space were temporarily suspended. There was a pointed but thus far non-invasive police presence. Officers stood at the edges of the small crowd, chatting and eyeing those assembling with a casual, almost paternal gaze.

'Right,' said Robert as they wandered over to the edge of the gathering and came to a stop. 'What now?'

Jess shrugged. 'Wait, I suppose.'

He slipped an arm around her waist and pulled her towards him. She felt herself resisting, then, embarrassed by her own reluctance, relenting, softening into him.

'When was the last time we were out like this?' she said.

He frowned. 'Last night?'

She rolled her eyes. 'No, like *out*. Like this. Like looking at fireworks or Christmas lights or something.'

'You think that's what this will be like?'

'No,' she said. 'But still.'

Edmundsbury's clock tower, which didn't so much loom over the square as perch squatly a little way above it, began to chime. As it did so, a black transit van with tinted windows rounded the corner and, allowing time for the small crowd to part, drove into the middle of the square and sat with its engine idling. For what felt like a lengthy few seconds nothing happened. The tension, Jess noted, was palpable, and people were, consciously or unconsciously, backing away from the vehicle. Jess did not feel particularly concerned. Far from being sinister, the van was actually, to Jess, a sign that something carefully considered was going on. It was too common a signifier – a vehicle not for a covert military team or highly organised terror cell but instead for a group of people who revelled in the idea that they might be mistaken for one of those things. It was the tinted windows, she thought, and the fact that they'd chosen a black van as opposed to a white one. For anyone conducting some kind of hostile act from which they hoped to escape, the primary concern would have been to select a vehicle that would blend in on the roads. This shiny black monstrosity would stick out a mile, suggesting that sticking out a mile was exactly what it was supposed to do.

It was difficult to tell whether the crowd was becoming more anxious during the slight delay, or if in fact it had caused people to relax. There was almost, Jess sensed, a slight feeling of impatience, as if everyone was waiting for the event to buffer and load.

She was about to say something to Robert when the rear doors of the van opened and five people wearing identical masks and office garb to the man at the party climbed out. They gestured to the crowd to move back, and the crowd, inexplicably obedient, obeyed. The power balance was not lost on Jess. This was not an anarchist gesture. This was a group of people for whom existing dynamics of authority were largely assumed. Even if they might have felt themselves to be outsiders, their marshalling of the crowd demonstrated that they still sought a power they envied in others.

They arranged the crowd at the front of the van, facing towards and past it. The back doors of the van were open and pointing away from the crowd. Everyone and everything were now directed towards the large expanse of pale wall that formed the top half of a café overlooking the northern end of the square. The angle of the building's roof meant that it had skylights rather than standard windows, leaving the upper wall as an unbroken rectangular expanse of whitewashed facade perfectly proportioned to become exactly what the men in masks now made of it: a cinema screen.

Jess, like the rest of the crowd, was at the front end of the van, and so couldn't see inside it, but the moment the familiar glow lit up the white space it was clear that the van housed a powerful projector. The men outside the van now numbered four. They arranged themselves two on each side of the vehicle, facing the crowd, their backs to the unfolding projection. They carried nothing, and something about their stance and the way they flanked the van implied an absence, as if weaponry were suggested but not present. She wondered if this was deliberate, or just the result of profound cultural association. It was an uncomfortable sensation, realising you'd noticed the absence of guns. Guns, surely, should be noticeable only when present?

On the wall behind the men, a word appeared: black, sans-serif, stark in the sharp light on the bare white wall.

Edmundsbury:

It remained for several seconds. Then, it was replaced by an image: full colour, but grainy and low-res, shot in weak living-room light, the camera not quite straight. It was of a young woman, kneeling on all fours on a sofa, naked, her rear towards the camera, her hand reaching back through her legs to her vagina. After maybe ten or so seconds, the image disappeared and was replaced by text.

We are The Griefers.

This was in turn replaced by another image: a woman in what looked to be her late teens, leaning over a sink, wearing nothing but a G-string, her right hand covering her breasts, her left hand holding her mobile phone, its camera pointed at the mirror, the starburst of flash cutting across her eyes and obscuring her face.

We want to ask you:

Another image, this time of a man, or rather, most of a man. His head was out of shot. His trousers were round his knees, his shirt unbuttoned to reveal a thatch of chest hair and a generous expanse of stomach. In the centre of the image was his erection, his right hand gripping it with unnecessary force, the veins on his arm standing out in relief, the head of his cock bulging out of the top of his fist.

What *don't* you want to share?

People in the crowd were starting to mutter. If this was some sort of art piece, they seemed to feel, it was in bad taste. If it was real, it was in worse taste.

The next image was of an email, the address of both sender and recipient crudely redacted with a red, photoshopped smear. Some of the text had been blurred but in the centre a single line stood out in relief: *no-one will ever find out*. The image dissolved in a slow fade, replaced by a screenshot of a bank account – the details again bluntly struck through with digital red pen, only the transactions visible. The amounts, Jess noted, were in the tens of thousands. This time the text appeared over the image:

Remember, Edmundsbury . . .

As it did so, the thick red lines across the bank details began to erase themselves, right to left. Just as a few letters became visible beneath, the image was replaced by the preceding one, the email, on which the red lines were again creeping off the page, revealing the back half of the redacted addresses. This was in turn replaced, quickly, before any names besides generic email services could be seen, by the erection image, only now the camera was edging upwards, with more of the man's face becoming visible, only for the image to vanish at the last moment, dissolving into the bathroom selfie, in which, now, the light from the flash was fading, airbrushed in real time, the woman's eyes becoming visible. Finally, the first image showed itself again: the kneeling woman, anonymous unless you happened to know her intimately, or unless you happened to follow the camera as it zoomed in, over her backside and shoulder, towards a mirror that Jess had not originally noticed, in which, faint and small, her face could almost be made out . . .

The image vanished. In its place, in close-up, filling the screen, a series of un-redacted profile pictures faded into one another. One or two looked familiar. Someone in the crowd shouted, 'That's me,' and someone else shouted, 'That's my wife.' Tight red squares appeared on the images, isolating the faces, cropping them, blowing them up. The fade-speed increased, until the images no longer quite seemed to be replacing each other but instead *becoming* each other, each face morphing to accommodate the next. As the speed increased, the impression was of a blur of faces, until the change from image to image was undetectable, the speed registering only as humming visual static, the shifting faces now essentially stable, one face, staring out at the crowd: the face of the masks worn by the men in the van. Finally, over the top of it, flashing white before the screen went black, came the statement Jess was by now expecting:

We are your face.

And then the projector snapped off. The men climbed back inside the van. The rear doors slammed shut. The van drove calmly away.

Jess slipped her hand from Robert's and rubbed her eyes, returning to herself after some moments away. When she blinked and looked at Robert, he was massaging his fingers, kneading away the force of her grip.

0010

Being Hugo Bennington, Hugo liked to say, was a tough job, but someone had to do it. For a while he'd said dirty job, but Teddy, his right-hand man and advisor in all things presentational, had cautioned him against the word.

Hugo operated in a complicated state of balance. His primary task was to be outspoken, but his other task was to watch what he said. Hence: being Hugo Bennington was a tough job. Quite whether anyone *had* to do it was more open to question. Hugo had, on many occasions, given quite serious thought to not doing it at all. But you couldn't just go around saying it was tough to be you. It sounded like you were whining, and Hugo hated whining. Indeed, a recent statistical analysis of Hugo's columns for *The Record*, carried out, ironically enough, by some whining liberal hoping to eviscerate Hugo through his use of language, had revealed that *whining* was his most commonly used term, beating out *liberal, conspiracy, politically correct*, and *'Multicultural'*, which Hugo always both capitalised and placed in inverted commas.

The trick to being Hugo was that both Hugos – outspoken and restrained – had to get out of bed at the same time and work in happy tandem through the course of the day. Not that Outspoken Hugo ever had a day off, of course. Give Outspoken Hugo a Pall Mall, a bacon sandwich, and a cup of coffee the colour of a person Restrained Hugo would caution Outspoken Hugo against mentioning, and Outspoken Hugo was good for several hours of good old-fashioned common sense. Restrained Hugo, on the other hand, was a different beast entirely. Restrained Hugo liked to sleep in late, let Outspoken Hugo get going, and then panic later, when Outspoken Hugo, left unsupervised, said something he wasn't supposed to say. This had, unfortunately, happened more than once, and the consensus in Hugo's party was that it needed to happen a whole lot less, and so measures had been taken. These measures took the form of Teddy, who, with Hugo's begrudging agreement, now let himself into Hugo's kitchen every morning and waited for Hugo to get up so as to ensure that all Hugos were present and correct, meaning Hugo had been forced to instigate a counter-measure by which, after brushing his teeth and getting dressed, he snuck out the back door for a fag and a few moments of peace – the word by which Hugo euphemistically described his first deep, burning haul of the morning, the protracted coughing fit and the lingering wilt against the wall with his fingers pressed into the space between his eyes while he waited out the inevitable head rush.

Hugo's health was complicated. To the casual observer, he appeared reasonably fit. He was slim, compact. His face, when not bloodless with almost fainting, often bore what appeared to be a perfectly healthy glow. He made efforts, at all times, to appear hale and hearty and possessed of what at least one newspaper column had described as an inexhaustible energy. The implications of this were, politically, critical. A great deal of his message was built around the idea that Britain was in a dreadful state, and that there was, as a result, a great deal of work to do. It was no good, according to Teddy, telling all and sundry how much difficult work lay ahead if you looked like you were about to crumple into an exhausted heap at the merest suggestion of effort. Instead, he had to project an aura of invincibility, an impression of infinite reserves.

The problem was that as well as being a perpetual font of youthful vigour, Hugo also had to remind potential supporters that he was just like everyone else. He was, according to his own personal branding, the man in the street. More importantly, he was the man in the pub. If ever he failed at being the man in the pub, was the fear, men in the pub would stop being impressed by him. This put pressure on Hugo's photo opportunities. The second Teddy got wind of a photographer, he parked Hugo behind a full English, or jammed a fag between his fingers, or hastily pulled him a pint of ale, even if it was barely ten in the morning.

The result was that Hugo's perky exterior was grossly at odds with his slowly corroding interior. Regardless of the glow in his cheeks, his campaign was killing him from the inside. His pulse sped up and slowed down on a schedule entirely of its own devising. Even when he slept he panicked, waking in the grey, dingy fog of near dawn to a hammering heart and what seemed like more sweat than any one body should healthily have produced.

He told himself this would all be reversible. The timeframe of the campaign was vague, but at some point, hopefully in the next year, it would be over. The by-election was yet to be announced because the incumbent occupant of the seat on which Hugo had his eye – the neither hale nor hearty Trevor Barnaby – was not yet dead and not yet retired, but soon, very soon, as everyone knew thanks to a series of well-publicised health scares, he would be at least one of those things, and Hugo would pounce. There would be a last desperate expelling of energy and then, finally, a moment of rest.

Deep down, though, Hugo knew this wasn't quite the case. It was true that the campaign hadn't helped, but it was equally true that the tightening grip of decay about Hugo's body hadn't just come from nowhere. His fears had diseased him. Hugo was a man very much in touch with his fears. He had to be, for they were legion. He could file every heart-flutter and stomach-plummet, every clutched breath and stumbling white-out, into its appropriate category: Illness (global); Illness (personal); Death (self); Longevity (others); Humiliation (self); Failure (self); Success (others); Impotence (self); Virility (others). He knew them, but didn't want to talk about them. Instead, he transmogrified them, bundled them into an all-purpose terror that people seemed to relate to. Everyone was scared, when you got right down to it. Hugo was old enough to remember the days when politics was about reassuring people. But those days were over. Now you had to keep them fearful. Who better to do that than a fearful man?

Fag finished, Hugo took a preparatory calming breath, eased himself through the back door, and wandered through to the kitchen, where Teddy was lounging at the dining table with his feet up on one of the chairs.

'Boss man,' said Teddy. 'Hugotron. The Hugh-ster. How goes it?'

'It goes fine,' said Hugo. 'Get your feet off my chair.'

'Totally,' said Teddy, not getting his feet off the chair.

Teddy was ostentatiously toned. His physique suggested not so much physical strength as an unswerving commitment to the expansion of his glamour muscles. He had a way of flexing his pecs with every motion. Even reclining, he kept his arms about six inches away from his torso, clearly attempting to convey the impression of throbbing power brought reluctantly to rest. Like his body, his tanned skin spoke not of invigorating outdoor activity but of expensive indoor labour – a shade somewhere between bad laminate flooring and a photoshopped sunset. He dressed in a uniform of hyper-advanced activity gear: skin-tight breathable running tops and dangerously revealing shorts. On his feet he appeared to be wearing a kind of moulded saliva.

'What on earth have you got on your feet?' said Hugo. 'You look like you've stood in a puddle.'

'Memo-skin footwear,' said Teddy. 'It mimics the experience of being barefoot. I literally can't feel my shoes.'

Hugo made his way over to the kettle, wondering, not for the first time, why Teddy's daily intrusion into his domestic life seemed to exclude the effort of making a cuppa.

'Cup of coffee?' said Hugo, somehow making it sound like both an offer and a request.

'No thanks. I'm powering down.'

'Do you mean sitting down?'

'No, I can power down standing up. I'm arriving at a moment of stillness.'

Teddy closed his eyes and took a long, deep breath.

'I feel totally re-energised,' he said.

'I thought you were powering down?'

'Oh, I've powered down. Now I'm re-energising. It's all about flow.'

'Are you going to have to power down and recharge or whatever repeatedly today? Because—'

'I'm striving for the non-habitual. Ask me how big my comfort zone is.'

'How big is your comfort zone?'

'This big,' said Teddy, pinching his index finger and thumb tightly together.

'Meaning you're never comfortable?'

'Meaning I'm embracing the unknown.'

'So you're uncomfortable and you don't know anything.'

'What do any of us really know?'

Hugo didn't have an answer for that. The things he knew he didn't want to know. The things he didn't know he didn't want to know either.

Having consumed as much as he was able to tolerate both of coffee (he couldn't, yet, stomach anything solid) and Teddy's surreal musings (an area in which a degree of solidity would have been appreciated), Hugo trudged back upstairs to his study, got himself comfy in the luxuriously padded swivel chair that faced his desk, and settled down to what he rather generously referred to as work, by which he meant the arduous task of wasting yet another hour examining the internet's opinion of him. Years ago, there had been a sense of excitement in being the subject of discussion, but this was quickly replaced by paranoia, and then, as the paranoia burned itself out, by grim resignation and even, although he couldn't quite admit it, morbid fascination, and so, for the past few years, Hugo's working day had begun with a deep-dive into the state of his auto-complete. Typing *Hugo B* into the search box was relatively pleasing in that *Hugo Bennington* tended to be a respectable fourth or fifth in line, but Hugo tended not to pause here, instead pushing on to *Hugo Benn*, at which point his full name jumped satisfyingly to the top of the list. Day after day, Hugo took exactly one second's pleasure in what he always thought of as a bloody and dramatic coup fought out in some unseen cyberspatial realm, only for his fantasy to rudely dissolve as, bubbling upwards from the bottom of the list, Google's suggestions for what might follow began to appear. *Hugo Bennington evil* tended to make a pretty rapid appearance, as did *Hugo Bennington ugly*, *Hugo Bennington sexist*, *Hugo Bennington racist* (naturally), and *Hugo Bennington must die*, which was, much to Hugo's utter disgust, the name of a radical left-wing punk band plying the Devon pub circuit. From here, a man with more self-control and, indeed, more self-respect than Hugo would have given up, hit the delete key, and watched all the suggestions vanish. But sadly, if that man existed, Hugo was not in touch with him, and so his fingers forged manfully ahead, bashing out the final letters of his name and watching as, against all his hopes, Google began to vomit up insult after insult, particularly if, or, more accurately, when, Hugo's fingers, acting largely on their own reconnaissance, added *is* after his name, at which point it always felt as if Google had opened a direct conduit between the filth of the world and every half-buried insecurity in Hugo's soul. *Hugo Bennington is a moron.* *Hugo Bennington is the antichrist.* These were the ones he clung to now: the vague, the uncreative, the mindless. But beneath them came an ever-evolving hierarchy of distressingly inventive ire. *Hugo Bennington is to humanity what dog shit is to shoes. Hugo Bennington is an aching scrotum. Hugo Bennington is a condom full of clap.*

Precisely why he wasted the start of each day masochistically updating himself on the extent to which he was loathed, Hugo couldn't quite say. Like everything else in his life, he had a suspicion that it stemmed from his fears. To the ever-growing list, he had, since the marked increase in attention he now enjoyed, added invisibility, irrelevance, superfluity. So long as people were angry, he thought, he could still be reasonably certain that he existed.

'Ten-minute warning, big guy.'

Teddy's voice from the bottom of the stairs gave Hugo an unpleasant jolt. The irony of Teddy, a child so fundamentally sub-par that it was a miracle he managed to dress himself, getting paternal with Hugo was almost too much to take. But such irritations were, in Hugo's experience, best borne in silence.

He shut down his computer, which now that it had fulfilled its primary purpose of reminding him exactly how much he was hated was effectively redundant, gathered his documents and briefcase, and made his way downstairs.

'Car's here,' said Teddy brightly.

'The car? Oh Christ, is it that time already?'

'Afraid so, dude.'

They stepped out of the front door and walked to an idling Mercedes. They both sat in the back, separated from the driver by a glass screen. From his obscenely futuristic backpack, Teddy brought out a fluorescent-yellow plastic thermos, unscrewed the lid, and began to drink.

'Oh God,' said Hugo. 'Can't you wait until we get to the office? The smell of that stuff makes me gag.'

'I time my nutrition to the minute, Hugo. Putting back breakfast throws my whole metabolism off.'

For approximately a year, Teddy had consumed no solid food whatsoever. Instead, his diet was composed entirely of a semi-liquid, neon-yellow goo called Fibuh, which he consumed four times a day at carefully scheduled intervals and which he claimed was scientifically calibrated to provide an even more rounded meal than the average rounded meal. Fibuh had been invented by a seventeen-year-old chemistry genius so socially awkward that he was unable to eat in the school canteen and so in need of remedial life-skills training that he was unable to prepare a sandwich. He'd therefore devoted his life to the design, production, and marketing of a product that eliminated both of those horrors and which also, conveniently, made him a millionaire. He claimed he was going to live to be two hundred years old because he was achieving optimum nutrition. A series of nutritionists claimed that as a result of never allowing his body to process solid food he'd be colostomised by forty.

Teddy took a long haul on his flask and came away with his upper lip painted bright yellow.

'Mmm,' he said, with a slightly uneasy satisfaction. 'Yeah.'

'You know that stuff smells exactly like melted plastic, don't you, Teddy?'

'Fibuh is actually flavourless and odourless,' said Teddy. 'Taste and scent are synthetically added as part of the production process.'

'Then why have they chosen to make it smell like a radioactive lunchbox?'

'It's actually supposed to smell like a canteen. Research has shown that the smell of dining rooms elicits a more stable hunger response than the smell of food itself.'

'It's eliciting a distinctly unstable nausea response in me.'

'That's because you haven't tasted it,' said Teddy, taking another haul and swallowing heavily, then blinking away tears and wiping his mouth with the back of his hand. 'So you don't have the right association. Once you taste it . . .'

'What does it taste like?'

'Chicken,' said Teddy. 'It's a joke.'

'How's that a joke?'

'You know, people always say everything tastes like chicken. Well, in the future, everything will taste like chicken.'

'That's it? In your brave new world of never having to consume solid food again, that's the only choice of flavour anyone will have?'

'Choice is unproductive,' said Teddy. 'It produces cognitive friction. People haven't got time for choice any more, Hugo. They want to get up, put on their clothes without choosing them, knock back some Fibuh, and get on with what's important.'

'But what about variety? What about surprise?'

Teddy shrugged. 'Outmoded concepts.'

Hugo was on the verge of pressing Teddy on what was, in terms of Hugo's political ambitions, a rather concerning view, but Teddy had clearly drilled down enough, and had shifted his attention to the street outside.

'Right, he should be around here somewhere,' he said. He twisted in his seat and squinted out the back window. 'No sign of a tail.'

'For God's sake, Teddy. Do we really have to go through all this—'

'Do you want to be seen with him?' said Teddy. 'Do you want to explain why you're having a meeting with him?'

'No.'

'Right then. OK, there he is.' Teddy pointed to a thick-set, shaven-headed man standing on a corner desperately trying to look inconspicuous by reading a newspaper in the middle of the pavement.

'Christ,' said Hugo. 'He's in disguise as himself.'

'Why's he wearing his outfit?' said Teddy. 'How many times have I told him: don't wear your outfit?'

'He doesn't have any other clothes, I don't think. He's like you. He gets up in the morning and chooses between four identical black bomber jackets.'

'OK, let's pick him up,' said Teddy. 'And Hugo? Strict fifteen-minute clock on this meeting. That Fibuh will be heading downtown and you don't want me trapped in a car when it pulls into the station. You know what I'm saying, big guy?'

'You're saying you've had your baby food and now you have half an hour before you shit yourself.'

'That's . . . I mean, I wouldn't put it quite—'

Teddy didn't get a chance to finish because Ronnie Childs was clambering awkwardly into the back of the car and trying to slot himself between Teddy and Hugo.

'Gents,' he said.

'Ronnie,' said Hugo, moving over.

Short, muscular to the point of being spherical, bald to the point of being reflective, Ronnie Childs was now wedged so tightly between Hugo and Teddy that his shoulders were up around his ears and what little neck he had was completely compressed into his bomber jacket. Unable to properly turn left or right, he attempted to greet first Teddy then Hugo using only the muscles in his face.

For several years, Childs had positioned himself as head of the East of England wing of a self-styled 'militia' called Brute Force. Brute Force's agenda was, in no uncertain terms, street-level race war. They wore a uniform of black bomber jackets, oversized black boots, and camouflaged combat trousers. They were all, to a man, feral. The problem was that they were also increasingly popular, so popular in fact that they'd started muttering about becoming a legitimate political party, meaning they presented, for Hugo and the rest of England Always, a double nightmare. On one level, they were political poison, roaming the streets making what Hugo thought of as the 'proper' Right look bad. On another level, they had the potential, if they insisted on their deranged plan to shed their bomber jackets and slip into some cheap suits, to leech votes. They therefore had to be convinced to work with England Always so as to secure as much of the vote as possible. However, because they were the last thing England Always needed to be publicly associated with, any connection between Hugo and Childs had to be conscientiously concealed and, in the event it was ever uncovered, strenuously denied, which was why, once a month or so, Hugo and Teddy had to go through the rather debasing rigmarole of hiring a car and a driver in order to pretend to Ronnie Childs that they were important enough to have a car and a driver, just so Childs would meet them in the car and not at the office.

'My boys aren't happy,' said Childs bluntly. 'And if my boys aren't happy, I'm not happy.'

'And we want you to be happy, Ronnie,' said Teddy, doing his empathetic face. 'What is it that's making you unhappy?'

Ronnie Childs was a man who spent his entire life tense to the threat of disrespect, and so he often, as now, tended to stare at people for quite a long time before responding, clearly trying to ascertain whether or not he was being mocked.

'It's these cunts in masks,' he said finally.

'Right,' said Teddy.

'They're fucking terrorists,' said Childs, trying to raise a hand to emphasise his point but finding himself straitjacketed by the seating arrangements.

'Are they?' said Hugo, genuinely surprised.

'They might be, for all we know,' said Childs. 'That's the point. We don't know what they are.'

Hugo looked over towards Teddy, seeking some kind of confirmation.

'It looks like they're political,' said Teddy. 'Whether or not that makes them—'

'Some bunch of cunts in masks are waltzing around fucking things up and freaking people out. And what are we doing? Nothing. Fucking nothing. Because you said before I get the boys to do anything about . . . anything, I have to ask you. Meaning we're just sitting on our arses.'

'Are you listening to this, Teddy? Ronnie here is sitting on his arse. We can't have that.'

'No,' said Teddy.

'I'm not the sort of bloke who just sits on his arse,' said Childs.

'Quite,' said Hugo. 'Look, it seems to me that what we need to work out first is who they are and what they want.'

'Well, good luck with that,' said Childs, 'when you can't even see their faces.'

'Right,' said Hugo. 'We can't see their faces and so we can't—'

'You can't see if they're Muslims,' said Childs.

'Shit,' said Hugo. 'That's true.'

'Whoa,' said Teddy, holding up a hand. 'Let's—'

'What?' said Hugo. 'It's what everyone's thinking.'

'But no-one's saying.'

'But that's my thing,' said Hugo. 'I say what everyone's thinking but no-one's saying.'

'Well, within reason. Some people are thinking things no-one wants anyone to say.'

'OK, what's the problem with saying that then?'

'It's anti-Islamic,' said Childs. 'Everything's anti-Islamic now.'

'No it isn't,' said Hugo. 'It's got nothing to do with bloody Islam. All we're saying is, if you can't see what colour people are—'

'I'm wondering if maybe we should kind of not keep saying it?' said Teddy. 'So as not to get too in the habit of saying it? Because that's how things slip out.'

'I don't understand what's controversial about this.'

'Well, what's controversial about it is that it kind of suggests that terrorism is something that's defined by the race of the person doing it rather than the thing they're doing.'

'But it is,' said Hugo.

'Not really, no. Because if you put a bomb in a school, you're a terrorist. Doesn't matter what colour you are.'

'I think that's a very semantic point.'

'Politics basically is semantics, Hugo.'

'That's an even more semantic point. Well done, Teddy.'

'I don't know what semantics is,' said Childs.

'You don't need to, Ronnie. Your life involves no semantics whatsoever.'

'You could tell by their hands anyway,' said Childs.

'That's true,' said Hugo. 'What if I didn't say faces? What if I said hands?'

Teddy looked at him a long time. 'Let's say nothing for the time being, OK?'

'Faces. Hands. It's a semantic point, isn't it?' said Childs.

Hugo looked at Childs for what he hoped was a long time but not long enough to make Childs angry.

'What's that thing they say?' said Hugo. '*We are your face.* What does that mean?'

'We don't know what that means,' said Teddy.

'Could be racial,' said Childs.

'Could be very racial,' said Hugo, who found himself agreeing with Childs slightly more often than he would have liked. 'Have we looked into that, Teddy?'

'No,' said Teddy, 'because like I was saying before . . .' He looked at his watch. 'We're T minus seven minutes on the bowel situation, Hugo. Ronnie: we need to drop you off here.'

'But we haven't—'

'We've heard,' said Hugo seriously. 'You understand what I'm saying, Ronnie? We've *heard.*'

'We've heard *very clearly*,' said Teddy, across whose face a thin film of sweat had developed. 'And now we're going to *plan*. And once we've planned, we're going to act.'

'What you need to do right now, Ronnie,' said Hugo, 'is *pause. Strategically.* You know what we're saying?'

'I can only hold back the lads for so long,' said Childs.

'I know exactly what you mean,' said Teddy. 'Boy, can I relate to that. But there's a time and a place. That's all we're saying.'

'Right,' said Childs.

'We're going to drop you here,' said Teddy.

'Maybe if one of you gets out,' said Childs, wriggling from side to side.

'No can do,' said Teddy.

'One of us might be seen,' said Hugo.

'Alright, yeah, good point. I'll just . . .' He clambered over Teddy and pushed open the door, then stumbled out onto the pavement. Looking briefly rage-filled, he then gathered his composure and opened his newspaper.

'He's reading his newspaper on the pavement again,' said Hugo, looking back.

'Driver,' said Teddy, tapping urgently on the glass partition. 'We're going to need to travel slightly faster than this.'

———————

'He's gone dark, is what you're basically saying.'

'Not totally dark, no. Like, he's still *there*. He's still pulling traffic. But nothing's really coming back and I can't see what he's doing.'

Trina nestled the phone into the crook of her neck and reached down to her mouse to click around some more. In front of her, the traffic-light colour codes of the Microtaskers that made up the bulk of Green's workforce reordered themselves, but left her none the wiser as to what the one on whom her attention had fallen might be up to.

'And he's usually productive?'

'Usually super-productive,' Trina said. 'He logs in all hours, shifts tasks like a machine. He was a day or two away from going next level.'

'And then . . .'

'Then this.'

'Maybe it's personal issues?'

'I thought that, but then . . . His traffic is just too weird. He hasn't dropped off the grid, which would suggest a sudden crisis, and there hasn't been the slow decline in productivity you'd associate with, you know, mounting domestic issues. It's like he's half-vanished, but he's still there.'

There was a pause on the other end of the line.

'Have you flagged him?'

'Not yet.'

'You're going to have to flag him.'

'I know, I know.'

'Who's your team leader?'

'Norbiton.'

Another pause.

'I can see why you'd be reluctant.'

'Right.'

'But I don't think there's any other way.'

She sighed.

'Fine. OK. I'm flagging him. Wish me luck.'

She put the phone down, navigated her way through the profiles in front of her, right-clicked, and added a flag. Seconds later, the system acknowledged her action with a little pop-up. Through the grinding monotony of her day, this was about as close as she would get to an event.

She sat back in her chair and rubbed her eyes, onto which were imprinted the scrolling colour-codes of Beatrice, her task-management system. She waited until the after-image faded before allowing herself to return to immediate time and space: the blank cube of her No-Go room, just big enough for a desk and a terminal; soundproofed, swipe-carded. To some, it would have been depressing. To Trina, this anonymous, isolated cell was what achievement looked like. She'd battled for this, and so never resented it.

Work at The Arbor was rarely, if ever, a process of collaboration. Thanks to the neurotically enforced Need To Know policy, nothing of significance was achieved in the open. Instead, projects were managed by designated individuals in flat-packed, portable cells programmed with a single set of entry credentials. The system's aim was to prevent data breach. Even if someone went rogue and started leaking, went the wisdom, they would only be able to reveal what limited information was known to them. A side effect of secrecy, though, was status. Your presence on the open floor, toiling away with all the other non-project workers, signified only the unimportance of your work. To be noticed, to be in the mix when increased responsibility was discussed, you had to be nowhere to be seen, working away on something only you could define.

She returned her attention to Beatrice, the neatly ordered interface that comprised the entirety of her working environment. In the top right-hand corner of her screen, a real-time figure advised her that productivity was exactly where she wanted it. Nonetheless, she played with the parameters, nudging sliders and dials and watching as the productivity rate updated itself accordingly. Below it, the icons and worker handles, each of which represented an anonymous worker coding away in their bedroom or lounge in various corners of Edmundsbury and, in some cases, the country, shifted colour. Green for the highly productive, amber for the average, a stern red for those not currently pulling their weight. At the bottom of the list, Tayz, the once-reliable worker she'd just been forced to report, remained stubbornly scarlet.

Thought and action were ruthlessly segregated in The Arbor. Ideas were generated by those whose position in the hierarchy allowed them to think. Once approved, those ideas were broken down, fragmented into a series of actionable tasks. Each task was a package, a container for a series of tiny, non-hierarchically arranged jobs that needed to be done, each of which was, by this stage in the process, so small, so insignificant, so utterly disconnected from the big-picture project of which they were part, that literally anyone could complete them. Even better, they could complete them from anywhere they had access to a networked computer. If you believed Green, which all Green employees unquestioningly did, it was an arrangement that suited everyone. Bulky, expensive offices had become redundant. Dull, inflexible office hours were a thing of the past. Microtaskers worked wherever they wanted, whenever they wanted. Because they were given a single micropayment for each microtask they completed, they worked as much or as little as they liked. The work–life balance,

Green proudly claimed, had never been more flexible.

The reality, as Trina knew, was a lot less utopian. She'd MT'd herself. She knew how many micropayments it took to approximate a full wage. She knew how many hours, daylight and dark, it took to complete enough tasks to pay the bills. Unlike so many of the faceless workers she currently controlled, however, she also knew exactly what it took to graduate from remote, piecemeal labour to the next level up.

Like any gamified and incentivised system of working, the aim of Microtasking was to win. The problem was that no-one knew what winning looked like, or how it might be achieved. This was, of course, no accident. With no clear sense of what constituted achievement, the only option was to achieve as much as physically and emotionally possible in the hope it might suffice. Shaped around distinctly primal impulses, the Microtasking ecosystem was custom-built to leverage morale. Because the work required of MTs offered no context, no sense of completion, and no fixed endpoint, a sense of achievement had to be synthetically added. Levels could be unlocked, payment could be incrementally increased, status could be offered and withdrawn according to productivity. MTs weren't just working, they were competing. At the end of the game, was the implication, lay the ultimate reward: an end to Microtasking, a position Inside The Building.

Rumours abounded as to what was required. MTs formed chatrooms and forums to swap speculation. Some said productivity was key. Others felt quality was what counted. Trina knew the truth: it was neither. Green had productivity on tap. Since the Microtasking system automatically weeded out anyone who botched more than a couple of tasks, quality was a given. Instead, what caught Green's attention were the very factors around which they based their own ethos: innovation and disruption.

The sliders and dials of Beatrice's interface, to which Trina, in her hard-earned No-Go room, now turned her attention, were her own design. During her time working and studying, she'd become interested in certain parameters. Beatrice, she'd realised, was automated, and as a result, it was predictable. Although its exact structures of punishment and reward could never quite be ascertained by the people it remotely managed, its rhythms and patterns could be unconsciously absorbed. Productivity would be highly stable, but would never exceed projections. Her solution, emailed to The Arbor via an admin address, was simple: a user interface designed for human play. Now, Beatrice's parameters incorporated the plasticity of human whim. In response, the workforce of Microtaskers was destabilised. In scrabbling to rebalance, they overworked. Productivity spiked. Trina was Inside The Building.

Her sense of achievement, though, was muted. All the time she'd been Microtasking, through every speed-fuelled working jag and Valium-cushioned comedown, The Arbor had been her goal. Breaking in had kept her going. Now she was in, now that she'd unlocked the level she'd craved, all she found was that a whole new set of goals had unfolded in front of her. Life in The Arbor, it turned out, was only marginally different to life outside it. The hours were more manageable, the pay more satisfying, but the conditions were painfully familiar. Even here, it transpired, no-one was on anything even approaching a traditional contract. Workers could be sunsetted without warning. She'd seen it happen. A little pop-up on your screen thanked you for your contribution. You clicked to acknowledge, your screen locked, and you were out. Workers were encouraged to keep an empty box under their desk so they could vacate without delay.

As if on cue, an alert box appeared on Trina's screen, causing her to experience, as always when these little windows sprang up out of nowhere, a momentary jolt of fear, followed by relief when she read the contents. *User: NORBITON requests your immediate presence at: An emergency huddle. Location: The Dialogue Den.*

She sent her computer to sleep and exited her No-Go room

using her swipe card. Outside, the open floor hummed gently with muted activity: the insectile patter of keyboards, the chirr of quickly dismissed alerts.

Bream and Holt, who prided themselves on allowing not a single second of non-productivity to burst the fragile bubble of their efficiency, were already present, reclining awkwardly on the beanbags Green provided for meetings in the misguided belief that they countered formality, tablets propped on their knees, styluses windmilling through their fingers while they fretted over the wasted moments lost to Trina's not quite instantaneous appearance. Perched on a slightly larger beanbag, repeatedly adjusting himself as the malleable floor-furniture rejected his portly form and deposited him onto the carpet, was Norbiton.

'Trina,' said Norbiton. 'Glad you could make it.'

'The alert implied it was compulsory,' said Trina.

'It is. I was using a standard idiom by way of a greeting.'

'Consider me greeted,' said Trina, lowering herself to the others' level.

'Right,' said Norbiton. 'All present. Let's begin.'

He turned a page on his defiantly retro legal pad and tapped the paper with a chewed biro. Bream and Holt exchanged glances.

'As all of you no doubt know,' Norbiton began, 'on Friday night, Edmundsbury experienced what for want of a better word we are currently describing as an incident. A group of people calling themselves The Griefers assembled—'

'We all know what happened,' said Bream.

'Great,' said Norbiton. 'Excellent. I was just making sure.'

'Let's move on,' said Holt.

'Well maybe if we start by—'

'We're all short of Meeting Minutes, is the point,' said Bream. 'So this has to be a very targeted meeting.'

'Fine,' said Norbiton. 'I'll get to the point.'

'Got to point out here that saying you'll get to the point only further reduces the speed at which you're able to actually get to the point,' said Holt.

'Noted,' said Norbiton. 'Anyway—'

'We're, what, two minutes in?' said Bream. 'And I'm hearing literally nothing.'

'Green are, as you can imagine—'

'Concerned?' said Holt. 'Because if you're about to say they're concerned, I think we can all safely say that we'd gathered that much.'

'Let's skip the concern,' said Bream. 'Drill down to the relevant detail.'

Norbiton, Trina noticed, was starting to sweat slightly.

'I heard you were a tough team,' he said.

'Kind of a tangent, no?' said Bream.

'My timer says three minutes,' said Holt.

'Wow,' said Norbiton. 'OK. So the thinking is that we need to cauterise this situation basically ASAP because otherwise—'

'Otherwise the town is going to flip out,' said Bream.

'What with the infrastructure and security concerns, etcetera,' said Holt.

'Right,' said Norbiton, running a hand across his brow and heaving himself back to an upright position on his beanbag, from which he had once again slid. 'Exactly so. What I'm trying to establish is—'

'You want traffic reports,' said Bream. 'You want access registers. You want a breach analysis.'

'That's exactly it,' said Norbiton. 'This is . . . This is great. I mean, I'm barely having to do anything here, so, you know, that's really great. Because that's my whole leadership philosophy, to be honest with you. Get out of the way, let the people do their thing. It's not even leadership, if we're being really fine-grain about this. It's more—'

'This seems, like, totally extraneous,' said Holt. 'Does anyone else think this is extraneous?'

'I think it's extraneous,' said Bream.

'Whew, this is quite a pace you're setting here, chaps. And Trina: when I say chaps I want you to know that obviously your gender is noted. No-one's being exclusionary here.'

Trina said nothing. Much as Norbiton might have been hitting the ground, she thought, he was not doing so running.

'Anyway,' said Norbiton, who was starting to sound breathless despite being semi-prone on a beanbag. 'Bream, what are the—'

'Can't tell you,' said Bream.

'Excuse me?'

'I assume you were about to ask about my traffic reports. But I can't tell you. You're not NTK.'

'Also,' said Holt, 'I am not NTK on Bream's traffic reports, so even if you were NTK, Norbiton, Bream wouldn't be able to say anything with me here.'

'Also not NTK,' said Trina, raising her hand. 'Although while we're on the subject, I would like to be NTK on more—'

'You're not NTK on it because you're not working on it,' said Bream.

'It's not, like, some sort of civil-rights issue,' said Holt.

Trina eyeballed Holt but swallowed her response. Whenever Bream or Holt made her angry, they tended to lay the whole angry black woman thing on her, which of course only made her more angry.

'Good,' said Norbiton. 'Great knowledge of the Need To Know policy there. That is totally noted and admired, OK, guys? But—'

'This meeting will be many seconds shorter if everyone uses the agreed acronyms,' said Holt.

'Trina,' said Norbiton, attempting to press on, 'maybe you could—'

'Uh uh,' said Bream. 'We're not NTK on what Trina does.'

'Yay equality, right?' said Holt, shooting Trina a smarmy, dead-eyed smile.

'So basically no-one can . . .' said Norbiton, floundering.

'Tell you anything?' said Bream. 'Not right now in this setting vis-à-vis the subjects that have thus far arisen, no.'

Norbiton set his pen down on his pad and folded his hands, which were, Trina noticed, shaking slightly.

'Sidebar question, OK, guys? If none of you can disclose anything, why do you have meetings?'

'We don't,' said Bream.

'We were actually a little baffled when you called this one,' said Holt.

Norbiton stared at his legal pad, on which he had written nothing. He started humming tunelessly. He took out his phone, thumbed the screen without turning it on, and then returned it to his pocket. Trina saw Bream soundlessly mouthing the words *system glitch* to Holt.

'I really need to . . .' said Norbiton. 'I mean, there's quite a lot of pressure to—'

'Get somewhere?' said Bream.

'Right,' said Norbiton. 'That.'

'You need to put in an NTK request in writing, by email,' said Bream. 'We will then respond as appropriate.'

'OK,' said Norbiton. 'But one of the reasons I called this meeting is because when I email you guys, I tend to get quite a lot of auto-responses, and so—'

'We'll prioritise as the situation demands,' said Holt.

'OK,' said Norbiton, suddenly and, Trina thought, misguidedly positive. 'Well, great meeting guys.'

Everyone stood up. As Bream and Holt left, Trina heard Holt say, 'I give him a month, tops.' Looking at Norbiton's face, it was clear he'd heard too.

'Hey Norbiton,' she said, after the other two had gone.

'What?' said Norbiton, failing to rise from his beanbag with any dignity and in the end just giving up and moving to an upright position through recourse to being on all fours.

'It's just that while I've got you, I need to talk to you about—'

'Look here, missy,' said Norbiton. 'We're in a fucking code-brown situation here. And no, before you say anything, that is not some kind of discriminatory remark. So unless what you've got to say to me is somehow *even more serious* than this business with—'

'You know what?' said Trina, cutting in before Norbiton had a chance to fully work himself up. 'Forget it. I'll catch you at a more . . . focused moment.'

Now that her morning had been interrupted, and given that Norbiton would no doubt be firing off at least one nuclear-priority email the moment he got back to his office, Trina decided she might as well take a break from her No-Go room and go through her emails at her workspace. Everyone who had a No-Go room also had a desk on the open floor. This was where they managed everything they regarded as distracting, by which people tended to mean everything that was not the project for which they had been assigned a No-Go room.

She sat down and opened up her mail client. She had forty-seven emails, most of which were auto-responses. Email at The Arbor was regarded as both antiquated and out of hand. Only managers, keen to keep some kind of record of their correspondence, bothered with it. Everyone else used IM. Consequently, most employees set global out-of-office responses even when they were in the office.

As Trina watched, an email appeared from Norbiton, advising them that he was requesting an NTK exception. Almost immediately, an auto-response popped up from Bream, who always cc'd all on his auto-responses.

Thank you for your email. Due to sustained inbox pressure, I am now only checking my email once a day. I aim to get back to you within one working day. Non-urgent emails will be deleted. If you have not heard from me in two working days, please assume you will not be hearing from me.

Right above it was an auto-response from Holt.

Thank you for your email. Due to the increased demands of managing email in the workplace, I only check my email once a day. Please regard this response as notification that I have already checked my email for today and will be getting back to you tomorrow. Non-urgent messages will be deleted.

Trina didn't cc herself on her auto-responses so that didn't pop up, but after about two seconds she saw another email from Norbiton, subject heading: *Auto-responses.*

Guys: Getting a lot of auto-responses here. Let's get these turned off, OK?

Then Bream's auto-response appeared again, followed by Holt's. Trina deleted both of Norbiton's emails and started working through the forty-seven below, most of which were auto-responses advising her as to people's email habits. Another email popped up from Norbiton with the subject heading *Hello?* and Trina deleted it without even reading it, along with the subsequent auto-responses from Bream and Holt.

'Jesus Christ,' said Bream from two desks back. 'There is a fucking gale-force dickhead blowing through this team.'

Trina turned round and spoke to the tops of Bream and Holt's heads over their terminals.

'Maybe we should turn off our auto-responses,' she said. 'Norbiton seems like he's on a hair trigger.'

Bream looked up, shrugged.

'What are you saying?' he said. 'That Norbiton's, like, *above* protocol?'

Holt said nothing. From his monitor, the tinny hiss of a YouTube video became audible.

'What are you watching?' said Bream.

'The new Teddy Handler,' said Holt. 'Have you seen it?'

'No,' said Bream. 'Ping me that.'

'Done,' said Holt. 'Trina: I'll cc you.'

Trina was about to say *please don't* but the link was already in her inbox, meaning she now, if for no other reason than to avoid unnecessary conflict, felt pressured to watch it. In the tightly patterned existence of The Arbor, conformity was a serious business, and for various reasons a long way out of her control, Trina was already regarded as something of an outsider. She had to take her opportunities of inclusion where she could.

Perpetually garbed in sleeveless workout vests that made his biceps pop, Teddy Handler had swelled outwards from his day job as a political advisor into an increasingly high-profile side role as raving proselytiser for the cult-like productivity movement. He ran so-called Teddycation weekends in corporate hotels during which he paced the stage braying into a head-mic, accompanied by impromptu whoops and throaty roars from the chino-clad white men who paid through the nose to attend. He was not, of course, the first of these dismayingly charismatic productivity gurus. The elevation of productivity and efficiency from help-ful ideas about getting things done to quasi-religious ends unto themselves had happened long ago, and tech had always had a bit of a guru problem in the shape of these huge-ego'd man-boys who promised to lead the precarious masses into one-size-fits-all bliss-fulfilment through endless and unquestioning daily grind. Trina's problem with Handler was the fact that he was, as far as she was aware, the first of these inexplicably revered figures to double as a political advisor to a party she regarded as being the National Front under a new name, and something about the way staff at The Arbor enthusiastically shared his productivity videos without ever stopping to question his politics left her nauseous in a way that far exceeded her usual background-level bullshit allergy. Not that not questioning someone's politics was unusual in The Arbor. If anything, it was something of a credo. Politics was the anti-tech, anathema to data. It was, as anyone would tell you if you were fool enough to ask, very much Outside The Building.

'Think outside the box,' said Handler on the video, flashing up a PowerPoint slide of the word BOX in huge letters. 'How many times have we heard that? It means we need to get creative, right? It's where genius comes from, right?' He paused dramatically.

Behind him, the PowerPoint slide switched to the word WRONG in even bigger letters than the word BOX. 'WRONG,' emphasised Handler, pointing dramatically. 'Why? Because newsflash: this ain't the sixties any more, guys. All that free thinking? All that blue sky? That shit is gone. And you know what I say? Good riddance. Why? Because we've been running an *outmoded paradigm*, that's why. What once was radical is now the norm. People have been thinking outside the box for so long that they don't even know where the box was to begin with or what it looked like or what was in it that was so bad they had to get out of it.' He clicked his remote. Behind him the words SHOW ME THE BOX appeared on the projection screen. 'This is what I say at my encounter sessions,' he said, gesturing behind him. 'When I'm Teddycating people, this is the first bit of Teddycation I throw at them. You should see their faces. They're like: *My box? But Teddy, I've spent my whole life trying to get outside the box!* And you know what I say? I say: Get in it. *Get in your box.* Why? Because if you ever want to have even a hope of thinking outside the box, you'd better be sure you know what it feels like to think inside the box. And if you want to do *that*, then you'd better be sure you can actually find your box in the first place. Because I'm working with people now who are so far out of the box they couldn't find their box even if they enabled some kind of find-my-box function on their phone. I say to people: that box isn't going to come to you. You've got to be out there, *hunting* the box, *tracking it down*, every day, just trying to get a *sniff* of the box, a *taste*, so that then, when you're onto it, when you've tracked that box down and backed it into a corner, you can *get right inside it* and ONLY THEN and ONLY IF YOU NEED TO, get back out of the box and do some thinking there.'

Trina closed the video and tuned out Bream and Holt's Handler-adulation behind her. It wasn't just Handler's politics that repelled her, it was the entire ideology these life-hacking white boys espoused. Unable to explain their privilege by any other means, they had convinced themselves and others that everything that had landed in their laps had landed there not through basic structural imbalance but through some sort of *philosophy*. Tech-bros weren't overpaid and over-lauded because they'd had everything handed to them on a plate, went the accepted wisdom, but because they'd *focused*, or *lived their vision*, or *actualised*. Because they'd done it, anyone could do it. Because anyone could do it, anyone who didn't do it had only themselves to blame.

An email arrived from Bream with the subject line: *Concerns re: Norbiton*. Bream had forwarded all of Norbiton's emails to Head of Corporate Efficiency Mike Grady and cc'd everyone Norbiton originally emailed as well as Norbiton himself.

'Kablammo,' said Bream. 'Someone get me a mop and some Mr Muscle.'

———

'Touchdown,' said Teddy, emerging jubilantly from the bathroom at the end of the hallway in Hugo's office building. 'You know what I'm saying, Hugo?'

'Regrettably, yes,' said Hugo.

'My body is such a clock right now,' said Teddy, easing himself into a seat across the table from Hugo. 'I mean, you could literally set your watch to my body.'

'Is that a good thing?'

'Oh, it's a very good thing. Our bodies are essentially mechanistic. They *want* to behave like machines. Basically because they *are* machines. If you just let your body be a machine, you free up your mind to be unlimited.'

'How do you . . . Actually, you know what, Teddy? I'm just going to accept that statement.'

'That's great, Hugo. Unconditional, open. I love it.'

'Now tell me about my day.'

They were in what Hugo rather grandiosely referred to as his conference room, but which was actually, officially, called Meeting Room Three, and available for booking on a rota basis by everyone who rented offices in his particular complex. It was a small, square room with laminated tables and plastic chairs and a whiteboard at the front. Teddy had asked about a digital projector but that was still very much up in the air.

'Well, obviously I've scheduled some you and me time,' said Teddy, tapping away at his tablet.

'Great,' said Hugo.

'But first, you've got a meeting with that Downton guy.'

'Oh Christ. Jones? When's he coming?'

'Ten minutes.'

'Ten minutes? For fuck's sake, Teddy, I haven't even . . . I mean, aren't you going to brief me?'

'Precisely what I'm about to do, big guy.'

'In ten minutes?'

'No briefing should ever be longer than ten minutes, Hugo. Otherwise it stops being a briefing and turns into a meeting.'

'OK, but let's not make this a briefing about briefings. What does Jones want?'

'Catch up, basically.'

'Catch up. That's it. That's your briefing.'

'I'd say strong bet he's going to want to mention Robert Townsend.'

'Robert who?'

'The guy who blogs about the estate.'

'Oh, *that* guy. And what should I say?'

'Tell him we're on it.'

'Right, but—'

'Time's up, big guy. He's on his way up. I'll be in your office.'

Teddy bounded up, performed a brief squat, exhaled powerfully, and made for the exit. Hugo turned his attention to his posture and positioning on his side of the table. Jones unnerved him. It would be important, he thought, to project a sense of control, of authority.

Hugo's link to Downton wasn't just complicated, the very nature of its complexity was itself a complication. His entire career, his entire existence, was built on simplification. His critics assumed this was because Hugo was simple, but Hugo, who prided himself on not being nearly as stupid as people seemed to believe, knew that his reliance on simplicity was one of the better examples of how astute he was able to be. In an ever-complexifying world, simplicity was a much sought-after and increasingly finite commodity, and people had a tendency to grab it where they could find it. For some, this took the form of what was effectively a culturally approved regression into infantilism. Teddy, for example, owned at least one adult colouring book, framed world events as extended riffs on *Harry Potter*, and had once told Hugo that constructing spaceships out of Lego helped him brainstorm. For others, it manifested as a form of nostalgia in which it was assumed that everything had been so much simpler before it all got so complicated.

Hugo, in his columns, in his talking-head television appearances, in his careful deployment of what he very advisedly called common sense, had become adept at synthesising these instincts. When he talked of present-day England and the ways in which it both disappointed and terrified him, he made it clear he was regarding it in contrast to another, historical England, which had once made him proud and secure. When he decried political double-speak and lambasted his rivals for their inability to construct a simple policy that could be conveyed in a simple sentence to . . . he didn't say simple people, of course, he said *ordinary* people . . . he was careful to communicate the idea of an implied alternative of clarity, directness. Through simplification, Hugo was selling reassurance. Through nostalgia, he was selling the political equivalent of escapism. And through reductive blame-mongering, he was, he knew, selling a potent combination of the two.

So when Hugo muttered to himself in the mirror before going on television, as he sometimes did, *keep it simple*, he meant it in a highly literal sense: keep not just what he said simple, but keep everything simple, and defend the simplicity he had created from the opposing political forces of nuance, subtlety, and doubt.

There were, however, elisions. Hugo's politics, given the backroom deals he continually found himself making with people like Ronnie Childs, were not exactly simple. Nor, given the Downton situation, were his finances.

Hugo was, even he would admit, awful with money. He liked the idea of it. He savoured the vocabulary of its accrual, injecting words like *portfolio* and *interests* with all the mouthwatering suggestiveness he felt they deserved, but actual financial success came only when he employed advisors who categorically refused to carry out any of his instructions and instead invested his money in industries and institutions they regarded as safe. Two or three of these investments, made with no supervision on Hugo's part, had become comparatively profitable, and one – Downton – which had begun snapping up local-authority housing contracts alongside big-ticket private developments, had become very profitable indeed.

Downton's courting of Hugo had begun in unspectacular fashion. They'd noticed he was a long-standing shareholder, they said, and they wanted to thank him by inviting him to some sort of dinner. Hugo had, naturally, attended. A more business-oriented meeting had followed, during which Hugo was encouraged to take advantage of a particularly attractive extra share package that had been put together just for him, as a way of saying thank you. To celebrate Hugo's taking up of this offer, another dinner was arranged, this time on a smaller scale, at which Hugo got to know Wallace, who headed up something to do with expansion, and Sterne, who did something involving planning. Both Wallace and Sterne sent follow-up emails jauntily expressing what a pleasure it had been to meet Hugo and suggesting they all get together in a less formal setting sometime. Hugo had agreed, because what possible reason was there not to agree? After all, Hugo's involvement in politics at this point was still strictly at the opinion end of the scale, so there couldn't really be said to be a conflict of interest. Even when, after listening to Wallace and Sterne bemoan the effect of certain, as they put it, *draconian* planning legislations, he had subsequently bemoaned the state of those very same regulations himself in one or two columns which ran shortly after, Hugo still didn't feel he was buggering about with any boundaries. The Downton connection was completely coincidental, just as it was coincidental when, a short time later, as England Always were reaching out to Hugo and Downton were beginning to feel out Edmundsbury Council with regards to rescuing the moribund Larchwood estate and turning it into something profitable, Wallace and Sterne chummily suggested to Hugo that they get together round a dinner table with one or two council types so they could all have a friendly chat about how they might be able to help each other out. The Larchwood was an embarrassment, a magnet for all the issues Hugo had been talking about, and redeveloping it would be exactly the kind of project he intended to very strongly support if, as he was beginning to suspect at the time would be the case, he decided to make a proper run at being an MP – a run for which, *were* it to happen, Downton, in a move that reflected nothing more than their deep personal and economic commitment to Edmundsbury and their wish to achieve at every turn what was best for the town, had agreed to provide substantial assistance with funding.

But then, the deal approved, the decanting had begun, and even Hugo had to admit that things had become murky. He saw less of Wallace and Sterne, who had both been shunted on to other projects. Instead, he began working with Jones, who had been tasked with overseeing the clearance of the estate, and whose style was to put a considerably less friendly face on things. Even more problematic was the impact of the mounting controversy surrounding the enforced rehousing of the Larchwood tenants on the increasing complications inherent in Hugo's carefully oversimplified politics. His message was clear: the ordinary white, working-class people of Edmundsbury had been forgotten, and what should have been rightfully theirs – jobs, housing, benefits, and the like – was now all going to immigrants and scroungers. This message had proved extremely popular, so popular, in fact, that once the decanting was under way, many of the residents saw in Hugo's political rhetoric a near-prophetic ability. The maths of the situation, after all, seemed obvious. Immigration had increased hugely, and suddenly they were being asked to move out. Within the space of a few months, Hugo's popularity soared. He had not, at that stage, even announced his intention to stand, but, such was the upswell of popular public opinion at a local level, he was able to spin the entire situation so that it appeared he'd be standing, somewhat reluctantly, because the people of Edmundsbury had asked him to; because, as he put it in one particularly emotive speech, they *needed* him to.

In many ways, Hugo should have been completely stuck. He had, after all, agreed with Downton to ensure the ongoing success of a project he'd tacitly agreed with his core voters to oppose. But the powers of paranoia and oversimplification were, Hugo found, more pervasive than even he could have imagined. The more Downton leaned on tenants in the Larchwood, the more convinced the tenants became of their own victimisation, and the easier it was for Hugo to point the finger elsewhere, a phenomenon that explained the apparent anomaly in Edmundsbury's opinion polls: Edmundsbury was home to fewer immigrants than almost anywhere else in the country, yet anti-immigration sentiment had never been higher.

The endgame, in Hugo's mind, was simple. Downton would successfully decant the estate and turn it into their new high-tech, digitally connected conceptual nightmare, and the people they displaced would be angrier than ever, and keener than ever to apportion blame, and Hugo would be right there to help them.

Before all of this could play out, however, there was the small matter of the few remaining hold-outs, who were, especially now that a certain degree of attention had fallen on the estate, making life uncomfortable all round, meaning that Hugo, who really should have been concentrating on more pressing matters, had no choice but to tolerate the increasingly common presence of Jones, a man with the unerring ability to rub Hugo the wrong way.

'Mr Bennington,' said Jones, who slid into the room like it was his own personal talk-space and started in with his bank-manager delivery without so much as a hello, making Hugo miss all the more sharply the days when his business dealings with Downton had revolved around languorous lunches with Wallace and Sterne. 'I understand you were keen to hear an update on progress?'

Hugo had not, as it happened, been keen to hear an update on progress. Or, he'd been keen to hear one, but he hadn't asked for one, leading him to conclude that Teddy had been up to his usual scheduling mischief.

'Well, more just a reassurance that there has actually *been* some progress,' he said bluntly, glossing over this slight area of confusion. His dealings with money men, Wallace and Sterne aside, tended to be somewhat gruff, largely because he had to maintain an air of irritability as a defensive cover for his ignorance.

'I think it's fair to say there has been a degree of progress,' said Jones, 'and that we anticipate completion according to deadline.'

'How many people are left?'

'A small and ever-reducing number,' said Jones, 'of which only two or three are proving particularly stubborn.'

'And who are those two or three?'

'Well, there's a, how shall I put it, an unconventional, or perhaps *alternative* family who seem quite convinced they should be allowed to stay,' said Jones, handing Hugo a piece of paper containing four names.

'Three parents and a child?' said Hugo, attempting to decipher what was in front of him. 'Should one of those read grandparent?'

'Like I say,' said Jones. 'An unconventional family.'

'Who else?'

'An older gentleman,' said Jones, handing Hugo another piece of paper. 'Particularly determined. And, if I might say so, distinctly disagreeable.'

Hugo looked at the information. 'Darkin,' he said. 'What sort of name is Darkin?'

'He's a great admirer of yours, actually,' said Jones, either because he felt that the question about Darkin's name was an unnecessary deviation, or because he'd read into Hugo's question another question, which he felt his comment about Darkin being a supporter of Hugo's went some way to answering.

'Clearly a man of intelligence and taste,' said Hugo.

Jones looked at him blankly. 'Perhaps you might like to go and meet him?'

'And say what?'

'You could discuss his options with him.'

'And what are his options?'

'Leave voluntarily or under duress.'

Jones smiled.

'You know,' said Hugo, 'I'm not entirely convinced it's such a good idea for me to get directly involved.'

'You're concerned, perhaps, about losing his vote?'

'Well, OK, yes, there's that. But also, how's it going to look if I go round there and lay out his distinctly limited options to him? Isn't that going to look—'

'Somewhat threatening?'

'Somewhat threatening, yes.'

'I suppose that very much depends on the manner in which his options are presented to him,' said Jones.

'And how do you propose I present them?'

'Oh, I'm sure a political man like yourself doesn't need advice from me about the uses of nuance,' said Jones.

'Well, like I say, it seems to me that this is a matter for Downton to handle directly. Putting the word about for you boys and protecting your interests in the right circles is one thing, but going down to the estate itself and—'

'There is another matter,' said Jones, who had a way of stopping tangents before they started.

'Right. What is this other matter?'

'Have you heard of Robert Townsend?'

'Rings a bell,' said Hugo.

'He writes a blog for *The Command Line*.'

'Oh yes,' said Hugo, torn between demonstrating he knew what Jones was talking about and then having to explain why he hadn't yet done anything about it, which risked looking ineffectual, or simply pretending he hadn't known anything about it until now, which risked looking ill-informed.

'He's been blogging about the Larchwood.'

'Mhmm.'

'He seems to want to turn it into some sort of *cause*.'

'Aha.'

'I'm just making sure you're aware.'

'I am very much aware,' said Hugo, who hadn't, he knew, given a particularly good impression of being aware.

'I'm sure it's something Teddy can deal with,' said Jones.

'Absolutely,' said Hugo, rankled at the idea there might be anything Teddy could deal with that Hugo couldn't deal with himself.

'Well,' said Jones. 'This has been helpful.'

'Yes,' said Hugo, who had no idea why this had been helpful. 'So just to clarify, in terms of moving forward—'

'Yes. Just let us know when you've been to the estate and we can plan from there.'

'I just told you,' said Hugo, 'I don't think it's a good idea to—'

'Perhaps you'd like me to clarify *your* options?' said Jones, somehow managing to use the absolute minimum of facial muscles necessary to shape the words.

'Don't threaten me, Jones,' said Hugo. 'Because I can just as easily clarify your options, if you know what I mean.'

'How about we both go away and look at our options,' said Jones slowly, 'and then get together sometime soon and talk them over?'

'What will that achieve?'

'Well,' said Jones, 'I think it will at least help to clarify who actually *has* options.' He looked pointedly at Hugo, then stood up and gathered his things before extending his hand. 'Pleasure to see you again, Mr Bennington.'

He left as he'd arrived: with barely a concession to Hugo's existence.

If there had been more time, Hugo probably could have unpacked his own apparently increasing insignificance into a fully expanded panic attack but, perhaps thankfully, the moment the lift doors at the end of the hallway closed on Jones's smug little face, Teddy was already darting out from Hugo's office with an expression worryingly akin to the one he'd worn not half an hour previously when he'd been on the verge of soiling himself.

'Teddy,' said Hugo.

'No time for pleasantries, big guy,' said Teddy, holding up a hand. 'We've got a situation.'

'Oh Christ. What kind of situation?'

'A Ken Henderson kind of situation.'

'Oh fuck me. What now?'

Ken Henderson was another prospective England Always MP with his eye on a seat in a small coastal town somewhere in Norfolk. Like many of the party's MPs, he had no political or media experience but was incredibly excited about political and media exposure, and so had a tendency to say shatteringly stupid things at wildly inconvenient moments.

Teddy slid an A4 printout across the table and waited while Hugo read it.

'He said all of this on camera,' said Hugo, gazing, head in hands, at the printout.

'Yeah,' said Teddy.

'I mean, I want to be absolutely clear on this. I haven't, you know, entered some sort of weird parallel dimension. I'm not having a fever dream. Ken Henderson said this, on television, in the actual real world in which we live.'

'I can play you the video file if you like,' said Teddy.

'God no,' said Hugo.

He studied the transcript again in the hope it might magically appear less depressing, but it remained stubbornly unchanged, which meant that, much as Hugo might wish otherwise, the facts of the matter remained depressingly real. Early this morning, no doubt hungover, and no doubt over-excited at being interviewed, Ken Henderson had shambled onto the BBC news and, stumbling between two equally offensive and outmoded terms, somehow merged them in his mouth and uttered the word *colouroid*.

'I mean, Jesus fucking Christ,' said Hugo. 'Colouroid? Is that even a word?'

'Nah,' said Teddy. 'I've already checked. Although, like, maybe that's a good thing?'

'Why is that a good thing?'

'Well, can it definitely be offensive if it's not even a word?'

Hugo thought about this. One of the unsettling effects of spending regular and sustained time in Teddy's company was that the border between the profound and the insufferably moronic began to feel dangerously porous.

'Alright,' he said weakly. 'Just give me the bullet points and tell me what to say.'

'Honestly,' said Trina, tapping away at the laptop propped on her knees, 'it's really good. You just need to—'

'You always say it's good,' said Kasia. 'But look: you're still changing it.'

'I'm just . . .' Trina hit the delete key. 'There. It's neater. See?'

Kasia rested her chin on Trina's shoulder and squinted at the laptop screen. She nodded, then hung her head over the plastic container of sushi in her lap.

They were sitting outside The Arbor, blinking in the sun, Trina's eyes not quite adjusting from screen-glare to sky-dazzle. Around them, the carefully sculpted and formed grounds of the facility unfolded with the kind of neat, modular order one would expect. Benches were arranged in little clusters, each with their own allotted tree. Other clusters contained chatting huddles of workers, but Trina and Kasia had this particular bench to themselves. Their daily lunches, the unspoken stratification they disrupted, had caused talk. Trina did what her colleagues called real work; Kasia was part of the service staff. The two strata, siloed in different quarters of the complex, rarely mixed.

'What?' said Trina, twisting from the laptop and spearing some of the sushi she'd balanced on the seat next to her.

Kasia shook her head. 'Just tired,' she said.

'Were you up all night on this?'

'Every night. Then come to work. Then up all night working.' Kasia rubbed her eyes with her thumb and index finger.

Trina reached out and rubbed Kasia's back.

'I have so been there,' she said. 'It's worth it.'

Kasia turned her head sideways to catch Trina's eye.

'Really?'

Trina sighed, leaned back on her hands so that the sun caught her face for a moment.

'Fair question,' she said.

With Trina's encouragement, Kasia was teaching herself code.

She regularly brought out her laptop over lunch so that Trina could scroll through and make corrections. For the first few months, Kasia's enthusiasm had been obvious. Recently, though, Trina had sensed a dwindling of Kasia's inner resources. It was a feeling she knew well. Between work and study, she thought, or work and other work, always chasing the image of your imagined future, you could lose space for your present self entirely.

'So I learn to code,' said Kasia. 'Then what? MT? Then . . . I don't know. Learn something else? I'm not like you.'

'Like me how?'

'I won't do something brilliant.'

'OK, first of all, I didn't do anything especially brilliant, and second of all, how do you know that?'

Kasia shrugged again.

'You're picking it up really fast,' said Trina, passing her the laptop.

Kasia scrolled through the strings of code, a faint smile teasing at one corner of her mouth.

'It gets like this,' said Trina. 'You're exhausted. You're doing the same thing over and over again. You think: why the fuck am I even doing this? Like, what even is the point? But it passes, you know?'

'I know,' said Kasia. 'Just . . . I need a day off. Or a week off. Or a holiday. Or something.'

'You know what kept me going?' said Trina.

'Speed?'

'Besides speed.'

'I think . . .' Kasia thought about it. 'I think you believe in yourself.'

'That's bullshit,' said Trina, replaying the Teddy Handler video in her mind as she spoke. 'All that fucking crap people come out with about believing in yourself and doing what you love and visualising and positivity and finding your bliss and all that shit. Fuck that. What kept me going was thinking about those arseholes in there.' She pointed at The Arbor. 'Because do you think they ever sat up at night asking themselves why they were doing this? No way.

They're all there because they just never questioned the fact that they should be there. And if they don't have to question it, I don't have to question it, and you don't have to question it either. It's not about thinking positive or motivating yourself, it's just about never stopping to ask yourself these kinds of questions.'

'OK,' said Kasia. 'Yeah. I see that. But still. What's the difference? Now I carry their shit around for them; maybe if I do this next year, I carry their code around for them.'

'Yeah,' said Trina. 'Maybe. But at least you take, like, fractionally more of their money. You know how much money these fuckers have? You should be getting some of that money. More of that money. Like, as much of it as you can reasonably take.'

Her voice had become louder and she had, without realising it, begun pointing at Kasia's chest as she spoke, as if admonishing her.

'I'm ranting,' she said. 'Sorry.'

Kasia shook her head, gave Trina a look that said she knew what Trina was really talking about.

Necessity, not ambition, had made Trina an MT. Some years ago, an ex-boyfriend by the name of Dustin had got slap happy. On the first occasion, she'd foolishly forgiven him. On the second occasion, she'd knocked out six of his teeth with a TV remote. Trina was not someone you could push around indefinitely. She'd left him crawling around the living-room floor, spitting blood, picking his incisors out of the sheepskin rug. Or at least, she'd thought that was where she left him. As it turned out, he'd had other ideas. He'd pressed charges, dragged her through the courts. It was her word against his, and given that he'd had the audacity to turn up to court in a wheelchair claiming nerve damage and post-traumatic stress disorder, his word had carried undue weight. She dodged an actual jail cell, but wound up with the next best thing: an electronic tag, a closely monitored curfew. Microtasking allowed her not only to work from home, but, fuelled by coffee, speed, Adderall, and whatever else was at hand, to study at the same time. Through days and nights that appeared endless, during which her entire sense of time distorted to the point where she simply slept and ate according to the rhythm of the tasks she needed to complete, Trina stretched her brain until she could calmly function with three windows open on her screen at once: the MT system, her coursework, and a third project, Beatrice, into which she had invested all her hopes for a new life.

In many ways, that new life was now hers. In other ways, though, it was as out of reach as ever. She wasn't using any of the coding skills she now possessed. Instead, she simply toyed with the parameters she'd created, manipulating the workforce from what was little more than a glorified personnel position. Worse, her future, now that it was here, was still forever curtailed by her past. For all their gushing about their disruptively meritocratic working practices, Green, as was explained to Trina by two eerily similar HR drones on the day of her induction, were not above basic arse-covering.

'Because what we categorically do not want here is a PR or litigation gangbang,' said HR guy number one, eyeing her from across the table in the windowless basement room into which they'd taken her to lay out her lack of options.

'Or both,' said HR man number two. 'A double gangbang.'

'We're being frank,' said HR man number one. 'We can be frank with you, right Trina?'

'Hey,' said Trina, 'nothing I haven't heard already.'

'Great,' said number one. 'That's just the kind of attitude we like here. Straight. No bullshit. So let's tell it like it is. Trina: everyone respects your abilities. But they also do not respect your . . . background.'

'Vis-à-vis the physical violence,' said number two. 'As opposed to your actual background.'

'Right,' said number one. 'Good to clarify that. Your actual background is very much respected.'

'I understand,' said Trina.

'So with that as a given,' said number one, 'we here at Green feel it's only prudent to put certain failsafes in place to ensure that any early-warning signs are not only noted but also acted upon appropriately and effectively.'

'By which he means,' said number two, 'that say one day a colleague is moaning about, I don't know, some perceived inequality or slight, and you happen to say, I mean, hell, I'm just making this up off the top of my head, something like, *If you don't shut up, I swear to God I'm going to come over there and*—'

'Insert violent intention here,' said number one.

'Right,' said number two. 'Could be anything. It doesn't even matter what it could be. The point is that we would have to take it seriously.'

'Because of your history,' said number one.

'Right,' said number two. 'Your previous, as I think it's sometimes called.'

They'd placed her on indefinite probation. The slightest misstep, the faintest of misunderstandings, and she was gone, ejected back out into the world, staring down the barrel of God knew how many more years ticking nameless tasks off an infinite checklist.

Trina finished her sushi and sucked up the last wisp of milk-foam from her latte.

'I'm done.'

Kasia nodded. 'Me too. Hey, look at this.'

Kasia thumbed the screen of her phone and tilted it towards Trina.

'Oh fuck me, Kasia. Is that a dick?'

'Dick pic.'

'Is that like a consensual dick pic or one of those ones where they just assume you want to see a picture of their dick? Like, you text them about dinner and their reply is a picture of their dick.'

'What are you saying? I asked for a dick pic?'

'A lot of people do.'

Kasia made a face. 'Not me. Who wants to see picture of dick?

But this guy, he sends me one like every day.'

'And are you, you know, getting daily dick from this guy in other ways too?'

Kasia made a face of abject disgust, tears of distaste welling briefly in her eyes while she imagined, then clearly unimagined, the prospect.

'You fucking kidding me?' She shook her head. 'Never.'

'But you know who he is?'

'Obviously I know. That's what makes the dick so disgusting.'

'So who is he?'

'Some guy. He looked round. Everyone was mister this and mister that. I gave him lunch. Then two days later, boom.'

'So how do you know it's him?'

'It's in his eyes. When I met him, I knew: this is a man who does something weird with his dick.'

'How did he get your email address?'

'It's not so difficult.'

'Do you think he wants to give you his dick in other ways?'

'Who cares?'

'Do you feel like if you have to look at his dick every day on your phone, you're less inclined to look at his dick in real life?'

Kasia thought about this, giving the question the attention she clearly felt it deserved.

'Depends,' she said. 'Sometimes, you know, seeing the dick, it makes you think of dick, so . . . But other times, yeah. You don't want to see the dick.'

'Maybe you need to develop some kind of code.'

'Or a day. A dick day.'

Trina snorted and gathered up her lunch things from the bench.

'Wait 'til you work upstairs with me,' she said. 'Every day's a fucking dick day.'

———

His meeting with Teddy concluded, Hugo took the opportunity to grab what he increasingly thought of as a quick sanity break by popping outside for a fag. He was, as ever after one of his strategising sessions with Teddy, both baffled and slightly scared; unable to recall exactly what had been discussed, or pinpoint what had been concluded.

The sense that he was being moulded into new and not necessarily positive shapes was one that had dogged Hugo for some time, and the more pronounced the sensation became, the more Hugo worried that he might in fact be hopelessly lost, until on particularly bad days he would go to bed and close his eyes and imagine that he could feel, physically, the internal compass of his self whirring wildly through its points.

In many ways, being required to form an opinion on a weekly basis about a subject of your choosing should have been a sure-fire way of creating and maintaining a bullet-proof sense of identity. But even Hugo, who by this point practically had a black belt in self-denial, knew that an erosion had long ago begun, and was now almost complete. The truth was, his job as a columnist was not to say what he thought, it was to say what people expected him to think, and as a result of his continual self-portrayal as an honest everyman, what people expected him to think was exactly the same as what they themselves thought, meaning that in reality, his job was to say what other people already thought so that they no longer had to feel guilty about thinking it.

The arrival of England Always onto the British political scene had happened just as Hugo was beginning to put all this together in his mind and ask himself whether anything he had thought, written, or done had been either genuine or of genuine note. When he died, he'd thought, what would be left of him? A handful of columns about waiting times in GP surgeries, the need for Muslims to conform to British values, the importance of wearing a poppy on Remembrance Day? Was that a legacy?

It was difficult, in retrospect, to figure out exactly who had approached and manipulated whom. Hugo had begun, gently at first, more stridently later, to praise the anti-European opinions of England Always's leader, Alan Elm. Alan, again in an informal way at first, and later in print, had returned the compliments, calling Hugo the voice of exactly the same man in the street that England Always wanted to represent. Somewhere in the midst of this flirtation, England Always, chests puffed with post-exit pride, had begun their transformation from a party concerned with redefining England's place in the world to a party preoccupied with people's place in England, and had moved from shaping England's post-Europe future to recapturing its pre-contemporary pomp. Brexit was over, but the energy it had accumulated had to be retained. Fears needed to be redirected. Hatred needed to pivot. The nation that England Always began to both diagnose and define was one Hugo not only recognised but remembered: the England of his childhood, of his frustrated and bitter dreams, an England in which he once again felt at home.

Eventually, a meeting had been suggested, and Hugo and Alan, over pints of ale and a curry in a Travelodge somewhere near Milton Keynes, where Alan was staying for a conference, had thrashed out Hugo's move from, as Alan put it, opinion to action. They'd sunk a few more ales. Hugo had got looser, Alan looser still. They'd made the shift from the political to the personal. Alan had talked about his first marriage. Hugo had talked about his only marriage. They'd talked about what they wanted, what they feared.

'We know what people say about us,' Alan had said that night, his tie loosened, the remains of the all-you-can-eat Indian buffet still clinging to his lips. 'We know what people think. But you know what? They're wrong.'

'I know that,' said Hugo, swishing the rubble from a desiccated pakora through a crime-scene streak of crimson dip. 'It's just political correctness gone mad.'

'Exactly,' said Alan. 'Can't say this, can't say that.'

He downed the rest of his pint and clicked his fingers at the waitress. 'Two more of these, sweet cheeks,' he slurred. Then he leaned closer to Hugo, beer and bhaji on his breath and the last glazed glint of complicity in his rolling eyes. 'We're alike, you and me,' he said. 'We could do a lot.' And then he slumped back in his chair, as if drained, and gazed out into the middle distance of the threadbare corporate lounge as if it were a landscape from which he drew deep and lasting inspiration. He took a long, extravagant sigh. 'Fucking niggers,' he said to no-one in particular. Hugo, woozy with ale, warmed by rare masculine understanding, had simply nodded.

During his time as a columnist of greater notoriety than regard, and now as a politician of greater exposure than ability, Hugo had been asked many times if he was a racist. It was the liberal media's default ploy, and a reflection of the fact that the word *racist* was now toxic enough that simply placing a person in proximity to it would irradiate their public persona as surely as it would undermine their message. His answer was always the same: of course he wasn't a racist, of course his party wasn't racist, and of course people who voted for the party weren't racist. He would then, deliberately, digress. He would talk about the importance of free speech, of democracy, of living in a society where views could be aired and heard in a civilised manner. Sometimes, if he felt more evidence were needed, he would point to the valuable contributions assorted ethnic minorities had made to the country, such as Indian food and Thai massage. Finally, he would say that England was, and had always been, a tolerant country, and that he was proud of that, just as he was proud of England in so many other, less fashionable ways.

But these were, Hugo knew, the things you had to say, and he said them in order to sidestep the possibility that he might say any of the things you were no longer allowed to say. Even as he was saying them, even as he was actually believing them, other ideas would flood into the foreground of his mind, as if the dam between his public self and his private reservoir of disgust had been breached. Because he could not, or felt he should not, release them, they pooled, and once they'd pooled they began to stagnate, thickening into a dark, brackish puddle. This, for Hugo, was the reality of tolerance: the continual, day-to-day, unrelenting swallowing of your own bile.

What *did* Hugo believe? He had to keep asking himself. His views, once so simple and easily expressed, now drifted in and out of focus depending on whom he spoke to. Was it Teddy who distorted things? Or was Hugo confused because the *world* was confused? If he, Hugo Bennington, an experienced commenter, an intelligent man, felt this baffled, this uncertain of his ability to navigate the modern moral mishmash of equivocations and evasions, then imagine how the average man in the street felt. That, Hugo always decided, was why England Always was important. It wasn't about white this or black that. It was about *clarity*.

But clarity was an increasingly precious commodity, and one, Hugo was coming to believe, over which Teddy had ultimate and not entirely positive control. Hugo's understanding of his own beliefs was intimately bound up with his understanding of Teddy's reframing of those beliefs, and his ability to track the ways in which his beliefs were being moulded was hamstrung by his inability to unpick the extent to which Teddy could be trusted. Teddy, after all, had begun his career with Alan. He'd been sent to assist Hugo only after Hugo's name had risen in stature rather faster than anyone could have predicted. And there was a fine line, Hugo thought, between assistance and observation, reconnaissance and outright sabotage. Did Teddy work for him? Or did he still work for Alan? Technically, Hugo thought, they both still worked for Alan. Hugo's suspicion, which had become ever more strongly held the more aware he became of Teddy's other activities and interests – his tech work and motivational speaking, his unfathomable productivity videos – was that Teddy worked for everyone and no-one. His approach, or, to use a word Teddy was more likely to use himself, his *philosophy*, was always to connect. The merits and complexities of his connections could, he seemed to think, be thrashed out later.

The more Hugo looked at it, the more he concluded that his life was travelling in a direction of ever more arcane ambiguity. His views and direction were uncertain; his sense of whom he could trust was itself increasingly untrustworthy. The irony was not lost on him. Every day, be it in print or in person, he reduced the world to its starkest black-and-white simplicities, yet with each passing, opinionated minute, the once-sharp lines of his reality seemed to blur that fraction further, until he was forced to spiral inwards, questioning again and again what he believed. What he found, once he was there, corkscrewed all the way in to the deep core of his wavering being, was a truth dark even to himself: the truth that, in the cold, lived reality of his life, when he stepped into a shop and was served by an inscrutable Indian, or when he stood in the pub beside necking, fondling queers, or listened to the babble of Middle Eastern and Middle European tongues as they clashed violently with the tribal boom-thud of rap from the open window of a passing car full of smug, grinning black men, Hugo felt a fear and revulsion stronger and deeper than he could ever let on, meaning that, far from being cautious of the ideological roads down which Teddy could sometimes be seen to be leading him, Hugo knew better than anyone just how badly he needed Teddy's spin. What Teddy was doing was simply a far more efficient version of what Hugo had always done himself: taking the unpalatable matter of who he was and moulding it into something the shifting, unrecognisable world could cautiously, guiltily, accept.

He inhaled deeply on his cigarette and tipped his head back against the wall to slowly release the smoke from his lips. It's OK, he told himself. You're alright. It's everyone else that's lost.

———

Trina arrived back from lunch to find Bream and Holt standing beside her desk.

'Shitstorm,' said Bream.

'Seal up your body cavities,' said Holt.

'This is re the emails?' said Trina.

'This is very much re the emails,' said Bream.

'Mike Grady emailed Norbiton and told him to shoot one and scare the hundred,' said Holt.

'And you know this how?' said Trina.

'Mike Grady cc'd the hundred,' said Bream. 'Presumably to advance-scare the hundred prior to the one being shot.'

Trina sat down at her desk. 'Bream: you emailed Grady.'

'Right,' said Bream. 'But I spoke on behalf of everyone. I think that was clear.'

'Look, Bream,' said Trina, 'I think on this one you're our lone gunman.'

'Hey, come on,' said Bream. 'Give a guy a grassy knoll.'

Norbiton stuck his head round his office door.

'You three,' he said. 'I'm calling a huddle. Right here. Right now.'

'You can't,' said Bream. 'You used your huddle quota this morning. Your allocation won't reset for another twenty-four hours.'

'Are you kidding me?' said Norbiton. 'Trina: confirm.'

'It's twenty-four hours,' said Trina.

'Email me,' said Bream.

'Copy that,' said Holt.

'OK,' said Norbiton, 'I'm going to play ball, but if I get a load of auto-responses I have to say a touch of negativity might start creeping into my day.'

Norbiton went back into his office and started pounding his keyboard. Trina logged on and fired up her email to find that Norbiton had sent a high-priority scheduling invite to her, Bream, and Holt.

'I didn't have time to turn off my auto-response,' said Trina.

'Me neither,' said Bream, not making any sort of move towards his desk. Holt just shrugged. From inside Norbiton's office a sort of war-cry went up. He came back out of his office and marched up to them.

'You lot are so fucked,' he bellowed. 'Do you even know how fucked you are? You are beyond fucked. You are quad-core, ten gig of ram, retina-display, twenty-hour battery life *fucked*. Bream: my office.'

'No can do,' said Bream.

'No can do? What do you mean no can do?'

'I used up all my Meeting Minutes at the huddle this morning and just now when I had to take time out to explain to you how huddles work. I can't do any kind of meeting now until next week.'

'Then why in the name of *fuckery* did you tell me to email you to arrange a huddle tomorrow?' screamed Norbiton.

'So I could respond by email to let you know I am out of Meeting Minutes and could we maybe do next week,' said Bream.

There was a slightly overlong pause while Norbiton digested this. Then he started laughing maniacally. He laughed all the way back to his office and slammed the door.

'Whoa,' said Holt. 'Norbiton's flashing a crash screen.'

Everyone went back to their desk to do emails and check their to-do lists. Just as they were all about to head off to their respective No-Go rooms for some real work, three Structural Facilitators rocked up carrying PortaWalls and began annexing an empty corner. Norbiton came out of his office and watched as they bolted the walls together and started hanging a swipe card-protected door.

'Think outside the box,' he said, gazing into the middle distance and smiling enigmatically. 'How many of you have heard that old chestnut?'

'Norbiton,' said Bream, his head popping up from behind his multi-display setup, 'I would urge you very strongly not to do this.'

'Think outside the box,' said Norbiton, putting his foot up on a chair and resting his elbow on his knee. 'That's what we say, isn't it? That's what we're all here to do, right? Well riddle me this: how can you think outside the box if you don't know where your box is?'

'What's happening?' said Holt to Bream. 'I mean, obviously, on a purely audio-visual level, I can appreciate what is happening but on a deeper, more meaning-based level I find myself very reluctant to accept what is going on.'

'Apparently Norbiton thinks he is the only one with a fucking YouTube account,' said Bream. 'Hey Norbiton. Take a fucking duvet day, OK? You're going to throw the whole morning out of whack.'

'Should we call Wellbeing?' said Holt.

'And say what?' said Trina.

'Norbiton is delusional,' said Holt. 'He is trying to pass off a You-Tube video that has had several thousand hits as his own original thought. That is the textbook definition of psychotic.'

'Folks,' Norbiton was saying, 'we, collectively, have lost our box. We've thought so far outside the box that we no longer know where our box is or what was in it or why we were supposed to get outside of it in the first place.'

'I just googled the DSM criteria for a mental breakdown,' said Bream. 'It's here under delusions: *believing a publicly available work of another person that has been seen by numerous others, e.g. a YouTube video, is in fact your own original thought.*'

Holt was on the phone. 'Hello? Yes, this is Holt on floor three. We've got a mental health-type situation. It's like that time Burgess said he wrote the whole of Wikipedia.'

'One of us,' said Norbiton, apparently unconcerned as to the attention levels of his audience, 'has to get back in the box.'

'Norbiton,' said Holt. 'You can't just build yourself your own No-Go room. It doesn't work like that.'

'I can't discuss that with you,' said Norbiton. 'You're not NTK on what I'm doing. *No-one* is NTK on what I'm about to get up to in that No-Go room.'

'All ready for you, chum,' said one of the Structural Facilitators, passing Norbiton a swipe card.

Norbiton strode forward. There was a beep as he swiped himself in. 'I may be some time,' he said stoically. The door closed and he was gone.

There was a long, slightly uncomfortable silence. Somewhere, someone opened a packet of crisps and attempted to eat them discreetly. Several people received emails. Several people in turn received auto-responses.

Bream said, 'Did, er, did those guys hook up any equipment in there?'

'Negative,' said Holt. 'Norbiton is in an empty No-Go room with no discernible purpose.'

Mid-morning, another team of Structural Facilitators rocked up brandishing power tools and stood slightly awkwardly around Norbiton's box. They were followed, with the sense of purpose and occasion for which he was renowned, by Dick Bangstrom.

'Oh shit,' said Bream. 'Say it ain't so.'

Dick Bangstrom was the smallest man Trina had ever encountered, and the man least at ease with his smallness.

'Heads up,' said Bangstrom.

Everyone did an overt heads-up over their screens.

'Some of you may know me,' said Bangstrom. 'I'm Dick Bangstrom. AKA The Interrobang. I have been sent from above.'

Bangstrom nodded pointedly while he let that sink in. No-one said anything.

'Both literally and figuratively,' he continued, 'I am way above your floor. I am a floor-five kind of guy both in terms of how I live my life and the fact that I am literally to be found most days on floor five. That's where the big chimps play, kids. Only, we don't play. If we did play, which we don't, we would play for keeps. Think on that. I've been sent down here by floor seven. That's right. The men upstairs. Half an hour ago, they called me up from floor five to floor seven and told me to get down here to floor three and not return to floor five *or* seven until I had done some very serious taking out of some very unwholesome trash. You know what they call you guys up there? The Troll Floor. This floor is averaging a new team leader every two months. It's at the point now where no-one will take a post here because they value their sanity too much. But not me.'

'You don't value your sanity?' said Bream.

'Who the fuck are you?' said Bangstrom.

'Bream,' said Bream.

'I've heard about you, Bream,' said Bangstrom.

'Still holding out for an answer re your sanity,' said Bream.

'Yes, I value my sanity,' said Bangstrom. 'The point is I do not fear its loss.'

'That does sort of imply you don't value it,' said Holt.

'Who the fuck are you?' said Bangstrom.

'Holt,' said Holt.

'I've heard about you too, Holt,' said Bangstrom. 'Matter of fact, I've heard about every last motherfucking one of you. I do not fear the loss of my sanity because I do not believe my sanity can be taken from me. Am I clear? We've sent some weak men down here. Not our fault, just a lot of weak men out there, it turns out. But no longer. I have been sent from above to break you shits down.'

He gestured at Norbiton's No-Go room. 'Let's get those walls down, boys.'

The Structural Facilitators took all of two minutes to unscrew the entire front wall and lift it clear. Inside, Norbiton was stripped to the waist and sweating profusely.

'Hey Dick,' said Norbiton. 'Welcome to the sweat lodge.'

Bangstrom shook his head sadly.

'Security,' he said, gesturing to two uniformed guards who had arrived behind the Structural Facilitators. 'Restrain this man.'

'We're going to have to towel him off first,' said one of the security guards. 'With that level of perspiration, we'll never get purchase.'

'You hear that, Norbiton, you sweaty fuck?' barked Bangstrom.

'You're literally too sweaty to be satisfactorily restrained. We're going to have to send you home packed in silica gel.'

'Do what you like,' said Norbiton. 'It doesn't matter. I see that now.'

'Please don't throw yourself a pity party, Norbiton. Try and leave here with your shiny little head held high, yeah?'

The security guards had repurposed a fire blanket and begun wrapping Norbiton up in it like a struggling cat at the vet's.

'You know why it doesn't matter?' said Norbiton, craning his neck to free his mouth from the blanket.

'Shut the fuck up, Norbiton,' said Bangstrom.

'Because of The Field, that's why,' said Norbiton. 'You think The Griefers are what we should be worrying about? The Griefers are nothing. Once The Field comes, you can forget about everything. There'll be no inside or outside the box. Everything will be The Field. Everything will be—'

'Let's get some of that fire blanket pushed into his mouth,' Bangstrom said to the security guards, who promptly gagged Norbiton with a dangling strap.

'Hey, Bangstrom,' said Holt. 'What's the—'

Bangstrom walked slowly over to Holt and stood menacingly in front of him.

'Go ahead and finish that question,' he said. 'I dare you.'

Holt thought for a moment, then nodded. 'I'm not going to finish that question,' he said.

'Do you have any other questions?' said Bangstrom.

'No,' said Holt. 'No more questions.'

'Does any *other* motherfucker,' said Bangstrom, turning to address the room, 'have any *other* motherfucking questions?'

Everyone looked anywhere but at Bangstrom. There were, it seemed, no more questions.

Trina wasn't one of these countrified cyclists you saw meandering with dangerous ease down the back roads. She was, in her own mind and in the eyes of others, a serious mover. At the end of the working day, she didn't just tuck her trousers into her socks and freewheel home with a priestly smile. She changed into black spandex and hit the tarmac at a vicious clip. She had, in a concession to her partners, both of whom had repeatedly professed their concern at the thought of her barrelling unprotected through the notoriously unforgiving kinks and turns of Edmundsbury's road network, reluctantly taken to using a helmet, but besides this she liked to be as exposed as possible, returning home, sometimes, with her skin chafed and tingling and deliciously sensitised from rain and hail. Code was all very well, she thought, but at the end of a day spent inside a machine, you had to get back out there in the world and feel a few things, otherwise you'd end up like Bream and Holt: weirdly eggbound and clenched with an anger they couldn't name.

She felt, as she shifted down through the gears and pushed upwards towards the kind of fluid velocity that both blurred the world and sharpened her own bodily periphery, a sense of evaporation, of vaporisation. Trina had grown up on comics, and she still, in her happier, more kinetic moments, imagined the world in their hyper-onomatopoeic vocabulary, so that, cycling home, she pictured behind her a jetstream of swooshes and vrooms, the sharp, angular letters spilling out from her back wheel and bursting into language behind her. You were never too old, she thought, for a superhero fantasy, and such fantasies, with their dreams of muscled, costumed impermeability, were never easier to access than when moving at speed.

She stuck to the main road back into town, weaving through the traffic when she needed to, opening up and roaring ahead whenever she could. She rarely went straight home. Instead, she orbited, picking roads at random, looping around her own centre of gravity until she felt herself change and lighten, the muscles in her back and shoulders suddenly and blissfully melting. It was a sensation she thought of, in keeping with her comic-book sensibility, as a literal transformation: all the plates and armour she wore through the day sliding back to reveal the body beneath. By the time she got to her front door, most days, she was herself again, and the people she lived with, the people she loved and was loved by, never had to encounter the person she was without them.

People moaned about the Larchwood Estate, of course, like they moaned about all estates, but Trina was more forgiving. She'd lived in nicer places in lives gone by and mercifully forgotten, but this was where she'd ended up being happy, and so inevitably there was a sense in which she'd projected that element of herself outwards, onto the fading walls and desiccated greenery of the ill-conceived and now no doubt doomed project she called home.

She sang out a greeting as she pushed her way through the front door, bringing the bike in with her and propping it in the hallway, where it dripped road-residue and oil into a thickening patch on the carpet. From the lounge, Mia and Carl both called back, while Bella gurgled something that may have been a greeting or may, more probably, just have been another expression of delight at her own ability to make sound. She found them on the sofa, Bella between the two adults, both of whom were playing a video game, and kissed them each in turn, Mia and Carl returning her kisses but also, as was their habit, leaning round her to eyeball the game in progress.

'Wow, sweat much?' said Mia, recoiling in mock disgust but smirking as she did so.

'Look at you two,' said Trina. 'Glued to the frigging screen while the baby just sits there.'

She kissed them all again, playfully rubbing Mia's head against her sweaty cycling top, then left them to it while she showered and found some comfortable clothes onto which little Bella could, if she wished, unproblematically throw up.

Trina's hour or so with Bella when she got in from work had

become something of a ritual. Of the three of them, Trina was, even by her own admission, the less dreamy in her approach to parenthood – no less loving, but perhaps less indulgent of the significance of her own feelings. It was also, in a way they all accepted and had discussed quite openly, restorative. Bella had been born when Trina was simultaneously Microtasking and studying, logging far too many hours at her laptop, exhausted and adrift in time. It was one of the benefits of Trina, Carl, and Mia's relationship that no one person had to pick up the slack when a partner got busy, but at the same time it was, as Trina had eventually confessed to Carl and Mia one evening, difficult in other, less expected ways. Suddenly, while she tapped away at a keyboard and completed tasks that would never, for her, add up to any kind of complete picture, Carl, Mia, and Bella came dangerously close to becoming a nuclear family. It was no-one's fault. It was simply something they hadn't considered, and Trina was as surprised as anyone at the odd jealousy and loneliness that began bubbling away as she watched them.

'I'm just becoming her aunt while you two play the happy couple,' Trina had snapped at Carl and Mia one night. 'You're probably teaching her to call you mummy and daddy while I just get to be Trina or aunty.'

It had, the moment she'd said it, sounded ridiculous, but she was glad she'd said it for exactly that reason.

Now she was at The Arbor, there was more of a routine. Carl was the stable centre, while Trina and Mia operated in a kind of rotation, each of them slipping comfortably into whatever role was required whenever either of them happened to get home. Mia was a Chorer – a job that was essentially like Microtasking, only the tasks weren't that micro and they couldn't be done remotely. Every day, when the hours suited, she logged into an app in which she had listed all the things she was prepared to do. Clients could then book her at a moment's notice and for very little money. Some people wanted their shopping done, their houses cleaned, their cars taken to the garage. Other jobs were more skilled. Last week, Mia had tiled a bathroom. The week before that, she had cleared some guttering. It was, essentially, the monetisation of an age-old unofficial economy. But of course, in this model, the developers of the app took a substantial cut, and the pressure to log in as much as possible was immense, meaning that Mia often ended up being out when Trina was in. It all just about hung together, but how the nukes, as the three of them referred to the drabber end of the family spectrum, managed it, Trina had no idea. Work was changing; the family was not. Something, Trina thought, was going to have to give.

'What news from the homestead?' she said, wandering back into the lounge and plucking Bella from the sofa.

'Nothing breaking,' said Carl.

Mia elbowed Carl and he shot her a recriminatory look.

'What?' said Trina.

Mia widened her eyes at Carl.

'Snitch,' said Carl. He looked from Mia to Trina. 'Forgot to say the other day. Some journo popped round. *Mia* here thought it might be important.'

'Journo? Wanting what?'

Carl shrugged. 'He asked about my accident. He asked about Downton. He asked if people were organising in any way. That was it.'

'And what did you say?'

'I said that Downton pop round and *make sure I'm alright*, and he seemed to understand what that meant, and then I said people were scared of reprisals for organising, but there were ideas floating around.'

'You're sure he was a journo? Did he have any ID? What paper does he work for?'

'He's a blogger. Robert something.'

'Townsend,' said Trina. 'I've read his thing. He's insufferable.'

'Have you read the comments though?'

Trina laughed. 'I *only* read the comments. Maybe that's the point. He's totally in love with himself, but at least he gets comments. Who else is getting any comments about this mess?'

'So we're cool?' said Carl with a smile. 'I haven't, like, *leaked*, or something?'

She kissed him on the top of the head. 'We're never not cool,' she said.

Trina took Bella through to the kitchen and sat with her at the table, telling her about her day, bitching about Bream and Holt and whatever else came to mind while Bella made what Trina thought were encouraging noises.

The kitchen, like much of the house, was relatively sparse – the dining table and its matching chairs simple, plain wood. Rather than attempting to merge their collective tastes, Trina, Mia, and Carl had opted instead to suspend them, leading to a home of uncluttered simplicity, the effect of which was somewhat undermined by all the once-niggling and now barely tolerable incidences of disrepair they had given up on ever getting resolved. Damp was a major issue. In places, the paintwork was coming away in crumbling hunks. The boiler rattled and groaned. Hot water could not be relied upon. In several places, the linoleum of the kitchen floor had come completely away, revealing bare, disintegrating floorboards beneath. Last month, a pipe in the flat upstairs had leaked, leaving a pale-brown splotch like an outsized tea-stain on the ceiling.

Tired of battling for the television when Mia and Carl were mid-game, and desperate for something on which to fix her gaze so that she wouldn't be forced to stare in mounting despondency at all the evidence of neglect around her, Trina had set up a small television in the corner of the dining area. She picked up the remote and turned it on, hoping for something mindless that would neither demand nor annoy.

'Let's see what we can find, huh?' she said to Bella, who, perhaps because this television was producing less noise and drama than the one next door, appeared uninterested, and who was contenting herself instead with the drawstrings that hung from Trina's hooded sweatshirt.

The problem with television as a medium for relaxation, at least as far as Trina was concerned, was that so much of it so rapidly and comprehensively annoyed her that she wound up more tense than if she'd just, as Mia had suggested far too many times that she should try to do, sat with Bella and savoured the moment. Following other notable trends in the direction of what, to Trina, was little more than faux-nostalgic, overly twee fantasy indulgence, British television had given itself over almost entirely to the perpetuation of a faded and frequently offensive English ideal. Clicking through the channels, grumbling softly to Bella as she went, Trina encountered first a programme in which everyone had to cook according to nineteen-forties rations, then a reality show based around the pressures of competitive knitting, and finally a much-discussed and supposedly narcotically addictive period drama set in the last days of the Raj in which glowing young Caucasians lay about on lawns wearing a uniform of pristine whites, picking at sandwiches handed to them by turbaned extras while professing to be ever so worried about the future. Unable to recognise either herself or any element of the world she inhabited in a single one of these shows, she decided to give up on all the regular channels completely and instead zone out with some news, which she hoped would prove less annoying than the tsunami of whitewashed nostalgia and chocolate-box history currently on offer everywhere else – a hope that was cruelly dashed the moment she was confronted by the smug visage of Hugo Bennington, a man whom Trina had actually, more than once, fantasised about killing.

'Fucking hell,' she said to Bella, around whom none of the family watched what they said, on the theory that they had no interest in raising a coddled child who only later had to learn the realities of adult life. 'He's everywhere.'

'Is it that man?' called Mia from the other room. 'Because if it is, don't watch it.'

'I'm hate-watching it,' said Trina.

'Well don't. It stresses you out.'

'Look,' Hugo Bennington was saying on the television, his face attempting a complicated admixture of sincerity and trademark bonhomie, 'no-one is more appalled by racism than me.'

'No-one?' said Trina. '*Everyone* is more appalled by racism than you.'

'Racism,' said Hugo Bennington, now adjusting his facial mixture more in the direction of to-this-point-and-no-further straight-talking authority, 'is abhorrent.'

'Wait for the *but*,' said Trina.

'But . . .' said Hugo Bennington.

'There you go,' said Trina.

'. . . I think we need to ask ourselves what racism is, and whether what Ken Henderson said was categorically racist, because I think if people actually listen to what he was saying . . .'

Trina reached in her pocket for her phone and began to scroll through Twitter. The abject horror she experienced whenever Bennington's face loomed into her field of vision was, in some ways, offset by the delight she took in watching her Twitter feed fill not only with the highly creative insults his every TV appearance inevitably inspired, but also with a scrolling chorus of criticism and disapproval without which Trina, left alone with the television, would have been at risk of losing all faith in humanity.

Twitter, for Trina, was the exact opposite of the brief overview of television to which she had just subjected herself. No-one was lying about on a lawn in cricket whites on Twitter, or at least, not on Trina's Twitter. Instead, they were, like her, watching and commenting on the offensive drivel currently spraying from the face of Hugo Bennington.

In the background, Bennington was still banging on about

England. On Twitter, which had now become Trina's foreground, a rush of comment and critique had begun – an ever-expanding stream that took in Bennington's politics; things he'd said previously in his column that his current appearance on television seemed to contradict; things he'd said as a politician which he now seemed to be forgetting; things other people had said about things he'd previously said which now seemed once again timely and relevant; playground insults about his voice and the fact that he looked as if he was losing the ability to dress himself and brush his own hair; and, of course, many links to the original comments made by Ken Henderson that had begun this whole fiasco.

All the while, on the television, Bennington was talking increasingly heatedly about the plight of white male politicians prevented from saying what they thought by the liberal constraints of mainstream media, conveniently ignoring the fact that he was, at that very moment, on national television, saying exactly what he thought.

'. . . and what we're saying,' Bennington was saying, 'is that we need to have a conversation about this. Not a slanging match. Not a guilt trip. Not a whole load of politically correct flimflam. A clear, rational, honest debate about what's happening in this country and what we can do about it. Because if you asked me what the most fundamental human right of every person living in England today is, I would say that it's freedom of speech. And I think a lot of people, if you asked them, would agree with me. But I also think a lot of people would agree that much as we might enjoy the *idea* of freedom of speech, we don't really have it. We're living in a censorious age, and if we carry on like this then we're genuinely, and this is going to sound strong but I want to make it clear to you just how strongly I feel about this, going to come dangerously close to what I honestly feel is a cultural and political purge in which a whole group of people, as far as politics is concerned, cease to exist.'

'A genocide of white men,' Trina said, bouncing Bella gently against her chest while she leaned back in her chair and felt the last cloudy wisps of her working day disperse. 'Maybe by the time you're grown up, Bella, that's something we might have achieved.'

'I can hear you,' called Carl from the living room.

'OK,' said Trina, briefly closing her eyes and letting herself drift a little. 'Not a total genocide. Just a controlled cull to keep the numbers down.'

She heard him chuckling under the din of the computer game. She scrolled through her feed a little more and then idly tapped out a post.

You can't even make up racist terms of abuse any more, she tweeted. *It's political correctness gone mad.*

Then, as an afterthought, she tweeted *#whitemalegenocide. Lol.*

She flicked through the channels again, then switched off the television. Bella, who had shown brief interest in Bennington's face only to quickly realise he was not worth bothering with, had quietened, and, nestled against Trina's shoulder, was beginning to doze. Trina reached for her phone again. Her *#whitemalegenocide* tweet had already garnered a substantial number of retweets. She thought of Mia, her orders to unwind. Fair enough, she thought. She'd satisfactorily distracted herself. Perhaps she could just enjoy the next few moments as they were.

1100

0011

'Robert. *Robeeerrrt.* Robbie-boy. The Robster. Robbing from the . . . I'm riffing. It's freeform. But let's streamline. How are you doing?'

'Fine, Silas,' said Robert, once again resizing windows on his laptop in order to achieve the minimum possible Blandford.

'I could have done this by email but I thought, what the fuck, let's make it personal. The buzz in the office is unbelievable, Rob. This piece is like if a fire emoji stopped being an emoji and became an actual fire. You know what I'm saying?'

Robert was thrown. Writing the piece had felt awkward, uncomfortable. His angle had eluded him. He'd tried it angry, tried it sentimental. He'd gone for dignified remove, then thought, fuck dignified remove, and tried his hand at spitting outrage. But then outrage had sounded too much like all the other outrage that littered the web and he'd worked his way back to what he hoped was a kind of dignified empathy. At the last minute, the events in the square, although he had not described them directly, had provided him with the perfect approach: the way in which the Darkins of the world (a phrase he'd actually used, but about which he was now less certain) were not only ignored but actually *obscured* by contemporary reality. Amidst the babble and froth of opinion and counter-opinion, he'd asked, what possible room could there be for a story like Darkin's, and what did that say about the future we were all shaping for ourselves? He'd sent it off on a hot whim, pulsing with achievement. Then he'd woken up in the morning and regretted it, gone over it all again, seen other angles, different positions, and, worse, obvious criticisms. Now here was Silas telling him he loved it.

'I . . . Really? I mean, people like it?'

'This piece is beyond that, Rob. It's beyond *like* or *dislike*. I've actually heard someone use the phrase *new dawn*.'

'In relation to my column? Are you sure?'

'Well, now that you mention it, no. But let's look at it another way. No-one in my office ever says *new dawn*. For your column even to have created an office atmosphere where a phrase like *new dawn* is able to unironically exist is like some kind of . . . new dawn.'

Silas's praise, Robert thought, was complicated. On one level, it was welcome, partly because any praise was welcome and partly because Silas was effectively, though Robert could rarely bring himself to admit it, Robert's boss. But on another level, it was *Silas*, a man whose intellectual and ethical shortcomings were so glaring that Robert practically had to adjust the contrast on his computer screen to take him seriously. The result was that Robert felt no less confused than when he'd woken up and gone back over the piece and asked himself if he'd erred. On the one hand, Silas loved it. But on the other hand, *Silas* loved it.

'I mean, obviously I wanted to write something powerful,' he said, feeling his way into being able to talk about what he'd written.

'Oh, it's powerful alright, Rob. It's seriously powerful. I'm actually overpowered by it. It's *over*-powerful. Which is apt when you think about it, because this is a piece that is also like, *over* power. You know?'

'I think I kind of know, yeah.'

'So let's get serious. We're running it as it is. It's long. It's grandiose. It's kind of windy in places. It's everything we don't dig. Which is why we dig the absolute fuck out of it. We're going to drop it in the ocean of culture like a fucking depth charge. But look, quick briefing, OK? Don't think there won't be pushback, because there will very definitely be pushback. But fuck the pushback, because this piece is *itself* a pushback, right?'

'What kind of pushback?'

'Oh, the usual pushback.'

'Like Julia Benjamin kind of pushback?'

'Like that, yeah. Only, you know, more so.'

'*More* so?'

'Well you didn't think it was going to be met with universal love and acceptance, did you, Rob? This piece is the future. When is the future not controversial?'

'I suppose I can't really see what's controversial about—'

'About being a man? About being white? About being English? Nor can I, Rob. Nor can you. Nor can the Darkins of the world, am I right? But the point is that it *is* controversial. And that's exactly what this piece is saying.'

As Silas was speaking, a rivulet of what felt like pure nitroglycerine had dripped, as if from a pipette, from the base of Robert's skull and into the opening of his spinal column, from where it had trickled, icily, mercilessly, all the way to his anus.

'Oh God, Silas. Jesus Christ. I mean, the column *mentions* those things, but I'm not saying—'

'What are you saying, Rob?'

'I'm just saying that we need to have a conversation about—'

'OK. I'll stop you there, Rob. Because people are going to ask you what you're saying. They're going to want comment. And if you want my advice, don't come out with a load of shit about *starting a conversation* or *trying to have a dialogue* or any of this other crap people say when they've finally managed to say something direct. This piece is not having a dialogue, Rob. This piece is saying, *Open your ears, fuckwads, I am here to speak.*'

Robert wasn't sure what to say. It would help, he knew, if he had a clearer sense of the column in his head. It would also help if he had some idea, however vague, of what Silas was seeing in the column that he himself had failed to detect. Because yes, OK, it happened to be about a man. An ignored man. An ignored, white, and actually, now that Robert thought about it, quite racist man. But that wasn't the same as . . . It wasn't saying . . .

'You know what?' he said, changing tack. 'Maybe it needs one more pass. Just tweak a few things.'

'Tweak a few things? That's what I'm saying, Rob. This is *raw*. This is from the *gut*. If you tweak it, you dilute it.'

'All the same,' said Robert, who, much as he might have been experiencing a near-radioactive level of concern and discomfort, was damned if he was going to undermine Silas's apparently genuine enthusiasm for something he'd written. 'Call me a perfectionist.'

'Hey,' said Blandford, holding up his hands, 'artistic attention to detail, right? I'm down with that. But seriously, Rob. I don't want to see you gut this thing.'

Robert had clicked open his piece and was skimming through it. It was no longer familiar to him. It had been distorted through the lens of Silas's reading, and from there through a series of further, imaginary lenses representing all the readings that were to come. Not only could he not recognise the piece, he realised, he couldn't recognise the version of himself that had written it, meaning he couldn't, by extension, trust the accuracy of the reading he was giving it now.

'People are tired, Rob,' Silas continued. 'They're fed up. They're worn down. They've had it with all this left-wing, liberal dogma. The new anti-authority is on the right, not the left. It's the new *punk*, Rob. People were crying out for this piece, and you've given it to them. That's why we're already seeing such a crazy response profile to it.'

'Response?' said Robert. 'What response? How are you seeing a response?'

'What? Oh, shit. Did I not say? It's up. It's live.'

'It's what?'

'It's out there, baby. The velociraptor has figured out the locking mechanism and is roaming the park.'

'But what the *fuck*, Silas? What about edits? What about me reading it over?'

'Yeah, yeah, what about this, what about that. You want me to level with you, Rob? This is the best thing you've ever written. Why? Because it's brave. And so we have a question. Why have you not written something this brave before? Obvious answer: because you're not, essentially, and don't take this the wrong way, a brave person. So – potential issue with this piece? Your moment of braveness fades and you go back to being not that brave. Solution? We *remove the option* of you going back to being less brave. I'm like the mother bird here, Rob. I've nudged you out of the nest and now I'm going to watch you fly.'

'Or plummet to the fucking ground.'

'That never happens, Rob. All birds can fly.'

'What are you talking about? You find baby birds on the pavement all the time with their heads smashed in.'

'Those are bad birds, Rob. They're defective. Are you a defective bird?'

'I—'

'*Are you a defective bird*, Robert?'

'No. I am not a defective bird.'

'Well stop *acting* like a defective bird and let's fucking *fly*, yeah? OK, I've got to run. Let's touch base later, because believe me this is going to go stratospheric.'

'Silas? Silas?'

But he was gone.

———

I t's . . .' Hugo stared at the A4 printout that Teddy had placed in front of him on the conference-room table. 'I don't even know what it is, actually.'

Hugo was not in the mood for this. He hadn't slept, then he'd overslept. His time without Teddy had been cut short. Now he felt like he was playing catch-up with himself.

'It's something,' said Teddy. 'I think we can categorically say that.'

Hugo scanned Townsend's column again. The experience of reading it was unnerving. He felt a weird, distorted familiarity, a kind of perverted recognition. It was, he thought, just one more thing in his morning that made the world feel strange.

'He sounds like me,' he said finally.

'He sounds a lot like you.'

'Is anyone pointing out how like me he sounds?'

'Not yet.'

'Maybe I should point that out?'

Teddy shook his head, gave Hugo a significant look.

'You're thinking kill it with kindness,' said Hugo.

'I'm thinking basically a bear hug he can't get out of.'

'Fine,' said Hugo. 'Fuck him, the little prick. That's not what I'm worried about, though, to be honest.'

'You're thinking about this Darkin bloke, I know. But you know what? Same deal.'

'Townsend's turning him into some sort of fucking *cause*.'

'A cause you're actually much better placed than him to champion.'

'But I can't just go out there and champion him. Downton will shit themselves.'

Hugo's fear of Jones was, he knew, unseemly, but it was genuine. He deliberately hadn't considered the specifics of what Jones might be able to do to him if he put his mind to it, but even if Hugo kept his visualisations vague the gist was clear enough. He pictured Jones opening his newspaper, or perhaps, like Hugo, being handed a printout, thinking a moment, his face as expressionless as ever, then morphing into semi-liquid form and pumping himself through the keyholes of Hugo's life. The shit Downton had on Hugo would act like an expanding foam: a quick squirt into a single crack and everything would be subsumed.

'Let them shit themselves,' said Teddy. 'At the end of the day, this guy's got, what, a few weeks of holding out left in him? You don't need to push him. You just need to make him feel like he's about to be pushed by someone else. Meanwhile, you wring your hands about the tragedy of it all.'

The trick, Hugo thought, was going to be to think as little as possible. That had always been the trick, really. Down at the pit of his stomach, the knowledge of what had to be done was always stubbornly present. His aim was to keep it there, in his gut, and never let it reach his head.

'It's hugs all round,' he said flatly.

'Big hugs,' said Teddy.

What a point it had come to, Hugo thought, when he was the man whose embrace was fatal. He couldn't tell if he felt thrilled at the power or depressed by the implications.

'Let's move on,' he said. 'Tell me about the TV thing.'

'Basically,' said Teddy, bringing up a series of completely unlabelled pie charts and associative diagrams on his tablet, 'you're off the scale right now, big guy.'

He showed Hugo a map of England covered in glowing orange conflagrations. 'This is your resonance slash amplification. See that? It's off the charts.'

'And that's good?'

'It's very good.'

'And people are saying . . . What are people saying?'

'I don't think we should get bogged down in detail here, Hugo. I don't think *what* people are saying is really as interesting and important as the simple fact that they are saying stuff.'

'I take it what they're saying is basically not good.'

'Oh, it's very good. It's just that its goodness isn't so much a direct result of the content and more an outcome of the act of saying it. Look at this.' He held up a line graph with an enormous spike in the middle. 'This is you on Twitter.'

'Look, Teddy, I know you think I'm very naive about all this, OK? But I've googled myself. I've looked on Twitter. I know what's going on. That spike is just a huge upsurge in people calling me a twat the moment I appeared on television.'

'Isn't it amazing?'

'How is that amazing?'

'Because it's free publicity. You can't buy this kind of amplification, Hugo.'

'But it's negative publicity.'

'No such thing. Negative publicity is like antimatter. It's an urban myth.'

'I don't think antimatter is an urban myth, Teddy.'

'Alright then, show me some antimatter.'

'Well, obviously I can't *show* you some antimatter, because it's—'

'Right. If you can't show it to me, it doesn't exist. You see what I'm saying? It might very well *actually* exist, but to all intents and purposes, it doesn't.'

Hugo felt a familiar wave of fatigue beginning somewhere around the backs of his eyes and then draining downwards through his face, neck, and shoulders. It was the consistency of honey and numbed everything it touched.

'Alright,' he said, massaging his eyeballs. 'Condensed version. Win, loss, or draw?'

'Well, I think we need to define—'

'How did it go, Teddy? Just how did it go? In simple terms. How do you think, given your analysis, it went?'

'I think it went very much as planned.'

'You know what, Teddy? I'm going to take that. That's great. It went as planned. Brilliant. Let's move on.'

'Although, saying that—'

'Sweet mother of Christ. What? What is it?'

'Well, there was one element which, although I would say it fell within the broadly defined boundary of being planned, was, within that boundary, not quite as planned as everything else.'

'And what was that element?'

'Right,' said Teddy, poking around on his tablet. 'So, basic Twitter search during the timeframe of you being on television, right? And we're getting all the usual buzz terms. Racist is right up there. Bigot. Lunatic. Plague-bearer—'

'Let's skip to the relevant detail here, Teddy.'

'I like it, Hugo. Yeah. So if we drill down through all the usual stuff, we get to this.'

He held up his tablet for Hugo to see. There, in front of him, was a screenshot of a tweet calling for white male genocide.

'What the fuck is that?' said Hugo.

'It's someone talking about white male genocide,' said Teddy.

'I can see *that*, Teddy. But, you know, give me details. Who is this person? Is this a death threat? Is this some kind of, I don't know, *organisation* we need be paying attention to?'

'Truly or hypothetically?'

'I'm going to take a gamble and say both.'

'Truly: er, not really. Hypothetically: I'm thinking maybe . . . Yes?'

'OK. Explain further.'

'This tweet was written by someone who is basically just some woman. Some black woman. She's not a somebody. But she has more than the average number of followers so we can't really say she's a nobody. And she's followed by some people who are sort of somebodies, in a kind of limited way. And some of those people retweeted this tweet. And so this tweet is . . . Well, it's not really a thing, but what I'm saying is that it could very easily *become* a thing, if we wanted it to.'

'Why would we want it to?'

'You remember last week when I was saying that what you really needed was a death threat?' said Teddy.

'Mhmm,' said Hugo.

'Well this is even better than a death threat. This is a genocide threat.'

'It says *lol* at the end. That doesn't make it sound very threatening.'

'Does it or does it not say white male genocide?'

'It does say that, yes.'

'And is that or is that not exactly the kind of thing you as an individual and England Always as a party have always feared and have always taken a very firm stance against?'

'Well, yes.'

'And wouldn't you say that, given your hitherto extremely firm stance with regard to exactly this kind of thing in a very hypothetical sense, you are pretty much *duty bound* – and I think you should say that if anyone asks, by the way – *duty bound* to take an especially firm stance when this kind of thing happens in a very real way to not just anyone but in fact to you yourself?'

'In some senses, yes. But in other, arguably more relevant senses—'

'Particularly at a time when certain *other* people are taking, as we've just discussed, kind of a notable position *themselves* on the whole, like, *white male plight*—'

'I know what you're saying, Teddy. OK? For once, genuinely, I know what you're saying. But—'

'You're angry about this, right, Hugo?'

'Obviously. It's just that—'

'Because I'm angry about this. I'm *fucking* angry about this, actually. And you know what? Alan's angry about this too.'

'Alan's angry?'

'Alan's very angry. And he assumes you're angry.'

'Well, you can tell him from me that I'm definitely angry.'

'I don't need to tell him, Hugo. I've already told him. And not just him. Everyone.'

'When you say *everyone*, Teddy—'

'So first thing, I tweeted a screen grab of the tweet from your account and then retweeted that from the England Always account. OK? So everyone's aware and everyone's on the same page.'

'Teddy, how do you—'

'And then I tweeted, from your account, just to be clear . . .' Teddy pulled out his phone and scrolled through until he found the relevant tweet. 'Three angry-face emoji.'

'That is at least . . . concise,' said Hugo. 'But just, if I could . . . I mean, let's just press pause on that for a moment, OK, Teddy? And let's just very momentarily divert and look at the issue of how you're able to use my Twitter account.'

'Oh, I guessed your password.'

'How did you guess my password?'

'Because your password is *password*.'

'That's . . . Alright, I can see how you might have been able to guess that. Let's look at it from another angle. *Why* did you guess my password?'

'Because I needed to send this tweet.'

Torn between admonishing Teddy for his initiative and simply moving on so as not to get bogged down in the quicksand of manic interpretation that so often seemed to be Teddy's speciality, Hugo decided, with reluctance, to take the path of least discussion. After all, he thought, Teddy was broadly right, even if, in his actual application of being right, he was so worryingly in the wrong.

'OK,' said Hugo. 'But for future reference—'

'Noted.'

'Let me finish, Teddy.'

'Totally, but at the same time—'

'For future reference, don't ever hack into any of my accounts again.'

'I didn't really *hack* into your account, big guy, I mean—'

'I'm going to change all my passwords anyway, so the point is moot. But understand that there's a principle, and—'

'Changing your passwords was going to be the next item on the agenda, actually, given the current climate. But whatever. I haven't told you the best bit.'

'What best bit?'

'With this genocide woman.'

'There's more?'

'Look at her *address*, Hugo.'

Beaming, Teddy passed a piece of paper over to Hugo, on which were written the woman's details.

'Well, what do you know?' said Hugo, peering at the piece of paper and experiencing, for the first time in far too long, the satisfying sense of things coming together in his favour.

He dropped the piece of paper on the table and grinned.

'Pat yourself on the back, Teddy, my man,' he said, with unusual warmth. 'Pat yourself on the back *very hard*.'

And Teddy, being Teddy, reached around, over his shoulder, and did exactly that.

———

'Bloody hell,' said Geoff, walking in with two bags of shopping, putting them down on the kitchen floor and taking a moment to examine Darkin's window, his hands on his hips, taking it all in. 'What happened here? Kids, was it?'

Darkin shook his head. 'Got stuck. I asked some bloke to put the window in and come give me a hand.'

'Stuck how?'

'Couldn't reach my stick.'

'How did that happen?'

Darkin looked down at his jumper, onto which, he now noticed, some of the contents of the sandwich he'd had for dinner last night had dripped, leaving a dark, sticky pickle-stain which he now, with the aid of a thumbnail in need of trimming, attempted to scrape away.

Geoff left the shopping on the floor and walked over to the sofa opposite Darkin, where he took a seat, leaning forward over his knees to study Darkin intently. Geoff was the only person Darkin knew who sat on his sofa without brushing it down first.

'What happened?' he said.

'Bloke from Downton,' said Darkin in a half-mumble. 'Came round here and moved my stick.'

'What?' said Geoff, outraged. 'Deliberately?'

Darkin nodded. 'Said I was *vulnerable*.'

'Did he now,' said Geoff. He flopped back on the sofa, this time exhaling through clenched teeth. 'Those shits.'

Darkin looked up from the pickle-stain.

'Don't say anything,' he said.

'I know, I know,' said Geoff. 'Code of silence, right? But still, those shits.'

They were both quiet a moment.

'Look,' said Geoff, 'I know I say this every time—'

Darkin shook his head.

'Why not? Seriously, chap. Why not at least consider it?'

'Because I don't want to.'

'But *why* don't you want to? You could do so much better than this place. You could have one of those little bungalows. They've got alarm systems. They've got wardens. They've got people what come and do your shopping. I mean, not that I mind doing your shopping, but . . . You know what I mean.'

'I don't want to because I don't want to,' said Darkin.

'I don't follow.'

'Look at me,' said Darkin. 'Look at this place. Look at the food I eat.' He pointed to the ticking kitchen timer on the coffee table. 'Look how I have to ration myself.' He shook his head. 'I've got one thing left that's how it was, how I want it,' he said. 'Staying here. Stopping here.'

Geoff nodded. 'Fair enough,' he said. 'But the minute you want me to give those bastards an earful, just say the word, right?'

Darkin nodded.

'Alright then,' said Geoff. He dug in his pocket. 'Here's your receipt anyway. I got all the usual. Here's your card too.'

'Ta,' said Darkin.

'Where would you be without me, eh?' said Geoff. He'd clearly meant it as a joke, but neither of them laughed. Sometimes, there were things Darkin wanted to say to Geoff that went beyond a mere thank you, but he never knew how to say them, so he just nodded quickly, and Geoff nodded back, and that was that.

Geoff drove a taxi for a living. He lived nearby. They'd met soon after Flo got packed off to the home. Darkin visited her twice a week until she died. Unable to manage the bus, he called himself a taxi. After a while, Geoff had given him his private number, done him a discount on the fare. Then he'd stopped asking for the fare completely. Once Flo was gone, Darkin didn't need the taxi any more, but Geoff had come round and knocked on the door, worried about him. He'd looked at Darkin, looked around the flat, and understood. He'd popped out to get Darkin some shopping. A few days later, he'd called again.

Geoff walked over to the kitchen area and rustled through the shopping bags, coming up with a packet of cigarettes which he tossed onto the sofa beside Darkin.

'Remembered the essentials,' he said. Then, turning to the window, 'You are going to get this fixed, though, aren't you?'

'Don't worry,' said Darkin.

'I do sort of worry, though, mate.'

'I just haven't got round to phoning,' said Darkin.

'You want me to phone for you?'

Darkin shook his head.

'This isn't about money, is it?' said Geoff. 'Because there are people what do it for free if you're, you know . . .'

'Old,' said Darkin.

'Above a certain age,' said Geoff.

'I'll sort it.'

'Suit yourself. But if it's still busted when I come back next week . . .'

He started pulling things out of the shopping bags – a loaf of bread, a tub of margarine, some cheese, a pint of milk. When he thought Darkin wasn't looking, he snuck a few things out of the fridge and into the bin. Darkin in turn pretended he hadn't seen.

'I can take this when I go,' Geoff said, knotting the top of the bin bag. 'I mean, since I'm heading that way anyway.'

'If you want,' said Darkin.

'Cuppa first, though, eh?'

Geoff picked up the kettle and took it to the sink. When he spun the tap, a phlegmy gurgle escaped. Water struck aluminium in a weak, spitting spray.

'Hello,' said Geoff. 'How long's it been like this?'

'It was fine this morning,' said Darkin.

Geoff tried the other tap, with a similar result.

'Maybe they're doing some work on the pipes,' he said, not sounding especially sure.

Darkin said nothing. No-one, he thought, was doing any work on the pipes, and no-one was likely to either. He'd had a distinct feeling, ever since Mr Jones's visit, that something was about to go wrong. Now, here it was.

———

Eschewing the awkwardness of a beanbag, Bangstrom had instead opted to stand over everyone while they looked blankly back up at him.

'Here's the download,' he said.

'Will this take long?' said Bream.

'Are you going to start?' said Bangstrom. 'Because let me tell you what I think about people starting: I don't like it. So let's stop with the starting before it even starts. Because *if* it starts, I will be very pissed off, and you do not want to see me pissed off.'

'Are you not pissed off right now?' said Bream.

'I am nowhere near pissed off right now,' said Bangstrom.

'So this is, like, your resting state?' said Bream.

'Let's be clear,' said Bangstrom. 'The Interrobang does not rest. Received?'

'Noted,' said Bream.

'Maybe you should rest,' said Holt. 'Maybe that's why you're so tense.'

'OK,' said Bangstrom, 'let's recap. My tension: not your concern. My rest or lack of rest: not your concern. Everybody clear? Now, as I was saying. The download. Green have concerns, which I have been asked to come down here and communicate to you in language you can understand, i.e. the language of implied physical violence, that this whole Griefer situation is not just a Griefer situation, it's actually also an MT situation, which puts you guys, i.e. you guys, and you Trina, in this room, right in the rifle sights, and I've been sent down here to train those rifle sights a little closer and, if necessary, take the kill shot.'

Trina could feel the cockiness drain right out of the room. Holt looked up from his tablet. Even Bream took a deep breath.

'Trina does all the MT stuff,' said Bream.

'Fuck you, Bream,' said Trina.

'Just stating a fact,' said Bream.

'It's not a true fact, though, is it Bream?' said Bangstrom. 'Because as we all know, given the way things work around here, all of us, whether directly or indirectly, do MT stuff, because all the stuff we do is, literally, given to the MTs to do for us.'

'When Green say this might be an MT thing,' said Trina, 'what sort of thing do they think it might be?'

'I'm going to answer that,' said Bangstrom, after a pointed panopticon glare, 'but I'm going to make it clear that my answer is not to be communicated to *anyone* who is not *right now* sitting here, because if that happens I will know it was one of you fucks who made it happen and I will make it my personal business to make sure every remaining day of your life is a day spent with shit raining down from on high, am I clear?'

Everyone nodded.

'Green think it might be an uprising kind of thing.'

Everyone in the room went a full ten seconds without saying anything annoying.

'Trina,' said Bangstrom. 'You used to MT, didn't you?'

Trina nodded. Inside her stomach, a geyser of anxiety became active.

'And then you worked your way Inside The Building and now you monitor the MTs. Have I got that right?'

Trina nodded again.

'So just confirm for me, if you can, an important point. Although the MTs don't work together, and don't know each other, and are all basically separate from each other, and although our operating system prevents them from ever seeing what each other is doing or collaborating in any way, they still talk to each other. Am I right?'

'There are forums,' said Trina. 'They're mainly places where people put the call out for work. But there's always chatter.'

Bangstrom nodded.

'Alright,' said Bream. 'Say the Griefer thing is basically an MT thing. Say all the Microtaskers are pissed off. I don't see what they'd achieve by having their little film showing in the town square. If they've found a way to pull data, why not just lock Green up for a few days and demand higher pay? Why cloak it in all this political mumbo jumbo?'

'Well, somewhat ironically for a bunch of people we've trained to think very, very small,' said Bangstrom, 'it seems they might actually be thinking quite big.'

'It's not enough just to make Green's life inconvenient,' said Trina. 'By doing this, they're undermining Green's whole business model, their standing, their brand value. Everything. They're saying: we made you. We can unmake you and remake you as we wish.'

'We are your face,' said Bream.

Everyone took a moment to consider this, or, Trina thought, to look like they were considering it while in fact taking a few moments to second guess the ways in which everyone else might be considering it. Ordinarily, Trina would have found this uncomfortable. Thanks to her role in what was effectively a glorified HR position in an organisation dedicated to all but erasing any need for a discernible HR structure, she rarely knew anything worth noting, and so spent much of her time cultivating the appearance of concealing what she knew so as to more effectively conceal the fact that she knew very little. Today, though, Trina knew something she was reasonably sure could not be widely known, namely that Tayz, the MT, had gone semi-dark and was, probably right at this moment, engaged in odd and unknowable activity. In Trina's mind, there was no question as to the importance and relevance of this information. The question instead was whether she should tell anyone now or simply run with it on her own. This, she thought, was the self-defeating ideology of gamification at Green. There was no way to progress by co-operating. What you needed was a crisis, and when that crisis came you needed to withhold the solution from your colleagues for as long as possible in order to, with luck, solve it single-handedly.

The problem was that she had already flagged Tayz's suspicious activity, raising the very real possibility that Bangstrom, in his rather unsettling determination to keep angling his lines of inquiry towards her, was not so much trying to find out what she knew as testing her to see if she planned on sharing.

'This may or may not be relevant,' she said, slightly experimentally, 'but the other day I flagged an MT. His activity was weird.'

Bangstrom gave no indication whatsoever that he had checked the flag, leading Trina to conclude that either she'd been right to assume he was sizing her up, or nowhere near strong enough in her estimation of just how ineffectual and determined to cover his own arse he actually was.

'Weird how?' said Holt.

'Essentially idle. But with sub-activity I couldn't monitor.'

'So why not upstream it for checking?' said Bream.

'Exactly what I did by flagging it,' said Trina.

'And the upshot?' said Bream.

'Haven't heard yet.'

'You didn't think it might be important?' This was Bangstrom – already, Trina thought, manoeuvring to deflect and apportion blame.

'I tried to raise it with Norbiton,' said Trina, 'but he was—'

'He was being Norbiton,' said Bangstrom.

'This is a long-standing MT?' said Holt.

Trina nodded. 'One of my best.'

'Aw,' said Bream, 'she says *my* like he's one of her kids.'

'Fuck you, Bream,' said Trina.

'Alright,' said Bangstrom. 'Trina: work on that.'

'On it,' said Trina. 'But I'll need more access.'

'Done.'

'Wait,' said Bream. 'That's it? You're just going to—'

'I'm just going to let the only person in this room who has even the remotest chance of getting somewhere go ahead and maybe get somewhere,' said Bangstrom. 'I mean, crazy, I know, but what can I say, I'm a maverick.'

'And meanwhile, we just—'

'Meanwhile, you two pricks take a few moments to reflect on your total lack of contribution to the situation, and then maybe a few further moments to reflect on how things might play out if your positive contribution levels continue to flatline, as they have thus far, at around about the fuck-all mark. How about that?'

Trina looked over at Bream, who was looking back at her with naked hostility. In the half-second that Bangstrom's head was turned, she shot Bream a wink.

'Fuck you,' said Bream.

'Fuck who?' said Bangstrom. 'Because if that fuck you is in fact a fuck me, then let me tell you, Bream—'

'It's a fuck her,' said Bream.

'Right back at you,' said Trina, unable to swallow the grin that had suddenly pressed upwards from her chest and burst open across her face.

'Meeting adjourned,' said Bangstrom.

They bottlenecked at the door, Bream bumping Trina with his shoulder. She turned to face him, staring him down, daring him a little.

'Have a nice day,' said Bream, pushing past her and through the door.

Safely sequestered in her No-Go room, in the brief seconds of heightened pause while her terminal booted up, Trina allowed herself three energetic fist pumps in quick succession. This, she thought, was it. This was everything she had so carefully constructed coming to fruition. It was the Beatrice system; it was her determination to grab herself a No-Go room; it was the endless hours and days pitch-shifting the parameters of faceless workers, calibrating, observing, waiting. It was her design, her plan, her hope.

She fired up Beatrice and clicked around in the dashboard. There was Tayz, still pulling traffic, still dropping down the levels. She wondered if, with the increased access that was either coming or perhaps even already enabled, she might be able to get into the specifics of what Tayz had been doing. The system, she knew, allowed it, but that kind of data had remained, until now, locked off to her. She pulled up his user profile, started graphing his history. Information unfolded in neat columns in front of her. Bangstrom, she thought with a little thrill, must have gone straight back to his office and unlocked her privileges. The temptation to now waste time exploring her own boundaries was immense. How far did this new-found reach go? she wondered. All the way? She shook her head, defogging her brain of misdirection. If Bangstrom had been so quick to grant her access, she thought, he'd be watching to see exactly what she did with it. He was almost certainly, right now, at his own terminal, in his private office, pulling up all her click trails, mapping her routes through the system, monitoring all the things she was about to monitor in relation to Tayz. Somewhere, probably, someone Trina had never encountered was watching Bangstrom watch her watch Tayz.

She got back down to it, scrolling, clicking, reordering. At what point, she wanted to know, had the change in Tayz's behaviour begun? She ordered his history by productivity, looking for the peak and the drop-off. The decline was more sudden than she remembered. He'd tipped into a new level, unlocked higher pay, then slumped. Maybe, she thought, it was something in his personal life, some kind of complication or distraction. But that didn't explain the activity. He was still, after all, working. She pushed into his packages, the individual microtasks that had been parcelled out to him, looking for the last thing he'd successfully fed back, finding a filename that looked like all the others – twenty or thirty digits of seemingly randomised upper- and lower-case letters – but with an extension she didn't recognise: .fld. Against the listed files in front of her gaze, she overlaid another list in her mind, a scrolling index of familiar file types: .c; .sh; .bak. Coming up blank, she clicked on the file, wondering if she could, from here, go into it and unpack it or if she would need to find out where it came from and access it that way. The listed files shunted decisively leftwards, replaced by what was now a blank screen. Cursing, she clicked back. Her system, glitching, didn't respond. She clicked again. A pop-up centred itself on her screen: *Thank you for contributing. Click to acknowledge.*

She froze. Her fingers, resting on the keyboard in front of her, began to shake. It was a mistake, she told herself, a system glitch. Bangstrom hadn't properly delineated her access levels. The system thought she was pushing beyond her remit and had locked her out. She'd clarify, get herself unlocked. It was fine.

She clicked on the pop-up. Her screen blackened, returned to a log-in state. She put in her password. It came back unrecognised.

She stood up and jerked open the door of her No-Go room, already fuming at whatever bullshit was unfolding. Outside, the two HR men from her induction were stood side by side, waiting for her.

'Hello, Trina,' said HR man number one. 'If we could just borrow you for a minute?'

People were looking up over their terminals. The room echoed with the click-clack of urgent IMs being fired off and opened. She felt hotly visible, exposed in the transition from her private room to the glare of the floor.

'Can I ask what this is—'

'Won't take long,' said the HR man.

'Literally no time at all,' said number two.

'Do I need someone with me?' she said.

HR man number one shook his head.

'I'm not going anywhere until I—'

Bream appeared behind them, inexplicably absent from his own No-Go room, doing his best to shape a face approximating sympathy.

'Word of advice,' he said. 'It always goes better if you don't fight it.'

———

To say that word of what was happening in Edmundsbury had spread quickly was something of an anachronism. All word spread quickly, regardless of any inherent urgency. But even by the standards of a high-speed time, it was noticeable that The Griefers and their odd, ad-hoc protest, if that's what it was, had been seized upon by opinionists up and down the country almost immediately. A collective nerve had been touched. Opinions kept on standby were suddenly and deliriously discharged.

DeCoverley's little gatherings had helped, as had Hugo Bennington and, probably, Robert's columns about the estate. Not so long ago, Jess thought, Edmundsbury would have been far enough off the commentarial radar for most people to think twice before unholstering their thinkpieces. Now, it occupied a tantalising hypothetical position. It was recognisable enough to the intellectual and political set that events taking place within the town seemed notable, but not so familiar that many of their readers could securely challenge anyone's interpretation of those events, meaning any columnist who'd once hopped on a train and spent two hours wandering around could now claim a unique level of insight. It was a perfect storm of opportunistic interpretation. Something no-one yet understood had taken place in a setting with which only a privileged or irrelevant few were familiar. All known yardsticks of veracity were therefore abandoned. If no-one knew what something meant, anything anyone said about it could be true.

For Jess, sitting at her office computer studying the chatter of comment, the available responses were predictable largely because the people offering those responses were so depressingly familiar. Here, for example, in a longish piece for a neoliberal, corporately sponsored web-rag called *The Non-Believer*, was none other than Ziegler, he of the misappropriated data and thinly veiled misogyny, putting forward the opinion that The Griefers, with their interchangeable white male faces and drably businesslike attire, were staging a protest not against the internet, but against the tyranny of identity politics.

For Rogue Statement, The Griefers' faces and uniforms, the quasi-military overtones of their arrival in a van with blacked-out windows, conveniently hinted at a fascistic aesthetic that the Theory Dudes were keen to exploit. As always, though, the simple recognition of observable fascism was not enough for a group still riding high from a recent, heavily circulated piece about the fascism of selfie-sticks, and so they had spun from their loose observations about The Griefers an overblown and frankly dangerous riff on the inherent fascism of public events in general, and, by extension, all protest, implying, although Rogue Statement didn't quite say it, that conformity was the last truly radical act.

Jacques DeCoverley, meanwhile, was worried less about fascism and more about what he termed the *encroachment of the contemporary*. What was happening in Edmundsbury, he said, was emblematic. *The modern world* could no longer be escaped, even in parts of England that once could have been relied upon to act as a haven from, one presumed, all the things DeCoverley had grandiosely left London to escape. Edmundsbury, he contended, had to defend its connection to what he slightly incoherently called *the ancient, unchanging real*. It needed to resist not only the encroachment of technology, but the encroachment of the *discussion* of technology. It needed to get back to a sense of *place* and *belonging*. It needed, he said, to *finger once again England's visionary soil*. How could it do that if not only technology, but *protests* against technology kept worming their way in?

'Catching up?' said Deepa, entering with her usual enervated energy and casual disregard for knocking. 'I'll spare you the trouble: the masters of the dude-iverse have not excelled themselves.'

She flopped into Jess's spare chair, tried three different arrangements of legs and arms, then gave up and stood again, wandering over to the window of Jess's office and peering out at the car park.

'Deepa,' said Jess, turning from her screen and fixing Deepa with a stern over-the-shoulder stare. 'Have you . . . *slept* at all?'

'What?' Deepa was back in the chair again, folding her hands, then unfolding them, then biting her nails, then seemingly noticing something about the nails that concerned her and studying them intently. 'No. Sort of. I mean, a bit. But mainly no.'

'Do you want a cup of tea?'

'I've had four coffees.'

'Do you want to maybe—'

'Take the edge off? No. I mean, thanks. But no.'

Deepa set strict limits around relaxation. She knew when she needed it, knew what she needed to induce it, but rejected it out of hand when thinking was required. For her, thinking was not contemplative. It was not even particularly focused. It charged and sprawled. Connections fired, multiplied, then dwindled.

'Everyone's focusing on the wrong thing,' she said. 'I mean, they're looking at the thing itself and not the thing that the thing is supposed to direct people towards.'

Jess nodded.

'People are like, oh my God, The Griefers. But they should be like—'

'Oh my God, privacy.'

'Right. They're looking for meaning in the masks but there isn't any meaning in the masks. The whole point is that everything of any significance in that event was already available. It was taken from elsewhere.'

'They're wearing a composite image. *We are your face.*'

'Right, *this is you.* This is your picture on the internet. This is the email you sent. This is all the shit you thought was private but isn't.'

'Or is but soon may not be.'

Deepa shook her head.

'That bit I don't buy though. The whole threat angle. The black-mail possibility. I mean, they haven't even said what they want.'

'Or what they've *got.*'

'Right,' said Deepa. 'Some pictures? I mean, *I've* got pictures. Everyone's got pictures.'

'You could have put together that little spectacle just as easily,' said Jess.

'I could. But, I mean, better, obviously.'

'Obviously.'

Deepa had extended her hand level with the floor and was now rhythmically flexing and clenching her fingers.

'Cramps?' said Jess.

'Partly,' said Deepa darkly.

'Partly?'

'The cramps are the symptom. They're not in themselves a diagnosis. It's like when people say, *Oh, I've got a cough.* Yes, but *why*? What sort of cough is it? Maybe it's bronchial. Maybe it's cancerous. Maybe it's fucking *airborne*, you know?'

'That's your mouse hand, Deepa. You've got trackpaditis.'

'My question is,' said Deepa, treating Jess's inexpert diagnosis with the disdain she clearly felt it deserved, 'what do they want? Or, no, actually, that's not my question. My question is, do they even want anything at all?'

'And if they do, why don't they just ask for it?'

'Maybe it's ideological,' said Deepa.

'Maybe the screening was one big public-information film. Like, *Remember, kids, the internet can be dangerous.*'

Deepa rolled her eyes. 'That's so *corny* though. Like, OK, they've appropriated the whole Griefers and Trolls idea from online and brought it offline in order to make everyone think about what certain behaviour actually means or the ways in which context has been allowed to determine morality, as in, you do this online, or you accept this online, or you *are* this online, none of which you would think is OK in some sort of offline, so-called real-world setting. *Fine.* But if that's their thing, then what separates them from all those yoghurt-weaving crusties trying to cast off their devices and get back to nature? Or put it another way: what's their alternative?'

'What if we're getting confused by the medium? And what if that's *exactly* the point they're making? What if they're saying: it doesn't matter that all this shit you do is online, it still exists, and it's still *you*, and one day someone, anyone, can remind you of it, meaning, basically, *remind you of who you really are*. Hence: *We are your face.* We are you. This is you. This is all of us. And the cosy little box we've all fashioned to pour our ids into isn't as secure as we thought.'

'You know what I'm thinking?' said Deepa.

'Honestly, Deepa? No. I don't know what you're thinking.'

'I'm thinking: *false flag*.'

'Oh, Deepa, Jesus Christ. Seriously? I mean, do we have to—'

'Think about it,' said Deepa.

'I don't have to think about it, Deepa. There's nothing to think about.'

'Say you're the government.'

Jess hung her head in her hands.

'No, hear me out,' said Deepa. 'Say you're the government and you want to force through, like, utterly draconian internet measures.'

'They're not from the *government*, Deepa.'

'Not *from* the government, no. But—'

'But what? You think the government of England just, like, *selected* a small town in England, where literally no-one actually lives, in order to stage some sort of, I don't know, *art happening*, which was seen by like *tens* of people, in order to instigate some national programme of—'

'Maybe this one's the tester. They're feeling it out. It's a trial run.'

'Deepa. Please. Do not go down this rabbit hole. Look. All the information is there. The masks. The appropriated faces. The snapshots of online behaviour. They're reflecting back. *We are your face.* I mean, come *on*.'

Deepa was eyeing Jess suspiciously.

'What?' said Jess after a significant pause. 'Why are you looking at me like that?'

'Because it's very *interesting*,' said Deepa.

'What's interesting?'

Deepa waved a hand vaguely in the air.

'This. This whole *angle* you've got here.'

'It makes sense, Deepa.'

'Yeah. If you're you.'

'What does that mean?'

Deepa angled her head to one side and somehow implied a roll of her eyes without actually rolling them. Jess shifted position in her seat. This was something Deepa was uncomfortably adept at: the sudden pinch-to-zoom, the shift of focus from paranoid global hypotheticals to astute interpersonal specifics.

'Your whole take on this thing,' said Deepa, her tone suddenly gentler, more patient, 'is that it's about the essentially pretty toxic nature of our behaviour on the internet, right? The way we kid ourselves that our behaviour can be digitally contained when in fact it can't, both in a literal sense, because we have no actual control over our data, and in a less literal sense, because that kind of shit has a way of always finding its way back. Yes?'

'Yes,' said Jess cautiously. 'That's . . . That's basically what I'm saying.'

'And you don't think,' said Deepa, 'that that in *any way* says more about you than it does about what's going on?'

Jess felt herself slump a little.

'Are you worried?' said Deepa, not unkindly, but not so gently that there was any question of her indulging any bullshit.

'No,' said Jess. 'God no. I'm *interested*. That's all. And maybe this is their whole point, right? We project. We see our own face in everything. I mean, God, you only have to look at the thinkpieces this morning to see everyone finding their own reflections in the headlines.'

'Maybe you feel guilty,' said Deepa.

'*Guilty?* You're shitting me, aren't you? Guilty about what?'

'I'm saying: say, just for argument's sake, that these Griefer guys actually plan to make everyone in Edmundsbury's internet usage public. Say that's really what they're going to do: lay us all bare, possibly literally, in front of each other, so that we can all get a good long look at the people we are, the people we live with, the people we love. Right? Say for a second that's what's coming. I'm saying: imagine that moment. Imagine it all pouring forth. Imagine the end of secrets. And then imagine how you'll feel. Horrified? Ashamed? Or . . .'

Jess knew what was coming even before Deepa got to the word, and so finished the sentence for her.

'Relieved.'

Deepa gave her an open-palmed *you got it* gesture and sat back in her chair with an air of commingled satisfaction and concern.

'Have you seen his latest column?' said Deepa after a while.

'Whose?' said Jess, off guard, the question nicking at the edge of her skin. 'Robert's?'

She had, of course, been thinking about Robert. Was it that obvious?

'Real change of pace this time round,' said Deepa.

'In what way?'

Deepa shook her head, then raised her hands.

'Not going there,' she said, standing up.

'Great,' said Jess. 'Thanks.'

'My pleasure,' called Deepa in a sing-song voice from the corridor.

There was still a qualitative difference between the way Jess navigated to one of Robert's columns when she was logged in as herself, and the way she did so when she was logged in as Julia Benjamin, but Jess was unnerved at the distinction's decay. Once, her feelings had stayed where she had put them. Jess had kept up to date with Robert's work so that she felt in touch with what he was doing, where he was in his thinking, and so that she could discuss it with him later, over dinner, or half-watching a television show on the couch. Julia went there looking for weakness, for an opportunity to argue. Slowly, because of the gaps in Robert's thinking Julia had been able to open up, Jess increasingly clicked through to one of Robert's columns with trepidation, and read them with a slight wince. Now, something in Deepa's grim tone had exacerbated that sensitivity. When Jess arrived at the piece and began reading, something in Robert's tone blurred the lines between her selves even further.

Robert had, for a long time, and certainly in the wake of his more recent success and visibility, dialled up a version of himself when he put a column together: a little sharper, a little more forthright, a little more perfectly positioned than he was able to be in person. The discrepancy – subtle enough to be detectable only to someone who knew Robert as intimately as Jess – had always annoyed her. Indeed, its existence in part explained her need to create Julia Benjamin in the first place. But she had always been able to detect one Robert in the other, and she had always taken a degree of reassurance from that, as if in continuing to recognise him a kind of anchor was established by which she was able to recognise herself. Now, though, Robert had widened the gap between the man he was at home and the mouthpiece he became in print to an alarming, chasmic degree.

The truth, Robert wrote, *is that Darkin simply isn't cool. His plight ticks not a single one of the boxes necessary to ensure the fashionability of his cause. He is simply a man – an old, white man – who has given enough, paid enough, shared enough, but who now receives nothing in return because society has moved on, and no longer regards the Darkins of the world as a worthwhile cause.*

She sat back in her chair and allowed her computer to go to screensave. It was a state she wished she could access herself: awake, running low-level processes, but disconnected, and available to receive new information only if woken in the correct way. She didn't want to think about this piece, she realised – didn't want to consider its meanings and implications, or palpate the sensitivities it stirred in her. Which was worse, she wondered: being unable to recognise her partner in what she read, or recognising him all too well?

She tried to imagine herself reading the piece as someone who had never met Robert, let alone lived with him, but doing so only returned her to the person she'd created in order to achieve just that: Julia. Everyone, she now saw, was doing exactly what she spent her time doing: donning a series of masks, creating convenient personalities they could inhabit. You were this person at work, this person at home, this person in print, this person digesting the ideas of another.

She wanted to text Robert, or phone him. Or, even better, go home and confront him with the absurdity of what she'd just read. But of course, she thought, she couldn't. This was the great side effect of Julia: she and Robert no longer argued. They had outsourced their disagreements, and in doing so created a space where they were happy, where the concerns that threatened their comfort were held at bay. The moment she went home and said what she thought, she would allow Julia into her home alongside what she now thought of as *public Robert*. Something would be irrevocably ruptured; some membrane would tear. The dark matter of their ideas would subsume them.

She pushed back from her desk and picked up her bag. On her way out, she tapped on Deepa's door and gave a little wave.

'Back later.'

Deepa, engrossed in her screen, raised a hand above her shoulder, but didn't turn round.

———

'One thing we want to be clear on,' said HR man number two as they steered Trina into the same windowless room she remembered from her induction. 'We've looked at your performance here and we have to say it's admirable.'

'We've also looked at your personal qualities and we want to make it clear we feel those are admirable too,' said number one as they took their seats opposite Trina. 'Not to mention your membership of certain minority groups, which although not admirable simply in and of itself does draw attention to the way you manage your membership of those groups and the unique challenges membership of those groups presents, which is admirable.'

'Is this going somewhere?' said Trina. 'Because nice though it is to be admired—'

'OK,' said number two. 'Here's the rub: Trina, have you checked your phone in the past, I don't know, thirty minutes, give or take?'

'No,' said Trina. 'I was busy with work.'

'What's your notification protocol?' said number one.

'My what?'

'Vibrations, sounds, alerts on screen, or total do-not-disturb blackout?'

'All silent,' said Trina.

'OK. Good to clarify that.'

'Clarify what?'

'Clarify the fact that unless you have physically looked at the screen of your phone and actually, you know, *gone through* your alerts, you won't know what has been happening, which goes some way to explaining why you haven't done anything about it.'

'Maybe you'd like to look at your phone now,' said number two. 'So we're all on the same page with reference to what has been occurring.'

Trina checked her phone. She had two hundred Twitter notifications.

'Jesus,' she said.

HR man number two reached in his pocket for a phone and tapped around on it before turning its screen towards Trina. On the screen was a snapshot of her tweet about Hugo Bennington: *#whitemalegenocide. Lol.*

'Is that your tweet?' said HR man number two.

'Yes,' said Trina, who now felt not only sick but alternately hot and cold and intermittently short of breath.

'Correction,' said number one. 'It's actually not your tweet. It's Hugo Bennington's tweet of your tweet.'

'Oh Christ,' said Trina.

'That's approximately what we said,' said HR man number one.

'Approximately,' said number two.

'It's my personal account,' said Trina. 'It's not a work account. And for fuck's sake, I didn't even *at* him. He must have searched. And I put *lol* at the end. Only an idiot would think I was—'

'Some kind of dangerous extremist threatening the English way of life?'

'Excuse me?'

'We're quoting,' said number two.

'Quoting directly,' said number one.

'Quoting *who*?'

'Multiple sources. On Twitter. On blogs. And, as of a few minutes ago, on a live radio phone-in.'

'I'm being called an *extremist*?'

'We're not saying we feel that's an appropriate term.'

'We're just quoting.'

'But this is obviously bullshit,' said Trina. 'I mean, you can see that, right? Anyone who isn't a moron can see that this is just—'

'It is what it is, is what it is.'

'Right. It's very much what it is, and we have to take it for what it is.'

'So let's move on and tell you about our problem.'

'*Your* problem?'

'Do you recall,' said HR man number two, 'the conversation we had when you first started here?'

'Oh fuck me,' said Trina. 'You're not serious. You're not seriously going to go there.'

'Let's make one thing very clear,' said HR man number one. 'We're going to go everywhere.'

'Right,' said his colleague. 'There is nowhere we are not now going to go in the name of getting this thing sorted out.'

'When you joined us, Trina, it was necessary to have a conversation about your past.'

Trina just shook her head, sicker than ever at where this was obviously now heading.

'Or more specifically, about the contents of your past.'

'Right. About your history of . . .'

'Let's say confrontation.'

'Right. Confrontation. And physical violence.'

'Which we are not judging.'

'Totally not judging.'

'Which we are dealing with strictly as a legal point of fact as it is noted on your record.'

'Exactly. Strictly that.'

'And which we have never had cause to bring up until now.'

'Unless you include then.'

'Right. Now and then. Those are the only two occasions.'

'That has no relation to . . .' Trina protested.

'We're not here to say categorically yes or no in terms of the relation between these two things,' said number one.

'We're here to point out that when you started here, we explained to you that, given your background, there were certain circumstances in which we would be forced to take your history into account. And this is obviously one of those circumstances.'

'Because what have we got here? We've got people saying, hey, HR guys, what is this Trina person like? Is this usual behaviour for her? Does this kind of outburst have any precedent?'

'And obviously we're thinking—'

'What people?' said Trina. 'What people are asking about me?'

'We're thinking, possible threat alongside previous demonstrable history of enacting that threat.'

'I don't have a history of genocide, for fuck's sake.'

'You have a history of violence.'

'Violence against men.'

'Let me ask you, Trina. Was your previous partner, the person you assaulted, a white man?'

'What?'

'It's not a trick question.'

'Very straightforward question.'

'I'm not answering that question, because it is *not fucking relevant*. Jesus Christ, this is madness. Can't you see what madness this is?'

'We're trying to establish some kind of precedent.'

'If he wasn't white it could really help you.'

'Because then we could say, yes, OK, she does have some history of violence, but it's not race-specific.'

'Whereas if he was white—'

'Fuck you both,' said Trina. 'Fuck you both completely. You creepy sanctimonious clones. You don't even have *names*, for fuck's sake.'

'We absolutely have names,' said number one.

'I'm actually a little hurt at the suggestion we don't,' said number two.

'But we'll probably let that slide because there are mitigating emotional circumstances.'

'Mitigating emotional circumstances? Let me clarify with you, OK, dickhead twins? There are no emotional circumstances. There are *factual* circumstances. I'm being witch-hunted. I might be in *physical danger*. Green should be protecting me, instead of—'

'We are protecting you.'

'And us.'

'No reason we can't do both.'

'Alright, alright,' said Trina, who much as she may have been angry was not in any way irrationally so, meaning she was aware of the battles that would help her and those that would not. 'What now?'

'We suggest you keep your head down.'

'That's it? That's your advice? Keep my head down?'

'We think it's good advice.'

'Don't you have some sort of *plan*?'

'Well, obviously we can't control what people say on the internet,' said number two with what was either a wry smile or a patronising sneer.

'Much as sometimes we might wish we could.'

'Right. We might wish it, but we can't actually do it.'

'And even if we could, there would be the whole question of whether we should.'

'Global tech company dedicated to free and safe use of the internet polices internet. You can see the inherent conflict there.'

'How about global tech company dedicated to free and safe use of the internet and the safety of their staff takes some sort of action, however small, to protect their employee from what is very obviously an attempt to curtail her freedom and safety?'

'How about global tech company dedicated to free and safe use of the internet and proud of their human-rights record defends off-the-cuff call for genocide?'

'Not really the same ring to it, right?'

'No ring at all, really. More like a heavy, clanking thud.'

'Why do I get the feeling that somehow sympathy is not really lying with me on this?' said Trina.

'Oh, we wouldn't want to give that impression. We're very sympathetic.'

'You see our faces? These are sympathetic faces.'

'But don't tell me,' said Trina, '*your hands are tied.*'

'To a certain extent, yes.'

'Sympathetic faces,' said number one, running his hand down his face before raising his wrists in a handcuffed gesture, 'tied hands.'

'Am I being disciplined? I mean, what's the position here?'

'The position is that there is not yet a position.'

'Right. No-one wants to rush to a position.'

'Green are waiting to see how this pans out, basically,' said Trina.

'Right.'

'Green are thinking they want to fire me, but they're also thinking what if the whole internet ends up coming down on my side and they just end up looking like the people who fired me.'

'The situation is very fluid.'

'Isn't it just.'

Trina stood up, calmer now, clearer on how things were going to be.

'Are we done here?' she said.

'I think for the time being, yes, we are done.'

'Right. Well, thanks for nothing, guys.'

'Our pleasure.'

———

By lunchtime, Robert was widely shared. It felt like being famous. In many ways, he thought, scrolling through notifications and new follows, this *was* fame, because this was how celebrity now manifested: no red carpet, no fizzing pap flash, just the hum of alerts, the skin-tingle buzz of being noted by unseen eyes.

Silas, who had already emailed with an update, was in raptures. He'd had to move an intern onto the comments thread full-time in order to keep up with even the rudimentary moderation system *The Command Line* employed. Quite what Robert felt about the fact that his piece seemed to have resonated especially strongly among people who expressed their enthusiasm solely through the medium of abusive messages and snuff imagery, he couldn't really be sure. In a way, it didn't matter. Resonance could no longer be neatly graphed along positive and negative axes. It was about volume, reach, impact.

At around one, Silas Skyped in for a catch-up.

'Robster. How's the man of the hour? Are you *basking*? Tell me you're basking.'

'I'm . . . I guess I'm kind of basking, yeah.'

'Are you really basking though? Or are you basking in that like super-English, *oh, what, me?* kind of way? Because how many opportunities does a guy get to truly bask, Rob?'

'OK. Consider me on basking standby.'

'Great. So anyway, update.'

'Right.'

'Basically: you're super hot right now. That's not a metaphor. I'm looking at a heat map of traffic and you're literally a hotspot.'

'That's great.'

'You're not *the* hotspot, of course.'

'No.'

'But you're in the mix. You're the plucky little hotspot that could.'

'That's really good to know, Silas.'

'But look. We need to capitalise on this window. Because it's a small and rapidly closing window. Less like an actual window you and I might be accustomed to seeing in the modern world, and more like one of those, like, slits they have in castles.'

'I think they were for archery.'

'Right. Exactly. That's perfect. You're in the castle, Rob, and OK, maybe you haven't got the biggest window, but you've got your little slit in the wall and you are firing your arrows through it like there's no tomorrow. Am I right? Maybe we could get that done as a cartoon or something.'

'Don't you think that would send kind of the wrong impression? Like, here I am in my ivory tower of pure privilege, raining down arrows on—'

'Own that though, Rob. I mean, really own it. The world doesn't need another cowering white man. You get me?'

'To a point . . .'

'Which is where this whole genocide thing comes in.'

'*Genocide?* Oh Jesus fucking Christ. Is this to do with Julia Benjamin? What's she said now?'

'No, Rob. Julia-whatever-her-face is yet to respond, although to be honest I can't wait until she does, because once she swings onto the scene you're going to go from hot to scorching. The bro brigade are already all over your piece. Once Julia Benjamin gets involved, they're going to be all over her too, and everyone else is going to be all over them being all over each other, meaning my heat-mapping software will basically *come*. But whatever. No, this is about the genocide woman.'

'What genocide woman?'

'You're not following this? This is literally happening right now, in Edmundsbury, where you live, and you have no idea? What have you been doing all morning?'

Robert had spent the entire morning repeatedly refreshing his notifications and link-searching reactions to his piece, and so had little sense of anything happening to anyone else. The reminder that there even *was* anyone else, or that any story besides his own might be the subject of discussion, came as something of a rude awakening.

'I've had a lot of correspondence to deal with,' he said. 'Wait, hang on. There's *another* fucking Edmundsbury story?'

'Yeah.'

'Not The Griefers, not me, but another one.'

'Right.'

Robert allowed this to sink in. It was as if, he thought, the universe was perpetually and stubbornly tilted against even his most modest success. First The Griefers stole his thunder, and now someone else, some *other* Edmundsbury inhabitant, was threatening to steal what miserable murmur of thunder remained. It felt like some grand, cosmic-level joke: all these things happening in Edmundsbury, where nothing ever happened, just as he'd been halfway successful in making something happen. The moment he realised this, though, was the moment he realised something else: whatever he felt about the piece, whatever he felt about what he'd uttered and unleashed, the thought of it playing second fiddle appalled him. The knowledge that people were reading what he'd written, *relating* to what he'd written, was uncomfortable, but not as uncomfortable as the idea of people failing to read it at all.

'Well?' he said, a little too sharply. 'What is it?'

'This woman. Trina James. Black woman. Lives in Edmundsbury. She was watching Hugo Bennington on television the other night, and she was, you know, tweeting away, as you do, and she kind of tweeted the hashtag *white male genocide*.'

'But not, you know, seriously?'

'Seriously or not seriously. What does it matter? It's words on a screen, Rob.'

'But I think there's a difference between—'

'OK: word to the wise. Do not go down that road. That road is available, yes. It may even appear the more sensible road. But none-theless, stay off it. Because this is a fucking godsend for you, Robert, and everyone knows you do not look a godsend in the mouth.'

'Why is this a—'

Even as he was asking the question, the only possible answer was shaping itself in Robert's mind. 'Oh Jesus, Silas. No. No way.'

'What do you mean no way?'

'I'm not weighing in on this.'

'Are you serious? This is *perfect*. This could not be more perfect if you'd designed the whole fucking situation yourself. If we're talking heat maps, she's like the frigging surface of the sun right now.'

'Because of a joke?'

'You know for one hundred per cent certain it was a joke?'

'Well, it obviously wasn't serious, was it?'

'No?'

'No!'

'Why?'

'Because no-one would say that seriously. No-one would actually tweet that they thought we should have some sort of—'

'A terrorist would. An extremist. A dangerous loose cannon or a member of some kind of cell.'

'A cell? A cell of who? A cell of dangerous Hugo Bennington-hating radicals? Everyone hates Hugo Bennington. *I* hate Hugo Bennington.'

'But you're not calling for genocide.'

'No-one's *calling* for genocide, Silas. For fuck's sake, you just cannot be serious with this.'

'Never mind my seriousness or otherwise, Robert. That's not what we're talking about here. I'm saying: how serious are you?'

'Serious about what?'

'Serious about yourself. Serious about your work.'

'My . . . I'm very serious, Silas. You know that.'

'Really? Because suddenly you look kind of . . . not serious.'

'Not serious? What, because I'm not taking a clearly not serious statement seriously?'

'Because you're not *backing up*. You're not doubling down.'

'On what?'

'On your manifesto.'

'My manifesto? It was a fucking *provocation*, Silas.'

'OK. So you've provoked. You've prodded the beast with a stick. Now the beast is awake. What are you going to do? You need to *own* this, Rob.'

'I don't know what you're talking about. Are you saying this woman, whatever her name is, who made the joke about—'

'The statement. She made a statement.'

'Who said whatever she said. Are you saying she's the beast I poked with my stick?'

'I'm saying you've started something. You've written this thing about sharing, and men, and unfairness, and everyone's gone, holy shit, listen to this guy, and now they're listening, and while they're listening someone *else* has said something that basically *proves your fucking point*. You think the people who liked your piece are going to be amused at this woman's genocide stuff? You don't think maybe they're going to expect some kind of response? And you don't think,

181

maybe, just maybe, that if no response is forthcoming, if you seem to have *no fucking opinion whatsoever* on the threatened *genocide of the white male species you claim to care so fucking much about*, people are going to see you as, oh, I don't know, *kind of a fucking fraud?*'

Robert had not seen Blandford angry before. Most of the time, he vacillated between childishly animated and affectedly unimpressed.

'Hang on, Silas. It sounds ever so slightly like I'm being threatened here.'

'Does it, Rob? Does it? You know what? Maybe you are. *By someone who's talking about killing every white man on the planet.*'

'But she's not going to actually *do it*, is she?'

'Is that the point? Do you actually seriously think that whether she actually literally goes out there and shops around on the black market, no pun intended, or maybe intended, I don't know, and manages to buy some sort of biological weapon that can be encoded with, like, skin-recognition technology, and then actually detonates that weapon, is actually literally the point of what is happening here?'

'There's a big difference between an allegorical bomb and a real one, Silas.'

'Yeah, maybe there is. And the difference is, in our line of business, only one really matters. You think if an actual bomb wiped out half the frigging population people would express outrage about it online? Do you think they'd even *look* online? To us, Robert, the allegorical bomb is the real bomb, and the real bomb is just an allegory. As far as opinion is concerned, *this is a real bomb*, and it has rolled in your direction, and if you don't do something about it the bomb's going to go off and there's going to be pieces of your brain all over the internet. Is that a clear enough image for you?'

'That's . . . That's pretty clear, yes.'

'Right. Good. That's clear. The threat is clear, and by threat I mean not *her* threat but *the* threat, the threat to you, and more importantly, by extension, the threat to me. So we're all clear and now you can go away and knock me something up, right?'

Robert nodded.

'You look completely morose. Why are you so morose? This is—'

'I know. A godsend.'

'It's a major godsend. Hold on to your pants, Rob. You're about to go supernova.'

Trina was not in the habit of panicking. If she cast her mind back through the times in her life when panic might have been a possibility, times that included both the threat and reality of violence as well as the possibility and actuality of poverty, she was unable to find documented even a single instance of abandoned reason. Pressure sharpened her up. A sense of crisis, real or imagined, helped her focus.

Something about this, though, was different. Her sense of alarm remained under control, but beneath the still waters of her ostensible calm a dark shadow of dread had become detectable. Walking out of the meeting with the HR men, she'd felt the sliding glances of passing co-workers. When she'd found herself a bench outside, alone, with ten comforting minutes to herself before the lunchtime rush, she'd taken out her phone to call home and found it clogged with notifications of violence. As the first of her colleagues began to drift out towards the tables for lunch, it occurred to her that some of the threats could well have come from people she knew, and that there was nowhere she could go to get away from what was happening.

She opened her contacts and tapped Mia's picture to dial her mobile. As she listened to the ringing, she realised she wasn't quite sure why she was calling her, whether it was for support or simply to warn her.

'Hey, babe,' she said when Mia picked up.

'You OK?' Mia said immediately.

'Do I have to not be OK to call?'

'At this time of day? Probably, yeah. What's going on?'

'I don't know,' said Trina. 'But it isn't good.'

Mia was quiet a moment. She would, Trina knew, be weighing her need to find out what was happening against her understanding of Trina's deep impatience with bringing anyone up to speed. 'How can I catch up?' she said simply.

'Are you near a computer?'

'Yeah.'

'Google me.'

Mia let out a long exhalation. She was holding back all her questions, and Trina loved her for it.

'Has anyone been round?' Trina said.

'What? No. No-one.'

'No-one at all? I mean, not even a tap at the door, or—'

'Well, there was the survey guy . . .'

There was the dread again, the wide shadow under the water's surface.

'What survey guy?'

'You know, that survey they do, about who lives here and what everyone's jobs are and all of that.'

'And this was when? This morning?'

'Couple of hours ago, maybe.'

'What did he ask about?'

'Does anyone claim benefits. Does anyone work. What do they do. Any children in the house. Religious beliefs. You know, all the usual stuff.'

'And you . . . What did you say?'

'I answered. It was a check-box thing. He just went down the list on his clipboard. I mean, I didn't . . . Shit. Have I fucked up?'

'No,' Trina said. 'No, don't worry. It's probably nothing. Probably just the Census or whatever.'

'What can I do?'

'Is Carl there?'

'He's changing Bella.'

'OK, so don't do anything. Just lock the door and sit tight. I'll be home soon.'

'I've got a job.'

'Go. It's fine.'

'Really?'

'We probably shouldn't turn any money down right now.'

Trina heard the rattle of a keyboard at the other end of the line and pictured Mia perched on the edge of the sofa with her laptop on her knees.

'Oh, babe,' Mia said, clearly landing on some article or other.

'It's fine,' Trina said. 'It's all going to blow over.'

'Sure. We'll batten down the hatches.'

'Yeah. Takeaways and movies and don't look at the internet for a couple of days.'

'Right.'

'Well, OK. I'll be home soon anyway.'

'OK.'

'Love you.'

Mia laughed. 'Now I *know* this is serious,' she said. 'Love you too.'

Trina stared at her phone for a moment after Mia's voice vanished, watching as the screen repopulated itself with further notifications. The worst of it was now skipping Twitter completely and heading straight for her inbox, meaning her personal email address was out in the wild. She thumbed and stopped at random, just to get a flavour. The message she opened contained a grainy photograph: a naked black woman noosed to a tree, her hands tied, her muscles slack.

For a moment, Trina's eyes blurred over, her vision pixellating like a bad video stream. She put her phone away and looked back up at the thickening crowd of distorted faces leaving the building and gathering around the lunch tables – the calm, unquestioning civility of her colleagues, the muted tribal behaviours. Here people were, she thought, going about their day with dignity, yet eviscerating each other behind screens.

Was everything that was happening, she wondered, really just because she'd made a joke on Twitter? Was Hugo Bennington, for years a journalistic punchline, now a one-man political farce, really influential enough to mobilise this kind of collective response with this kind of ferocious immediacy? Measured in the half-life of internet time, her tweet was dormant history, yet it was only now attracting widespread attention. Yes, she thought, perhaps that was simply because Bennington had only now seen it and only now marshalled his forces of bigoted darkness. But she hadn't even mentioned him in that tweet. Was his vanity searching really that thorough?

But then again, the simplest explanation was usually the right one, and bigotry was the simplest and oldest and most obvious explanation of all, one that didn't need the weight of some murky and paranoid conspiracy theory to explain it. Even the survey-taker at her house, she thought, could just as easily be down to the usual machinations of the anonymous bullies. She wasn't the first woman to be doxxed.

Turning it over in her mind, tilting between distinctly modern paranoia and depressingly old-fashioned oppression, didn't make her feel any closer to the truth, but it did make her angry again, and as she felt herself enraged, her vision sharpened, the scene in front of her shifted from low res to high def, and faces were once again faces, with one in particular emerging from the anonymity: Kasia, walking towards her, carrying two Tupperware boxes of today's lunch.

'Hey,' said Trina, taking one of the proffered boxes and prising off the lid to reveal a noodle salad. 'Thanks.'

Kasia perched on the edge of the bench beside Trina and began poking at her noodles.

'Everyone is talking,' she said.

Trina nodded. When Kasia didn't expand on this observation, Trina said, 'You don't have to sit here. I get it.'

Kasia frowned. 'I said everyone is talking,' she said. 'I didn't say I'm listening.'

'You're not even a little bit curious?'

Kasia shrugged lazily. 'Twitter thing,' she said. 'I don't care. It's stupid.'

'This thing? Or Twitter in general?'

'Twitter. The whole thing. Everybody . . .' Kasia did an exaggerated mime of someone clumsily thumbing text into a mobile phone. 'For what? Just gossip.'

Trina nodded. 'Maybe,' she said.

'Definitely,' said Kasia, battling a wayward tangle of noodles into her mouth. 'Who cares.'

'Can I ask what people are saying?' said Trina.

'Oh, you tweet this thing. Everyone tweets things back at you. Blah blah blah.'

'Right.'

They ate without saying anything for a few moments, either because there was little to say or simply because the food was difficult to consume while talking. Trina hadn't thought she was hungry, and hadn't thought she wanted to stay any longer than was necessary at The Arbor, but now she was eating she realised she was starving, and now Kasia was here she became aware of how alone she'd felt. These, she thought, were the moments that mattered – the ones that, amidst the violent slippage of private and public worlds, needed to be defended.

'What are Green doing?' said Kasia.

Trina shook her head in disgust. 'Covering their backs. I think they're waiting to see how it shakes out.'

'But you have rights.'

Kasia said this weakly, clearly aware it wasn't true.

They ate their noodles. Trina's urges were battling each other. A sense of mounting urgency, of the need to be active, was pulling her away, but a sense of easy familiarity, of being somewhere safe and known that protected her and knew her back in turn kept her perched beside Kasia on the edge of the picnic table. Everything that was swelling and rising online, she thought, would wash rapidly into everything she valued offline. These quiet, unnoticed interludes would be her only breakwater.

'Hey,' said Kasia, 'you want dick update?'

'God no,' said Trina.

Kasia got out her phone with a grin.

'I said no,' said Trina. 'You know the word *no*, right?'

'I know what's good for you,' said Kasia with a distinctly sadistic grin. 'When life gives you lemons, look at dick.'

'Is that a traditional Polish expression?'

'*Ta da*,' said Kasia.

Kasia's anonymous correspondent had upped the creativity factor considerably. Where before his dick had simply been photographed in proximity to a conveniently scaled object, now a small domestic scene had been created: a dining table set with a bunch of sunflowers, napkins in little wooden rings, dinner plates, and a full set of silver cutlery. In the middle was a silver platter ringed with glistening roast vegetables. In the middle of that, resting on a neat green bed of what may have been parsley, was a dick.

'Oh my *God*,' said Trina.

'Right?' said Kasia.

'I mean . . . What am I even looking at here?'

'It's a charming domestic scene.'

'What is he, like, lying under the table, with his dick through a hole?'

'He is like, come on darling, table is set for dick.'

'His dick is enormous,' Trina said, peering more closely at the image. 'I mean, look at it in comparison to that dinner plate.'

'Optical illusion,' Kasia said. 'Must be.'

'You think it's a fake dick?'

'Or fake plate. Fake everything.'

'Oh no. Hold up. You're saying this guy took the time to *craft* everything on that table so as to more effectively show off his dick?'

Kasia shrugged. 'Why not?'

'Doesn't that seem . . . I don't know, *insane?*'

'Men and their hobbies,' said Kasia.

'You do know,' said Trina, more seriously, 'that men's primary hobby is fucking up women?'

'Meaning what?'

'Meaning are you sure you're OK with this?'

'OK how? He sends dick. I laugh. Everyone's happy.'

'Has he ever asked for anything from you?'

Kasia rolled her eyes. 'Your paranoia is making me paranoid,' she said.

Trina nodded, let it go. She realised that this would, now, be another thing she would need to pay attention to: the extent to which she forced her fears on others. Paranoia was one thing, infectious terror something else entirely. If she wasn't careful, she thought, she could wind up toxic, isolated. She needed to contain what was happening and keep it from the people she loved.

She patted Kasia's thigh.

'Fair point,' she said. 'Sometimes a dick is just a dick.'

———

There was nowhere to park near Nodem. This struck Jess as odd but failed to occupy more than a fleeting moment of attention. She found a space a few streets away and walked from there.

She was several paces into her journey before she noticed the comparative lack of people, and several paces further on from that before she began to experience a sense of unease. Maybe, she thought, it was simply her own feelings catching up with her. She hadn't given adequate air time to her internal doubt, perhaps, and so now, displaced, it was manifesting around her as an emotional mirage. Only when she rounded the corner did she realise that the source of the atmosphere, unlike her still-humming post-thinkpiece enervation, was not inside her at all, but real and external, all too tangible in the street ahead: three men – squat, shiny-headed, thick-necked. Their insignia, stitched neatly onto their black bomber jackets, was grimly familiar even at some distance.

She watched as they waved at a passing old lady.

'Afternoon, madam,' one of them said.

The woman didn't reply, instead pushed on, scarfed head turned down towards the pavement. As she passed Jess, she muttered under her breath, 'Thugs.'

As Jess approached, the men stepped back to allow her room on the pavement. They were wearing utility belts, she noticed now – black webbing straps lined with pouches and clips. She wondered if they were armed, or simply giving the appearance of being armed; if those sinister, unknowable pockets held blades and foldable batons, or cigarettes, shopping lists, breath mints.

'Afternoon, love,' said one of them as she passed.

'Fuck you, fascist,' she said in response.

The men exchanged looks. She toyed, briefly, with the idea of leaving it at that, but it was not the kind of day and she was not in the kind of mood for leaving things at that.

She said, 'What are you doing here? What do you want?'

'You haven't got anything to fear from us, love,' said one. 'We're just here to keep people safe.'

'Don't call me love. I'm not your fucking love.'

'Feminist, is it?'

'I'm amazed you even know the word,' she said. 'You Nazi scum.'

'These are dangerous times,' one of the men said. 'We're here to protect women like you.'

This last was too much. She walked away in disgust, shaking slightly.

'You'll come around,' another of the men called after her. 'You'll be glad of us soon.'

At the end of the street, she could see the blacked-out windows of Nodem and she kept them as her focus. When she stepped through the door into Nodem, she was once again icily calm. Once inside, though, she was briefly thrown. Even when she volunteered for the refuge, which had seen a marked uptick in visitors in recent months, she had never been in Nodem when all the terminals were taken.

'Bloody hell,' she said to Zero/One at the counter. 'What's all this?'

'It's The Griefers,' he said. 'People are scared to go online. They're coming in here just to do their shopping. It was bad enough after the screening thing, but now, what with these letters . . .'

'Letters?'

'Take it you don't really look at your snail mail.'

'Who does?'

'Well, everyone, now. Go home and see for yourself.'

She wanted to ask more, but stopped herself. She wanted to target her energies, shape something narrow and attentive from the noise.

'I'll find you a terminal as quick as I can, yeah?' said One/Zero.

Jess nodded. She almost said *no rush* but there was, she felt, actually a rush.

'You want a brownie while you wait?'

'Sure.'

He passed her a floppy disk with a square of brownie perched on top.

'On the house,' he said. 'To keep your energy up while you wait.'

She picked at the edge of her brownie, watching with vague, distanced interest while a man in grime-streaked chinos bearing what appeared to be a hastily assembled bundle of possessions – a bulging holdall from which clothes protruded, a laptop trailing its charging lead – babbled at Zero or One, gesticulating desperately as Zero/

One attempted to steer him gently towards a quieter corner.

'Like, you guys are running a great show here. OK? That is totally noted. It's admired. No-one's trying to throw off your show. But what I'm saying is there are things you need to know. There are things you don't know that you really need to know because if you don't know them—'

'Hey,' Zero/One was saying kindly, laying an arm across the man's shoulder. 'That's cool, man. That's totally cool. But maybe if we just—'

'No,' said the man, shrugging off the proffered arm and stamping his foot to emphasise the word. 'No. You have to listen. You can't—'

'How about a brownie?' said Zero/One. 'You look like you could use a brownie. And maybe a coffee? Anything you want, dude. Seriously. Just come over here and we'll talk about it.'

As Zero/One led the man over to a relatively out-of-the-way corner and continued soothing him, his partner took over counter duties and caught Jess's eye.

'Weird energies,' he said simply.

Weird energies indeed, Jess thought. At what point had the velocity and mania of physical events begun to match that of their online counterparts?

A terminal became free and she settled herself at the screen, executing her basic sequence: firing up, logging in. The moments of reflection as Nodem's in-house operating system ground into life stretched out just beyond the comfortable, leaving her to contemplate the counterintuitive state of reversal that Nodem engendered: emotional hyperspeed buffered by a digital crawl. This, she thought, was probably how things were supposed to be: feel first, execute later; delayed communication as self-protective procedure.

Her screen teemed with indecipherable windows and boxes – the system running its own little executables and micro-programmes, chasing and unpacking itself with unstable efficiency. The timer vanished, appeared again, became a slightly different timer, and then, finally, a cursor. She ran her programme of habitual clicks. Web address, email account, username, password. It was the work of a few brief, semi-conscious moments to become Julia Benjamin. Through rote actions, Jess brought herself up to Julia's speed. Ordinarily, having revved up, she was able to roar straight out onto the open highway of Julia's voice. Today, though, her velocity propelled her not onwards, but suddenly, violently, into a sheer brick wall. The moment Jess became Julia, the moment she opened up Julia's notifications and began composing, in her head, the latest of Julia's by now quasi-famous comments, Jess's anger slipped from her grasp and, turning and shifting, became something else instead: a kind of depressed frustration, a disappointment, a drained and dissipated force.

It was a feeling that had been tugging at her for some time, but now it centralised, and it did so, she thought, because Julia Benjamin had centralised. Once, Julia Benjamin and Byron Stroud and all of her other personae had felt like an expansion. Now, increasingly, Julia dominated, and her domination was reductive. Yes, through Julia, Jess was able to express her anger. But where, Jess thought, was she able to express her knowledge? For all the web's gilded rhetoric of open discussion and pluralised voices, wasn't this, the demarcation between the body of an article and the comments that were literally and figuratively beneath it, the most stringently policed and least porous and ultimately most telling border of all?

She thought again of her bodily fear and brewing potential aggression in the presence of Brute Force. She thought about how, simultaneously, her work in the face of this undeniable physical manifestation felt inadequate, theoretical, and yet so necessary, so vital. She was angry with an intellectual boys' club for both exacerbating and ignoring an all too real threat. But how did supplementary bile in the comments sections go any further towards dismantling the connections she knew existed? Her work, she knew, would help make this clear. But was this, any of this, really her work?

She looked at the neatly ordered taxonomy of her comment

history, struck by the way its polite reverse-chronology masked the increasing violence of its development. You couldn't consider one future, she thought, without other futures looming into view. What about the as yet unmaterialised realities closer to home? What about her and Robert? One day, surely soon, this glossed-over, secret tension would reveal itself, and all the structures they'd put in place to contain it would sunder. She pictured the inevitable split, felt the subterranean yawn of upcoming aloneness. She imagined reaching for him in their bed, turning at the sound of his voice in the kitchen, or starting at what she thought was his breath beside her ear, and then, always, finding nothing, slamming up against the awful, amputated emptiness of life in the aftermath: Robert gone; parts of her gone with him.

But even as that imagined future emerged from the future she'd imagined before it, another was already becoming visible. The world she'd first envisaged: intellectually and morally void, strip-mined by self-serving opinion, more divided and unreal than ever, and Robert at the heart of it, bloated by his own success, drunk on all the things he'd once professed to abhor. She'd have to live with him, she thought. She'd have to live with the imagined voices of all the people who wondered why she lived with him. And of course, she'd have to live with herself, because the only way of living with the Robert that would inevitably emerge, knowing she had failed to change him, would be to choke back hunks of her own matter.

If they talked about this, it would wreck them. If she didn't express herself, it would build within her and wreck them anyway. There was no option, she thought, but to go on.

That didn't mean, however, that she had to go on as she was indefinitely. Her every expressed thought did not have to be a response to *Robert's* thoughts. She didn't need to nest what she said beneath what Robert had said. She could make that break, and from there, over time, edge away.

She clicked out of the page she was on and redirected. It was time, she thought, to get back above the line.

———————

M en in mud-clagged boots and reflective vests came to see about the water. They to-and-fro'd, shaking their heads, exchanging glances. They called Darkin *chum* and left footprints he wouldn't be able to clean.

'Backed up, chum.'

'External.'

'Not going to be easy.'

'Not going to be easy at all.'

They spun the tap, flushed the toilet, crawled under the sink and took a wrench to the U-bend.

'I was hoping it was gonna be something simple, chum.'

'Isn't, though, sadly.'

'Anyone you can stay with for a couple of days?'

Darkin shook his head, unsure if he believed anything they were saying. Their insignia didn't say anything about Downton, but he couldn't be sure how much reassurance that implied. Everyone worked for everyone, now. Companies were all tied up with each other.

'Is it a blocked pipe?' he said.

One of the men sniffed speculatively. 'Could be. Could be a leak. Could be several things, to be honest.'

'Hard to say until we look,' said his colleague.

'Can you look now?' said Darkin.

The men laughed, exchanged glances that suggested everyone thought they could just look now.

'Look now, he says,' said the first workman.

'We wish,' said the second workman.

'Well, when?' said Darkin.

'How long's a piece of string?'

'Depends on the access.'

Darkin was about to ask who needed to give them access but thought better of it. He knew exactly who needed to give them access.

'Could be out on the road,' said workman number one. 'In which case, it's council. Or it could be down there in the square. In which case—'

'It'll be Downton,' said Darkin.

The men exchanged another glance.

'Just you here, is it?' said the second workman.

Darkin nodded.

'No plans to move?'

'No.'

'Lot of people moving from around here.'

'Not me.'

'You've got just enough coming through for the odd cup of tea,' said the first workman. 'Not much more though.'

'Not enough to flush the toilet.'

'Shower's probably out too.'

'It's going to be tough, chum.'

'We'll get it sorted but it's going to be tough on you till we do.'

The first workman walked over to Darkin's spare sofa, black scuffs from his workboots marking his progress from the kitchen's lino-leum to the lounge area's threadbare carpet. He sat down with the sigh of a man who hadn't sat down in too long.

'My nan lived round here,' he said.

'Did she,' said Darkin. He didn't make it sound like a question because he wasn't asking to know more.

'You should see the place she's in now,' said the workman. 'Ever such a nice place. Plenty to do. Proper safe as well, like. She loves it.'

Darkin didn't say anything.

'Bloke like you could get one of those places easy,' said the workman. As he said *like you*, he cocked his head towards Darkin's stick, as if that said everything anyone needed to know about who Darkin was.

'They do all these adaptations.' The other workman was joining in from afar, calling out from under the sink, where he was having a last look. 'Baths, showers. It's amazing what they can do now.'

'My nan toddles over to the day room every evening and has her dinner there. It's like a bloody holiday, I swear.'

'When can you fix the water?'

'Alright,' said the workman on Darkin's sofa. 'I was only saying.'

'Days?' said Darkin. 'Weeks?'

'I just thought maybe you didn't know what you could get these days, that's all.'

'Not months, surely?'

'Depends what we find when we get in there. Like I say, though, if you were in one of these—'

'Tell them I'm not going anywhere,' said Darkin.

'Eh? Tell who, chum?'

'Tell them they can turn off all the bloody water and the electric to boot and I'll still be stopping here.'

'I don't know what you're on about, mate. All's we were saying was—'

'Don't bother saying it again,' said Darkin. 'I heard it fine the first time. Just sort the water out and leave it at that.'

'Look, I'm sorry if I . . .' The workman stood up, palms raised, placatory.

'I just want my water fixed,' said Darkin.

'Gotcha. We gotcha, chum. Alright? Don't worry. We'll get it fixed.'

Darkin nodded, eyeballing the man.

'We'll be back soon as,' said the man, moving to the front door, where he was joined by his colleague.

'Right,' said the second man. 'Soon as.'

They closed the door behind them. In the silence, Darkin could hear that they'd left the bathroom tap dripping. The sound measured out a faint, slightly erratic pulse through the flat. It weakened, slowed, then came to an eventual silence. Maybe he'd got the workmen wrong, he thought. Maybe they really were trying to help. This was what happened. Everyone always said they were trying to help, even when they were fucking you over. Once you no longer knew who was helping, it was safer just to assume no-one was.

Somewhere just outside his flat, a pipe rumbled deeply. Everything, thought Darkin, was too connected. One pipe led to another. What was yours led always to what was someone else's.

His kitchen timer screeched from the coffee table, cutting across the muttering pipe. He slid a cigarette from the pack and lit up. Downton had underestimated his capacity for waiting.

————————

Robert was at his computer when DeCoverley rang. He had been there for hours, battling his way into the article Silas had demanded on the genocide woman.

As with the Darkin piece, Robert had already, in the time that had elapsed following his chat with Silas, tried a number of different angles. The fact that he now seemed to have to do this with all of his writing was beginning to concern him. Surely, he thought, he should have had an angle *before* beginning a piece? Surely it was his intended angle that dictated what the piece would be? In the past, he had seen something, observed something, and known what he thought about it. Then he had shaped those thoughts into ideas his readership could easily grasp. Now, an entirely different process had taken over: one of triangulation, extrapolation. Rather than dealing directly with what he encountered, he had to circle, inspect, consider the possible ramifications, and then select, from all the possibilities, the approach most likely to achieve success. If he'd had time, he might have drawn certain conclusions from his discomfort, his inability to place himself in relation to his subject, but the truth was that he didn't have any time at all. This was another concerning factor in his rapidly morphing career. Once, no-one had been waiting for him to say anything, so he could take his time saying it. Now, Silas, along with everyone who had hungrily devoured the Darkin piece, wanted more, and quickly. Worse, they already seemed to know what they wanted Robert to say, despite the fact that he was no longer sure if he knew that himself.

Robert had been able to press on with the genocide piece because he had convinced himself that all the issues and discomforts he was experiencing were simply the unintended side effects of the very things he'd been chasing all this time: attention, resonance, success. Of course there was more pressure now, he thought. Of course things seemed more complicated, more pressured, less satisfying. And of course he was now expected to weigh in on discussions he previously would have stayed out of. It was because he was notable. People *wanted* his perspective, *valued* it. What was he going to do? Whine about his freedom? Push away the audience he'd spent so long attending to because he was marginally less confident about the issues he was expected to address? The idea was ridiculous. He was on the cusp of a breakthrough. Like Silas had said, he needed to capitalise. Comfort and certainty were irrelevances, luxuries. Everyone faked it until they made it.

Thinking about his audience had helped Robert clarify his role, and in clarifying his role, he had begun to clarify, for himself at least, his stance. Yes, the issues were thorny, nuanced, complicated. But that was precisely why his audience would be clicking on his article: because they wanted someone to *make sense* of it all. Everyone reading about the genocide woman, he thought, would experience the same discomfort, the same sense of barely tangible disquiet. But then they would push that discomfort aside. Why? Because it was too complicated, too difficult, too *controversial*. This was why,

Robert had concluded, the entire narrative of white maleness, particularly white working-class maleness, had been so comprehensively hijacked by the Hugo Benningtons of the world: because people on the left, in their middle-class, white-guilt-riddled, virtue-signalling Twitter bubbles, were too uncomfortable talking about it. Silas was right: with his Darkin piece, Robert had started something. Now he needed to continue it.

By the time his mobile rang and he saw DeCoverley's name scrolling across the screen, Robert had worked himself up to a pitch that went beyond mere relevance and tipped all the way into importance. His perspective wasn't just significant, he had concluded, it was *vital*. In this context, DeCoverley's phone call seemed like a sign, a confirmation. This was what happened when you crossed over the threshold of notability and became a recognisable figure: Jacques DeCoverley sidestepped the formality of email and called your mobile.

'Glad I got you,' said DeCoverley. 'You must be insanely busy.'

'Swamped,' said Robert, lounging back in his chair. 'To be honest, I'm desperate to get some actual work done but people keep asking me for work.'

'A feeling I know all too well,' said DeCoverley, a touch defensively. 'I'll get right to the point. We need to talk about this Julia Benjamin woman.'

'Oh God. You too?'

'Haven't you seen?'

'Last I looked, she seemed to have been a bit slow getting to my latest column.'

'Do a Google search instead.'

Robert typed *Julia Benjamin Robert Townsend* into the search bar. The top two results related to her comments on his *Command Line* articles. The third was a website called *Mapping the Morons: An Ecosystem of Masculine Opinion*.

'Oh my fucking God,' he said, clicking the link.

'I think we can both agree this has gone far enough,' said DeCoverley. 'Lunch tomorrow?'

Not since her time with Dustin had Trina been afraid to go home. And no, this time the danger didn't *reside* in her home, and this time, at least, much as she didn't want to go back to her address, she still wanted to be with her family – but in her mind, the locus of threat was shifting. Yes, it was something that was edging inwards from the outside, and yes, it was, in so many ways, external to her. But if she looked at it from the point of view of the people she loved, the reality was that she was the problem, the one bringing all of this to their door.

Yet even as she thought this, clicking through the gears, feeling the increasing and satisfying resistance to her pedalling feet, the bike smoothly accelerating as she locked into her pace, it struck her that the pressure to blame herself for what was unfolding would only increase in the coming hours and days. She knew the cycle because everybody knew the cycle. It played out daily, varied only by the identity of whoever was currently at the heart of it. The controversial statement, the backlash, the brief period of optimistic resistance, the inevitable humbling apology. To imagine herself as the source of what was happening was, she knew, to accept the terms of a game that was designed specifically with her loss in mind. Worse, it was to accept that what was happening to her was happening because of what she had said. Even in the midst of her disorientation, Trina could see that this was a lie, and could see that even by beginning to believe it she was starting down a road not of acceptance and repentance, but of self-doubt, complicity, and capitulation. The cause of what was happening was far bigger than a tweet. It was structural, historical. She hadn't *caused* the vitriol that was being directed at her. The vitriol was extant, searching for a place to put itself. Hugo Bennington needed to pretend he was arguing solely with her in order to hide the fact that he was arguing with everyone he thought of as being like her: namely the swelling, imagined mass of everyone who was not like him.

At home, she propped her bike in the hallway and walked into the lounge, still unbuckling the chin strap of her helmet. Carl was on the sofa, his laptop on his knees, his crutches propped against the cushions beside him, looking up at her with an expression that mirrored back to her everything she'd spent the day trying not to feel or acknowledge.

'Mia brought me up to speed,' he said.

'Where's Bella?' said Trina.

'Nap time,' said Carl. He stood up and hugged her. 'How are you doing? Are you OK?'

'I'm fine,' she said. 'I'm totally fine. It's all bullshit.'

'Trina . . .'

He had his hand raised, either slowing her down or making some sort of apology.

'What?' she said.

'I wasn't sure how much to look,' he said. 'But I had to look.'

'It's fine. How could you not look?'

'I don't know whether to show you this or not.'

'You'd better show me. If I don't know about it, I can't fight it.'

He passed her the laptop. She sat down and stroked the trackpad to wake it up. On the screen, she saw the *Daily Record* website, its headline filling a third of the screenspace:

'White Genocide' Tweeter Lives in Sink Estate Threesome With Benefits Scrounge

'Oh Jesus,' she said. 'Jesus fucking *Christ*.'

All day, she'd proudly held her tears at bay. Now, with the

magnitude of what was happening to her starkly rendered in a screaming headline, the effort was too much. She sobbed into the front of Carl's shirt while he held her.

'I know,' he said simply. 'I know.'

———————

*I*t's me.'

Jess gave her usual greeting as she came through the door, reminding herself, reassuring herself. There was no answer. Robert, she assumed, was upstairs in his study, no doubt either stewing over Julia Benjamin's latest assault on his standing or squeezing out another bitter stream of opinion in response. She liked, she realised, the sense that she could see him without seeing him, that she could picture, to a reasonable degree of certainty, his posture, his expression, his state of mind. This, she thought, was the real triumph of Julia Benjamin: she knew, in so many senses, where Robert was. Now, she had shown everyone else where he was as well. Robert would be feeling exposed, uncomfortably located within intellectual space. Later, no doubt, he would come downstairs and explain events to her, recounting in conveniently distorted detail all the things she already knew.

She went through to the kitchen, hung her laptop bag on the back of a chair, and found the day's snail mail in a loose heap on the worktop. Robert had clearly gathered it from the doormat and then promptly ignored it. She sifted the envelopes. The top two or three were the drab Manila of quotidian officialdom. It struck her that mail these days was reserved for the extreme poles of bureaucratic communication: the hopelessly routine or the terminally serious. All the grey areas in between had been digitised.

Beneath the inevitable bills and statements, however, were two envelopes that immediately caught her attention. They were identical save for the addressee: one for her and one for Robert. Spurning the dimensions and materials of official communication, they were the size of personal letters. The address, rather than being visible through a clear plastic window, was printed directly onto the thick, textured cream of the envelope itself. The seal was of the kind requiring licking. This human trace, now near-absent from daily communication, unnerved her. She slid her little finger into the gap at the end of the seal and ran it along the crease, the paper yielding along a neat line. Inside, she found a sheet of matching notepaper, folded once. When she opened it, she found it contained only a web address, printed in small black lettering at the centre of the page. It was the by now familiar Griefer address, *weareyourface*, appended with a single, sinister word: */you*.

She slid her laptop from its padded satchel and fired it up, engaging the security measures that by now were second nature: her anonymous browser, her surveillance detection. She typed the website into the address bar and was directed to a page that took an extra second to load, suggesting either bandwidth-heavy content or high traffic. It was, she noted, an unlinked addition to the main Griefer page, unlisted in the site's menu, accessible only by using the full address. When it loaded, she was confronted by a black screen, in the centre of which was the same morphing, animated face that The Griefers had used during the performance in the town square: the strobing composite that formed the basis of their masks. Now, though, the animation, the fade between faces, was slower. Individual identities could be briefly recognised, like cards fleetingly glimpsed as someone ran their thumb down a deck. Occasionally, the animation seemed to stutter or lag, threatening, momentarily, to come to a complete standstill. She wondered if this apparently randomised hang-time was due to the number of people looking at the page, or perhaps a glitch in the animation itself. Scrolling down below the shifting image to the text below, though, she found it was not a flaw at all, but the point.

The morphing face, said the text below the animated image, which was addressed, grandiosely, to the people of Edmundsbury, now functioned as a kind of lottery or roulette. At some point, according to a randomised algorithm, it would stop, thereby selecting a single face. That face, the people of Edmundsbury were advised, would be the face of the person The Griefers had chosen. They would make a website dedicated to that individual. On that website, which would be publicly accessible and widely promoted, would be everything that person had ever done on the internet: their photos, their private chats, their emails, their financial transactions, their search histories. Everything they both did and did not want to share. Then the roulette would start again, until, at an unspecified time, another person would be named. The process would continue indefinitely, people were told, unless someone in the town took it upon themselves to stop the randomised targeting in the only way The Griefers would allow: by volunteering themselves. If, The Griefers said, one person decided to step forward and release their entire history, in whatever manner they saw fit, the selection process would end.

Volunteering was simple, the website advised. All you had to do was click on the link at the bottom of the page, the one labelled *submit*.

Jess hovered her cursor over the word, stroking it, watching it change colour as she touched it remotely. She emailed Deepa the link with a single word in the message body: *thoughts?*

'Robert?' she called from the kitchen. 'Have you seen this?'

Again, there was no answer. She picked up the letter and walked to the bottom of stairs, realising as she did so that she was succumbing to an old and probably atavistic habit: the urge to share an event with him, to bridge the distance through mutual experience. She put one foot on the stairs and opened her mouth to call his name again. As she did so, a muffled roar escaped the closed door of Robert's study.

'That fucking *bitch*!'

She heard something being kicked or thrown, followed by another guttural, impotent cry. She took her foot off the stairs and stepped back, saying nothing, a sound of her own pressing up from her chest and catching at the back of her throat, half laugh, half yelp of fear. She was, she realised, tingling slightly, thrilled and appalled at what she'd done.

She thought of the strobing roulette of faces, imagining her own among them. Things were out of her hands, she thought. Events had their own momentum. All she could do now was submit to their furious logic.

0100

From his vantage point on his sofa, through his habitual cloud of fag smoke, *The Record* spread out on his knees and the thick scent of the unflushed toilet creeping out from under the bathroom door and mingling with both the fug of the lounge and the foreign tang of his own unwashed body, it seemed clear to Darkin that things were worse than ever. His personal, localised water issues were just the nearest, most observable symptom. Out there, beyond his front door and broken kitchen window, beyond even whatever obstruction was at work in his pipes, the world was going to shit. Worse, the world as Darkin imagined it had moved. Once, it had been *out there*, far away, encroaching but never quite arriving, and Darkin had comforted himself by assuming he would likely be dead by the time it drew near. He had been wrong. Edmundsbury was front-page news.

White Male Genocide, read the *The Record*'s blaring headline. A black woman living on his very estate in some sort of sex commune had suggested, on the internet, that white men should be sought out and killed. According to *The Record*, this woman was not alone. She had supporters, or, as the article chillingly put it, followers.

Over the page, Edmundsbury figured again. Masked men had apparently been terrorising the town. Dressed as office workers, the men had assembled in the town square, threatening, from what Darkin could piece together, some sort of blackmail, telling people, *We are your face.*

Hugo Bennington, of course, had seen this coming. Now that it was here, he was tackling it head on. What was at threat here, he said in his latest column, was not simply the day-to-day security of a small English town, but a *way of life*, and the extent to which this way of life was or was not defended had wide-reaching and potentially ruinous implications for the whole country. After all, he said, we could all, surely, regardless of where we lived and how we lived our lives, see something of ourselves in Edmundsbury and its people. And so, while it might seem to more metropolitan readers as if the events in Edmundsbury had little to do with them, in fact those events had *everything* to do with them. Edmundsbury was under attack. By extension, England, and everything it represented and stood for, was under attack too.

And yet, Bennington went on, wasn't it so often the case that in times of adversity, the very best of British spirit was sure to be on display? In this, again, Edmundsbury was no different to the rest of the country. When threatened, it revealed its best self. Just look, Bennington said, at a man named Darkin.

Here, stunned by the sudden and unexpected appearance of his own name, Darkin halted, retraced his steps. Bennington couldn't, surely, be talking about *him*?

Darkin, Darkin read, lived on the Larchwood Estate, and had recently been the subject of a ridiculously popular article by the up to now infuriatingly PC 'blogger', Robert Townsend. Here, Bennington said, in the midst of all this creeping threat, was an ordinary man who was, like Bennington himself, unafraid to tell it like it was, to stand up, possibly at great risk to himself, and sound the alarm against the creeping danger of our increasingly 'progressive' society. It was inspiring, said Bennington, a lesson to all of us. And more importantly, it was demonstrably effective. Up until he met Darkin, Bennington pointed out, Robert Townsend was peddling the same old soap-box platitudes as everyone else, blithely ignoring the obvious threats to everything he claimed to hold dear. But one encounter with one ordinary man prepared to speak the uncomfortable yet undeniable truth of his existence had changed him, and now Townsend was beginning to see the limits and flaws in his own opinions – moving, Bennington said, towards an outlook of maturity and distinction on which Bennington wished to be the first to commend him. Was it possible to imagine, said Bennington, a more persuasive and timely reminder of the power of one man's opinion than Darkin? In these frightening times, Bennington concluded, it was the Darkins of the world who needed to be heard. All of us, each and every one, had to search for the Darkin inside ourselves.

By the time Darkin reached this conclusion, which he had to read several times in order to confirm he was not hallucinating, his hands were shaking – a state not helped by the fact that at that moment, as if he were not already sufficiently on edge, the kitchen timer on his coffee table went off and caused a further spike of adrenaline. He put the newspaper down and fumbled for a cigarette. The cigarette lit, he leaned back into the enfolding familiarity of his sofa and tried to think.

His first response was fear. Everything he had read up to the moment he encountered his own name had contributed, in his mind, to the belief that danger was creeping in from every side and convening outside his door. There were hooligans in the town. Somewhere on the estate, a murderous black woman was whipping up some kind of race war. It was all, he thought, perilous enough, close enough, real enough, without suddenly seeing himself at the centre of it. What if the hooligans and the people who wanted to kill white men also read Bennington's column and saw in it, as Bennington seemed to have intended, some kind of example? And what if, on seeing this example, they decided to come right to his door and make of him an example of a very different kind?

But beneath the surface-level fear and the initial, gut-level response, a deeper, warmer sensation was at work. Reading about himself, seeing his name in print, and, most importantly, seeing Bennington very publicly taking up his cause, Darkin felt in his chest the unexpected glow of a long-forgotten pride. Not for years, not since Flo died, had he felt important. He hadn't, he thought now, sitting on his sofa, the breeze from his broken window gently stirring the stagnant atmosphere of his flat, even felt important to himself.

Hugo Bennington, the only politician Darkin had ever admired or believed in, was on his side. Bennington knew him, cared about him. He would, Darkin felt sure, when all of this reached whatever boiling point it was moving towards, protect him. That knowledge, that certainty of support and promise of attention, warmed him, and gave him something he had reconciled himself to never having: hope.

Hugo took a long haul on his cigarette and held the tar in his lungs for a length of time that was almost, but not quite, painful. Thanks to Teddy's desperate inability to gauge the moments when Hugo needed to be alone, Hugo, in much the same way as he'd started sneaking out his own back door in the mornings, had been forced to get creative with his fag breaks. Nipping out into the car park no longer cut it. Instead, he had to wend his way down a back alley and loop round the corner of a neighbouring building. Teddy was not a man who understood the notion of breaks unless they fulfilled some sort of purely physiological purpose. As far as Teddy was concerned, all time had to be leveraged at all times.

Hugo had to admit, though, that after a lengthy period of being an undefinable presence in Hugo's life, Teddy had undeniably come good with this tweet business. Hugo had had his doubts, of course. Much as he loathed the stranglehold of PC bullshit that prevented him from expressing his opinions in public, he still harboured a distinct discomfort with public opposition to people of the non-white persuasion. It could so easily go wrong. The moral high ground, on which people like Hugo had long been denied any sort of comfortable position, seemed always within reach to a woman like this Trina James person, who was, Hugo thought, not just a black but the worst kind of black: the angry kind. But that, Hugo reminded himself, was exactly why this woman needed to be taken on, indeed, taken *down*. Hugo wasn't the sort of person who believed in segregation or ethnic cleansing or whatever it was Ronnie and his boys were going on about. Hugo believed in live and let live. Or at least, he honestly believed that was what he believed. What bothered him was when people like this Trina woman got it into their heads that somehow the rules didn't apply to them and started getting in everyone's faces with their anger. *That* was the point at which he felt the need to take some kind of stand.

He tossed his fag end on the ground and squared his shoulders. Inside, Jones was waiting. For once, Hugo felt not only prepared, but confident. The tide was turning. Things were slowly, but perceptibly, coming under his control.

'Ah,' said Teddy, leaping up as Hugo wandered into the conference room. Jones was already there, as glacially inscrutable as ever. Hugo wondered what Jones did to relax. Played the harpsichord and ate people's brains, probably. He tried to get a read on Teddy's slightly over-zealous welcome. Was he relieved that Hugo, who had deliberately held his arrival in abeyance so as to make Jones wait, was finally there, or had they been talking about something Hugo wasn't supposed to hear?

'Mr Bennington,' said Jones with a thin smile, failing either to stand or extend his hand.

'Don't get up,' said Hugo.

Teddy, who had stood up, now sat down.

'We were just shooting the breeze, weren't we, Jones?'

Jones said nothing. Hugo eased himself into a chair and opted also to say nothing. A silence unfolded that was faintly competitive.

'What can we do you for?' said Hugo finally, when it became

clear that Jones was prepared to wait indefinitely if it meant holding onto whatever petty power was available.

'A simple matter of reassurance,' said Jones.

'Fire away,' said Hugo, affecting an air of genial warmth.

'This . . . *woman*,' said Jones.

'Which woman?' said Hugo.

'The genocide woman,' said Jones.

'Ah yes.'

'Is this a situation you have under control?'

'Absolutely,' said Hugo.

'Because it seems to be generating rather a lot of attention,' said Jones. 'And I'm not sure I'm entirely comfortable with that.'

'Well, we can't have you uncomfortable, can we?' said Hugo.

Jones opted not to answer this.

'I have to be honest,' said Hugo, 'I'm rather surprised at your discomfort.'

'How so?'

'Well, given that we see this as basically the opportunity we've been waiting for . . .'

'You see unprecedented national attention and what appears to be a brewing race war as an opportunity?'

'Well, the race war has been brewing for a very long time,' said Hugo. 'Which has always been our point. And as for the attention, well, I don't like to spew clichés but, you know, there's no such thing as bad publicity.'

'We don't really see this as *publicity*,' said Jones. 'And we don't really see this as a situation that *requires* publicity. If anything, we see this as a situation that would benefit from being resolved with a minimum of attention.'

'I think the mistake you're making is that you're assuming your situation and our situation are somehow the same,' said Hugo.

'I think the mistake *you're* making is that you're forgetting just how dependent your situation is on our situation,' said Jones.

'Wow, *smackdown*, right?' said Teddy.

'Shut up, Teddy,' said Hugo.

'Noted,' said Teddy.

'Maybe I'm not being clear,' said Jones. 'When I say we're uncomfortable, I mean that we're . . . displeased.'

'With what? With this woman?'

'With this woman. With the way you're handling this woman, which seems to be an exercise in fanning the very flames we'd like to see put out, and also with your words about a certain tenant, this Mr . . . Darkin.'

'Ah yes, I was wondering when you'd get to that.'

'The very tenant, I might remind you, with whom I asked for your assistance just the other day. Only, instead of assisting me, you now seem to have taken up his cause.'

'Well, I do feel *some* responsibility to my supporters,' said Hugo, unable to make the statement sound anything but profoundly sarcastic.

'Exactly our concern,' said Jones. 'Perhaps, with this Mr Darkin character, we've reached the point at which your interests and the interests of Downton Homes diverge.'

'It seems to me that the whole point of politics is to balance what appear on the surface to be divergent or opposing interests,' said Hugo.

'Like you have with this woman, you mean?'

'No. In that situation, I think what's needed is some good old-fashioned opposition.'

'I don't feel we're any further forward here, Mr Bennington,' said Jones.

'Look,' said Hugo. 'You want these people out. I get that. I want them out too. But if you think that me being seen to side with you in terms of kicking people out is in any way good for anyone, then you're obviously far more naive than I'd imagined. I've got an opportunity here for what is basically a win-win situation all round.

So why don't you let me work my side of the fence while you worry about working yours?'

Jones smiled.

'Politics is admirably ideas driven,' he said. 'But business is very much results driven. As long as that's understood—'

'Oh, we're very results driven,' said Teddy. 'I mean, if you want to see some graphs . . .'

'I'm not talking about the kind of results you can plot on a graph. I'm talking about the kind of results you can literally build on.'

'I think that's understood,' said Hugo. 'But what you need to understand is that we're still very much committed to achieving those results. It's just that we plan to achieve them without completely abandoning the things we ourselves need to achieve.'

'As long as those things continue to align,' said Jones.

'Let's just bear in mind,' said Hugo, 'that much as you might like to throw your weight around with regards to offering or withdrawing your support for my campaign, which I assume is what you're implying with all this vague talk of interests, your project is going to take a hell of a lot longer to complete than mine, and while you're completing it you're going to want someone who's sympathetic to your cause in a position where they might actually be able to help you, so let's stop pretending that my getting elected is solely of benefit to me.'

'Of course,' said Jones. 'But let's also not pretend that you're the only one who can help.'

Hugo thought about this for as long as he could manage without giving the impression he'd been thrown by it.

'Hang on,' he said. 'How many people are you backing?'

'Like I said, Mr Bennington. We're very much results driven.'

'And I've just told you I am very close to getting you those results.'

'Then I don't see that there's anything to worry about, is there?'

'No,' said Hugo, believing nothing of the sort.

Once Jones had slithered back to his lair, Hugo slumped in the cheap plastic office chair and ran his fingers idly across the Formica of the conference table. When Teddy came charging in, Hugo held up a hand.

'Not now, Teddy,' he said. And then, a little more plaintively, 'Please.'

'Whoa,' said Teddy, backing up with his hands raised. 'Mood crash.'

'I'm powering down,' said Hugo.

It was true, he thought, he was. The problem was that he was not powering down in the Teddy sense – cycling his energy, preparing himself – but in the drabber, more unwilling sense: struggling to extract a last drop of power from his own dwindling and finite charge.

Teddy slid into a seat opposite Hugo and drummed his fingers on the tabletop.

'I'm going to power you right back up,' he said.

'Unless you've got a ready supply of new body parts, a replacement brain, a time machine, and an entirely new soul, Teddy, I'm afraid I don't think that's going to be possible,' said Hugo.

'The BBC want to do a profile.'

Teddy was positively aglow. Somewhere deep in Hugo's engine, a set of crocodile clips were applied, a weak jump-start initiated.

'Like, *At Home With Hugo*,' said Teddy. 'The full works.'

Teddy wrapped up his drumroll on the tabletop with a little flourish, fashioning his fingers into two cocked pistols, which he fired, slightly disconcertingly, at Hugo.

'Who's doing it?' said Hugo.

'That woman who always does them. What's her name? Vivian.'

'Vivian Ross.'

'That's her.'

'Christ.'

'What?'

'I hate Vivian Ross. Everyone hates Vivian Ross. And you know what? She hates me too.'

'She's a challenge, I'll give you that.'

'She'll make mincemeat out of me,' said Hugo, sounding morose even to himself.

'You know what I'm hearing here, Hugo?'

'What?'

'I'm hearing a lot of resistance. I'm hearing a lot of obstacles.'

Hugo sighed. He was hearing a lot of resistance and obstacles too. In addition to his long-standing taxonomy of personal fear, he thought, he now needed a catalogue of everything that was working against him. Pressure from without, a draining of the spirit from within.

'Don't you ever get tired, Teddy?' he said. 'I mean, I know you're young and healthy and fuelled by weird liquid. But don't you ever just think . . . fuck it?'

'Listen to me, big guy, OK? You're flagging. I get that. It's noted. We'll schedule in some impromptu downtime just as soon as this phase plays out. But you know the mistake like ninety-nine per cent of people make in this situation? They go downtime in the uptime. Because this is where it gets gritty, Hugo. This is where it quite frankly gets tough as fuck. Yeah, things are knotty. But things are always knotty right before you totally unknot them. You see what I'm saying?'

'No.'

'I'm saying: we've got a lot of balls in the air. Do you want to be the guy that lets them drop?'

'Maybe they're just dropping of their own free will, Teddy. Maybe neither I nor any other guy has any actual power to effect the dropping of the balls, because in the end it's all just gravity. OK, but let's name some of these balls. You've got the old bloke. Ball A. You've got Townsend banging on about the estate. Ball B. You've got this genocide woman. Ball C. You've got Jones. Ball D. And you've got these Griefer people, who right now aren't even a ball – they're more like a strong wind affecting the trajectory of the balls. OK? Now. Into this admittedly ball-rich and high-winded scenario, we've got Vivian whatshername. We've got this BBC profile. And what I'm saying is that the way things are at the moment, this isn't about actually *catching* any of the balls. If anything, catching one of these balls and being left standing there holding it would be no different to dropping one. What this is about, Hugo, is keeping all the balls in the air, keeping them moving, faster and faster, so that all people can see are the balls.'

'You're saying—'

'I'm saying, everyone else has to catch at least one of these balls.'

'Whereas I—'

'Just keep throwing them around. I mean, shit, while we're at it, let's throw a few more in there. Right?'

Hugo nodded. 'Everything's in play,' he said. 'It just needs agitating.'

'Right. Stirring up.'

'All I need to do,' said Hugo, 'is go on there and just—'

'Show people the balls. *Dazzle* them with the balls.'

'Like, look at this situation.'

'Look at this *chaos*.'

'Look at what we're having to *deal* with here.'

'Like, for you, the situation *is* the solution. The game is the endgame.'

'I'm a free agent.'

'You're pure chaos, big guy.'

'But I'm also the calm inside the storm.'

'Exactly. You know how I see this?'

'How do you see this, Teddy?'

'I see it like, you're at home, but you're not even that relaxed. You're maybe in your kitchen, grabbing a quick cup of coffee because you've got, like, literally half an hour to yourself right now.'

'Like, this is what passes for relaxing in the crazy, hectic life of on-the-go power-monger Hugo Bennington.'

'A cup of instant coffee in a chair that isn't even that comfortable.'

'Saying something like, I've got half an hour.'

'OK. Setting: nailed. Vibe: nailed. Let's talk content.'

Hugo was sitting forward now, leaning across the conference table, entirely drawn in.

'Obviously,' said Teddy, 'this is very much focused on the genocide. You need to be clear: this is your issue.'

'For me, this is a defining issue. It goes to the heart of—'

'Yes, say heart. It ups your empathy rating.'

'It goes to the heart of our campaign.'

'Don't say campaign.'

'Why not?'

'It comes across kind of campaigny. You need to be, like: I feel incredibly strongly about this issue whether it's in a campaign context or not.'

'So it's more sort of: regardless of the campaign.'

'Say something like: this isn't about politics.'

'Maybe I could even say politics slightly disparagingly?'

'Yeah. *Politics*. Eyeroll.'

'Making the point that there are actually people out there who want to make this about politics.'

'Yes! Like, fuck those people.'

'Scoring points.'

'Oh, I love that. You're not trying to score political points here.'

'Unlike *some* people.'

'Those *other* politicians.'

'With their politics.'

'Right. Not you. You're all about the principle.'

'I feel like we need to get the word duty in here somewhere.'

'Oh, totally. But make it *our* duty, not your duty. It's more rallying.'

'When we see something like this, we have a duty to do something about it.'

'Collectively.'

'We have a duty to say: *no*.'

'Can we use the expression *line in the sand*?'

'You don't think it's kind of a cliché?'

'I do but I think it's a good one.'

'How about we forget the sand but keep the line? As in, *where do we draw the line*?'

'It's like you're saying to the interviewer, and by extension the viewers: where do *you* draw the line?'

'I'm all for tolerance.'

'Good. You're literally all for it.'

'But—'

'Don't say *but*. The minute you say something like, *I'm all for tolerance* or *I'm as appalled by racism as the next man* or whatever, everyone on Twitter immediately tweets that they feel a *but* coming. And then as soon as you say *but*, they all tweet that they just tweeted that you were about to say *but* and they think it's hilarious.'

'I'm all for tolerance. The question is, where does tolerance end?'

'With genocide, that's where.'

'Serious genocide.'

'We need to get the estate in here, Hugo.'

'I want to talk about that guy. That old guy.'

'Agreed. Push the old guy.'

'Because he's vulnerable.'

'But that's not why you're pushing him.'

'Right.'

'I mean, it is, but not in the way that it sounds.'

'He needs protection.'

'He shouldn't need protection, but he does.'

'It's frankly an outrage that he needs protection.'

'I like it. You're just assuming he needs protection because who wouldn't assume that given the situation?'

'It's obvious.'

'Obvious to *you*, but not to everybody.'

'Look at where we are.'

'Nice.'

'Actually having to protect a vulnerable old man from—'

'From his *neighbour*.'

'This vulnerable old man, who has never asked for anything—'

'Right. Hang on. Tie this back to the woman. Because she's . . . Well, her boyfriend—'

'Right. Benefits.'

'Can we play with the word *benefits*?'

'There she is, *soaking up the benefits of the welfare state*, able to live happily and freely in a tolerant society that turns a blind eye not only to her race but to her lifestyle choices, her beliefs. A society that allows her to express those beliefs freely. And what does she do? How does she use what she's been given? To spread hatred. To fuel intolerance.'

'While just a few doors down—'

'While a few doors down, on her very doorstep, this vulnerable old man, who has never asked for so much as a penny, who keeps himself to himself and bothers no-one, is *living in fear*. Is that fair?'

'Boom.'

'Is that equal?'

'Preach it, big guy.'

'Is that the kind of free and fair and tolerant society we want to live in?'

'Hell no.'

'No.'

'High-five me, Hugo.'

'You know what? I think I will. Bang. High five. And fuck you, Vivian Ross.'

'**B**ecause no-one's saying, let's not have debate, right?'
'Right, exactly. If anything, we're saying, let's have more debate.'

'Better debate.'

'It's about the *quality* of debate, is what this is about.'

Robert and Jacques DeCoverley were sitting in one of Edmundsbury's numerous chain cafés, all of which masqueraded as independents by overstuffing themselves with mass-produced bric-à-brac artfully scuffed to a uniform vintage.

'I love this, Robert,' said DeCoverley, taking an exploratory sip of his double espresso and breathing deeply through his nose in the manner of a man merrily at large in the world and soaking everything up. 'I mean, this is why I felt I could reach out to you. We're like flint and tinder here, wouldn't you say?'

Robert was unsure who was the flint and who was the tinder in that analogy but decided it was best to agree without complicating the issue. Not complicating the issue was essentially Robert's mission for the day. In a brief space of time, everything had become hopelessly complicated, and now his capacity for complexity was exhausted.

Much of the noise in Robert's head concerned Julia Benjamin. She had, for quite some time, been a continual background hum in his consciousness, an irritating tinnitus drifting occasionally to the fore. Now, though, she was a full-tilt roar, a near-symphonic distraction.

Apparently unwilling to constrain herself to her rightful place in the comments section, Benjamin had made her own website. Here, she said in a brief and hugely pompous introduction, she would be *mapping* (her term) the connections between apparently disparate expressions of self-serving white male opinion and then extrapolating what she called an *ecosystem*. Taking Robert's original post about Darkin as a jumping-off point, she had highlighted a series of key words and phrases that she had then mapped not just across Robert's column, but across a number of other columns from the same recent time period, including, to Robert's dismay, a piece published by Hugo Bennington the morning *before* Robert had written about Darkin. The linguistic and rhetorical connection with Bennington made, Julia Benjamin was then able to produce a graphic breaking down Robert and Bennington's shared columnistic mode and the common ideological assumptions underpinning their arguments. As if this wasn't bad enough, Benjamin had also taken the time to connect various key indicators from Bennington's column to all sorts of dubious forums and message boards discussing everything from men's rights to white power where those exact same indicators were deployed and where, Benjamin triumphantly pointed out, Robert's column about Darkin had *also* been widely shared, the end result being that she was able to establish a clear connection between Robert's recent drift from a broadly left-of-centre position and the fact that Brute Force were now physically intimidating people on the streets of Edmundsbury. More targets would follow, she promised. Everyone, from Stefan Ziegler to Jacques DeCoverley to Rogue Statement and back again, would be implicated.

Sadly, this was not the only horror with which Robert had begun his day. Upon opening his emails and checking through the notifications by which he kept tabs on mentions of his own name, he'd quickly been alerted to the fact that Hugo Bennington, of all people, had also written about him, in that morning's *Record* column. Far from taking reactionary aim at Robert's ideas as Robert might have hoped, Bennington had instead opted for the more damaging and embarrassing course of *praising* Robert and, in a particularly unpleasant move, welcoming him into some kind of shared political fold, which in light of the Benjamin website now read less like the fiendish bit of politicking it so clearly was and more like a damning evidential footnote to Benjamin's charges.

And what did Robert have out there? What piece, this morning, stood as his contribution to the chaos of positioning happening all around him? Some strident defence of a worthy cause? Some valiant trumpeting of his own rigorously right-on stance? No. He had a lengthy rant about political correctness, double standards, and the genocide tweeter.

'Because what we *don't* want,' said DeCoverley, 'is to leave ourselves open to the accusation that we're trying to shut down debate.'

'God no.'

'That's why we need to be clear: we *love* debate. We welcome it. The point is that *this* . . .' – he made a little line in front of him with his forefingers, as if literally underlining his point – 'is not debate.'

'We're actually trying to *have* a debate,' said Robert, 'and what's happening? We're being threatened.'

'And not just us,' said DeCoverley. 'Because one thing I feel very, very strongly about here is that this is about so much more than just us. It's about . . .' He pinched his lips as if his own thought had given rise to a swell of emotion within him. 'It's about the future.'

'Not our future,' said Robert, 'but *the* future.'

'Right,' said DeCoverley. 'The future of free intellectual discussion in Britain.'

'And not just Britain,' said Robert. 'Because we're talking about the web here. And if all intellectual discussion is going to take place on the web, then we're really talking about the global future of free intellectual debate.'

'Benjamin's just a symptom,' said DeCoverley.

'Right. And by treating the symptom . . .'

They both sat back, contemplating this for a moment.

'I mean,' said DeCoverley, after a period of reflective introspection, 'it's not even as if I'm angry, you know? I mean, I *am* angry, but that's not the overriding emotion here. I was talking about this with Lionel Groves just the other day and he of course agreed completely. I feel *saddened*. Don't you?'

'Oh yes,' said Robert. 'It's sad all round.'

'I mean, there are mornings when I wake up and I just frankly despair, don't you?'

'Oh God, I mean, recently I've been questioning why I even bother.'

'I think people like Julia Benjamin think what we do is easy,' said DeCoverley.

'Or that we're *privileged*.'

'Oh God, yes, that word. *Privileged*.'

'That's the word that really bothers me.'

'As if, you know, just because I've had the benefit of a private education,' said DeCoverley.

'Exactly,' said Robert, keen to gloss over the fact that he had not, in fact, had the benefit of a private education, but noting secretly, just in case credentials were called for in the future, that he was demonstrably less privileged than DeCoverley.

'I've literally spent my whole life sharpening my mind,' said DeCoverley. 'And now I'm supposed to apologise for that?'

'No way,' said Robert, ignoring the obvious point that if DeCoverley had really spent his whole life sharpening his mind there would now be nothing left except a whittled stub and a heap of shavings.

'It's almost as if,' said DeCoverley, 'the very fact of having some kind of audience is seen as a privilege in itself, when really it's a terrible burden.'

'Yes,' said Robert. 'Wish that we could all just express ourselves in a quick online comment without having to go through all the work of crafting a decent piece.'

DeCoverley nodded. 'And the *opprobrium* we have to deal with.'

'Yes, so *privileged* to have to deal with all this shit every day.'

'And I know what people say,' said DeCoverley. 'They say: oh, but look at you, a white, virile, handsome man . . .'

'Who are you to complain?'

'As if we couldn't possibly have anything to complain about!'

'As if we don't have *feelings*, for fuck's sake.'

'You know, Robert,' said DeCoverley, seemingly settling in to his subject, folding his hands in his lap and addressing not quite

Robert's face but instead a vague mid-space somewhere just over Robert's left shoulder, as if reading his lines from a distant autocue, 'the honest truth is, if you're a man of the left, like myself, like yourself, and if you've devoted yourself, as we have, to any kind of credible intellectual left-wing project, you see this all the time. That's what's so *saddening* about the whole thing, don't you think?'

'The pointlessness of it,' said Robert, taking a guess because he wasn't exactly sure what DeCoverley was talking about.

'Because what do we want, Robert?' said DeCoverley, tearing his eyes from his imaginary teleprompt and fixing his gaze directly on Robert. 'We want *change*. We want *alternatives*. What we want, Robert, is a *better world*. Am I right?'

'Absolutely,' said Robert. He was struggling to think of anyone who might seriously want a worse world, but he felt the point was probably unhelpful.

'And our great gift,' DeCoverley went on, 'as well as our great curse, is that we can *see* that world.' DeCoverley leaned forward across the table, locking eyes with Robert and pinching his fingers together in the space between them as if literally holding up a piece of reality. 'Do you think everyone can see it, Robert? Of course they can't. They can see, at best, their tiny little piece. And a lot of people can't even see that. So what do they do? They look for the obvious. I'm black therefore I'm oppressed. I'm a female therefore I'm oppressed. It's all just noise, Robert. And because of all that noise, people are incapable of *listening*. They're ignorant of the fact that there are people like us, people who want to help them, people who want to help us *all*. Is Julia Benjamin going to change anything? Can Julia Benjamin see the world as it is, as we can?' He shook his head. 'Of course not.'

'It's about the greater good, isn't it?' said Robert.

'Go on,' said DeCoverley.

'Well, what we're doing is important. It's important in all sorts of big-picture ways. And here's Julia Benjamin, or one of her cronies, or whoever, saying, hey, this doesn't take account of me. And you know what? Maybe it doesn't. Maybe it doesn't need to. Because maybe it takes into account *more* than that, meaning that Julia Benjamin isn't just irrelevant, she's—'

'Dangerous,' said DeCoverley.

'And not just dangerous to us, dangerous to . . . Well, everything, really.'

'We've got a responsibility here, Robert.'

'That's how I'm starting to see it, yes.'

'A responsibility to *act*.'

'Completely.'

'Not just for ourselves, but for the *principle*. Or, actually, many principles.'

'Yes. The very *notion* of principles.'

'Exactly. So. What are we going to do?'

'What?'

'What are we going to do?'

'Do?'

'Do. About Julia Benjamin. What are we going to do about her?'

'Right.'

Robert thought about Julia Benjamin. He felt his hatred shifting, coating itself not in its usual exterior of guilt and uncertainty, but in a new patina of righteous ire. He hated her, now, on behalf of others, in the name of *principles*.

He thought of Silas, their conversations over Skype. Slowly, through the fog of indignity and inflated purpose, an idea began to form.

'So,' said Robert slowly, allowing himself the maximum possible time to develop a coherent line of reason, 'Julia Benjamin wants to kick back against this supposed tyranny of male opinion. Am I right? She thinks we're misogynists. She thinks we're some kind of *establishment*.'

'Laughable,' said DeCoverley. 'But true, yes.'

'She thinks we're the enemy.'

'Definitely.'

'But what if there was another enemy? A . . . A *worse* enemy?'

'Go on.'

'My editor at *The Command Line* said something interesting. He said that once what he called the bro brigade got wind of Julia Benjamin, they'd be all over her. I've been waiting for it to happen but suffice to say it hasn't happened.'

'But what if it *did* happen, is what you're saying.'

'I'm saying: what if Julia Benjamin, who has been merrily commenting away, exercising her right to free speech at the expense of *our* freedom of speech because she genuinely seems to think we're the absolute worst the world has to offer, suddenly got a glimpse of people who were *genuinely* the worst the world had to offer, and who genuinely wanted to oppress her?'

DeCoverley made either a gun or a steeple by interlacing his fingers with the forefingers extended and then pressing the forefingers against his lips. It was a pose Robert had seen him strike for at least two separate author photographs.

'It's very interesting in terms of reversal,' said DeCoverley. 'And I think it's kind of *psychologically* interesting too, don't you?'

'You mean in terms of . . .'

DeCoverley stopped tapping his fingers against his lips and returned his hands to his lap, where his thumbs started to make little circles around each other in a way that Robert found distracting.

'What does Julia Benjamin really want?' said DeCoverley.

'Attention,' said Robert. 'It's literally that simple.'

'But go deeper with that. What is attention, really? What is the ultimate attention? The attention we all essentially crave?'

'Fame?'

'Being fucked,' said DeCoverley. 'Don't you think?'

'Well, she certainly seems—'

'Uptight?' said DeCoverley. 'I should say so. Imagine her, sitting around her house on her own. I imagine that she's terribly ugly, don't you? A person who really, in a different existence, had she not so determinedly undermined such important intellectual work, would be worthy of our sympathy.'

'Well, I have to say I find it rather difficult to sympathise with her at this point, but I sort of see what you're saying, yes.'

'Now, obviously, we can't arrange for her to be fucked . . .'

'God no.'

'But what you're proposing is, I think, a *kind* of fucking, just as it is also a *kind* of attention. It's almost . . . *therapeutic*, no? And I think it would ask Julia Benjamin a very valuable question: *is this what you want? Is this really what you want?*'

'Like, OK, you want this? Well, here it is, have it.'

'And now that you're getting it, do you like it?'

'I bet she loves it,' said Robert. 'That's the thing. All those men piling onto her . . .'

'All that *abuse*.'

'You want to be a bigshot intellectual? Well, *this* is what being a bigshot intellectual feels like.'

DeCoverley laughed. He was not, Robert had noticed, a man who laughed often, and so when he did it was with the air of a man dancing at a wedding: hesitant, concerned about his veneer of cool, yet aware that if he didn't certain judgements would be made.

'And how,' he said, 'do you propose putting this little lesson into practice?'

A kind of prickling heat had begun to creep into Robert's body, working inwards from the edges, his skin flushing first and then, seconds later, his organs and muscles feeling uncomfortably warmed. He wondered if it was the coffee, or perhaps the weather. Later, when he was alone and looking back on his lunch with DeCoverley, he would know the feeling for what it was: shame.

'Well, as it happens,' he said, slightly hesitantly, 'I do have a degree of experience that might be relevant here.'

'Oh yes?' said DeCoverley.

'There was . . . There was all that stuff with Jess a while back. I mean really . . . Really full on.'

'Ah yes,' said DeCoverley, 'I remember.' He paused before adding, 'Terrible, obviously.'

'Oh, horrendous,' said Robert. 'I mean, yeah. Just totally awful. But—'

'But we're not suggesting quite that level of—'

'No, absolutely. But maybe if we just went to a few of those—'

'A few of those places where that kind of thing flourishes.'

'A few forums. I mean, I know some of the ones that—'

'Of course you do.'

'And actually, as it happens, my work seems to have . . . I mean certainly not through any deliberate attempts on my part, but—'

'You have a degree of influence.'

'Not that I'm proud of it, of course.'

'Of course not. But it's testament to your reach.'

'Exactly. And anyway, once we—'

'Once we set things going—'

'Yeah,' said Robert, sweltering now, the temperature inside his skin bearing no relation to the temperature around him. 'After that, we'd have nothing to do with it.'

'Fascinating,' said DeCoverley with a smile. 'You know, Robert, this could actually end up being an extremely important cultural intervention. It reminds me, in fact, of the chap your girlfriend ended up on the wrong side of. Ziegler. I know him a little bit, actually. Fascinating man. An *important* figure, in a lot of ways. What was his point at the time? That sometimes hyper-masculine culture serves as a kind of catalyst? Or even, which I think is the case here, as a kind of corrective?'

'Something like that,' said Robert.

'We should bring him in,' said DeCoverley. 'I mean, not now, but afterwards. You and I could co-author something, maybe with

Ziegler, maybe even with Stroud. What do you think?'

'Like a sort of collective?'

'A loose collective. A merging.'

'Sure,' said Robert, reaching for a glass of water.

'I mean, I've been thinking for a while that there's a book in the whole vexed question of masculinity,' said DeCoverley. 'All of this just makes me think I should bring it forward.'

'A book on . . . masculinity?'

'Masculinity as a kind of abject,' said DeCoverley. 'A new taboo. My stance would very much be: feminism, *yes*. But equally: *men*. N'est-ce pas?'

DeCoverley reached over and patted Robert's shoulder.

'Exciting times, Robert,' he said. 'Exciting times.'

———

Mildly hypnotised, Jess and Deepa watched the sequenced dissolve of faces on The Griefers' /*you* page. The speed was inconsistent. Faces hummed in a strobing blur, then stuttered and lagged at random moments. Each hangup brought a glitch in Jess's breath. Was *this* the face? Or this one? Any of these faces, Jess thought, could suddenly become hers. She could find herself, without warning, confronted by her own gaze, staring into her own static eyes, unable to do anything but watch as who knew what elements of her digital and personal history were amassed into a ruinous public archive. What, she wondered, would unsettle her more: the leakage of everything she'd done into the places from which she'd withheld it, or the simple sight of it all collected, catalogued, for her to see?

Deepa's computer speakers emitted a rhythmic, scratching rustle – the sound of an antique dip-pen moving across heavy, textured writing paper, a ninety-minute video of which was playing in one of Deepa's browser tabs.

'No no no,' said Deepa, almost musically, clicking around the Griefers' website, inspecting the shuffling faces and blunt, hyper-linked instruction to *submit* at the bottom. '*Noooo* no no no no.'

The ASMR video – scrabbling, insistent – was getting under Jess's skin. Now Deepa was going in with her whole talking-to-the-cursor schtick and Jess wasn't sure she could take it.

'What?' said Jess. 'No no no what?'

'Touchy touchy,' said Deepa, in a tone that suggested mere distanced observation as opposed to accusation.

She went back to inspecting the webpage, opening up chunks of embedded code and picking around in the strings. Jess decided to let Deepa go through her own sequences rather than hurrying her.

'It's just an animation,' she said finally. 'Very simple. They've put some stutters and slow-downs in it to make it look like it's happening in real time but it's basically just a looped video.'

'But it gives the impression of some kind of artificial intelligence, parsing people's data histories at random.'

Deepa shook her head. 'Just an impression. It's bollocks.'

'They could still have all that stuff though. I mean, just because the front end they've put together is kind of basic—'

'Doesn't mean they're not sitting on all the data at the back end, no. But then we're saying, what, that a bunch of boys so enamoured with their own mythos that they stage a kind of masked *thing* in the middle of town might choose *not* to show off the brilliance of their hack?' She shook her head.

Jess stood up and paced the room, stretching. When she briefly closed her eyes, the faces remained, like the after-image of a harsh light.

Deepa took her hands from her keyboard and sat back in her chair. 'This isn't making me feel paranoid,' she said. 'And I'm *very* uncomfortable about that.'

'You don't trust how not frightening it is,' said Jess, tuning into Deepa's distinctly individual wavelength.

'*Right*,' said Deepa, bouncing a little in her chair. She had a ten-dency to get excited when her idiosyncrasies went unchallenged. 'Because obviously these guys *could* frighten, and *want* to frighten, and sort of *are*, in some ways, frightening, but then you look at it and think, yeah, but are you going all the way though? And if not, why not?'

'I'm torn between wanting them to go all the way and, obviously, not wanting them to go all the way,' said Jess.

'Yeah, yeah,' said Deepa. 'Because if you go all the way, at least you've gone all the way. I mean, it would be disruptive and awful and shaming and probably sort of violent and maybe offensive in a kind of town-level fappening kind of way but at least it would be committed and it would be in the name of something, whereas if you go out there with your dicks swinging around going, oh, we're going to go all the way, and then it turns out that not only are you not going all the way but you don't even really have any, like, *way* to go, then that's just . . . shit.'

Jess experienced a delay in processing what Deepa had said – the words piling haphazardly in her mind, shaping themselves into meaning only when all of them had arrived.

'Whatever they're doing and however or wherever they're doing it, the feelings they're producing in people are real, so you want what they're doing to be real as well, to *merit* the feelings. Other-wise, it's just, what? A prank, basically. A big empty joke that leaves everyone feeling shitty but that changes or achieves nothing.'

'At least if it's for real, then there's a *point*, meaning that even if I hate the point, and I think I probably do hate the point, I can con-cede that they *had* a point, right?' said Deepa. 'Otherwise, like, don't waste my time by not having a point. Don't say you've got some kind of AI roulette system when all you've got is a GIF and a limp dick and you're just pissing on my leg and telling me it's raining.'

'But then equally there being no point could be the point,' said Jess. 'They're called The Griefers, right? What if it's all just for the lolz? Maybe their whole point is there's no point to anything.'

Deepa thought about this.

'I'd rather be properly attacked than distracted by student-level subversion,' she said.

'Say it's real,' said Jess, pausing in her pacing to lean against the wall. 'How everyone feels about it is going to depend very much on who it lands on, and what gets leaked.'

Deepa nodded. 'As in, full marks for exposing corruption or something.'

'But *nul points* if it's just another shaming exercise.'

'Another cache of nudes for the schoolboys.'

'Either way,' said Jess, 'it's invasive.'

Deepa leaned forward, peering again at the faces. There was that switch again, Jess noted: dissonant, full-spectrum manic interpretation right down to narrow-bandwidth concern.

'It's the volunteer element that bothers me,' she said after a few seconds of observation. Then she nodded, as if she'd quickly run her own answer past herself and found it satisfactory.

'Me too,' said Jess.

'They must know, unless they're very, very stupid, that the minute you suggest someone should volunteer, the whole town is going to pressure someone to volunteer?'

'Maybe that's the point. Maybe the whole thing builds to a kind of public burning.'

'And then what?'

'Flip it, maybe? Let everyone bully someone into disclosing and then leak everything about all the bullies?'

'Kind of moralistic.'

'Also kind of short-sighted. Because by the time they made their point about collective morality—'

'Someone would already have been shamed.'

'Exactly. Whichever way you cut it, someone potentially suffers so that they can make their point. Which is all very well if that someone turns out to be some privileged, powerful, corrupt, scheming piece of shit for whom no-one has any sympathy, but quite frankly we've seen no evidence of that being their agenda at all. I remember thinking at the screening thing, when they all got out of the van: these aren't people who are suspicious of power. They love power – the feeling of it, the idea of it. This is just the same. They're holding something over people. If their point is that power is unevenly distributed, their solution sucks, because their solution is just: grab more power.'

'OK,' said Deepa. 'But they wouldn't be the first movement or protest to go down that road.'

She swivelled in her chair so that she was facing Jess, the blur of avatars still visible over her left shoulder, pulling Jess's gaze from Deepa's, which suited Jess because Deepa had very obviously gone into scrutiny mode.

'This is all very theoretical,' said Deepa.

'You can't be serious, Deepa.'

'I'm very serious.'

'You can't seriously be saying, *you*, Deepa, who only very super-ficially inhabits the fully analogue, non-theoretical dimension, that we're being too theoretical about this?'

'Not we. You.'

'Me?'

Deepa nodded.

'You're saying, what? That I should think less? Be more practical? What?'

'Say it's real,' said Deepa. 'And say it's you.'

Jess had been about to say more, but pulled up short. She nodded, let out a long exhalation that wasn't quite a sigh, more a tentative measuring of her own stability. There was, she noticed, a flutter of uncertainty, a warp in the waveform of her breath.

'It's like a one-in-fifty-thousand chance,' she said.

'Is it?'

'How many people are there in Edmundsbury? How much data is flying around? How many other—'

'Say The Griefers really do have all this information on everyone. Say that right now, as we speak, they're sifting around in it. And say they do go ahead and select someone to expose. You really think they're going to do that randomly? Because let's be realistic. If you select someone randomly in this town, what you're likely to get is a load of shopping lists, some round-robin emails about how the family are doing, some low-level porn, and maybe some extramarital activities. It's not like we're in the fucking seat of power here. What kind of impact is leaking that even going to have? It's not exactly going to make headlines. But say on the other hand you *went through* what you've got, picking out the best stuff, selecting people for whom exposure actually *means* something, maybe even people who might be open to a bit of blackmail or manipulation. I'd say that list is shorter, wouldn't you?'

'I see your point,' said Jess. 'But even if you put me in that company, I still don't see why they'd pick me over, what, politicians? Green?'

'You really think they've got that kind of weaponry?'

'You really think they've got the weaponry to get through what I've done?'

'I think we don't know. And I'm not you but if I *were* you that would give me pause for thought.'

'A minute ago, you were saying you weren't frightened. Now you're saying I should be frightened?'

'I'm saying it would worry me if you weren't even a tiny bit scared, because that would suggest either that you're far too confident, which obviously is totally dangerous, or that you don't give a shit any more, which is frankly even more dangerous.'

Jess slid down the wall until she was sitting on the floor. She drew her knees up and wrapped her arms around them, clenching herself.

'I don't want to see this go bad for you, Jess,' said Deepa.

'It's not going to go bad for me.'

237

Deepa said nothing, merely held Jess's gaze.

'It's not,' said Jess again. 'Or, I mean, what if it does, you know?' She shrugged.

Deepa shook her head.

'Don't get beyond caring,' she said. 'It's a shitty place to get to.'

'I'm not beyond caring, Deepa.'

'Good,' said Deepa. 'Because neither am I.'

Jess nodded, looked away for a few seconds, thrown by the stern, almost admonishing compassion in Deepa's gaze. For a while, neither of them said anything. The noise of the anachronistic pen on rough paper seemed louder in the stillness, giving Jess the feeling of ants weaving through the hairs on her arms. She felt tender, she realised; raw.

'Aren't you *curious* though?' said Deepa.

Jess looked up.

'You've got a very suspicious glint in your eye, Deepa.'

Deepa leaned forward, suddenly energised.

'Don't you want to meet this a bit more . . . *head on*?'

'You don't mean *submit*?'

'Not me.'

'Me?'

'Not you either.'

Jess let her eyes roam the room while she gave herself a moment to consider the possibilities. She took in the computer screen over Deepa's shoulder, the roulette of faces still spinning its way through Edmundsbury's inhabitants, and then the wall behind the computer: the array of Deepa's digital lost. She was back on Deepa's wavelength again, tuned in to her thinking.

'What if they don't buy it?' she said. 'What if they know it's bullshit?'

'Then we know they're for real.'

'And if they do?'

'They're bluffing. And the game is over.'

Jess swept her finger round the room.

'Given the material you have to hand,' she said, 'how long will it take you to make a person?'

'You tell me,' said Deepa. 'You're the one that's done it before.'

———————

Robert left his lunch with DeCoverley, who had sent him off with one of his customary wistful gazes and an embrace that felt to Robert more like having a heavy cardigan briefly draped over his shoulders than any kind of meaningful physical or emotional exchange, fizzing with a combination of dread, guilt, and excitement that would have been invigorating were it not so problematic. He was appalled at himself, yet thrilled at having the means to appal himself so completely.

He tried to remember the last time he'd felt a similar feeling of power. The attempt was depressing because, as he thought about it, he began to wonder whether he had *ever* experienced a genuine sense of power. His whole life, it seemed to him now, had been a kind of deflated capitulation. Now, suddenly, an issue had arisen in which he was invested, of which he, and he alone, was genuinely at the centre. For so long, he'd written about others from a distance, and tailored what he wrote to the imagined tastes of still more distanced others. This, now, was about *him*. The power of autobiography, so much in vogue, and so infuriatingly out of reach to a man like Robert, was now available to him. Even as he squirmed at the exposure, he thrilled at the potential.

He was driving, he realised, extremely fast with no real idea of where he was going. Leaving the café, climbing into his car, Robert had been fairly certain he was heading home to immediately put his plan into effect. But now that he was on the move and alone, he was beginning to think that home was the last place he should be heading. If he was going to do this, he thought, he shouldn't do it from his personal computer, not with all this Griefer business going on. He pictured, briefly, the sinister facial scroll, unwatched while he went about his business, slowing, stuttering, and ultimately coming to a halt on his own image, triggering some online dam-burst of disclosure, a portrait of his obsessions and ire. No, he thought. Things were too close to him now. He needed to manage and express everything elsewhere.

Nodem looked, from the outside at least, like a sex shop from the eighties: the measures it had taken to preserve its anonymity had formed their own distinct identity, one that was about as subtle as a flashing neon sign. Once inside, the only surprise was how busy it was. Robert had always assumed that, aside from a few paranoid weirdos, Jess and Deepa were the only customers. Today, though, the place was heaving – populated not, as Robert might have imagined had he pictured the place populated at all, with ivory-pale, goateed goths and twitchy, eye-contact-averse geeks, but, if one excepted the unshaven, wild-eyed man in the corner mumbling something about fields, with regular-seeming members of the public. This was the most observable effect of The Griefers he'd yet encountered: the desire for secrecy had gone mainstream. Even casual users of the internet now felt they needed to operate behind an extra layer of protection. But then, he thought, a degree of romanticisation was almost certainly at work. Everyone wanted to believe that what they were doing was worthy of observation, that it merited protection, because everyone wanted to believe that what they were doing was important. No-one wanted to accept the drab reality of their online lives: that there was little or no need for privacy because nothing they were doing was of any note or merit.

This, of course, was where Robert differed from everyone else. He had purpose. The work he did was vital, and what he was about to do depended very much on secrecy and anonymity.

He was, he realised as he made his way to the counter and was directed to a recently vacated terminal by a scruffily bearded youth, experiencing the world at a greatly increased distance and sense of remove. This, he told himself, was what it felt like to be a mover, an impetus. He felt, following his experiences reading both Julia Benjamin's webpage and Hugo Bennington's *Record* column, as if everything related in some way to him. Everyone, he imagined, was talking about him, reading him, forming an opinion about him, and so he was, in that sense, more involved with the people around him than ever before. But at the same time, he was no longer, or so it seemed to him, an ordinary person. He was, in a whole new sense, a subject.

He made his way to his appointed terminal, sat down, booted up, and observed the resulting slow-motion chaos on his screen. If he was to get through this experience without pulling his hair out, he was going to have to radically downgrade his expectations of immediacy. He tried to relax, pause a moment, leaning back in his chair and folding his hands behind his head while he waited for the spinning timer to disappear from his screen. The sense of ease, however, was short-lived, replaced by a panic so acute that his previous enervation felt like a warm bath by comparison. There, right in his eyeline, was Jess.

He'd considered the possibility she might be here, of course, and he'd already planned what he might say should he find himself having to explain his own presence, but her face had been obscured behind her terminal when he'd arrived, and after completing a scan of the room and failing to see her, Robert had entirely relaxed, meaning he now, on feeling her gaze lock briefly with his, felt undefended, and panicked. He looked down at his screen, wondering if he could pretend not to see her. On finding himself unable to resist looking back up again, he realised that all he had achieved by looking away was to appear guilty.

Chastened by his own awkwardness, Robert now felt unable to confirm whether Jess was looking or not. As a result, he had

no option but to assume her observation, so that his every routine keystroke and page navigation became freighted with awkward
implication. He couldn't just do what he'd come here to do, he
realised. It would look too quick, too furtive. He needed to make it
look as if he'd come here to do many things, all of which lay ranged
along a scale of significance.

He took a few minutes to faff around with his emails, sending
another one off to Byron Stroud. Given that Robert had never once
heard back from him, this was somewhat presumptuous. In light
of the way things were playing out with Julia Benjamin, though, it
was also important. Support from Stroud could turn what might
be seen by some as a petty little tantrum into a fully legitimised
resistance movement.

Emails done, he turned his attention to the real task at hand,
already, in his mind, justifying what he was about to do as if he'd
already done it. For a moment, he wondered whom his silent justifi-
cations might have been aimed at. Certainly not himself, he thought.
He had already, not minutes ago, confirmed that there was nothing
for him to justify. To Jess then? He didn't even know if she was looking. If she was, she wouldn't actually be able to see what he was doing.
No, his explanations were directed elsewhere, to some more nebulous
force. The state of feeling himself to be watched, he realised, had
only highlighted the extent to which he *already* felt watched, regardless of whether Jess was sitting in front of him. It was an extension,
he thought, of being read, being discussed. The gaze under which
he operated was diffuse, but unwavering. Observation had become
a kind of higher power, towards which he directed all his unspoken
explanations, his reasoning, his excuses. Everything he did, he now
imagined himself defending afterwards. In doing so, he was able to
form a defence before he even did the thing he thought he might
have to defend. *What this is about*, he heard himself saying in an
interview sometime in the near future, *is the principle. Sometimes, in
defending a wider principle, you have to set aside a few smaller ones.*

It really was that simple, he thought: a matter of identifying what mattered most. How many people, he wondered, were genuinely able to do that? How many people, in trying to tackle an issue, ended up bogged down in the shrapnel of smaller distractions? And how many people, finding themselves in that situation, lost sight of the issue completely? Not him, he thought. He would not make that mistake. The success of his work highlighted the accuracy of his eye. He had identified the right issues all along! All he needed to do now was trust in the ability for which he'd been recognised.

He googled, clicked, opened a message. It was strange, seeing addresses and names he recognised from the *from* section of Jess's emails suddenly active in the *to* section of his own correspondence. But that was life, he thought to himself whenever guilt tugged at his sleeve. It was fluid. There could be no absolutes.

———

When Jess glanced up from her Nodem terminal to see Robert skulking guiltily into the café like a man on a sex holiday plucking up the courage to buy a blow job, she knew instantly, with one hundred per cent certainty, that whatever he was doing was awful. When he sat down at his own terminal and looked up and briefly caught her gaze before darting his eyes downwards in a parody of nonchalance that would have been comical were it not so sad, she knew that whatever he was about to do related, directly or indirectly, to her.

Within the context of the café, she decided to ignore him. She wanted, in an interpersonal sense, to communicate to him his own irrelevance. She also wanted him to think she wasn't looking. In reality, in the virtual context in which they were both now operating, her gaze was forensic.

She killed time by checking the emails of her personae,

beginning with Stroud. His inbox was predictably full of requests. People wanted his hot take. He'd reached the kind of critical mass in the opinion-sphere where his silence on a given subject was felt as an absence. Nothing could truly be said to have happened, she thought, until all the usual subjects had commented on it. This was particularly true, it seemed, of The Griefers' most recent threat, with which the majority of emails to Stroud seemed to be concerned. What was Stroud's interpretation of the scrolling facial lottery? Could Stroud say, with a certainty both missing and longed for elsewhere, what it *meant*?

She clicked her way through, weighing things up, trying to kid herself into the kind of egocentric excitement Stroud would experience at the idea of his own critical indispensability. It was something she'd become more adept at channelling, this distinctly male intellectual entitlement, this assurance that the world required your explanatory insertion in order to understand itself. Today, though, it evaded her.

An email from Robert. The subject line: *Unity*.

Byron, said Robert, *I hope this email finds you well. I know I emailed you recently and you have not yet had a chance to reply, so forgive me for writing again, but this is about a separate matter, one I hope you will agree is important.*

I don't know if you've been following my work at The Command Line, *where I've been writing about the plight of a soon-to-be-decanted housing estate in Edmundsbury called the Larchwood. In case you haven't had a chance to catch up, you can read some of the key pieces here, here, and here. Again, I'm not sure how up to speed you are with my work and the hugely passionate response it has received, but if you take the time to look through the comments you'll notice that one commenter in particular – Julia Benjamin – whose most unpleasant comments you can read here, here, here, here, here, and here, not to mention here, and even here, has taken it upon herself to challenge and undermine my work at every opportunity. This, of course, would be concerning enough were it simply confined to my own writing, but in fact many other writers have been targeted, including Stefan Ziegler, Jacques DeCoverley, and the radical anarcho-theorist collective Rogue Statement.*

I think you'll agree that this is a matter of grave concern. The outcome of this situation has very real ramifications for both quality of debate and freedom of speech. Myself, DeCoverley, and Rogue Statement are all in agreement that some form of stand must be taken and this conspiracy to dismantle and destroy vital intellectual work must be stopped. We feel that the best way to achieve this is through unity.

Byron, I have checked the comments on your pieces and I have noticed that Julia Benjamin has not yet targeted your work. Believe me when I tell you, though, that this is merely a temporary luxury, as she quite clearly has it in mind to target all successful and notable male commenters. I was therefore wondering, and I speak here on behalf of the others, who I believe will also be emailing you, if you would offer us your public support. This is an issue with implications for all of us, and one against which we need to take decisive action before the threat becomes overwhelming.

In solidarity,

Robert Townsend.

These frightened little men, she thought, organising against some phantasmal image of a woman simply because she'd threatened the imagined sanctity of their ideas. And all the while, outside, in the world they claimed both to consider and to depict, events were occurring that shrank their fears to irrelevance. Perhaps that potential irrelevance was why they were doing this: because their biggest fear was that their biggest fears were insignificant; because their biggest fear was insignificance itself.

Except, she thought, they weren't simply *these men*. Not any more. One of them was Robert, and in fact had always been Robert. Could she still dismiss as forcefully the ideas and behaviour of someone she knew so intimately, even if that behaviour no longer quite aligned with the man she knew?

Through the distaste she experienced at Robert's responses, she tried to find again the flavour she'd once enjoyed – one that had once been strong enough to mask the sourer notes beneath. He'd erred. Wasn't it, in the end, really that simple? Couldn't anyone, including her, find themselves caught up, out of reach of their own best judgement?

She minimised the entire web browser, her screen returning to the comforting all-black backdrop of the Nodem desktop. Then she sat back in her chair and rubbed her eyes with her fingers for a few seconds, mentally minimising first the café around her, then the street outside the café and the street where she'd encountered Brute Force, then Edmundsbury, taking with it her home, her office, Robert, and finally the world, leaving only the comforting blankness of whatever reality remained when life's deceptive overlay was removed. Here, in this space, when everything that existed to her had been temporarily erased, there were no connections. Nothing related to anything else. Nothing meant anything. There was only silence.

She was trying, she knew, to strip away the forces that had confused them. In doing so, she had imagined that she would find something fundamental still present – some foundation or core that remained undamaged. But it was lost to her. What remained was not truth at all, or even reassurance. Just blankness – the void she'd filled with imagined meaning.

When she removed her fingers from her eyes and began to blink away the blur, the process reversed itself. The world, formless and vague, emerged darkly at the edge of her imagination. From there, she built inwards, peopling the town, the café, until Robert was once again in front of her, and in front of him was once again the tightly bordered simplicity of her screen. There was, she thought, no attainable respite or refuge from the tangle.

The interconnectedness of just about everything, the ultimate illusion of all distinctions, the transparency and porousness of all the borders we erect to keep things separate, were not new concepts for Jess. For the first time, though, it seemed as if their reality was something she experienced not just intellectually, not even emotionally, but physically, as if in this brief instant her body had become both the subject and expression of everything she knew to be true. These were the last collapsing divides: the world and herself; her thoughts and her body. The thing she had spent so much time trying to understand and dismantle was not only everywhere, but everything. It was opinion columns and internet ire; it was politics; it was fascist thugs on the street; it was her relationship; her work. It was the hypothetical and physical space in which all these things existed, in which she existed, and it was, because it was all of these things, also *her*, right down to her deep tissue: muscular, biological, and real.

In returning her gaze to her surroundings, she had, accidentally, caught the gaze of the babbling man who seemed to have become a fixture. In the short time since she'd seen him last, he'd clearly slipped into further decline. A rash of stubble peppered his face. His eyes were bloodshot, darting from side to side as if attack might arise from any and all directions. He was bouncing his knees according to entirely different rhythms, humming a little tune to himself in a half-whisper. On what appeared to be some kind of physiological schedule, he took a phone out of his pocket, stared blankly at the entirely blank screen, and then put it away again. She wondered if he was sleeping here, or perhaps out on the streets, nearby, coming here for the coffee and brownies Zero and One were charitably providing him.

'I'm getting phantom alerts,' he said, taking her accidental eye contact as an invitation to engage.

She gave him a sympathetic smile, then looked away, wary of a distracting and uncomfortable exchange.

'It's where you think you're phone's vibrating, but then when you look it's turned off,' he clarified.

She smiled again, keeping one eye on her screen.

'I used to work at Green,' he said. 'Maybe I still do. I don't know. It doesn't matter.'

She nodded, still refusing to engage.

'Nothing matters,' he said.

She looked over to Zero/One, widening her eyes in the universal shorthand for an unspoken distress signal.

'It's The Field,' the man said as Zero/One, with touching gentleness, encouraged him out of his chair and began to lead him towards a back room. 'Everything's The Field, so nothing matters.'

Once he was gone, she returned to Julia Benjamin's website – waiting, like a spider tense to vibrations along the strands of its web, to see if anything Robert did triggered anything she had in place. She found herself wondering how they had got here. There had been, she remembered, once, an intimacy – one that had existed in the very space they now used as a forum of harm. She remembered how they used to text each other at parties, even when they were standing side by side, maintaining a closeness right under the gaze of the people they were speaking to; how, for a long time, they'd sustained a cautious flirtation over Twitter, each of them thrilling a little at what was both concealed and suggested in that tentative public affection. When, she wondered, had a channel of affinity become a vector of hostility? Text messages and tweets had become open-ended, all-night conversations in bed. Then the bed had become a place for sleeping, and the dinner table a place for talking about what happened online, until finally the internet was a place to work out what happened at the dinner table, in bed, between minds that now couldn't reach each other. Now, here they were, yards apart in a public place, dealing each other deeply private, deeply personal wounds.

Imagining the trail that she and Robert had no doubt left as they unravelled, she found herself thinking again of those scrolling faces and the hidden activity for which they were avatars, imagining The Griefers now as they arguably should always have been seen: as archivists, keepers of the essential information by which our future selves would come to know the world as it had been. The archaeologists of the future, she thought, would have no need for unearthed remains and the dusty rubble of crumbled buildings. Ruins, currently so aesthetically praised, so anxiously guarded, would be meaningless. Instead, like the spill of mangled debris from a blasted aircraft, there would be a long, scattered trail of personal wreckage: pixellated selfies on half-corrupted servers; the hieroglyphic arcana of ancient blogs in disused formats; a litany of updates and reposts; videos watched; songs downloaded; the record of domestic items purchased and delivered long outliving the buildings and homes at which they'd arrived. For the future historians of who we were, Jess thought, the problem would not be a lack of data, it would be the feedback howl of informational noise. From the distortion, patterns would emerge that, now, as we made them, were dark to us.

As she refreshed the inbox of Julia Benjamin's website, she realised that she was awaiting an alert or confirmation: an automated message advising her of what she knew already to be final. She took a deep breath. There was that little spinning sand timer again, buffering her between two states: connection and disconnection, presence and absence. As long as the sand timer spun, nothing could really be said to have happened. She and Robert could buffer forever.

Perhaps, she thought, she would be wrong. Perhaps she only imagined what Robert was doing to be related to her because now she imagined everything to be related to her. In the mess of connections, causes, positions, there was still a chance for Robert to do nothing. If she was wrong, she would admit to herself that she had been wrong. The admission would be easy, she imagined, because it would be fuelled by relief.

The sand timer blinked, vanished. A new notification arrived in Julia Benjamin's inbox. The sender was painfully, nauseatingly familiar: a particularly feral group of anti-feminist woman-haters that had led the attacks on her after Ziegler. They were wise to Julia Benjamin's site and, judging by the message, already going to work on her. She looked again at the top of Robert's head and knew exactly what he had done.

Her response manifested not as feeling but as sound. There were no words in her head, only a faint, granular hiss, like the run-off of an old tape after the music fades. She thought of The Griefers' facial dissolve, the hyper-blur of identities they'd harnessed and unleashed. She saw again Deepa's wall of female figurants, her assemblage of images at once diverse and singular. She thought again of that imaginary archive: the data-trail of lives lived and abandoned. She clicked out of her messages and scrolled through old files and abandoned ideas, personae imagined and rejected. She began gathering the parts together, assembling them, giving form to something new and hybrid. Then she plugged in a thumb drive, moved the pieces across, and gave them a name that was a corruption of her own: Jasmine.

This was how things ended, she thought, but also how they began: with neither a bang nor a whimper, just a click.

———

Vivian Ross, Hugo thought, was your basic bitch nightmare. Taller than Hugo, with a gaze that suggested she was accustomed to looking down on her interview subjects in every conceivable way, she rebuffed his attempt at a cheek-kiss and instead extended her hand, crimson nails pointed straight at his heart.

'I thought we'd do this in the kitchen,' he said, ushering in first Vivian Ross, then a cameraman, then a boom operator, and then some bloke with a clipboard who, Hugo assumed, directed or produced or something.

'Let's get some establishing shots,' said the man with the clipboard to the cameraman, who immediately zoomed in on Hugo's front door and then tracked from there into the hallway.

'I'd prefer it if you didn't actually show the door number,' said Hugo. 'Or the street.'

'You probably have to be careful,' said Vivian Ross, which, Hugo noted, was not the same as saying they would be careful.

'Get this,' said clipboard man, pointing to the carpet. 'And this,' he added, pointing to the door through to the kitchen.

'People like detail,' said Ross. 'Close-ups of door handles, a mug on the kitchen counter. That sort of thing.'

'Softens things,' said the man with the clipboard.

'Come on through,' said Hugo, wandering into the hastily cleaned kitchen. 'Shall I put the kettle on?'

'Looks best if we both have a drink,' said Ross. 'More convivial. But I don't drink hot drinks. So make me a cup of tea and then don't be offended when all I do is hold it.'

'Right,' said Hugo, turning to the kettle, already finding her bossy and unappealing.

He filled the kettle and found a couple of mugs. He didn't offer anything to the men he'd decided to think of merely as the crew. If he started asking what everyone wanted and remembering who took sugar and then handing round mugs, he was going to lose focus.

Tea prepared, Vivian Ross holding her mug ornamentally in cupped hands over crossed legs, Hugo also holding his mug but now, due to Ross somehow psyching him out with regard to hot drinks, not entirely comfortable drinking from it, they sat at one corner of the dining table, clipboard man having quickly vetoed a strict across-the-table arrangement as too formal and confrontational.

'Wouldn't want it to get confrontational,' Hugo said.

Vivian Ross said nothing.

'And, ready,' said clipboard man, holding his hand in the air while the cameraman angled his equipment towards Hugo in what Hugo imagined as an unflatteringly tight zoom.

'Um, are we just going to start straight away?' said Hugo.

'We were told your time is tight,' said Ross.

'Oh, it is,' said Hugo. 'Very tight. I just thought it was usual to go over—'

'It can make it seem stilted,' said Ross. 'You know: too scripted. I like to keep it fast and loose.'

'Right,' said Hugo.

'Which I'm sure is what you prefer too?' she added. 'What with your dislike of spin and formality and media slickness and the like.'

'Absolutely,' said Hugo. 'Fast and loose is my middle name. Names. My two middle names.'

'And three, two . . .' said clipboard man.

'Oh,' said Hugo. 'Blimey, let me just—'

'Hugo Bennington,' said Vivian Ross, suddenly cracking out a surprisingly warm smile she'd apparently been keeping under wraps until it was needed. 'Thank you so much for having us in your home. I know how busy you are.'

'I . . . Hello,' said Hugo. 'Absolutely. I mean, yes.'

Beneath Hugo's shirt-collar, discrete beads of sweat were starting to organise themselves into an insurrectionary army.

'It's been quite a week for you,' said Ross.

'Well, yes,' said Hugo. 'But such is politics. It's a fast-moving world and you just have to move with it or be left behind.'

'Is that something you fear? Being left behind?'

'No,' said Hugo. 'Not at all.'

'Because that's a common criticism of your party, isn't it? That you're a throwback, a bunch of dinosaurs.'

'Well, if loving my country and calling for a return to what I see as its values makes me a throwback,' said Hugo, who had answered this charge so many times that he sometimes woke up in the morning unconsciously repeating this mantra, 'then yes, I'm guilty as charged.'

He laughed. Ross didn't. He stopped laughing and she smiled. He hated her.

'And what are those values, exactly?' she said.

'Respect, for one,' said Hugo. 'Integrity. Pride in our landscape, our people. Control over our borders, our laws. I think the English are fundamentally—'

'Our people?' said Ross.

'*The* people,' said Hugo. 'The people of England. It's about putting the needs of our country and the people in it first.'

'And do you have a sense of what those needs might be at this point in time? I mean, what, for you, are the most pressing needs?'

One of the most critical skills for any politician speaking in public, Hugo had always thought, was the skill of enumeration. It communicated control, orderliness, a systematic approach. The moment a question like this arose, his right hand shot up in front of his face in a reflex gesture, fingers curled into his palm, thumb extended.

'One,' he said, shaking the thumb. 'Self-protection. We need to get control of immigration. We need to get control of our culture. We need to ensure we're all, literally and hypothetically, speaking the same language.'

Those should, he thought, have been three things. Instead, he had bundled them all into one and was still gesticulating with his thumb.

'Two,' he said, hastily extending his forefinger. 'The economy. Why are we giving money away? Why are we allowing people to drain our resources? People like healthcare tourists and benefits cheats. Three, liberty. We need to fight for our basic freedoms, which are being eroded.'

'And what do you think those basic freedoms are?'

Up shot the thumb again.

'Freedom of expression. Freedom of belief. Just . . . Freedom, basically.'

He'd somehow managed to enumerate this last, vague repetition of *freedom* as if it were a further point, meaning he now looked like a man who madly enumerated mere words in a desperate struggle to imbue significance.

'You talk a lot about freedom of speech.'

'Oh, absolutely,' said Hugo, pleased at the opportunity to reset. 'It's something I feel incredibly strongly about. I mean honestly, this culture of offence. Look, all we're saying is that we need to have free, open debate, and not have the terms of that debate continually dictated by a single minority group. It's just common sense.'

'So this whole notion of offence, for you—'

'It's ridiculous.'

'It's ridiculous that people are offended?'

'It's ridiculous that the idea people might be offended by something is becoming a de facto reason not to say it or write it, yes.'

'Should people be able to say whatever they like then?'

'Of course people should be able to say whatever they like. Do you want to live in a country where you're not able to say what you think?'

'Well, it just seems to me that there's something of a conflict between the fact that on the one hand, you're complaining that you and other members of your party are somehow discouraged from voicing your views, while at the same time, you've also spoken out very forcefully this week against someone who has tweeted—'

'OK,' said Hugo, 'I see what you're saying. But let's be clear: this tweet was a death threat.'

'Was it?'

'You don't think genocide involves death?' Hugo decided to deploy his trademark, *am I the only one around here who thinks this is crazy* laugh, which he always used in tandem with a kind of glance around an imaginary audience. 'Your conception of genocide must be very different from mine.'

'I'm not disputing the definition of genocide with you, I'm just questioning why you appear to be advocating one rule for yourself and another rule for someone else.'

'I'm not advocating any kind of rule other than the rule we already have, which is the rule of law. Incitement to violence is against the law. Racial discrimination is against the law. It really is as simple as that.'

'What about the violence that has been threatened towards the woman who tweeted that statement by people who claim to be your followers and admirers?'

'Well, like I say, I believe in the rule of law, and so I do not in any way condone—'

'But you're rather slower to condemn threats of violence by some people than you are others, wouldn't that be fair to say?'

'No. I condemn all threats of violence in the strongest terms.'

'So for any of your supporters out there watching—'

'Don't . . . threaten violence. There. Simple.' Hugo was about to say *but*. Remembering Teddy's advice, he caught himself at the last moment and reshaped it into a *now*. 'Now, I'd just like to pick up on this idea that some people are treated more severely than others,' he said. He was still, he thought, just about clinging to the last tattered vestiges of his easy-going persona, but he was, he knew, close to a severe and no doubt costly break in etiquette. Just *who*, he asked himself repeatedly, did this woman think she was? 'Because let's imagine for a moment, if we may, the response from the general public if a white man had tweeted, however humorously, about a genocide of black women. I mean, can you even *picture* the outcry?'

'Are you saying you as a white man want the right to tweet, perhaps humorously, about killing black women?'

'No, I'm not saying that. Why on earth would I want to tweet about killing black women?'

'Well, you seem to be very concerned about—'

'I'm saying that we live, whether we like it or not, in a new orthodoxy, and political correctness is all very well—'

'But—'

'No *but*. If you'd let me finish. Political correctness is all very well in theory, *providing* it doesn't become so entrenched that we can no longer have a free and open debate.'

'You mention there the, if you like, average white man,' said Vivian Ross. 'And you have in fact this week brought up the case of a particular man, a Mr Darkin, who coincidentally lives on the same estate as the woman whose tweets we were just discussing.'

'Well, I mean, you just couldn't make it up, could you?' said Hugo. 'Talk about a perfect illustrative example. Here's this woman and her, shall we say unconventional family, at least one of whom is claiming benefits, tweeting this appalling vitriol, for all we know on a mobile phone or a laptop that was paid for with taxpayers' money, and meanwhile, just a few doors down the road, we have a perfect example of the very person against whom she wants to take violent action: an old, vulnerable man, a man who has no doubt worked hard all his life, and who is facing eviction. Now, he's not on Twitter, is he? He's not promoting himself. He's not lapping up the media attention. He's not enjoying the benefits of the so-called welfare state while at the same time completely contradicting what I think everyone would agree are the basic values of English society. And yet his plight is very real.'

'In that he faces eviction because the estate, the Larchwood Estate to be exact, is to be torn down and replaced with—'

'There's no room, is there?' said Hugo, deciding he needed to interrupt Ross more frequently. 'Let's just come right out and say it. In the shiny, brave, new, happy-clappy future, there is simply no room for the Darkins of this world.'

'Is it an issue of space then?'

'Absolutely. Look, Britain has in the past however many years seen the biggest rise in immigration since the Second World War. And meanwhile, we're evicting people from what was supposed to be social housing to make room for more housing. Are we supposed to believe that that's some kind of *coincidence*?' Hugo scoffed. 'I mean, pull the other one, quite frankly.'

'The estate has been bought out by a private housing organisation. I suppose I just wonder if this is really an issue of space, if we can really tie this situation back to immigration, or if this is more an issue of—'

'The Larchwood Estate was an experiment,' said Hugo, who by now was thinking, what the hell, why let her complete any sentence at all. 'Can we agree on that? It was an experiment in community. It depended on shared values. Shared ideals. And yes, come on, let's say it like it is: a shared *culture*. Now, I'm not alone in thinking that the Larchwood, as an experiment, has been a failure. Go out there and ask some of the residents. Ask local councillors. Ask charities. It fundamentally has not worked. Now, let's look at what we're left with at the end of this experiment. We're left with a vulnerable old man facing eviction, stuck in his flat not knowing what's happening, afraid to go out, afraid to speak his mind, afraid of his neighbours. And a few doors down, we've got this woman, this unconventional family, spewing hatred and violence. Hatred and violence, I might add, that takes as its primary target this vulnerable old man. Now, I ask you: is that the kind of society we all signed up for? Is that the kind of world we want to live in? I think that from this isolated example of a failed, shall we say *inclusive* experiment, we can draw further, more broad-reaching conclusions about the extent to which we have all been subject to a similar, but larger, country-wide experiment. And I think *that* experiment, the great politically correct, multicultural, multisexual, come-one-come-all melting pot of British culture we now find ourselves signed up to, in which some of the most fundamental tenets by which we live our lives – tolerance, respect, family values, and what have you – are not only called into question but actively, even violently undermined, has been a similar failure. Mark my words. What is happening on the Larchwood Estate is indicative of a wider malaise. It is symptomatic. There will be more and more situations just like this. So you'll understand, with that in mind, why I take this so seriously. Because how we handle this one sets a very real precedent for how we handle the ones that are to come.'

'But aren't you conflating—'

'I'm not conflating anything, darling. These things are already conflated. The problem is that people like you—'

'I'm sorry, people like me?'

'People like you in the liberally biased media refuse to report these things as they actually are.'

'But it's almost as if you're saying that this old man is *directly at risk* from this woman tweeting.'

'Well, he is.'

'I don't think you can necessarily—'

'You don't think a vulnerable old white man living next door to someone who has called for the violent execution of white men is in some way at risk?'

'Well, I almost think it sounds as if you're—'

'That poor man,' said Hugo. 'Terrified, no doubt. And, while we're on the subject, let's not even think about the horrors that await him once the PC brigade get wind of this.'

'The—'

'He's an emblem, isn't he? His views, his background. This is a man very much in need of protection.'

'But you're just stoking the fires of—'

'I'm saying to the local community: this situation is happening right on your doorstep. Turning away and pretending it's not happening is no longer an option.'

'But you're not advocating—'

'I'm calling for positive community engagement,' said Hugo with a smile. 'Now surely you're not going to criticise me for that?'

'And what do you say to people who say that, far from promoting positive community engagement, you're actually deliberately stoking the fires of racial hatred and then manipulating the fallout for your own political gain?'

'Well, I don't tend to pay much attention to crackpot—'

'But you do recognise, don't you, that those who said, back when your party's main thrust was leaving Europe and curbing immigration, that all you had really done was conceal your racism behind popular mainstream political issues, are now pointing to the speed with which you've turned on this particular black woman as evidence of *exactly* the kind of bigotry you've always fervently claimed your policies remained uninfected by?'

'I don't think I really follow.'

'The accusation is that you've shown your true colours.'

'Well, unlike most politicians, showing my true colours is actually something on which I happen to pride myself.'

Hugo looked at his watch and then towards clipboard man, deliberately cutting clean across Vivian Ross as she began to form a follow-up question. 'Not to tell you your job or anything, my man, but time is ticking on. Shouldn't we do a bit of the old touchy-feely stuff before you have to go?'

Ross's mouth fell open in what Hugo could only imagine would prove a profoundly unbroadcastable response. Clipboard man, however, was already talking over her.

'He's right. That's enough of the hard stuff. Let's wander around the house and talk about hobbies.'

Hugo smiled at Ross, who was categorically not smiling back.

'Would you like to know a little bit about my hobbies?' he said.

———

'That fucking—'

Trina was raging in the lounge. Hugo Bennington's face,

polished with self-satisfied, orchestrated outrage, stared straight down the camera and into her life.

'Alright, alright,' said Carl.

'Don't you see what he's done?' she shouted. 'He's basically just told anyone who's watching to get down here and forcibly stop me from *killing an old man*.'

'That's . . . Well, basically, yes,' said Carl.

'*Unconventional family*,' spat Trina. 'Soaking up the benefits of the fucking . . . I work at *Green*, for fuck's sake. He's made me sound like—'

'I know,' said Carl. 'I know.'

'We can't stay here,' she said.

'Well, hang on,' said Carl.

'No,' said Mia. 'No hanging on. Trina's right.'

'Look at what's happened to me online,' said Trina. 'We know our address is out there. At least one person's already been round. Bennington's basically made it sound like it's everyone's collective responsibility to . . .' She muted the television and sat down on the sofa, already feeling herself begin to focus, to think, keeping Bennington's silent face in her field of vision as a focal point for her rage.

'I won't be driven out of my home,' she said. 'I won't have Bella and you two driven out of your home. We can go under our own steam and come back when it's all died down.'

'Admit it,' said Carl, 'we're not going to be able to come back.'

'Oh, come on,' said Mia. 'Don't be melodramatic. These things always burn out in a couple of days.'

Carl shook his head. 'Don't you get it? Downton will evict us. This is all they need.'

Outside, someone dropped a bin bag into one of the bins with a heavy thud. They all started, checked each other, softened again. It was impossible to know how safe you'd previously felt, Trina thought, until the sudden, plummeting moment when your entire sense of security fell away.

She looked back up at the television. Bennington was now roaming his house, pointing at this and that. With the sound off and context stripped away, it seemed, to Trina, like the final insult. Hugo Bennington, unraveller of lives, pointedly touring the homely comfort of his kingdom.

'Smug fuck,' said Mia.

Neither Carl nor Mia had at any stage in the whole unfolding nightmare blamed Trina. From the moment everything had detonated online, one thing had been tacitly agreed between the three of them: none of this was Trina's fault. Resentment was reserved for Bennington alone.

'Question is,' said Carl, 'where do we go?'

'Why don't we just check into a hotel?' said Mia.

'How are we going to know how friendly the hotel is?' said Trina.

'My parents would take us,' said Carl.

'Let's call that plan Z,' said Mia.

'Oh, for God's sake, they're not that bad,' said Carl.

On the TV, in silence, Bennington had led the interviewer into his lounge and was seemingly talking her through an array of artisanal objects he'd laid out on the couch. What was it about fascists and bad art? Trina wondered. Why were they always taking time off from tyranny to faff around with some chintz?

'Not that bad?' said Mia. 'They literally hate me.'

'They love Trina,' said Carl. 'That's all. They don't *hate* you.'

'Shut up,' said Trina, scrambling for the remote. 'Everybody shut the fuck up. Where's the remote? Where's the fucking remote?'

'Beside you,' said Mia. 'Jesus, will you—'

Trina flapped her hand at Mia and un-muted the television.

'It started out as a hobby, yes,' Bennington was saying. 'But I almost feel that word's a little inadequate these days. I mean, I've been making these for so long now—'

'The attention to detail is really quite extraordinary,' said the interviewer.

261

'Oh, I go to huge effort to achieve verisimilitude,' said Hugo. 'The whole point is that the scale is literally the only thing that's different. Everything else is . . .'

'Why the fuck are we watching this?' said Carl.

Trina ignored him. She'd stood up from the sofa and was now right in front of the television, squinting, following Hugo's proudly pointing finger as he offered the interviewer and the viewers at home a guided tour of what he seemed to be describing as his 'art'.

'It must be very calming,' the interviewer was saying.

'Absolutely,' said Bennington. 'I just shut everything out and . . .'

Trina felt as if peripheral perceptions were draining away. Her hearing, her vision, her whole self, were now trained on the objects Bennington was holding up in turn: a miniature cutlery set, a shrunken dinner plate decorated with imitation parsley.

'Jesus fucking Christ,' she half-whispered at the screen.

'What?' Mia said. 'What am I missing here?'

'I've seen all of this,' Trina said, pointing at the shrunken dinner set. 'I've seen all of these things before.'

———

On the other side of action, Jess thought as she drove home from Nodem, the quiet blankness of the Edmundsbury suburbs scrolling past her, lay emptiness. There was a superficial buzz, a sting in her eyes from screen-glare and fought-back tears, a faint, lingering tingle at her outer edges as she contemplated the consequences of what she'd done, but beneath it she was drained, almost blank. Once, Julia had been her expressive extension, her gobby stand-in. Now, away from the safety of the digital, the roles were painfully reversed. Something alive in Jess had been externalised, fragmented, and lost. Julia was no longer her outlet. Instead, Jess was merely what remained in Julia's aftermath: Julia's guilty, exhausted hangover.

She cracked the window and lit a cigarette, accelerating slightly as if raw momentum might counterbalance her confusion. In a way, she thought, that had been her whole approach: move fast and break things, look back later and try to learn – the disruptive logic of the Silicon Valley tech bros.

The emptiness was expansive. She didn't just feel it, she lived in it, breathed it. She didn't know what she was going home to. The uncertainty howled like a high wind across a blanched and desiccated landscape. She would pull into the driveway, she thought, open her own front door as a semi-stranger, and call out to the stranger inside, *It's me.*

Perhaps as a means of taking control, she refused to return in the way that she'd imagined and become accustomed to. She sat in the driveway, smoking and stewing. When her throat was suitably raw and her nerve endings sufficiently sharpened by the nicotine, she stepped through the front door and said nothing. She found Robert in the kitchen, neither cooking nor drinking wine, just sitting at the table with a notepad and a furrowed expression.

'Hey,' she said, easing herself into the opposite chair and reeling at the space between them.

'Hey,' he said, looking up and assembling the components of a smile in not quite the right order – beginning with his mouth and then clearly trying, and failing, to match the light in his eyes to the muscles in his face.

She felt as if everything had been laid bare. They were stuck, she saw, in a silence of their own making. Robert would not talk about what he had done. She would never be able to disclose that she knew what he had done. If either one of them revealed what they knew, the other would know the means by which it was known. Only the public domain was available to them. If it wasn't out there, it couldn't be cited.

'How are you?' he said.

'Pretty good,' she said. 'How about you?'

'Pretty good.'

She nodded.

'Congratulations on your piece,' she said. 'Seems to have been pretty popular.'

He looked at her for longer than the simple statement required. He was always sensitive to what she didn't say. Saying his work was good was not the same as saying it was great. Saying it was doing well was not the same as saying she wanted it to do well. Now she was saying less than ever, and it showed, but she had no idea what to say in order to gloss over the things she didn't believe.

'Popular,' he said.

'Yeah,' she said. 'I mean, that's good, right? You must be pleased?'

Without recourse to reality, she was trapped in the realm of the hopelessly weak utterance: diluted, vague, inadequate.

'You sound . . . less than pleased,' he said.

'No, I'm . . . I'm really pleased, Robert. It's great.'

His name felt awkward in her mouth: foreign and indigestible, gristle amidst a bolus of meat.

'Have you read it?'

'Of course I've read it. I thought it was great. Very powerful.'

She kept thinking about him in Nodem – his guilty creep into the café, the ease with which he'd drawn on the sources of her own harassment in his moves against Julia Benjamin. She wondered if he'd stored that information in his mind even then, when he was privately downplaying and then publicly condemning her situation, or if this was a connection he made only at the last minute, in desperation.

'And what about the other thing?' he said.

'What other thing?'

He looked away, found something of sudden interest in the notes on his pad. There was a long pause in which he seemingly weighed the possibility of not telling her what he'd written, despite the fact that she could take out her phone at any moment and google it.

'Silas asked me to weigh in on the whole genocide thing.'

The statement hung in the air for a few moments. He couldn't look at her, she noticed. In that inability or unwillingness to connect, to be seen, she gathered all she needed to know about the form his weighing-in had taken.

'Don't say anything,' he said.

'I didn't say anything.'

'You were about to. But don't.'

'But why would I—'

'Because you always do.'

The atmosphere had gone from awkward to ugly. Here they were again, she thought, poised on the precipice of an argument. How many times had they been here? How many times had they backed off? And then how many times had they ended up having the argument anyway, by different means, as different people?

'Are you OK?' she said.

'I'm fine,' he said. 'Why?'

'You just seem kind of . . . defensive.'

'*Defensive?*'

It was the wrong word and she knew it. In this world, in this reality, Robert didn't have anything to be defensive about. Now he would become defensive about his defensiveness.

'I mean, not—'

'Why would I be defensive? What would I have to be defensive about? Jesus Christ. All I've done is write something about this old man, this poor old man, and people are acting like I've—'

'What people?'

'People online. That Julia Benjamin woman. You.'

'I haven't said anything.'

'You've thought it.'

'*Thought* it? Robert, you're being totally paranoid. Are we seriously going to have an argument about something you think I've thought but haven't actually said?'

'Oh come on, Jess. I know what you think about things.'

'What's she said? This Julia woman.'

He waved a hand in the air as if dismissing the question. His lip curled in disgust.

'The usual shit,' he said.

She caught the twist in his lip, the catch in the back of his throat as he spoke, the venom he injected into the word *shit*, and recoiled. He hated her, she realised. Before, he had been irritated, then angry, then exasperated. But all of that had congealed now. His feelings were simple. She felt, quite suddenly, as if she might cry. In order not to cry, she had to remind herself of her own feelings about Robert. Did she *hate* Robert? It was easy for him to hate Julia – she was not, to him, a person, just a phenomenon. Robert was right here in front of her – the man she knew intimately. Maybe that was the problem, she thought. She now knew him *too* intimately. She knew his responses, his positions, his hasty and bitter thoughts.

'But you can ignore that, right? I mean, fuck it. It's just some commenter on the internet.'

At this, he flared up.

'Just some commenter on the internet? Are you serious?'

'What?'

He lifted a finger and aimed it in her direction.

'When *you* were getting all that shit online, Jess—'

'Oh fucking hell, Robert. Don't. Don't even make that comparison.'

'Why not?'

'Because it's totally different.'

'How is it different?'

'No-one has harassed you, Robert. No-one has threatened you.'

'They've threatened my career, my livelihood, my integrity. Are you saying I shouldn't be angry about that?'

'Of course I'm not saying you shouldn't be angry about that. I'm just saying—'

'What? What are you saying?'

'I'm *saying*, if you'd let me finish, that it's different because—'

'Because I'm a man and she's a woman, that's what you're going to say.'

'Are you serious? I mean, seriously Robert, is that what you think?'

'Seems pretty obvious to me.'

'What I was *going* to say, before you *interrupted* me, Robert, is that it's different because you're not *scared*. You might be annoyed, or embarrassed, or infuriated, or whatever, but at the end of the day you're not *scared*. That's the difference. No-one's *threatening your life*. No-one's sending a *wreath* to your fucking house. No-one's saying they're going to come round and *rape* you.'

'So, what? That's the line now? So long as you don't actively threaten someone, anything you say to them is basically OK?'

'Hasn't that pretty much always been the line? Like, that is basically the law you're describing there.'

'She keeps talking about how I'm a man. She hates me because I'm a man. How is that different from hating someone because they're a woman?'

'Disagreement isn't harassment, Robert. Come on. You know this.'

He sat back in his chair, evidently trying to calm himself down, but doing so in a way that drew attention to his efforts, as if, she thought, she was supposed to respect the fact that he was trying to calm himself down; as if, in calming himself down, he was making some sort of statement about the ways in which she was *not* calming herself down.

She realised she was now furious.

'What have you said about the genocide woman?' she said. 'Because please tell me you haven't gone out there with a whole load of white man apologia about—'

'About not threatening to kill people? Yes. Yes, I have, actually. And I don't see why that's such a controversial fucking position, quite frankly.'

'Well, obviously you do or you wouldn't be being so defensive about it.'

'I'm *not being defensive. Stop saying I'm being defensive.*'

'You're being *fucking* defensive, Robert.'

'I'm making *connections*,' he said. 'It's that simple. Old white man no-one cares about, perfectly reasonable white man trying to do something about the situation – me, in case that wasn't obvious – and some woman going round talking about killing white men.'

'*Some woman.*'

'Oh fuck off. Don't *you people* me. You know what I mean. It's a figure of speech. You know what? This is the problem.'

'What's the problem?'

'We can't talk about anything any more because all we can talk about is the *way* we talk about things.'

'Who do you mean by *we*? Us? Or everyone?'

He didn't answer. He couldn't answer, Jess thought, because he didn't know. He could no longer define those kinds of differences: the two of them in their kitchen, arguing about his work; the world around them, arguing about everything else. It was all the same to him. The world was his world only. Everything else was just context.

'Maybe you don't mean us,' she said finally. 'I mean, what do we really talk about? Nothing.'

'We talk all the time,' he said.

She shook her head.

'We don't,' she said. 'We just chatter. We don't say anything.'

She saw him soften, sadden. He looked suddenly hopeless, at a loss, and she knew exactly why. It was because he had no recourse to opinion. His life had become a problem about which merely commenting was inadequate. He'd lost the safety of observance.

'I mean . . . Do you . . . Do you want to talk now?' he said.

She looked at him, pained by the fact that he looked frightened. She was frightened, she realised, and registering his fear only increased her own. But she suspected they feared different things, or that even if their fear was a single, shared obstacle, they were now on opposing sides of it, unable to see each other through its distortions. She couldn't determine which was more terrifying: how unfamiliar Robert now was, or how completely he'd become the person she'd long identified – the one who wasn't quite there when she was fearful, the one who empathised more rapidly with some old man he'd met only once than he did with the woman he supposedly loved. They couldn't talk about it, she realised, because they *had* talked about it, and now neither of them could admit to what they'd uttered.

And yet, she thought, she had to try it, if only to know that she'd tried it. The offer of communication was there. If she didn't test it, feel it out, she'd never know what they might have been able to say to each other.

'What were you doing in Nodem?' she said.

He froze, momentarily caught up in the question. He experienced her question as a command, she thought, and on receiving the instruction, because his answer was elusive even to him, whatever programme that controlled his response briefly locked up, and gave her all the answers she needed.

'Nothing,' he said after a moment. 'Just work.'

She could, she knew, have pressed him, but she saw there would be no point. The things they had said and done publicly could not be said in private. The people they were when they were apart could not be reconciled with the people they became when they were together.

And so neither of them said anything, and it was worse, she thought, far worse, than anything they might actually have said.

Trina's initial excitement about Hugo Bennington's extracurricular photographic activities had quickly waned. She should not, she thought, have told Mia and Carl about it until she'd given it more consideration. Now, obviously, they were all for leaking the pics as quickly as possible, deflecting attention away from Trina and onto Bennington's predilection for thrusting the image of his dick into fields of vision unconsenting to its arrival. But Trina had quickly spotted the dangers associated with this plan. Bennington would guess, immediately, the source. He knew Kasia's name, where she worked. Clearly, he also knew someone at The Arbor well enough that he'd been able to get Kasia's information simply by asking for it after a guided tour. If Bennington's contact thought so little of handing over employee data at Bennington's request, it seemed unlikely they would suddenly develop a conscience when it came to, for example, firing or publicly humiliating a low-level, easily replaced service worker.

But then, when Trina thought about this, she also thought about herself, about her family, and about the wider fact of Hugo Bennington as a cultural and political phenomenon. This was a man who was deliberately fanning the flames of racial hatred, who was making life in England unsafe in real and terrifying ways. Imagine, she thought, if he continued, if the tensions increased, if TV and online rhetoric became street-level physical violence. Would Kasia's friendship come as any comfort when neither of them felt safe to walk the streets? Perhaps this was simply what such situations demanded: the ruthless counterweighting of micro and macro; the dissolution of the personal into the political.

There were other issues besides moral discomfort. Bennington, for so long portrayed by the left-wing commentariat as little more than the court jester of contemporary politics, a man to be both laughed off and ignored until, conveniently, he simply disappeared, had genuine power and reach, and his hold on both was tightening. Trina had a couple of thousand followers on Twitter. Bennington had just under thirty thousand. Between its web and print editions, *The Record* had a monthly readership of around twenty million. The result of *The Record* embedding Trina's tweets in its article was that Trina's Twittersphere, which she had always regarded as being a comparatively safe private space, was thrown open to a skewed and distorted demographic who then weaponised her only outlet against her.

And this, she thought, was Bennington operating at the level of mere political opportunism. How far would he go, she wondered, if she made the fight personal, if he saw in her actions not just an opportunity for professional gain, but an imperative for personal defence?

The feeling of needing help was disappointing, awkward, and the source of a resentment unlikely to dissolve with time. It made her loathe Bennington all the more, for putting her in a position where her own resourcefulness seemed insufficient. But nothing, she felt, should come at the expense of realism, and right at this moment, realism dictated that she was not going to be able to extricate herself from this predicament without assistance, and that the support usually and so readily available to her – the support of Carl and Mia and, in a different way, Kasia – was not, this time, going to cut it.

She had, for the past hour or so, from the moment Bennington came on television through to the moment she recognised his ridiculous miniatures, been thinking about Robert Townsend. Yes, he was pompous, and yes, he would enjoy the opportunity to be Trina's white knight in a way Trina would find unpalatable, but the fact remained that he was, as things stood at the moment, one of very few commentators to show sustained and active interest in the Larchwood Estate. Moreover, his platform was stronger than ever. In the past few weeks, Trina had noticed not only a growing audience for his blog, but a swelling interest in the estate itself. And besides, she thought, he had, unlike basically anyone else, *been here*, asking questions, making an effort, at least, to understand.

She hadn't read his last couple of blogs, and so decided, before reaching out to him, to catch up on where he was with things. His most recent column occupied a large portion of real estate on *The Command Line*'s homepage. The headline read: *Speaking Out: Robert Townsend Takes Down The Genocide Tweeter*. The numbers on the share icons were through the roof. Within approximately a sentence, she knew her plan to call on Townsend for support had been hopelessly misguided.

She recognised not a single element of Townsend's article. The woman who was supposedly the subject bore no relation to her. The columnists who, according to Townsend, were supposedly engaged in a conspiracy of PC silence bore no relation to the legions of outraged white men who, far from keeping silent, were in fact bombarding her with violent noise. Nor, now that Trina thought about it, did the person who wrote this particular column bear any relation to the person who for so long had defended the interests of the Larchwood Estate. Everything was coming at her bent and tinted, as if through a distorting prism. She was, on one level, reading about herself, but it was a version of herself she had played no part in constructing. Her own words, and by extension her identity, her name, her very existence, had been appropriated, twisted, refashioned and repurposed until all recognition or ability to identify had been denied her. Apparently, all she was supposed to do now was read placidly as versions of herself were created, described, and decried in print, or sit back on her sofa and watch in passive semi-slumber as people she had never been were trotted out and casually denounced on national television. Where, she thought, was she supposed to go to refocus and un-distort the picture? Twitter, where even the briefest second of activity would trigger a new onrush of rabid, slavering violence? Television, onto which she hadn't once been invited?

She pushed her laptop off her knees and onto the bed beside her and covered her face and eyes briefly with hands warmed by the heat of her overworked computer. She felt, as she had before she looked into Townsend's latest work, alone. Indeed, she thought, she was probably more alone now than she had been a few minutes ago. Before, she had assumed that all her enemies were on the right. Now, even people who just yesterday she might have relied upon to be halfway sympathetic were falling over each other to abuse the woman they had collectively decided she was. It was a familiar, bitter position. White people always decried injustice when it was safe to do so, and when an audience in the cheap seats could reliably affirm their righteousness. But when injustice was actually occurring, when their intervention was both necessary and fraught with risk, they vanished or turned hostile.

Townsend had no insight into his own power. That was what made him so dangerous. To him, everything was mere hypothesis. He was, Trina thought, working with the ideological equivalent of Beatrice. He manipulated the sliders and parameters of controversy in order to achieve the perfect conditions for his own success. No doubt thrilled at the extent to which he was able to tweak the emotional and intellectual reality into which he injected himself, he remained blind to the fact that what he was really adjusting was not some generalised and nebulous intellectual atmosphere, but the hard reality of Trina's life. In upping the controversy, he limited Trina's safety. He was merely playing, but she was the one living with the results.

As Trina picked her way through these thoughts, it struck her that, as familiar and predictable as so much that was occurring might have been, one element, one crucial factor, was in fact not the same at all. The moment she homed in on this detail and recognised its difference, she felt her conception of the factors surrounding it shifting in turn, until, quite suddenly, having deliberated so thoroughly on all the ways that what was happening to her was in no way new, she found herself alive to all the ways in which recent events were strange in a particularly sinister way.

If there had been one constant in Trina's life and the way she had repeatedly found herself treated, it had been the idea, tacitly supported by those around her and, for a while, internalised and normalised in her own psyche, that her voice was irrelevant, that her ideas and opinions were somehow worth less than the ideas and opinions of everyone else she worked with, schooled with, dated. To make herself heard, Trina had always been forced, sometimes literally, sometimes metaphorically, to raise her voice. In many ways, the present predicament was no different – the usual babble of white male voices amidst which there was little or no room for her own. But at the heart of it, she thought, sitting up, straightening, coming out of her slump and into a sense of attention, a new and unusual consensus was at play. Her voice, her opinion, which had always been treated as if it was largely irrelevant, was suddenly powerful, so much so – and on this everyone, from Bennington to Townsend to the frothing attack dogs of the Twittersphere seemed in complete agreement – that it was dangerous.

How many times had she fought to be taken seriously? How many times had she had to restate her point in meetings, just to achieve a simple acknowledgement from the likes of Bream and Holt? How many times had she seen one of her ideas, initially ignored, appropriated by a colleague and then suddenly praised? And now, amidst all that background and experience, here she was effectively being told that one single tweet from her personal account had the power to destabilise British society overnight? No, she thought. There was no way, after a lifetime of disregard by the powers that be, that she was suddenly going to lay claim to that kind of significance.

She thought about Downton, the easily graphed increase in their intimidation tactics; about Tayz, the file she'd clicked on, the speed of the lockout; and suddenly, without quite knowing why, about Norbiton: his meltdown, his babbling, the thing he'd shouted before Bangstrom had him gagged. What had he called it? The Field? She saw herself clicking on the file again, just before her screen locked, remembered trying to parse the extension as she did so: .fld.

Her phone started humming. The vibration played out down her spine, jolting her, causing momentary panic. The screen showed a withheld number. The last thing she needed now was a gravel-voiced threat delivered straight into her ear. But at the same time, it could easily be important. What if someone was reaching out to her? And anyway, did she really want to give the impression that she was cowering away, afraid to answer her phone?

She scooped it up, hit the button to take the call.

'Yeah,' she said sharply.

'Don't hang up.' It was a woman's voice, calm and commanding. 'I'm a friend.'

'Do I know you?'

'No, but I know you. I know you need help.'

'What makes you think I need help?'

'Oh, I don't know, maybe the fact that I've helped about a hundred people through similar experiences and so like to think of myself as being a pretty good judge of when someone does or doesn't need my help.'

'What experiences?'

'Online harassment, violence, public shaming. I'm going to send you a link that will take you to a secure portal that will explain more. Follow the instructions and I'll see you soon.'

'See me where?'

'Follow the instructions.'

'Why should I trust you?'

'Who else are you going to trust?'

'How about no-one?'

'OK, put it another way. What other plans do you have?'

'I have plans.'

'Really? Because from where I'm sitting, all you've done is sit in your bedroom reading Robert Townsend articles.'

'How—'

'Wave at your laptop.'

Trina looked at her laptop. The camera was activated.

'You're not alone,' said the woman. 'There's lots I can do. There's lots they can do. They have a head start. Be smart, let me help you, and we can get you out of this.'

———————

Pained by scrutiny, Robert sought refuge in distraction. He'd muttered something vague to Jess about work, then come up to his study to stew. Someone had sent him a link to Bennington's TV appearance, and now he was watching it through for the third time, squinting as if in harsh light, reassuring himself that what he was seeing was a distortion, not a reflection, of his own recent work.

The Darkins of the world. Hugo had used the phrase in his column. Now he had used it again in his interview. Robert's own words – words he had hesitated over even as he wrote them – were now part of Hugo's lexicon. Robert could already imagine the glee with which Julia Benjamin would map them on her website, the conclusions she would inevitably draw. And would she even be wrong in those conclusions? he wondered. Would he be able, if asked, to explain away the fact that Hugo Bennington, *Hugo Bennington* – a man Robert had always regarded with a distanced, confident disgust – was now ventriloquising his own work?

He closed the window containing the video of Bennington's TV appearance and sat back in his chair, exhausted, deflated, shaken. Just a few hours ago, he thought, he'd thrilled at the shrinking distance between himself and his chosen subject. Now the collapse of that space appalled him. He could no longer look upon Bennington as an alien species, could no longer scoff at the sheer idiocy of his pronouncements, because the gap he'd always relied upon had vanished. There was no foreignness when he looked at Bennington now, no sense of the other. There was only a deep and awful recognition, a familiarity that even a day ago would have been unimaginable. He pictured the ways in which his column about the genocide woman would be read in light of Bennington's comments, the kind of audience it would now reach. Things he'd never said to himself, barely even *thought* to himself, would now be heard and interpreted by thousands. In the moments following Bennington's BBC profile, fingers up and down the country would be tapping words like *Larchwood* and *Darkin* into their search engines. Other columnists, other opinionists, would be racing to catch up. But Robert, whose piece had already secured a sufficient readership to push it to the top of the search results, would be way ahead of them. The achievement he'd always dreamed of and fought for so long to make real – clickbait gold, the assured virality of the tuned-in com-mentator – was now the very thing he couldn't undo. He'd wanted to be read. Now he was unable to control the readings.

It was imperative not to back down. Of course, there would be a degree of pushback on his piece about the genocide woman. But capitulation would prick the bubble of attention. His audience, the one he'd long pined for and long imagined himself to deserve, would desert him as swiftly as it had adopted him. He needed to stand firm. He needed, as Silas would say, to own it. His head start on the issue would make everyone else's columns look opportunistic, while his would retrospectively appear ahead of its time. Undermining it now would be akin to disowning his own gift for prophecy. What light would that cast on whatever he wrote subsequently?

His piece on the genocide woman had only really been a further defence of Darkin, hadn't it? Surely no-one expected him, now that this vulnerable old man was suddenly being directly threatened by a trendier and superficially more PC opponent, to simply turn his back or, worse, hop the fence and join the genocide movement out of nothing more than some utterly misplaced notion of righteous-ness? Hadn't his very point, in the first place, been about the ways in which the Darkins of the world had been unjustly maligned and ignored in favour of hipper, more attractive causes? Wasn't it exactly this shift towards a politics of identity, as opposed to a politics of class or economics, that had effectively rendered the whole left-wing movement so fragmented and impotent?

This, he was coming to understand, was the new reality of his job, and the natural endpoint of his career arc. He'd begun by reporting what was happening. He'd graduated from a focus on what was happening to a focus on what he *thought* about what was happening. From there, what was happening had come to have less and less bearing on what he thought, until all that mattered, to borrow a choice phrase from Lionel Groves, was that he thought at all. Now, what he thought *was* what was happening. His opinions and those of others were events unto themselves, supplanting their real-world counterparts and models. In this world, it didn't actually matter what he thought, and mattered even less what people felt about it. What mattered was the nurturing and manipulation of an environment in which his thought could flourish, in which discussion was its own reality. Silas was right: hatred, pushback, dissent were all just modified matrices of the only things that meant anything: impact and volume.

He had not been able to shrug off Jess's gaze, he realised – the one he'd imagined in Nodem, the one he'd seen confirmed downstairs at the kitchen table. *What were you doing in Nodem?* he heard her ask. He regretted, now, going on the offensive. What was *she* doing in Nodem? What, even, was her work? He tried to remember the last time they'd spoken about it, but was unable to call any specific moment to mind. How easy it was for Jess, he thought, to sneer at his public pronouncements, when all the while she was able to work without any scrutiny at all. Who, in the end, judged what she did? At what point did she ever, even for a second, open herself up to the kind of mass peer review he had to endure on a daily basis? Yes, there had been that one time, her brush with public disapproval, and look how she had milked that! Did she expect him to withdraw from public view simply because she had?

His rage had crept up on him, somehow only reaching his conscious mind once it had swelled beyond the point of being contained. Of course he was questioning himself, he thought. Of course he was subjecting himself to scrutiny. It was because *Jess* was questioning him. It was her gaze he felt now, thinking about Bennington's TV appearance. It was *her* disapproval he directed at himself in the wake of his success. He thought again of the word she'd used: *popular*. That was what she really hated, he thought. She could dress it up in all the ideological garb she liked, but in the end, it was the attention that bothered her, and because it bothered her, he'd let it bother him.

He heard her on the stairs, pausing for a moment outside his door. She knocked gently, opened the door just enough to poke her head through. She couldn't quite look at him, he noticed, and so he looked at her all the more forcefully.

'Deepa called,' she began.

'Did she now,' said Robert.

'She's asked me to pop over there. Something she's working on, needs a bit of help with.'

'Fine.'

'I don't know how long it will take. You know Deepa.'

He shrugged.

'Maybe . . .' She faltered a little. 'I mean, maybe if it goes on late I'll just stay the night.'

He nodded.

'Fine.'

'OK then.'

'OK.'

She closed the door behind her. He felt a twist in his stomach, a flutter in the centre of his chest. He could, he knew, have gone after her, or better yet not let her go at all. But he hadn't, and didn't feel able to. He *wanted* to be angry, he realised. He didn't want any other feelings to get in the way.

You haven't been attacked, Robert. You haven't been threatened.

He kept coming back to this. When she'd said it, it had simply sounded pedantic, but now, reshaped by the conflicting currents within him, it sounded mocking. He thought again of his Skype call with Silas: *You're nobody until somebody hates you.* Jess didn't seem to care if he was hated, if he was pilloried, if he was mocked. What would she care if he was threatened?

He turned back to his computer and woke it up. From the magma of his thoughts, something cool and rock-like was emerging. Fuck her, he thought. Fuck everyone.

He opened up a Word document, paused for a second in the face of the blank page, then pressed on with the difficult business of composing a death threat to himself.

0101

Darkin's first thought, as the tapping at his broken window drew his attention and he looked up at the wide, dome-headed profile that lurked at the jagged hole, was that Downton had dispatched the heavies to turf him out.

'Mr Darkin?'

Ever since he'd read about himself in *The Record*, Darkin had been waiting for a visit of this kind. He wished, sharply, that he'd done something about the window sooner.

'What do you want?'

'Didn't mean to frighten you,' said the man, holding his hands up. 'Just thought we'd say hello and introduce ourselves. We're going to be outside.'

'Doing what?'

'Keeping watch.'

Darkin pondered this for a moment.

'What sort of watch?'

'Hasn't anyone told you?'

'Told me what?'

The man rolled his eyes.

'Typical,' he said. He turned away from the window and shouted to an unseen companion. 'Hey, Tel. Get this. He doesn't even know.'

'You're kidding,' said a voice near Darkin's front door. Then another face appeared in the window – oddly similar to the first one. They were both, Darkin now noted, wearing the same black jacket too.

'Hello, mate,' said the second head. 'I'm Tel. This is Pete. We're here to protect you.'

Darkin wasn't sure how to respond to this.

'Protect me from who?'

'Haven't you been watching the telly?'

Darkin shook his head.

'You're all over the telly,' said Pete.

'All over it big time,' said Tel.

'But you're not to worry,' said Pete.

'Yeah, we're supposed to tell you that. You're not to worry now that we're here.'

'And who are you?'

'Brute Force,' said Pete. 'You've probably heard of us.'

'Can't say I have.'

'Really? Well, I mean, you should've, to be honest, but never mind. We're a protection force. Security, like.'

'For who? For Downton?'

'For people like you. And us.'

Apparently sensing Darkin's confusion, Pete began explaining the situation to him loudly and slowly. Darkin lit an unscheduled cigarette and listened dispassionately, his opinion as yet unfixed.

'You know that Hugo Bennington, right?' said Pete. 'Well, he was on the telly. Talking about you.'

Darkin thought about this. He couldn't decide if he was sorry he'd missed himself being discussed on television by Hugo Bennington – a genuine celebrity – or if the news that he'd graduated from the pages of *The Record* to the TV screens of people up and down the country was something about which he ought to be uncomfortable. He thought about Downton. If they hadn't noticed the newspaper article, he thought, they would definitely have noticed this.

'It was BBC,' said Pete helpfully. 'Like, proper news. This woman was interviewing Bennington in his house and he started talking about that other woman, the one who's been saying all that stuff about killing people. He was saying how worried he was about you.'

'Worried about me?'

'Well, you're vulnerable, aren't you? I mean, not being funny, but if a load of people came round here wanting to do a genocide, there wouldn't be much you could do about it.'

'I suppose not.'

'And so anyway, our boss, Ronnie Childs – do you know him?'

'No.'

'Proper patriot. Wants to really clean this country up. Know what I mean? Anyway, he phoned me and Tel here, and he said, look, we've got a duty to protect this man, and of course, me and Tel had both been watching and we both agreed. Next thing you know, here we are.'

'Do you think I need protecting?' said Darkin, who had now been told he needed protecting so many times that he was beginning to think there might be something in it.

'We all need protecting,' said Tel, popping his head round the window frame.

'But you maybe need protecting a bit more,' said Pete. 'After all, me and Tel can probably take care of ourselves.'

'We can take care of a few others too,' said Tel.

'But who . . .' said Darkin.

'Take your pick,' said Pete. 'These men in masks. That darkie woman, what's her name.'

'You think she's going to—'

'Probably not her specifically,' said Pete. 'That's the thing about these race-war types: they're all cowards. They just sit at home and let their followers do all the work.'

'And you think some of them might—'

'Well, she's as good as told them to, hasn't she? I mean, that's what Hugo Bennington was saying on the telly last night. That's why he feels you need a bit of protection.'

Darkin thought about this.

'Well,' he said to the men at his window, 'lucky you're here, I suppose.'

'You just take it easy,' said Pete. 'Me and Tel have got this under control.'

'Is . . . Is there anyone out there?' said Darkin.

'What, right now, you mean?' said Pete.

'Yeah.'

Pete turned away from the window and quickly checked over the expanse of the estate below.

'Nah,' he said. 'Not yet.' He shrugged. 'Won't be long though.'

———

The atmosphere in Deepa's kitchen, Jess thought, as the three women – Jess, Deepa, and Trina – busied themselves with coffees and cereal and bits of toast, stepping aside for each other, awkwardly and slightly tentatively sharing limited space and resources, was not exactly one of unchecked, open solidarity. Not that it was hostile or uncooperative either. It was simply that behind the obvious and now rather inescapable fact of their working together, there were, Jess knew, multiple, overlapping degrees of suspicion and reluctance.

She had, perhaps inevitably, stayed the night. It was late by the time she'd arrived. Introductions had been awkward, strained.

'Jess lives with Robert Townsend,' Deepa had said bluntly. Trina had rolled her eyes, angled herself away in her armchair.

'I know,' Jess had said, unable to think of anything else that might be of use. 'Believe me, I know.'

It was a partial truth. She had not, at that point, read Robert's latest article. Nor, even after reading it, could she fully know what it must have been like to read it from the position of being the article's subject. After less than an hour, Trina, clearly exhausted and shaken,

286

had gone to bed, leaving Jess to vent at Deepa for putting them in a room together.

'I mean, for fuck's sake, Deepa,' she'd said. 'What am I supposed to do? Apologise for Robert? Is that why I'm here?'

She was angry at Deepa because there wasn't anyone else to be angry at. Unless, of course, she counted herself. Somehow, though, that wasn't a road she felt able to go down just yet. There would be time, she knew, for self-recrimination, for the kind of interrogation she perhaps should have conducted sooner, but just at this moment it seemed indulgent.

'Fuck no,' Deepa had said. 'You're here to help. Simple as that.'

With Trina asleep, however, the details of that help remained vague. After perhaps half an hour or so, Deepa also turned in, leaving Jess on the couch, wrapped in a distinctly shabby single duvet, catching up with the Trina story on her phone and failing to forget about Robert. If they separated, she thought, *when* they separated, this would be all that remained of him in her daily life: his public profile, the toxic energies of his web presence. The reasons for their falling apart would be always at hand, but the person she'd actually parted with would be lost – erased by the phenomenon Robert had become.

Being in Deepa's house, Jess thought as she began to drift into a restless sleep, was a strangely unsettling experience – a vision of a potential future Jess now realised she feared. She'd always admired Deepa – her resolve, her commitment to what interested her over and above what was probably good for her. But something about the way she lived spoke of an immersion, even a retreat, that Jess found frightening. Almost every surface bore some scrap of Deepa's work – photos from which she was trying to make identifications; articles she'd printed off and highlighted; scribbled notes on repurposed scraps of paper. It was something Jess knew she had in her: the possibility for exclusion, perhaps even obsession; a drift into the digital at the expense of the human.

Now, at the breakfast table, Deepa's difficulty in engaging with the stuff of daily life was all the more apparent. She was, by her own admission, unused to guests. Through her work helping harassed women, she regularly provided shelter, but these were passing moments – women that arrived late at night, slept in Deepa's study, and then left in the morning. With people to feed and conversation to make, Deepa was uncomfortably adrift, her role as host barely extending beyond a casual gesture towards the toaster, next to which half a loaf of bread sat defrosting. And yet in a way, Jess thought, it was admirable. Deepa knew where her talents lay. She helped people only with the most pressing details of their crises. Because she never pressed at her or their boundaries, she remained undistracted by the extent to which those boundaries could shift.

Trina, on the other hand, seemed to represent a different pole of existence entirely. Even as she strolled into the kitchen, wiping the night's sleep from her eyes, her hair pressed flat on one side and her borrowed T-shirt crumpled by slumber, she was on the phone to her family, speaking with an easy, concerned warmth entirely at odds with the stern eye she cast at Jess. Jess envied this too, she realised – this comfort with family life, this sense of an intimate network. When she had been in a similar situation to Trina, who had she called? Who had she leaned on? Robert, she thought – a man she'd had to lean on in all the wrong ways in order to extract the support she needed.

Trina pulled up a chair to Jess's right, at the end of the breakfast table, and watched the steam curling off her cup of coffee without saying anything. Deepa was either oblivious to tensions or, more likely, uninterested in the way personal politics might play out in her kitchen.

'This is way earlier than I usually prefer to encounter anyone,' she said. 'Don't take it personally.'

'Don't worry about it,' said Trina.

Drinks were pointedly sipped. The sound of Jess nibbling a corner of toast seemed suddenly cacophonous.

'So,' said Jess, 'what's the plan?'

Trina looked over at Deepa, posing a silent question that made Jess feel childishly wounded.

'She's cool,' said Deepa. Then, to Jess: 'Bennington's only the tip of the iceberg, is what we're now thinking,' said Deepa.

'Green?' said Jess.

'What makes you say that?' said Trina sharply.

'I know you work there. I know something's going on there.' She shrugged. 'So I'm guessing.'

'What do you know about what's going on there?' said Deepa.

'Nothing,' said Jess, who had spent her pre-sleep hours making connections in her mind that now, by daylight, seemed tantalisingly out of reach. 'But there's a guy hanging out in Nodem, maybe even living there. He says he works or worked at Green. He keeps talking about . . . Fields?'

Again, Jess noted, the little glance between Deepa and Trina.

'*The* Field,' said Deepa.

'That's it,' said Jess. 'What is it?'

'We don't know,' said Deepa. 'We just know that we're not sup-posed to know. Which, of course, makes me very keen to know. Trina: any idea who this guy in Nodem might be?'

'Norbiton,' said Trina. 'It must be. He got sunsetted after babbling about The Field.' She shook her head. 'He'll be no use to anyone.'

'Do you think Bennington and this Field thing are connected?' said Jess.

'Maybe,' said Deepa. 'Maybe not.'

'And The Griefers?' said Jess.

'I'm hoping we'll know more when we get onto our other little plan,' said Deepa.

'Other plan?' said Trina.

'Little something we've been working on,' said Deepa. 'Kind of a test.'

Trina didn't ask more, and Jess was glad of the rebalance this occasioned. Maybe it was a side effect of her non-argument with Robert, but her sensitivity to exclusion felt uncomfortably heightened.

'We could spend all morning bringing each other up to speed,' Trina said.

'Agreed,' said Jess, toughing out the dismissal this statement seemed to imply. 'Tell me the Bennington plan.'

'I may have dirt on Bennington,' said Trina, a little too slowly, drawing the words out, as if uncertain Jess would understand or still unsure that Jess could be trusted.

'OK,' said Jess.

'He sends dick pics,' said Trina.

'That's an understatement,' said Deepa. 'These are dick pics with a Hollywood budget and an auteur director.'

Jess was looking between them, undecided as to whether or not she should laugh. Deepa and Trina remained deadpan and so she decided to follow suit.

'I'm trying to picture it,' she said, 'but . . .'

Trina pushed her phone over. Jess picked it up, rotated it a few times to find the best aspect ratio.

'Is that . . . What is that? A dinner service? And then in the middle . . . Wait, his dick can't be—'

'He makes miniature objects,' said Trina. 'He talked about them on the TV profile. The plate, the cutlery, the gravy boat, the ring of parsley. It's all miniaturised.'

'Oh my God,' said Jess.

'Right?' said Deepa.

'Just when you think you've truly explored the outer limits of fragile masculinity, something comes along that just—'

'Recalibrates your whole sense of scale?' said Deepa.

'Did he send this to you?' said Jess to Trina. 'I mean, surely he's not that stupid?'

'Sadly not,' said Trina.

'And therein lies the problem,' said Deepa.

'He sent them to my friend Kasia,' said Trina. 'She's shown them to me a few times but never said who they were from. Then, when I saw him banging on about his handicrafts on the telly last night, I put it all together.'

'You don't want to throw her under the bus,' said Jess.

'Right. Because why should I?'

'You shouldn't,' said Jess. 'You shouldn't have to.'

'So I had to go to the source,' said Deepa. 'Given this guy's password is *password*, it took like ten minutes to grab the lot.'

'And you want to leak them,' said Jess.

'But with a plausible explanation as to where they came from,' said Deepa. 'Which, luckily, we kind of have.'

'The Griefers,' said Jess.

'Bingo,' said Deepa. 'It's perfect. The whole town's braced for some kind of leak. It's the perfect alibi. Problem is: platform. We can't get the pics onto The Griefer website. Even if we use their submission thing, we have no idea how long it would take. And given that we still don't know who they are or how this all ties together—'

'Why trust them?' said Jess.

'Exactly.'

'You think this is what The Griefers wanted all along?' said Jess. 'Like, not to release anything themselves, but just to create the perfect conditions for everyone else to release everything, with The Griefers conveniently taking the blame on everyone's behalf? Maybe that's what they mean by *we are your face*?'

'Maybe,' said Deepa. 'Maybe it's not about The Griefers themselves at all. Maybe they're not the movement. They're just creating the conditions for a movement.'

Jess nodded. 'Or maybe—'

'Fascinating though this speculation is . . .' said Trina.

'Sorry,' said Jess.

'The problem is, we can't just leak the pics ourselves either,' said Deepa. 'One, because we'd be exposing ourselves, and two, because no-one would see them in time for it to help us.'

Jess shrugged. 'Send them to a newspaper,' she said.

'And say what? Have some pictures of a politician we obtained completely illegally?'

'So, what? You want to—'

'We want to go through someone The Griefers might conceivably reach out to,' said Deepa. 'Someone with a platform. Someone with a degree of intellectual credibility. But someone who can't themselves be compromised.'

'Me?' said Jess.

'Kind of,' said Deepa.

'Oh Christ,' said Jess.

'And she's there,' said Deepa.

'I'm not,' said Trina. 'What are we talking about here? Who are we talking about?'

'Jess contains multitudes,' said Deepa drily.

'That's not exactly an explanation,' said Trina.

'It's a long story,' said Jess. 'Look, Deepa. I see your plan, OK? I do. It's smart. It makes sense. But—'

'Please don't *but* me here, Jess.'

'I just—'

'I know. You don't want to muddy the water. You want to keep Stroud pure for all the other stuff you've got him doing. But come on, Jess. The waters are already muddied. And don't just look at this from the perspective of now. Look at it from the perspective of *hence*. Stroud's getting some attention. After this, he'd be getting like ten times the attention. He'd have *everyone's* ear.'

Jess was shaking her head.

'It's too risky,' she said.

'How is it risky? Jesus, Jess, you couldn't ask for a more obscured trail. All people are going to see are the dick pics. The minute they drop, everyone will be clamouring at *Bennington's* door. And you know something else? That's just looking at it from the point of view of the Bennington situation. What if we do end up with more on The Griefers? What if this Field thing turns out to be something? We'd need someone who could get the information out there who—'

'Already had a track record of getting the information out there,' said Jess.

'Look,' said Deepa, 'I could do the whole appealing-to-conscience thing. I could do the whole *opportunity to really make a difference* speech. I know you're not immune to that stuff. But even if you think of this strictly from your own point of view, it's a good thing. You could take Stroud to a level he'd never have been able to get to without—'

'Without Bennington's dick,' said Jess.

'Exactly,' said Deepa.

Trina's phone beeped with a message.

'That better not be anyone other than your family,' said Deepa sternly.

'It's Mia,' said Trina, a flutter of panic at the edge of her voice. 'Brute Force are at the estate with a load of townspeople.'

'What?'

'Hang on,' said Jess. 'Your family are OK, right? You said they're in a B&B.'

'Yeah,' said Trina. 'Flat's empty. They're getting this off Twitter.'

Deepa reached across the table and pulled her laptop towards her. A rattle of keys, a couple of searches, and she was looking at a grainy livestream, broadcast from someone's phone.

'Jesus Christ,' she said.

Jess and Trina moved their chairs around the table and sat either side of Deepa, the three of them peering closely at the screen. The footage was shaky, the sound distorted. They could make out the jostle of a crowd, the tinny hiss of layered voices punctuated by duelling shouts.

'That's the stairway up to my flat,' said Trina.

Deepa put her arm round Trina.

'They're safe,' she said gently. 'Just remember that.' She looked round at Jess, her eyes hard.

'Jess,' she said.

Jess nodded. 'Alright,' she said. 'Give me the pictures.'

Deepa smiled, patted Jess's leg. As she did so, the hissing din from the laptop's speakers seemed to order itself, the crowd-shout becoming rhythmic, based around a single word.

'What the fuck are they saying?' said Trina.

'Submit,' said Deepa. 'They're chanting *submit*.'

Trina had her hands on her head, as if seeking shelter or attempting to contain what was inside it.

'Where are we with the other thing?' said Deepa.

Jess dug in her pocket for her thumb drive and passed it to Deepa. 'Her name's Jasmine,' she said.

——————

Darkin watched the dial of his timer tick round towards the hour. Outside, he could hear Pete and Tel chatting. Sometimes, one of them had a cigarette and the smoke wafted in through the broken window, sharpening Darkin's own urge and stirring in him the temptation to abandon the discipline of the timer. Checking his fag packet, though, he found that supplies were worryingly low. He was also out of milk and down to his last three or four slices of bread.

'Oi,' he called out to Pete and Tel.

'Yeah?' Pete's head appeared again at the window.

'How about one of you pops down the shops for me?'

'Couldn't do that,' said Pete.

'Why not?'

'Abandoning our post, innit?'

'Yeah,' came Tel's voice. 'What if something happened while one of us was at the shops?'

Darkin decided not to push it. Outside, he heard Pete and Tel muttering about not having signed up to be carers.

'Excuse me.'

The voice outside sounded both tentative and angry, as if not yet sure how concerned or annoyed to be. It came from a short distance along the walkway. It was a man's voice, briefly unrecognisable, then reassuringly familiar.

'Help you, mate?' That was Tel – calmer, Darkin thought, than the person he was addressing.

'I'm just here to see my friend.'

'Hey,' Darkin called. 'Hey, Geoff.'

'Darkin? Are you in there?'

Darkin pulled himself up from the sofa and made his way to the window.

'It's alright,' he started to say. 'I—'

Outside, he heard Tel say, 'He's busy.'

'Easy, Tel,' said Pete.

'Geoff?' said Darkin, now at the window and craning his neck to see along the walkway.

'If Darkin lets me know he's fine, then I'll be on my way,' Geoff was saying. 'But I don't think it's up to you to—'

'Not going to tell you again,' said Tel.

'Take it easy, Tel,' said Pete. 'Remember what we talked about.'

'Get your . . . Get off me,' said Geoff, sounding frightened now.

'Easy,' said Pete. 'Easy now.'

Darkin had managed to angle himself across the sink so as to peer through the hole in the window. Tel had Geoff by the scruff of the collar. Pete was attempting to get between them.

'It's OK,' said Darkin. 'He's—'

'Don't fuck with me, pal,' said Tel.

'Tel,' said Pete. 'Let's calm this down, OK?' Then, to Geoff, 'He's on a hair trigger, mate. If I were you I'd—'

Geoff caught sight of Darkin through the window and twisted

awkwardly in Tel's grip to try and get to him.

'Hey,' Geoff said. 'Darkin. What's going on? Why are these blokes—'

'Let him go,' said Darkin.

Geoff made a sudden, forceful push towards Darkin, stretching his hand past Tel's shoulder, knocking Tel slightly off balance as he did so. Tel's stance shifted. He dug in with his heels, got a better grip on Geoff's collar, and then dashed the side of his head against the wall. The sound of bone on brick made Darkin's stomach flip. When he tried to shout, his throat caught.

Geoff's legs went out from under him. He hung briefly by his collar, held up by Tel's fist. Then he righted himself and twisted away. Tel, at Pete's insistence, loosened his grip and allowed Geoff to stumble a few steps back.

'You shouldn't have done that, mate,' said Pete. 'You've set him going now.'

Geoff had his hand up to the side of his forehead. A thick rivulet of blood had sprung from the edge of his hairline and was running down towards his eyes.

'Fuck,' said Pete.

'Fucking thugs,' said Geoff, backing unsteadily away. 'I'm calling the . . . Darkin. Darkin? I'm calling the police, OK? Don't worry. Just hold on there and—'

'That's right,' said Tel, 'call the fucking police when we're the ones here to help your mate, you little prick.'

From across the square, the sound of more people could be heard – massed footsteps on one of the stairways.

'Back inside now, mate,' Pete said, turning to Darkin. 'Told you they'd be here, didn't we? Bet you're glad we turned up now, aren't you?'

'Why did you do that?' said Darkin.

'Heat of battle,' said Pete. 'These things happen. He'll be fine.'

'What's that noise?' said Darkin.

'Just like Bennington said,' said Pete. 'Only a matter of time before they got your address and came looking for you.'

'But I haven't done anything,' said Darkin. 'I don't even know—'

'You just sit tight,' said Pete. 'We've got this.'

Darkin backed away towards the sofa but then thought better of sitting down. The only room with a lock was the bathroom.

Whatever the complexities and intricacies and, frankly, even the realities of what was happening, Hugo reminded himself as the car pulled up to the edge of the Larchwood Estate and he took in a pleasing vista of strobing blues and pig-penned protesters, one thing was certain: a full-blown shitshow was in effect. Everything else was just details, all of which could be unpicked or further obscured over time. He had, very successfully, brought chaos. Now he could appear to bring order.

His arrival was anything but impromptu. He and Teddy had sat for a considerable time in the back of the car several streets away monitoring the entire unfolding fracas over social media so as to arrive at the most perfect possible moment: tensions still high, anger not yet drained from the protesters, but the police very much on scene; physical violence and unchecked aggression already definitively in the past.

Watching Teddy load up forum chat, rolling news, and live-streamed social-media footage of the Larchwood on his tablet, Hugo's sense was that things had gone better than he ever could have imagined. This was the reality of seeding chaos: you could initiate, you could trigger, you could marshal key elements with a reasonable degree of control, but all you could really do after that was watch and hope. Hugo had done a lot of hoping in his life. In the main, circumstances had tended to fall short of expectations. Today, the near-impossible had occurred. From the tangle of Hugo's loyalties and obligations, the mess of triangulations in which he could no longer confidently locate himself, a pattern had emerged that even Teddy, with his graphs and diagrams and prediction engines, could not have foreseen. The people of Edmundsbury had taken Hugo's outrage about the genocide woman on one hand, and their unsettled paranoia about The Griefers on the other, and drawn a conclusion that now seemed obvious: that the genocide woman should be the one to submit. Because where was the fairness, someone had pointed out in a particularly emotive Facebook post highlighted by Teddy, in some innocent member of the public exposing themselves to potentially global scrutiny, against their will, despite the fact that their internet behaviour had harmed not a single soul, when all the while, right under everyone's noses, this woman, this extremist, was using the internet in ways no-one could possibly defend? Here, as if confirming Hugo's previous concern that certain forces could never truly be controlled, Ronnie Childs had stepped in. The people of Edmundsbury, he'd said, having created a Facebook group specifically for this discussion, should not only rally at the Larchwood to protect the old man, they should also, while they were there, gently, peacefully, suggest that this woman turn herself in. Even if she refused, he said; even if, with half the town non-violently beating down her door, she still somehow managed to resist, The Griefers, who, Childs reminded everyone, saw everything, would understand what was being said: that the people of Edmundsbury had, democratically, selected someone to submit. Within minutes, perception of both The Griefers and Brute Force had shifted. Before, they had been merely a threat. Now, they could help the people of Edmundsbury purge their town of a radical and unwanted element.

What Childs couldn't possibly have known, of course, flushed with pride though he no doubt must have been at his own political brilliance, was that Hugo had no intention of letting him act on anything like his own reconnaissance, and even less intention of allowing him to gain any hint of localised power. Instead, Hugo regarded Childs as little more than bait. Much as Hugo wished he lived in an England where the plight of an ageing white man and the demonstrable presence of a hostile race vigilante were enough, in themselves, to galvanise the general public, he knew, with regret, that one thing was certain to attract violent protest more certainly than any other: the presence of Brute Force. Already enraged by Hugo's inflammatory TV appearance, he thought, local do-gooders would be on a hair trigger when it came it to the Larchwood. The arrival of Brute Force would stir them into rash, undignified action. And just to be sure they knew Brute Force were there, he'd taken the precaution of tipping them off. Anyone these days, it seemed, could set up an account in a forum or two, alerting the rabid anti-right to the arrival of a few neo-fascist thugs on their doorstep. And so it had proved. Who won or lost, which causes were or were not represented, was irrelevant. All that mattered was that Hugo was able, as he now would be, to use the words he wanted to use: *clash*, *violence*, *unrest*.

And so, perhaps prematurely, Hugo was treating this little excursion into the Larchwood as a victory outing. No, the situation was not entirely wrapped up, and yes, there were still one or two variables that might play out in unwelcome ways, but the signs, as far as Hugo could see, were very good indeed. Now, as what was admittedly a strategic self-fulfilling prophecy came true, the smug liberal media that for so long had treated him as a sort of besuited monkey hammering away at politics and only occasionally making sense through blind chance alone, would be forced to accept that his vision of the future was one that needed to be acknowledged. Moreover, once the dust had settled and it became clear that Hugo had not only concretised the conditions required for his particular brand of politics to be successful, but also both cleared the more stubborn tenants from the Larchwood and established a public perception that would now greatly favour its re-evaluation and ultimate destruction, Jones would be forced into a deferential position from which he would find it markedly more difficult to be a self-satisfied prick – a position Hugo very much intended to exploit.

'OK,' said Hugo as the car eased up to the kerb and he took in the scene, 'I'm seeing an ambulance.'

Teddy didn't look at the ambulance but instead checked his tablet for news of it.

'I'm not seeing anything that would suggest an ambulance,' he said.

'I'm literally looking at the ambulance, Teddy.'

Teddy tapped around. 'Looking at it doesn't tell us anything,' he said.

'It tells us it fucking *exists*,' said Hugo.

'Right. An ambulance exists. I could have told you that without seeing one, no? It's irrelevant. That ambulance could just be there as a matter of protocol. Visual confirmation of its presence is, like, literally useless at this point.'

'Maybe we should briefly speculate,' said Hugo.

Teddy looked up, nodding. 'You're saying: let's quickly explore the possibilities of that ambulance.'

'Very quickly. As in, before I go out there and potentially look like a literal ambulance chaser.'

'Possibility one: it doesn't mean anything. Possibility two: some-one has been hurt.'

'What if that someone is the old man?'

'Basically great. That's the best possibility.'

'What if he's seriously injured?'

'Tragic, but you saw this coming.'

'But if it's the genocide woman?'

'She brought this on herself. It's a lesson.'

'OK. I'm going to get out of the car.'

He opened his car door and stepped smartly out. Exiting cars in public was something, Hugo thought, he was going to have to get used to. This particular exit could have gone better. It took him a couple of undignified shuffles to get fully upright. But still, it wasn't bad, and there would be many more exits from many more cars in far more public settings in the future.

It was exactly the right degree of shitshow. A few press had arrived, at least two with TV cameras. A handful of lefty protesters had been contained behind some police tape and were bleating weakly about fascism. A few yards further down the road, a second cordoned area housed a group of protesters holding signs saying things like *Darkin Is All Of Us*, and *We Are The Darkins Of The World*. Beside them were the rather sheepish-looking *Submit* brigade, who weren't saying anything at all, and who looked, Hugo thought, thoroughly uncomfortable – beset, he assumed, by a post-adrenaline moral hangover. In the middle of these factions were two police vans and an ambulance, their lights still flashing in such a way that Hugo could, he saw, opportunistically position himself in front of the universal visual shorthand for unfolding drama.

'I'm seeing *optimum* disruption here, big guy,' said Teddy, strolling round the car to join Hugo. 'Some damage, some chaos, no actual body bags.'

'Let's not even think about body bags, OK, Teddy?'

'Mr Bennington,' said an enthusiastic young journalist trotting up to the car as Hugo stepped out. 'In what capacity are you—'

'I'm here as a concerned citizen,' said Hugo. 'That's first and foremost. I'm also here as someone who cares about this constituency and cares about the people who live in it. I fully expect to be briefed by the police, at which point I will comment, but as it is—'

'Mr Bennington, what do you say to people who—'

'Like I said, I'm anticipating a briefing by the police. Any comment before that time would be premature.'

'. . . who accuse you of manipulating the situation—'

'No more questions, please,' said Teddy, extending an arm in front of the journo. 'We'll have more for you when we've been briefed.'

Teddy jogged on ahead to prime the police. Playing for time, Hugo slowed his pace and fell back on a tried and trusted tactic: the slow walk while he took it all in. He raised his head as if scenting the air, looked slowly from left to right as if absorbing every detail. He tried, through his facial expressions, to attach the suggestion of an appropriate emotional response according to whatever he appeared to be looking at: dignified respect when his gaze wandered across the police vans; a moved and hopeful gratitude as he met the gaze of some of the self-proclaimed Darkinists; and then a kind of stoic anger mixed with a gentle shake of the head to indicate pity when he took in the small group of anti-fascist protesters. The *Submit* group he passed over without visible response. He had not yet decided what he felt about them, or what he was going to say, if anything, about their cause, and so, for the time being at least, they were effectively not there.

'Fascist!' shouted some oik from amidst the protesters. The outburst seemed to enliven the hitherto slightly sorry-for-themselves group and they started up with a chant – *Oh! No! We won't go! Why don't you go, Hugo?* – which at least, Hugo thought, had the benefit of not being entirely predicated, as these chants tended to be, on either his stupidity or his physical resemblance to maligned fauna.

He felt profoundly uncomfortable. This was the grubby, undignified side of politics. To Hugo, politics was television, it was speeches, it was columns in sympathetic organs. Not slinking uneasily past a bestial, heckling throng. But through his disgust, his resentment, his awkward and shameful sense of inadequacy, even Hugo knew that to betray his revulsion was to telegraph his weakness. The more uncomfortable he felt, the more dismissive he had to appear. The more he faltered, the thicker the mask of disdain he was forced to paste across his straining face.

He found Teddy leaning a little too casually against the side of the police van and chatting amiably to an officer.

'Hey, big guy,' said Teddy, still irritatingly at ease. 'This is Sergeant Gates.'

'Pleasure,' said Hugo, extending his hand. 'Are you in charge?'

'I'm the senior officer, yes.'

'Well, first of all, please accept my thanks and admiration for responding so quickly and controlling the situation so rapidly. You'll be charging this lot, I assume?' Hugo jerked his head with stage-managed disgust towards the anti-fascists.

'What with?'

'I don't know, breaching the peace? Resisting arrest?'

'They were never arrested.'

'Why weren't they arrested?'

'They hadn't done anything wrong.'

'You're telling me that you've got two police cars and an ambulance here because nobody did anything wrong?'

'I didn't say *nobody* did anything wrong. Looks like a couple of those Brute Force boys assaulted someone. Plus a flat has been broken into.'

'Whose flat?'

'The Twitter woman.'

'I see.'

'We've got the Brute Force boys in the back of the van. Meanwhile, that lot over there' – he gestured towards the *Submit* mob – 'helped with the flat break-in, but we can't narrow it down to specific suspects, so we'll probably have to let that go and just take the Brute Force blokes.'

'Right,' said Hugo, who wasn't entirely sure any of that would be quotable to news sources. 'Any news of a tenant by the name of Darkin?'

'He's fine. He'd shut himself in the bathroom for safety, so couldn't be much help as a witness, but he hasn't been hurt.'

'Shut himself in the bathroom?'

'Says he heard the commotion break out and decided to make

himself safe. Seems pretty terrified, poor chap.'

'So he actually didn't see anything at all?'

'No. God knows what the poor old boy thinks happened. He's pretty shaken up.'

'As in, he literally has no idea?'

'I don't think so.'

Hugo considered this.

'I think I'll go and pay him a visit, if that's alright.'

The Sergeant shrugged. 'Nothing to do with us.'

'Thank you, Sergeant,' said Hugo, turning away and motioning for Teddy to follow while he walked towards the estate's central square.

———

Darkin's first act after leaving his bathroom was to light a cigarette. In his haste, he'd locked himself in there without taking his fags with him. As soon as he heard the police shouting through his broken window, he'd shot the bolt on the bathroom door, brought himself awkwardly and painfully to a standing position, and shuffled back through to the lounge, where he'd collapsed into the familiar and reassuring comfort of his sofa and lit up.

Now he was sipping a cup of tea kindly prepared for him by the bobby, contemplating all the sources and subjects of his terror. How long, he wondered, before the mob came back? Suddenly, Downton, for so long the thing he'd feared and loathed beyond all else, seemed the lesser of available evils.

The police officer popped his head round the open door.

'Someone here to see you, if you're up to it.'

'Who?' said Darkin, his fears rearing up, coalescing into a single sensation.

'Hugo Bennington. You know him?'

'From the paper?'

'That's him. Says he'd like to personally make sure you're OK, if that's alright with you?'

Darkin nodded, his anxiety reshaping itself into relief, and then, when the reality of the moment caught up to him, an awkward nervousness. He'd never met anyone well known before.

The police officer stepped aside. Standing behind him, right there on Darkin's own doorstep, was Hugo Bennington. He was slightly smaller than Darkin had imagined him, less intimidating than he managed to appear in his pictures and columns.

'Well, you must be the famous Mr Darkin,' Bennington said, crossing the room. 'What an honour. I'm Hugo Bennington. Don't get up.'

Bennington turned and took in the flat. His lip curled, his nostrils briefly flared. He swallowed once, hard, then mustered an uncertain smile.

Darkin looked at the floor for a moment, ashamed.

'It's usually tidier,' he said. 'And the water's been out.'

'Oh, you should see my place,' said Bennington. 'You live alone?'

Darkin nodded, pointed towards the sofa so that Bennington could sit down.

'Wife's gone,' he said.

'As in dead?' said Bennington.

'They took her away,' said Darkin. 'Then she died.'

'Mine's gone but still alive, sadly,' said Bennington, giving Darkin an awkward wink.

He wandered across the lounge towards the sofa, making a point, Darkin thought, of not studying the coffee table too closely and then, once he was lowering himself onto the sofa, not allowing too much of his body to touch the cushions.

'A smoker, I see,' said Bennington.

'Don't see the point in giving up now,' said Darkin.

'I've never seen the point,' said Bennington, taking a packet from the pocket of his suit jacket, lighting up and inhaling deeply. 'Got to go of something, right?'

It was strange, Darkin thought, locating his still-burning cigarette in the ashtray and returning it to his lips for a long, stabilising haul, seeing a man he'd always imagined as being somehow different or distinct behaving in such familiar ways. He tried to imagine any other politician coming round, chatting and smoking.

Bennington was looking around him, his features now under control, his expression harder to read.

'Been here long?' he said.

'Since they built it.'

'Really?' Bennington shook his head. 'Don't meet many like you any more.'

'Like me?'

'People move around a lot more now, don't they? They don't stay in the same place.'

'I thought about moving,' said Darkin. 'Me and Flo did anyway. But then when it was just me I didn't see the point.'

'Flo's your wife? I mean, was.'

Darkin nodded.

'You must have a lot of memories,' said Bennington.

'Wish I had fewer,' said Darkin. 'You want my advice? When you get to my age, make sure you go gaga. Or better yet: don't get to my age.'

Bennington nodded.

'No kids?' he said.

Darkin shook his head.

'Me neither,' said Bennington. 'A blessing, as far as I'm concerned.'

'Never liked them,' said Darkin. 'Flo was more keen, but . . . it didn't happen.'

'Last thing I need in my life is more people to hate me,' said Bennington. He nodded towards Darkin's window. 'The mob do that?'

'Nah. It was like that already. Been meaning to get it fixed, but—'

'In your own time or not at all, right?'

Darkin smiled. 'I'm a stubborn fucker,' he said.

'You must be,' said Bennington. 'Not many people have been able to hold on here. Must have really dug your heels in.'

'I don't like being pushed around.'

'Me neither,' said Bennington. 'Gets tiring after a while, though, no?'

Darkin thought about getting himself out of bed tomorrow, pulling himself upright, possibly falling, trying again. He thought about Geoff, wondering if he'd ever be back, picturing the supplies in the kitchen dwindling to nothing in Geoff's absence. Then he thought about the mob: if and when they'd be back, whether Downton would beat them to the punch. How many days after tomorrow, he thought, would he still be wondering all the same things?

'Gets you down after a bit,' he said.

'Makes me sick,' said Bennington. 'People like you, the way you're treated.'

'Wait until you're someone like me yourself,' said Darkin. 'It'll make you even sicker.'

Bennington shook his head. 'A man like you,' he said, 'driven out of your home.'

Darkin frowned. 'I'm still here.'

'Are you?' said Bennington.

Darkin wasn't sure what he was supposed to say to this.

'I mean, don't get me wrong,' said Bennington. 'I hate it. I hate these bastards. Coming round here, making old men afraid, forcing you out. I mean it. I want you to know how angry I am.'

'But they've gone,' said Darkin, a little weakly, barely believing it himself.

'Gone?' said Bennington. 'They're still down there, mate, chanting away. The police have got them cordoned off but how long's that going to last? I mean, OK, they're behaving themselves now, but you think they'll keep that up when the police are gone? When there's no-one else to stop them? Those two chaps from earlier were literally the only people on your side, and the police have taken them away.'

'I won't bother anyone though,' said Darkin. 'I'm not in their way.'

'Oh, but you are,' said Bennington. 'We all are.'

Darkin thought about this. It was something he'd always known, but only in an incidental way. Maybe he'd always just thought he'd be gone before they got to him.

'I mean, I wish I could just snap my fingers and reverse everything,' said Bennington. 'But we've got to keep you safe, chap.'

'But Downton . . .' Darkin began.

'Never mind Downton,' said Hugo. 'What can they do except work within the ridiculous system we already have? It's not their fault what's happening to housing. It's not their fault we're running out of space. If anything, they're trying to do something about it. And I tell you, they've been very helpful in this situation.'

Darkin was thinking about Jones: the walking stick placed just out of reach, the thinly veiled threats.

'Helpful?' he said.

'Well, ordinarily, getting you out of here would take months of bureaucracy. You know what these people are like. But I had a chat with them as soon as I heard what was happening. I said: look, this guy's vulnerable. He's unsafe. He's been targeted by a radical faction, by *militants*. I said: we need to do something to help this chap or it's going to be on all of our consciences. Anyway, I must have touched a nerve, because you know what? They agreed. They've found you a place already. A safe place. One of theirs. And they said you can do a straight swap. Because you own this place, don't you? So rather than having to wait for the sale to go through while you sit here with a broken window and no water and, you know, a whole horde of thugs outside, you can just move into this new place and sort everything out afterwards.'

'Always just figured I'd die here,' said Darkin.

'I understand that,' said Bennington. 'And there's probably a part of you that thinks: what difference does it make if I die of natural causes or if some, excuse my language, but some fucking radical gets in here and kills me? And you know what? Man to man, me to you, I'd agree with you. But you know what else I think? Why give the bastards the satisfaction? Why let them win? You could be tucked up in a lovely, secure place, with other people like you, comfortable, warm, all of that. Last laugh's all yours, right?'

Darkin managed a smile.

'Look,' Bennington said after a suitable pause, 'I've got to dash, sadly. No rest for the wicked, eh? But someone from Downton will be round very soon and they'll talk you through the whole move. I've said to them: look, he's not to spend another night in this place on his own, right? I'm making it my personal business to make sure you're safe. So here's my card.' He took a crisp white business card from his pocket and slid it across the coffee table towards Darkin – *Hugo Bennington, England Always*. 'I want you to call me if there's any problem at all. I mean, literally anything. I've got you covered.'

He stood up and held out his hand.

'Thank you,' said Darkin. 'You've . . . I mean, no-one else has—'

'I know,' said Bennington. 'Take care of yourself, chap. I'll come and see you in your new place. No, no. Don't get up. I'll see myself out.'

He gave a little wave and let himself out the front door, leaving Darkin alone on the sofa, sensation still not fully returned to his legs, the adrenaline still lingering in his system after hearing all that racket and clamour on the stairway and then sitting in his bathroom, braced for the crash of his front door, the heavy thump of someone shouldering their way into the last little room he could honestly call his own. He leaned forward and lit another cigarette, no longer caring how long it had been since the last one. He remembered them taking Flo, when she'd got too bad to know what was going on or who anyone was, saying it was *for her safety*. He remembered squaring up to the social worker, the police officer, the doctor, saying, *I'm not ready, I'm not ready to give up on her yet,* and them saying, *You tried your best, anyone can see you tried your best.* He remembered the shame he'd felt at having to let her go, at being cuffed and led outside, still shouting, defeated. Then he remembered visiting her in the home, helpless as he watched her fade and die.

They could have this place if they wanted it so badly, he thought. He'd be alright. He'd be looked after. Let the next generation worry about what to do. He was done.

A knock sounded at the door. A voice he recognised, calling his name. Jones, he thought, the man from Downton. *Here to help.* He ground out his cigarette in the ashtray and reached for his stick.

The kitchen timer went off, alerting him to what he already knew: that everything was out of order, cruelly reversed and unbalanced, the alarms sounding only to confirm it was all already over.

———

The work of sustaining the fantasy that he'd helped Darkin, or, if he hadn't, that he'd at least acted out of some sense of greater good, began as soon as Hugo closed Darkin's front door behind him, and continued a few seconds later when he passed Jones on the stairway and acknowledged him with only the faintest wink. After that, the work of sustainment was matched by the effort of suppression – the arduous tamping down of doubts, fears, regret, that would characterise much of Hugo's later life. In the years that followed, his conscience would see-saw, but his resentment would remain at a constant pitch. His meeting with Darkin was not, as he'd envisaged, the moment his political career evolved into the phenomenon he'd always imagined it to be. Instead, it was the moment that career ended, his last truly political act.

Having passed Jones silently on the stairs, Hugo found Teddy waiting for him at the bottom of the stairwell, not, as he usually was, tapping around on his tablet and giving off an air of contented distraction, but instead standing unusually still, looking right at Hugo.

'Job done?' he said.

'Done,' said Hugo. 'Jones is—'

'I know,' said Teddy. 'I just checked in with him.'

'You . . . Well, great. Everything's sorted then. I'll just go and give the press a bit of a speech, and then we can—'

Hugo made to step past Teddy towards the entrance to the Larchwood, where he'd left the press and the demonstrators and where he'd imagined himself delivering his defining address. Teddy, though, deploying the corralling gesture he so often used when telling journalists there would be no more questions, held his arm across Hugo's path.

'Slight change of plan, big guy,' he said.

'But what about—'

'Situation's very fluid,' said Teddy.

'Fluid? Teddy, we've knocked this out of the fucking park. We've killed not just two birds but basically a whole *flock* with, OK, maybe not *one* stone as such, but with *very few stones*, Teddy. I mean, we're practically home and dry here.'

'Let's chat in the car,' said Teddy, steering Hugo down a side alley, away from a future Hugo had been imagining for a very long time.

'Is it bad news?' said Hugo. 'What is it?'

'Good news and bad news,' said Teddy, still leading Hugo quite firmly to the end of the alley, which opened out onto a backstreet on which a car – not *the* car, Hugo noted, but *a* car: an unremarkable people carrier – was waiting with its engine running. Teddy opened the door for Hugo, ushered him inside, then climbed in behind him and slid it shut.

'I'll give you the good news first,' he said.

'I would have chosen the bad news first,' said Hugo. 'That way, the good news will sort of put a positive spin back on the—'

'The way this is going to play out, it's more like after the bad news there is no more news.' said Teddy.

'I see,' said Hugo, suddenly unable to distinguish between the sensation of the car pulling away and the weightless, floating unease in his stomach and bowels.

'The good news is that the by-election date has just been set,' said Teddy.

'Oh my God,' said Hugo.

'Yup. Turns out all this fracas with The Griefers and the Larchwood and Twitter and what have you was even more of a godsend than we thought. Trevor Barnaby's released a statement announcing his retirement. He says he no longer feels qualified or equipped to deal with Edmundsbury's changing status as a *modern town*.'

'Bloody hell,' said Hugo, momentarily forgetting that subsequent bad news was promised. 'Teddy, this is amazing. This is more than we ever could have . . . I mean, did you maybe think this might happen? You know, when we were planning . . .'

'I hoped things might get a bit much for Barnaby, yeah,' said Teddy.

'God,' said Hugo. 'Imagine being so bamboozled by your own constituency that you just . . . chucked it all in. You know, this is so perfect for us, Teddy. We've gone on and on about how the political establishment are out of touch, how they're not equipped to deal with what's happening, and now he's basically admitted it. We need to pounce on this. I mean, what's our next move? I need to confirm that I'll be running, of course.'

'Well . . .' said Teddy.

And there it was, thought Hugo: the bad news, delivered in a single, hesitant word.

'Fuck you,' said Hugo immediately. 'Try it. Just fucking try it, Teddy, you scheming *shit*.'

Teddy held up his hands. 'This isn't a power play, Hugo.'

'No? Then what the fuck is going on? Is this some bullshit that

Alan's pulling? Because if he thinks he can nail this constituency without me . . .'

Teddy fired up the screen on his tablet and turned it so that Hugo could see it. The moment he looked, Hugo experienced a sudden and seemingly permanent exsanguination.

'Is this your dick?' said Teddy, pointing to the screen of his tablet, on which was displayed a photograph of Hugo's penis peeking out from a clearly shrunken bookshelf of Penguin classics.

Hugo said nothing, merely stared dumbly at what was, undeniably, his own image.

'Is this your dick?' said Teddy, scrolling down to reveal a picture of Hugo's penis reclining across a computer keyboard the length of which it somehow exactly matched.

'Teddy—'

'Is *this* your dick?' said Teddy, continuing his apparently infinite scroll and pulling up an image of Hugo's penis as the centrepiece of a traditional, though miniaturised, roast dinner.

'Where did you get these, Teddy? Because if you're blackmailing me, let me tell you—'

'Hugo, I'm getting these from the *web*. These are *out there*, big guy. They're out there all over the place. Your dick is trending on Twitter. I've just done a resonance graph of recent events in Edmundsbury and your dick is so big you can't even see anything else that has happened. You want to see a heat map?' He tapped away on his tablet again and turned it back around to show a map of the British Isles rendered entirely in red. 'Areas where people are not talking about your dick are shown in green.'

'But there's no . . . Oh.'

'Yeah. Oh.'

'I don't understand how—'

'Is your password still *password*?'

'I was literally about to change it. I just didn't have—'

'And did we or did we not, Hugo, I think more than once, but certainly at least once, have a *very clear* conversation about The Griefers, and what they were threatening to—'

'Wait, is that who's behind this? That bunch of masked fucking—'

'Apparently. Them and a columnist called Byron Stroud, who seems to have a hotline to their intel, by which I mean your dick.'

'Right,' said Hugo, steeling himself. 'OK, this is embarrassing. Right? But like you always say, there's no such thing as bad publicity. At least people are talking about me. We can *spin* this, Teddy, like we always do. I've been a victim, *a victim* of this . . . I don't know what it is but let's say campaign. Let's say *witch hunt*. And yes, it may be embarrassing, but this is my chance to stand up for—'

Teddy held up his hands. 'I thought exactly that,' he said. 'And if this was just, you know, a bunch of hackers pulling some dick pics off your hard drive, we might have been able to go down that road. But this is no longer about that.'

'What's it about?'

'Well, since this Byron Stroud guy went live online with the exclusive, other people, *other women*, have come forward.'

'What other women?'

'Women saying you've been doing this for years, sending them stuff, and they've never said anything because they were worried about—'

'What fucking women?'

'Hugo, after your BBC profile, did you send a picture of your dick to Vivian Ross?'

'Oh fuck me.'

'Because tell me you didn't and I'll go out there and bat for you, Hugo.'

'I . . . She was such a bitch in that interview. I mean, you watched that interview, Teddy. She was a *cunt* in that interview. I honestly think, if we put it to the public, you know, like a poll, most people would agree that she was a fucking cunt in that interview, and that she deserved—'

'Was the picture an effigy of her detached head impaled on your penis?'

'It's a *joke*. It's a fucking *joke*, for fuck's . . . Look, if I had *actually* impaled her head on my cock, which, I might add, I very much wanted to do, then I would see your point, but, Jesus Christ, we're talking about a picture here.'

'She's charging you with indecency.'

'She's . . . What? How's that even a crime?'

'And threatening behaviour.'

'How did I threaten her? This is insane, Teddy. This is totally insane.'

'Sure is, big guy.'

Hugo held out his hand for the tablet.

'Give me that.'

'You really want to look?'

'Give it to me.'

Teddy handed it over. Hugo scrolled through the images. It was, he found, a comprehensive overview of his work. He tapped on the address bar and googled himself. In a final act of ironic efficiency, no doubt as a result of conflating *Hugo Bennington miniature models* and *Hugo Bennington dick*, Google's top suggestion was now *Hugo Bennington miniature dick*.

How maddening, he thought, to know that this, of all the possibilities, would be his undoing. It was, in many ways, his ultimate fantasy: his dick writ large, mapped over England's topography. He'd always feared the slow fade from public attention. Instead, he'd been undone by irrelevance's opposite. He'd gone *too* public. He'd become an attention supernova.

He sank back into the car seat and tugged at his tie. He desperately needed a smoke but couldn't face the inevitable battle that smoking in the car would entail. This age of fucking *sensitivity*, he thought. What was he supposed to do – castrate himself? When he met a woman he fancied, he fantasised about shoving his dick in her face. When he met a woman he loathed, he also fantasised about shoving his dick in her face. Was that no longer normal? Was that something for which he was supposed to *apologise*?

This, he thought, was the society he lived in: a society where a decent, upstanding man could at any moment be lined up in front of what was effectively an internet firing squad and summarily executed for the simple crime of doing what he'd always done: sowing fear; terrifying the cosseted, preening, effete, and ultimately unrecognisable excuse for a nation England had ultimately become. Because dear God if there was one thing Hugo had learned through all the years he'd spent banging on about how much he loved England, it was how much he hated England: its hordes of immigrants; its filthy street markets of foreign tat that babbled with every language except the one Hugo himself spoke; its prancing, marrying queers; its blaring, feral, feminist bitches; its querulous, faggy politicians with their gelled hair and flashy soundbites – *that*, he thought, *that* was the platform on which he should have stood: not England Always but England Eroded, England Besmeared.

'Alright,' he said, 'I can see a way out of this.'

Teddy shaped his face into the first expression of sympathy Hugo had ever seen him attempt.

'That's . . . That's awesome, Hugo. I mean, don't let the bastards grind you down, right? But . . . we've been having a bit of a chat—'

'Who's we?'

'Me and a few people.'

'What people?'

'Well, people in the party. A few of Alan's people. Alan.'

'Alan? What's he chatting to you for? He should be chatting to *me*.'

'Oh, he's chatting to you in spirit, Hugo. Like, big time. He wants that to be really clear.'

'What do you mean in spirit? Is he using a fucking Ouija board?'

'I mean, you know, spiritually he is with you, even if—'

'Physically he's not with me at all.'

'Physically or, more relevantly, publicly.'

'Fine,' said Hugo. 'Fine. I get it. He wants to distance himself. I understand. If he wants me to go out there and—'

'He doesn't, big guy.'

'He doesn't what?'

'He doesn't want you to go out there.'

'OK, I mean, that's probably wise in the circumstances. Maybe just release a statement and—'

'He doesn't want you to release a statement. In fact, he's actually pretty directly instructing you not to release a statement of any kind.'

'What, and just let this whole bloody scandal—'

'Just let him handle it.'

'Let him—'

'Let him handle you, basically.'

'Handle me.'

'Fire you.'

'Fire me.'

'Basically, yeah.'

'Fire *me*.'

'Sorry, big guy.'

'So because I sent a few pictures of my dick to a few fucking—'

'Well, that's a big part of it.'

'What's the other part?'

'The other part is really about moving forward.'

'Moving forward to *where*, Teddy? We can't just keep saying things like moving fucking forward if we never—'

'It's a very fluid picture.'

'How can a picture be fluid? The whole point of a picture is that—'

'It's dynamic, big guy.'

'What's dynamic?'

'You've got us this far, and that will be very clearly noted.'

'Noted? And what far? How far? Where are we?'

'We're entering the next phase.'

'What is the fucking next phase, Teddy?'

'It's really not something you need to—'

'Look, if you and Alan think you can edge me out without so much as a—'

'To be honest, it doesn't have an awful lot to do with us.'

'Excuse me?'

'It's not really a decision that's being taken at that level.'

'There is no other level, Teddy. That's all the levels. You think England Always is some kind of global syndicate with—'

'Not England Always, no.'

'Not . . . Oh fuck me. You're kidding.'

'They want to make it very clear that this will in no way affect your stock options, Hugo.'

'*They.* They being . . . *Downton*? Downton now get to decide—'

'Well, between Downton and Green—'

'Where do Green come into this? Since when do we . . . Please tell me this isn't all about the estate, Teddy. Because I have *handled* the estate. That situation has been completely dealt with. The mad genocide woman is gone. That old codger is about to be gone. Downton should be kissing my arse. I *solved* that estate for them, and now—'

'Now you're kind of too closely linked to it.'

'Too—'

'Like, people kind of associate you with the whole thing. It's making Green a bit edgy.'

'How do Green figure in this?'

'Green are central to Downton's plans, Hugo. Without Green, there's no vision. It's just . . . an estate, basically. And on top of that, you know how central Green are to Edmundsbury. They basically re-infrastructured the whole town. Look, you've nailed it. You've locked this town down. Between the estate stuff and the Twitter thing, you've swung it big time. That's what I mean about getting us so far. But are you going to get us *all the way*, Hugo? Are you going to be able to work with Green and Downton on building *the future*? No offence, big guy, OK? But your brand isn't really future. It's past. We needed to lock down the past. But now we've done that and we need to lock down the future. You don't go out there and offer to govern the world as it is. You *define* the world you want to control.'

'But I'm the one with all the traction, Teddy. That's what you're forgetting. You think people in Edmundsbury are excited about England Always? They're excited about *me*. I'm the local boy. I'm the face they know. I'm the guy that has been here for them, personally, through—'

'That's not entirely true, big man.'

'What? *Of course* it's fucking—'

'The Griefers have queered the pitch. People's fears are changing. They're looking to different people to assuage those fears.'

'Christ,' said Hugo. 'You utter, utter scheming shit. You don't seriously think that *you're* the person they . . . I mean, what, you and your little techno-cult? Your little fucking geek club? You can't make a political movement out of life-hacks, Teddy, OK? It's all very well going on about thinking in or outside the box to a roomful of techno-freaks but that is not going to translate to a national vision of—'

'The efficiency movement is the fastest growing movement in the country.'

'The *efficiency movement*? Since when did it become a *movement*? What are you, like Occupy or something? What are you going to occupy? Desk chairs?'

'People want an efficient England, Hugo. That's what they really want. They don't want a load of ideology. They don't want to get wrapped up in party politics. They want a country that runs smoothly. We can help with that. Green can help with that. Downton can help with that. You know what's always held the efficiency movement back? Its image. People think it doesn't respect the past.

They think we're slash and burn. It frightens them. But now, thanks to you, they look at me and go, hey, this is a guy who can fix the future but who we totally trust not to completely trash the past. Meanwhile, what's the biggest criticism people always level at England Always, at you, at Alan? That you're *stuck* in the past. That you can't even *see* the future, let alone deal with it. So . . .' Teddy brought his hands together, fingers gradually interlacing.

'How in the name of *Christ* does that in any way coincide with any of the issues England Always have been campaigning about? How is that going to strengthen cultural identity? How is that going to bring down immigration? How is that going to manage the spread of militant Islam? How is that, basically, Teddy, going to do *any of the fucking things people want us to do*?'

'Oh, it's going to do those things, big guy. It's going to do those things like no other political party has ever done those things before.'

'Bullshit.'

'What's the best argument for curbing immigration? Efficiency. The less immigration we have to manage, the more time and money we'll have to manage the things that really matter. What's the best argument for making sure everyone in England speaks the same language? Efficiency. Because if everyone speaks the same language, we won't have to waste time dealing with people who don't understand what's going on. What's the best argument for controlling the spread of radical ideologies that run counter to basic English values? *Efficiency.* Because if we allow militant ideologies to spread, then the country will collapse into anarchy. *No-one wants anarchy*, Hugo. No-one wants chaos. They want consistency. They want a safe, predictable, efficient country that runs like a well-oiled machine. That's what they want, Hugo, and *that's what we can give them*, and now we can give it to them without taking away all the stuff they love about the past.'

Hugo leaned forward, placed his elbows on his knees, and clamped his palms to his temples. He was assuming the brace position, he thought, in preparation for his inevitable crash landing into a world he neither recognised nor wanted.

'How long have you been working with Downton?' he said.

'I'm sorry?' said Teddy.

'You'd already briefed Jones. All you needed was for me to deal with the old guy and then you could step in. How long did you have that cooked up with Downton?'

'As I think Jones told you,' said Teddy, 'Downton are very fluid in terms of their working relationships. They have a lot of—'

'And Green?'

'I've always been popular at Green, Hugo. And now that they're starting to look at political consultancy—'

'At what?'

'We've been doing some amazing things with the data from your campaign, big guy. I mean, really groundbreaking. I honestly think that when we start mapping the info I've collected with the stuff Green have captured from the . . . from their other projects, we can . . . well, not just change politics but change everything.'

'People don't want change,' said Hugo. 'You said so yourself. They want the status quo. They want to vote for people who promise to protect them against change.'

'We won't be offering *change*, as such,' said Teddy. 'We'll be changing the way sameness is presented.'

Hugo sat back in his seat and eyeballed Teddy.

'You know who I think would be interested to hear all this?' he said. 'Robert Townsend, that's who. Lot of traction he's been getting on this estate thing, Teddy. Imagine if he were to find out the whole story. Not all at once, of course. Bit by bit. From an anonymous source. Maybe one of these Griefer people, for example. That would be interesting, wouldn't it? Just imagine if one of these Griefer people started dribbling out info to Robert fucking Townsend. Pretty uncomfortable all round, don't you think?'

'That's not going to happen, big guy.'

'Really? Tell you what, Teddy. Why don't you get Jones on the phone and I'll have a little chat with him about what I know, and who else might find out what I know, and the position I'm in as a *very popular*, I mean, really *very popular indeed* columnist, to make people aware of—'

'Have you spoken to *The Record* recently, Hugo?'

'No. Why?'

'Lot of changes at *The Record*. Lot of modernising. You know they've been losing money, I take it? Without a huge new advertising client, they'd have been in all sorts of trouble. I mean, luckily that client has in fact been found, but, you know. Changes will need to be made.'

'What client?'

Teddy smiled at Hugo.

'Jesus Christ,' said Hugo. 'Downton.'

'Going to be difficult to get much editorial agreement on anything that might spook the money men,' said Teddy.

'But that doesn't stop me going to—'

'Robert Townsend? Well, no. But I think you'd better be quick. My sense is that the particular website he works for has something of an uncertain future.'

'You bunch of shits,' said Hugo flatly. 'You bunch of tech-freakazoid, money-grabbing, self-satisfied *shits*.'

It felt hopeless, he realised. He was reduced – *they* had reduced him – to pointless, impotent insults. Without a mouthpiece, without a platform, he was just another ranter, another skin-sack full of opinions, the man in the pub who no one in the pub would vote for.

'Well, hurrah for progress,' he said, turning away from Teddy and looking out of the window as Edmundsbury, a town still languishing in ignorance about its own rapid slide into an unwanted future, wheeled drably past the car window.

'You want my advice?' said Teddy.

'No.'

'Ride this out, big guy. Just ride it out. Few years, you'll be back.'

'Fuck you.'

'Everybody loves the redemption narrative, Hugo. You do the public apology. You do the rehabilitation. You do the moving memoir. You go on some kind of health kick, maybe get into yoga. You come back refreshed and forgiven.'

'Maybe,' said Hugo. 'But come back to *what*, exactly? I mean, do you even have any idea what you're doing? What things will look like when you're done?'

'Hell no,' said Teddy boisterously, bouncing his translucent footsheaths on the floor of the car, a huge and dismayingly infantile grin breaking across his features as he reached into his bag and pulled out a thermos of Fibuh, which he poured enthusiastically into his face with a carefully and ostentatiously flexed arm before drawing the back of his hand across his lips and smearing his mouth with dribbling Day-Glo fluid. 'That's why this is so much *fun*!'

———————

Power, Robert thought to himself, standing in his kitchen, sipping coffee, had taken new, almost unrecognisable forms. Once, the measure of a man's reach had been dependent on his presence, his access, his ability to be where others couldn't go. Now, the ultimate demonstration of influence was the degree to which you didn't need to go anywhere at all. There were no press buses, no thrumming nerve centres of media activity. Real power looked like this: a man stood in his kitchen in his socks, commanding outcomes from a place of seclusion.

He'd attempted, briefly and half-heartedly, to follow events on the estate, but he'd felt, at this remove, as if knowledge of what was happening was simply passing through or washing over him, arriving and leaving with no discernible cognitive or emotional imprint. Such minor scuffles, he thought, were for local hacks – pressured men in crumpled clothes who needed the illusion of an event as a bulwark against their own irrelevance. It was old-world stuff, a dead pursuit. Anyone could *report*. The world needed people who could *interpret*.

The remote and nebulous events at the Larchwood were rendered all the fainter by the immediacy and pace of Robert's online life. The response to his death threats had been reassuringly strong. Within an hour, Robert's tweet publicising his own plight had received over a thousand retweets. His follower count had begun to tick steadily upwards. Noted public intellectuals like DeCoverley and Ziegler had shared the threats on their own accounts, expressing their solidarity. Lionel Groves had used the occasion of Robert being threatened as a springboard for a series of tweets about kindness and humanity. Rogue Statement had messaged Robert to say that they would be doing a piece on how the hostile response met by liberal men who dared to question the orthodoxy of identity politics was itself a new and insidious form of fascism. *The Command Line* embedded Robert's tweeted screenshots of the death threats on their homepage along with a statement making it clear that they stood in full support of any *Command Line* writer subjected to this kind of abuse simply for, as they put it, *speaking out*. Silas, from his own personal Twitter account, called Robert one of the bravest men he knew. The hashtag *#solidaritywithRobert* had quickly gained traction. That the death threats were manufactured no longer mattered. They were out there – observed, discussed, commented upon – and so they were real.

Yet the question of what was happening with Julia Benjamin still bothered him. How much better his day would be, he thought, if as well as feeling confident, as he now did, of the widespread support and admiration he commanded online, he could be sure of the widespread condemnation and hostility attracted by Julia Benjamin.

Naturally, he'd already checked her website. Some small part of him had been hoping for a 404 error, some obvious and graphic hack. To his disappointment, though, nothing had visibly happened. Not only was her website still there, in all its infuriating glory, but it had apparently gathered something of a community around it. The unthinking, shallow solidarity appalled him.

His phone buzzed with an unknown number. He thumbed the screen to answer.

'Robert Townsend?'

The voice was mechanised, augmented. A prickling chill launched itself from the base of Robert's spine to his scalp.

'Yes?' he said tentatively.

'We've been following your situation,' said the voice. 'We're allies.'

This, Robert thought, was what the power he'd just been imagining sounded like: the grainy, technologically disembodied voice of a man alone in a room, watching.

'You've made enemies,' said the voice.

'So it seems,' said Robert, thrilling a little at the gravity of the statement.

'Yesterday, we received an anonymous tip-off,' the voice continued, 'about someone called Julia Benjamin.'

Now Robert realised who he was speaking to: the women-haters he'd set on Julia Benjamin. They clearly had no idea the tip-off had come from him. The word *allies* echoed icily in his head.

'I see,' he said. He was reluctant to say anything, hesitant to commit. So long as he only listened, he thought, he could never be said to be complicit.

'We went to work on her.'

'And?'

'And there's no *her* there.'

'I don't think I quite—'

'No traces. No personal data. All her activity is routed.'

'You mean, she's—'

'Usually with these bitches we can find things. Personal things. Addresses. Phone numbers. We got nothing.'

'Are you telling me she's—'

'I'm telling you she's not what she appears.'

'I see.'

'I'm telling you she's clever.'

A faint sense of dread was gently stroking the hairs on the back of Robert's neck. *How* clever? he wondered.

'Are you saying—'

'I'm saying my guys tried everything. Worked all night. These are smart guys. Experienced guys.'

'But you got nowhere?'

'We got nowhere. That's never happened before.'

'I see.'

'And so we had to ask ourselves: what kind of cunt are we dealing with here?'

'That's a question I've been asking myself.'

'And you know what we think?'

'What do you think?'

'We don't think she's a woman at all.'

Deep inside Robert's psyche, an idea found its tessellating partner with a click he could not so much hear as feel, like vertebrae massaged into alignment.

'Just thought we'd let you know.'

'Thank you,' said Robert.

'Stay safe, brother.'

The line went dead.

Robert placed his phone carefully on the kitchen table and settled himself into a dining chair to think. It all, he thought immediately, made awful, stomach-turning sense.

Julia Benjamin was a man. Of that, he was now certain. But *which* man? That was the question. Someone he knew? Perhaps, he thought with a lurch, it was DeCoverley. He remembered their coffee together, remembered that it had been DeCoverley who'd suggested it, DeCoverley who'd encouraged him into action. Had DeCoverley set him up? Would DeCoverley now expose everything he'd done, the lengths he'd gone to in order to out-manoeuvre Julia Benjamin? No, Robert thought, it didn't make sense. DeCoverley was a slippery operator, but he was nowhere near cool enough to pull off that kind of deception in person. And besides, anonymity didn't suit DeCoverley. No-one with that kind of ego could tolerate invisibility. The culprit would be someone already comfortable with operating in the shadows, someone with at least a partial track record of obfuscation and evasion, some-one . . . Robert sat forward and banged the table, feeling at once enlivened by his own powers of deduction and nauseated at the depth of the deception . . . Someone *unreachable*. Someone who was *never seen in public*.

He sat back in the chair, aghast and suddenly drained, thinking back over all his nauseating, grovelling messages to Byron Stroud; reiterating in his mind the awful, denuding admission inherent in the message he'd sent about solidarity. All this time, he thought, trying to get Stroud's attention, his approval, and all he'd been doing was humiliating himself before the very person bent on his humiliation.

He took a long, steadying breath. The shock was acute, seis-mic. He typed Byron Stroud's name into his phone's browser and thumbed through the results. What he saw appalled him. Stroud, he saw, had not confined himself to ruining Robert. His targets were multiple, his hunger for exposure and success unquenchable.

Stroud, Robert gathered, had united himself with The Griefers. In doing so, he had tapped The Griefers' access to the town's data and used it to humiliate Hugo Bennington, releasing a chum-stream of dick pics into the shark-pool of the web. Uptake had been frenzied. Bennington was finished.

Robert placed his phone on the table and considered the situa-tion. What was at stake here, he thought, was everything. Principles, privacy, order. The threat was vast, its implications and ramifications unthinkable. Robert was no admirer of Hugo Bennington, but that, now, was irrelevant. This was a time of conflict – a time, almost, of war – and in times of war you had to set aside your differences. You had to take a long, hard look at what was happening and decide who your real enemies were and where your loyalties needed to lie.

Beneath the thrill of honour and duty, though, fear was already at work in Robert's consciousness. Stroud had The Griefers on side now. The damage they were capable of wreaking was incalculable. This, Robert saw, was Stroud's devious trap. He had, through provocation, drawn Robert into courses of action that were difficult to defend. The moment Robert moved against Stroud would be the moment Stroud made all the things Robert had already done known. The email to the men's rights group, the death threat against himself. If Robert took the bait, Stroud and The Griefers would make him known in ways he was barely even comfortable knowing himself.

The solution, Robert realised, was not to take on Stroud or The Griefers directly. Instead, he would need to rely on what was at stake: the principle. Unable to attack, he would have to defend. And because he was defending himself, he thought, in advance, against something that had not yet happened, but which could and surely would happen, one day, soon, not only to him but to everyone like him, he had no choice but to defend the person to whom it had *already* happened.

He went upstairs, Skyped Silas.

'Robert,' said Silas. 'How's the man of the hour?'

'I want to write about Hugo Bennington,' said Robert.

'*Interesting*,' said Silas. 'Your angle being . . . ?'

'Social responsibility. Justice.'

Silas nodded. 'I like it,' he said. 'I like it a lot.'

'I mean, I'm not defending him,' said Robert.

'No. Of course.'

'I'm just saying: what's the greater evil?'

'Completely.'

'I'm saying: where does this end? Witch hunts? Trial by Twitter?'

'You're saying: an Englishman's hard drive is his castle.'

'I'm saying: some things are sacred.'

'This could be incendiary, Rob.'

Briefly, Robert wondered if he should share what he by now not so much wondered as felt he knew for sure: that Julia Benjamin was simply Byron Stroud by another name. The moment he thought about sharing it with Silas, though, was the moment he realised there was nothing to share. If he disclosed what he knew, he'd have to admit the means by which he knew it. That, he thought, could never happen.

'And by the way,' said Silas. 'Congrats on the death threats.'

'Congratulations? Do you mean commiserations?'

'Commiserations? You're nobody until some anonymous coward threatens to kill you, Rob.'

'I thought you said I was nobody until somebody hated me.'

'But it's like, how much do they hate you? You might have people who hate you but if the next guy's got people who hate him enough to try and kill him, you're always going to be playing second fiddle, you get me?'

'I get you, Silas.'

'Look, Rob. I love this, OK? But we need to talk logistics.'

'Logistics?'

'I was going to call you about this later but then you called me first and disrupted the narrative, which I love, by the way, because that's totally what I'm all about, but now I'm readjusting and just dropping the news where it fits. Bombshell is: I'm leaving *The Command Line.*'

'Shit, Silas.'

'I know. Let's just be in the moment with that for a second, really live it out. I mean, I have great memories here. And more importantly, people have great memories of me, so, you know, it's going to be hard on everyone. But I think we'll get through it.'

'Why are you leaving?'

'Well, that's the good part, because I'm not actually leaving against my will, or on any kind of downer or anything. Like, I haven't scandalised myself, which is totally great. I'm leaving because I'm off to pastures new. And by pastures, I obviously mean money and power.'

'That's great, Silas. Congratulations.'

'Gotta say, Rob. Your work was actually a really big part of my getting offered this gig. So, you know, well done me on spotting your work and nurturing your talent, basically.'

'Well done you.'

'I'm kidding, Rob. Jesus Christ. Are you on methadone? Can't you see where I'm going with this?'

'Not totally, no.'

'I'm saying, how about you come with me? Honestly, considering I'm about to offer you a massive fucking pay packet, your inability to read between the lines is kind of disturbing.'

'You mean, move my column elsewhere?'

'I mean, whole new column, Rob. This one's done what it needed to do. You want to write about some estate in some fucking nowhere town the rest of your life? Come on.'

'Where are you—'

'*The Record.*'

Robert, as the words left Silas's lips, just about managed to maintain a face that suggested a degree of positivity. But deep in his core, he felt only the sudden and unceremonious removal of something load-bearing and structurally integral. A hollowness bloomed inside him, and he felt himself collapsing into it.

'Wow,' he managed to say, through a backwash of rising nausea. 'That's . . .'

'I know. No words, right? It's huge. Stratospheric.'

'I thought . . . I mean, not to dampen the whole . . . the whole thing, or anything but . . . I mean, what about the disruptiveness of the web? I thought print was—'

'Right,' said Silas. 'All of that: totally. And that's going to be a big part of my remit at *The Record*. *The Record* wants to modernise, Rob. They want to get with the times. I mean, yeah, they've got a website. But so what? They're talking about reach, amplification. They've got this new investor. They're suddenly flush. They want to change it up. They want people like you and me to help them. And they want to *pay* us, Rob. They want to pay us an absolute shit ton of money.'

'I'll . . . I mean, I'll have to think about this, Silas.'

'Think about it? Are you fucking insane?'

'It's not that I don't appreciate the offer, it's just that . . . *The Record*? I mean, seriously? They're everything I loathe. Literally.'

'Which is weird, because they love you.'

Silas was talking, Robert felt, directly into the cavernous void in Robert's centre, his voice echoing through the inner emptiness, searching for something onto which it could cling.

'Really?' he said.

'Oh God,' said Silas. 'Are you serious? You were all they talked about. Did I think you'd come with me, did I think you'd be interested, what did I think you might write about, blah blah blah.'

'So . . .' said Robert, shuffling forward a little in his seat. 'What exactly is it about my work that you think attracts them?'

'Well, it's direct,' said Silas. 'It's forthright, it's principled, it's fresh. It has a really rapidly growing tribe around it. It's hot, basically. What's not to like?'

'I don't exactly think of *The Record* and think—'

'You know what, though, Rob? *The Record* know that. And they want to change it. Like, that's exactly what's at the heart of their new mission statement. All these old ways of doing things, the old left, the old right, some clapped-out old socialist arguing with some lumbering old Tory. They're over. You think anyone gives a fuck about those distinctions any more? It's all about personal brand integrity. It's about people who aren't afraid to break it down. It's about people who call it like they see it without getting bogged down in all that outmoded identity crap.'

'You sound like Hugo Bennington.'

'You think someone like you makes a whole career off a few columns? You think that's sustainable? You get yourself in *The Record*,
Rob, and I promise you: other things will happen. Big things. I'm
talking TV and radio. I'm talking you as a full-on public intellectual. You've got to follow the money, Rob. That's where all these
other trumped-up little idealists go so wrong. You want to get read?
You want to get noticed? Start hanging with the big bucks.'

'But I mean, if I choose to stay at *The Command Line*—'

'What do you mean stay at *The Command Line*? There's not going
to be a *Command Line*.'

'But—'

'How the fuck can there be a *Command Line* without me? *The
Command Line* is coming with me to *The Record*, Rob. I'm taking
my whole platform to them. That's the point. That's always been
the point. You think our business model was a lifetime of being
the punky outsider? Our business model was punky outsider to
rich-as-fuck insider in under five years. That's the fucking Tao of
Command Line, baby.'

'So there isn't really—'

'Anything for you to think about? No, not really. Well, yes, there
is. You can take this massive fucking opportunity the biggest-selling
newspaper in Britain is tossing your way, or you can go back to
plying your wares across a series of struggling websites for nowhere
near enough money to live on.'

'And I could write about whatever I wanted?'

'Of course you could. I mean, I wouldn't necessarily run it, but
how would I stop you writing it?'

'So you'd decide—'

'Think about it more this way: you know how to write, and I
know what people want to read. I will *guide* you. You want to grow,
don't you, Rob? I mean, somewhere, way back in time, you must
have had some sort of life plan, and that life plan must have been a

fraction more ambitious than just knocking out blogs.'

'You always said they weren't blogs.'

'OK, they weren't blogs. But they weren't not blogs either.'

'I'll be the laughing stock of the internet. Jesus, can you imagine this news on Twitter?'

'Of course I can imagine this news on Twitter. That's exactly why I'm suggesting you do it. People will go fucking insane. By the time your first column runs, your readership will include all the existing *Record* readers, all your loyal readers, all the people who hate-read *The Record*, all the people who hate-read you, and all the people who specifically want to hate-read your move to *The Record*. That is a fucking hell of a lot of people, Rob.'

'It's a hell of a lot of hate, is what it is.'

'I know,' said Silas gleefully. 'Jackpot, right?'

'I don't know what to say, Silas.'

'Say: why of course I want to bring my ideas to *The Record* and get paid like four times as much money for them, Silas. What an excellent plan. Thank you so much for suggesting it to me.'

'I—'

'What are you going to do, Rob? Take a stand against everything that's happening on your own? Deal with death threats on your own?'

Robert said nothing. Maybe, he thought, he could just continue to say nothing until the situation resolved itself. But that, he reminded himself, was not his job. Out there, in the rest of the country, in the wider world, millions of people were saying nothing. Anyone, he thought, could say nothing.

He tried, in the few seconds he felt Silas might allow him to come up with something, to re-establish a connection with what he thought of as his principles. He had, he felt sure, started out with some. Strong ones too. But looking inwards, he could find only the hollowed depression where they'd once rested, in which had gathered a stagnant puddle of bile. He thought again about boundaries, scales, hierarchies. So Julia Benjamin or Byron Stroud had made a website. What was that compared to a column in *The Record*?

'OK,' he said.

'Sorry, Rob. Your voice went like, weirdly quiet there. Try that again?'

'I said, OK. I'm in.'

Silas nodded, a smile splitting his face.

'There you go,' he said. 'That's the Rob I know and, well, don't love, exactly, but certainly have a degree of warm feelings towards. This is going to be amazing, Rob. You and Bennington. Tag team. Left hook, right hook.'

'Wait. You're . . . You're keeping Bennington?'

'Are you serious? Of course we're keeping Bennington. He's everywhere. I've just commissioned an art critic who's going to compare Bennington's dick pics to the self-portraits of the old masters. It's you and Bennington against the world. Get me something in the next couple of days. I'll get the contracts pushed through and we're away. Next stop: funky town. Am I right?'

'Sure,' said Robert.

'Catch you later, Robster.'

He vanished with a blip. Robert closed the Skype window, his screen now filled with nothing but the blank expanse of an unfilled Word document, the mucilaginous reservoir of bile burning a hot little hole in his guts. By reflex, he thought about texting Jess, but then realised he had no desire to. She would only, he thought, undermine it, undermine *him*. That was why he'd felt so uncomfortable about the *Record* job – because he knew what she would say, could imagine the way in which she'd look at him when he told her. How many of his decisions, how much of his internal guilt, had been filtered through the same foreshadowing of her response? Without that response there, he thought, without having to confront these energies of doubt at home as well as online, his life would be so much simpler. No more tying himself in moral knots, no more justifying over dinner what he'd expressed at his laptop. No more *apologising*. All the complexities, the guilt, the awkwardness, the inadequacy, had fallen away. Spared the friction of intimate critique, his life would be an easy, unopposed glide. There was nothing further to negotiate. He was a free man: at liberty to do all the things he'd always abhorred.

0000

In the liquid light of evening, the sun low and golden in the sky, Jess became aware of the dirt streaked across her windows – diesel stains, smears of grime and dust. Outside the car, Edmundsbury's unchanging face moved slowly by. For so long, Jess, along with most other people in the town, had fixated on all the ways the place had changed, how it was always changing, evolving away from the people who lived in it, clung to it, tracked its yielding to some smooth-surfaced, digital future. Now, numbed by the rapidity with which her life had stopped being her own, Jess felt over-sensitised to all the ways in which the town had remained the same. So much had *happened*, she thought. Surely the buildings should have reorganised themselves, the streets shuffled over to new co-ordinates. And yet Edmundsbury was as Edmundsbury as ever, the houses in their neat suburban rows, the cars behaving as expected at traffic lights – no flash of alteration, no seismic reordering of small-scale lives.

And yet, she thought, it *was* a different world. Things she had been sure of yesterday she could no longer confidently assert. She felt herself transplanted, uprooted in space and time. Her emotional topography had shifted. It pained her that the landscape had not kept pace.

'I just want to go on the record as being deeply sceptical,' said Deepa.

No-one said anything. Deepa was already on the record as being sceptical. They'd thrashed it out countless times through the afternoon, while they'd worked. Everyone knew everyone else's position.

'OK,' said Deepa. 'You all just ignore that. That's fine.'

'Your scepticism is noted, Deepa,' said Jess.

'But we're going anyway,' said Trina.

'I told Zero and One we'd go and listen,' said Jess, catching Deepa's eye in the rear-view mirror. 'Beyond that: no promises.'

'It'll be pointless,' Trina said. 'Norbiton's glitch-out at The Arbor was next-level. You'll get no sense out of him. But still, we have to go.'

The mood in the car was difficult to gauge. Certain small battles had been won. Bennington had been comprehensively humiliated. The tension at the estate seemed, for the moment at least, to have dissipated. The Griefers had gobbled up Jasmine and spat her back out to the public. But these passing victories had merely cleared the stage for larger concerns. Rumours were already in the air about Bennington's successor, Teddy Handler, who in the coming days would be setting out his 'vision' for the party. Violence, temporarily suppressed in Trina's life, could resurface at any moment. The Griefers, having swallowed Jasmine in all her incompleteness, seemed as unknowable and unsatisfactory as ever. Meanwhile, online, Trina was enjoying a slight respite from hostility, but only because that hostility was now directed elsewhere. Vivian Ross, plagued by threats and exhortations to resign, had been forced to close her Twitter account. Energies had been redirected, but not stopped.

Most of Jess's work on Jasmine had been done the previous night, on Deepa's sofa, long after Deepa and Trina had gone to bed. Jess, still processing the day's events and unable to sleep, had itched for something on which she could focus. She'd begun by scrolling through the archive Deepa had created: forgotten and ignored images pulled from far-flung corners of the web, disparate women photoshopped into eerie similarity. Isolating physical characteristics from scattered examples of her digital nameless, Deepa had created a facial template. When this template was applied, the images all seemed to depict the same woman, albeit one who had never actually existed. Because Deepa had wiped the metadata from the images, they were released not only from any sense of personhood, but also from time and place, from narrative. Using discarded networks and histories from her early work constructing her personae, Jess had fashioned for the images a new context, a chronology. Deep into the night, towards morning, as the downward pull of Jess's eyelids had become almost irresistible, Jasmine had begun to cohere.

She introduced herself to the wider world via a covering letter. She was an ordinary woman, she stressed, a person with nothing to hide and much to dispose of. She had been through a breakup. Now she was resetting.

In the age of connection, Jasmine said, separation had lost its simplicity, its finality. Once, you were alone with your memories. Now, late at night, after a few too many glasses of wine, perhaps with a nostalgic song playing at low volume on the stereo, you could make your way back through it all: the archive of who you'd been. The laughing, sun-pinkened couple on the beach, sunglasses pushed up into after-sea hair, sipping each other's cocktails and angling their heads towards each other for the shared selfie, still existed. Somewhere, those first tentative emails were still being sent: the one where you said how much you'd enjoyed meeting each other; the one where you suggested meeting again; the one to a friend, announcing, with all the vagueness and symbolism the statement always carried, that you'd 'met someone'.

As these messages and images infinitely recurred, other moments, rendered as data, joined them. The long, now-unbearable expressions of love. The canoodling passport-booth snaps. The songs and quotes shared on social media. The first concerns, expressed to friends. The requests for advice. The negotiations of separation. The terse disputes about possessions forgotten or lost in the breakup. How could you become the person you needed to be, Jasmine asked, if the person you no longer were was so readily at hand?

Picking her way through all of this, late one night, Jasmine said, she had decided to delete it all. Why torture herself, she'd thought, by poring over it again and again, reliving moments that now were gone and which could not be replaced? She wanted to get on with her life, to make changes. She didn't want to know what he was doing on social media; didn't want to see him happy with someone else; didn't want him to see her, in whatever emotional state she happened to find herself, looking back at him and the people they once were. She wanted, she'd thought, to self-erase, to begin again. But then The Griefers had arrived, and it had struck her that, rather than destroying everything, she could instead release it, give it away. Once it was everyone's, she said, it would no longer be hers.

The Griefers, Jasmine pointed out, had only asked for one person to submit. They had not said anything about the submission of one person becoming, by extension, the submission of everyone that person knew. She had therefore redacted her archive. Her friends, her partner, her family, remained anonymous. She hoped, she said, that The Griefers and the people of Edmundsbury would be happy with that, and respect her reasons for keeping some things private.

Only when Jess had read it all back this afternoon, when she'd hit the submit button on The Griefers' website and watched the sliding status bar that signified Jasmine's disappearance into the world, did she recognise the woman she'd made. It was a paradoxical moment. As soon as Jasmine became familiar to her, Jess became unfamiliar to herself. Was this what she contained? Was this who she was? From this loss of self-recognition, a new fear emerged. Would others, looking at Jasmine, see the Jess she was unable to see in herself? The moment this fear appeared to her, though, the second she reached out and touched it, it dissipated. She pictured Robert, reading over Jasmine's letter, perhaps composing a quick piece on his thoughts, and she hoped that moment of recognition came, hoped that, for once, he saw her, even if it was just at the moment she vanished.

Jess parked one street over from Nodem, in almost the exact spot she'd used the day she'd run into Brute Force. As they began to walk, the streets quiet, the houses around them no doubt concealing anxious and baffled townspeople trying to parse the day's events, Jess found herself unable to determine what she was hoping for. A sizeable part of her wanted no further trouble; a not-insignificant part of her wanted nothing but trouble.

They turned the corner into another quiet, unguarded street. Ahead of them, the lights were on in Nodem, thin, glowing shafts slipping between the gaps in the blackout blinds. The sign on the door said, *Closed.*

Trina tapped on the glass. Zero/One opened the door and, looking past Trina to Deepa and Jess, both of whom he knew, stepped aside to let them in.

'Trina,' said Trina, holding out her hand.

'One.'

From behind the counter his other half waved amiably.

'Zero,' he said.

Trina turned to Jess and Deepa.

'You're shitting me,' she said.

'Welcome to Nodem,' said Jess.

'Hey, guys,' said Deepa.

'We're going to head out back,' said the man who, for the time being at least, was One. 'I mean, the less we know, the less anyone can ask us, right? If you need us, shout.'

Jess turned her attention to the corner of the room, where the man she'd encountered here twice before was sitting on the floor in a corner, using his jacket as a cushion. He had a laptop and mobile phone beside him, as well as a curling, overly thumbed copy of a self-help book called *Stop Whining and Start Winning.* He had, quite clearly, gone without sleep for some time.

'Hey, Trina,' he said.

'Hey, Norbiton,' said Trina, taking in the scene. 'How's things?'

'Oh,' he said, in a desperate parody of offhand brightness, casting a hand vaguely about his surroundings. 'You know.'

'Shit,' said Trina, visibly softening. 'I'm sorry, Norbiton.'

'No-one to really blame but myself,' said Norbiton. 'And anyway, I should apologise to you.'

'Forget it,' said Trina, walking over to Norbiton's corner and sitting down on the floor in front of him. 'Those pricks would drive anyone mad.'

She looked up at Jess and Deepa, who had hung back, slightly awkwardly, and made the necessary introductions.

'All we need are some beanbags,' said Norbiton with a sad smile. 'We could have a huddle.'

'Why *are* you sitting on the floor, Norbiton?' said Trina.

Norbiton held up his self-help book.

'I'm changing my perspective,' he said, suddenly enthused. 'Sometimes, by, like, literally changing your perspective, you also—'

'I get it,' said Trina. 'Norbiton, are those the clothes you left the office in?'

'I'm not allowing myself to take them off,' said Norbiton. 'I have to stay in the moment it all went wrong. When it's time to take off these clothes, I'll know.'

He picked up his mobile phone from the floor and held it out to Trina, his lip wobbling slightly.

'I'm getting phantom alerts,' he said. 'I keep looking and there's nothing there.'

'Wish I had the same problem,' said Trina. 'When I look, there's too much there.'

Norbiton nodded. 'Too much,' he said simply.

'Norbiton,' said Trina gently. 'You've been talking a lot about something called The Field.'

'Too much,' Norbiton said again.

'You've been talking too much?'

'*It's* too much.'

'Too much to talk about?'

He shook his head. 'Too much to know,' he said.

'What is it?'

'I don't know,' he said hopelessly.

Jess could feel the disappointment in the air. Trina slumped a little, almost imperceptibly, but then, clearly aware of the signals she was sending Norbiton, reset herself.

'What *do* you know?' she said.

'That's good,' said Norbiton. 'Accentuate the positive. Don't dwell on a worker's inabilities; emphasise their abilities. Say: *We love what you've done with X*, and then follow it up with: *Maybe you could take what you achieved with X and apply it to Y.*

'Norbiton,' said Trina, 'were you NTK on The Field?'

Norbiton shook his head.

'Hang on,' said Jess. 'NTK?'

'Need To Know,' said Norbiton.

'It's how things work at The Arbor,' said Trina.

'I used to think it was paranoia,' said Norbiton. 'But it turned out it was part of it.'

'Part of what?' said Trina. 'The Field?'

Norbiton had become distracted by his dead phone, tapping at it uselessly, then wiping the screen on his grimy trousers.

'Norbiton,' said Trina.

She looked back at Jess and Deepa, raising her eyes skywards and shaking her head slightly.

'Can I ask you a question?' said Deepa.

Norbiton shrugged.

Deepa walked over and knelt in front of Norbiton. She raised her index finger and pulled down the lower lid of her eye.

'Do the whites of your eyes look like this? Like, would you say this is a normal white of the eye?'

Norbiton squinted into Deepa's eye.

'What's normal?' he said.

Deepa nodded. 'That's exactly what I think,' she said. 'And you know what else I think? I think sometimes normal's the problem.'

Norbiton's eyes widened. 'Yes!' he said. 'Yes, that's what I think too. In fact, during my time at The Arbor, it was something I tried to escalate.'

Deepa laughed knowingly. 'How did *that* go?' she said.

Norbiton shook his head. 'Terrible,' he said. 'It went terrible.'

'It always goes terrible,' said Deepa. 'That's the problem. Look at this.' She unlaced her trainer, peeled off her sock, and waggled the toes in front of Norbiton's face.

'My God,' said Norbiton.

'You see what we're dealing with here?' said Deepa.

Norbiton nodded seriously.

'You see the extent of this thing?' said Deepa.

'I do,' he said. 'I really do.'

'I'm not like the others,' said Deepa.

'No,' said Norbiton.

Trina had stood up from the floor and come to stand beside Jess. She nudged Jess in the ribs and, when Jess looked round, widened her eyes. Jess held out her hands in a gesture she hoped came across as *I know, but what can we do?*

'What are we talking here?' said Deepa. 'False flag?'

'I wish,' said Norbiton.

'Wow,' said Deepa.

'I know,' said Norbiton.

'Do you?' said Deepa seriously. 'Do you *really* though?'

Norbiton gestured around himself, his hand coming to rest on his worn-out clothes, his drained and useless hardware. He gave Deepa a significant look.

'Got you,' said Deepa. 'So how did we get here? That's my question.'

'That was my question,' said Norbiton. 'And that's how I got here.'

Deepa nodded. 'Too many questions.'

'I thought . . .' said Norbiton. 'I thought, let's open things up, you know?'

'Talk about it.'

'Right. Have a *dialogue*. Maybe *co-operate*. All this . . .' He waved a hand vaguely. 'NTK. Who knows this. Who knows that.'

'You were like: be free.'

'I thought: initiative, right?' said Norbiton. 'That's what they always say. Get ahead. Disrupt.'

'Right,' said Deepa.

'But it was backwards.'

'It always is.'

'NTK wasn't the input. It wasn't even the process. It was the *output*.'

'Jesus.'

'I know, right?'

'Participation without understanding,' said Deepa.

'Without *knowledge*,' said Norbiton.

'There was a resistance paradigm,' said Deepa.

'Only, I didn't know there was,' said Norbiton.

'Walled gardens within walled gardens,' said Deepa.

'Oh, the works,' said Norbiton. 'The co-operation instinct, iterated prisoner's dilemmas, opt-in versus involvement, satisfaction versus engagement . . .'

'The illusion of freedom,' said Deepa.

'What don't you want to share?' said Trina.

Everyone looked at her.

'Norbiton,' she said, visibly mustering patience, 'after you left, Bangstrom took over.'

'That guy,' said Norbiton, his face darkening.

'He started going on about the MTs, talking about how maybe they'd organised, unionised, or something.'

'Code brown,' said Norbiton.

'Bangstrom got het up because I'd flagged an MT on the system,' said Trina. 'The one I tried to tell you about. Some guy called Tayz. Usually, like, insanely productive, but suddenly idle. Still logging on, still obviously pulling traffic, but not doing anything. Just . . .

watching. Bangstrom gave me the go-ahead to check it out but when I started digging around in his files I got locked out. Next thing I knew, I was whisked off to HR.'

'You, of all people,' said Norbiton. 'Soaking up the wrong info stream.'

'Of all people?' said Deepa.

'What?' said Norbiton.

'You said of all people. Why her *of all people?*'

Norbiton looked at Trina.

'Fuck,' said Trina.

Norbiton nodded, smiled, began his gentle humming.

'What?' said Jess.

'I was part of it, wasn't I, Norbiton?'

He nodded.

'*Beatrice?*' she said, her voice suddenly sharp.

Norbiton smiled.

'Who's Beatrice?' said Jess.

'Not who,' said Trina. '*What.* Beatrice is the software we use to package out work to the MTs and monitor what they're doing. It allows a degree of control but also a degree of . . . Well, let's call it what it is and say manipulation.'

'Opt-in,' said Deepa. 'Participation is voluntary.'

'But gamified,' said Trina.

'Were you the only person who used Beatrice?' said Deepa.

'I *designed* Beatrice. I used it more than anyone, *knew it* better than anyone. Jesus fucking *Christ*, the amount of times I asked for a promotion and the amount of times they told me what I did was *just* HR.'

'NTK,' said Norbiton.

'I couldn't know what I knew,' said Trina.

'That's how it works,' said Norbiton.

'Were *you* NTK on what I was doing, Norbiton? Because I remember in meetings you going on about how you weren't NTK

348

on anything any of us were doing, but now that seems like it was bullshit.'

'Outcomes,' said Norbiton. 'Significance. But not details. Not process.'

'So you couldn't see what I was doing, but you could see—'

'I was told to think of myself as a conduit.'

'Between what and what?' said Trina.

'Between you and the higher floors.'

'Me? You mean, the stuff I was doing with the MTs?'

'How you were doing it. What it was doing to you.'

'The effect on the overseer,' said Deepa.

'Right,' said Norbiton.

'Don't tell me,' said Deepa. 'It was for wider roll-out, right?'

Norbiton shrugged. 'I assumed.'

'Phase one is In The Building,' said Trina. 'Phase two takes it Outside.'

'To where?' said Deepa.

'To the community,' said Trina. 'That's right, isn't it, Norbiton? That's where it goes next?'

Norbiton didn't answer.

No-one said anything. Oppressed by the overview, they sought solace in meaningless detail. Norbiton ran his thumb across the dead screen of his phone. Jess noticed a scratch on her arm, the cause of which she was at a loss to recall.

Deepa took a breath, then stood up.

'Thank you, Norbiton,' she said.

'Pleasure,' he said.

'Wait,' said Jess. 'Deepa, hang *on*. There's still—'

'There's nothing more we need to know,' said Deepa.

'There's *loads* we need to know. There's . . . Trina, help me out here.'

Trina shook her head.

'Deepa's right,' she said. 'That's it.'

She turned to Norbiton.

'You going to be OK, Norbiton?'

He shrugged, as if the concept were meaningless.

'Take care, Trina,' he said.

They walked slowly out past the counter, Jess barely able to bite her tongue.

'Hey in there,' called Deepa in the direction of the back room. 'We're off.'

Zero or One's face appeared through the beaded curtain at the back. He tilted his head in Deepa's direction.

'Coming over tonight?' he said.

Jess turned to look at Deepa, who was, for the first time in all the time she'd known her, in the midst of a furious blush.

'I . . . Tomorrow?' she said hurriedly. 'Probably tomorrow.'

'Cool, hon,' said Zero/One.

They stepped out into the empty street, the door clicking shut behind them. Jess stared pointedly at Deepa, unable to entirely mask her smile.

'Well, aren't you the shady one,' she said.

Deepa said nothing, just turned and began walking.

Jess contained herself until they were driving, then ruptured.

'OK, Deepa,' she said. 'What the *fuck* was that?'

'What?'

'*Everything.* I mean, what were you even *talking* about in there? We went there to get *information*, Deepa. *Answers.* Instead, we've got . . . I don't even know what we've got, actually. What have we got?'

'Weren't you listening?' said Deepa.

'Of course I was listening. It's just that I don't have the first idea what I was listening to.'

'Trina,' said Deepa, 'you got it, right?'

Trina nodded. Deepa gestured towards Trina as if that were all the proof she needed. Again, Jess felt that little stab of non-belonging.

'Don't be smug,' she said.

Deepa rolled her eyes.

'Green were leveraging their own workflow,' she said. 'They made people think they were working on a project when in fact they *were* the project.'

'OK,' said Jess, trying to keep her eyes on the road but her brain on what it was being asked to digest.

'They made a system of hierarchical knowledge look like a system of networked knowledge. They wanted to know exactly how much people needed to know in order to participate.'

'Within that system,' said Trina, 'there was another system.'

'The MTs,' said Jess.

'Right,' said Deepa. 'And within *that* system, there was another test.'

'Trina,' said Jess. 'That I at least gathered. Trina was monitoring, but also being monitored.'

'The aim was wider roll-out,' said Deepa. 'They want to take what they've been doing and *apply* it. They're scaling up.'

'Scaling up to what though?' said Jess.

'The Larchwood,' said Trina. 'The engineered community. That's where the tech's going, right?'

'Right,' said Deepa.

'Jesus Christ,' said Jess.

'Only, there's a problem,' said Trina.

Deepa nodded, giving Jess a slightly exasperated look.

'The Griefers,' said Jess.

'Bingo,' said Deepa.

'So, what?' said Jess. 'The Griefers are what Green think they are? They're the workforce gone rogue? Like, they've figured out that they each have all these tiny bits of information, and—'

'No,' said Deepa, 'because we know they're not that.'

Jess nodded. 'Because they swallowed Jasmine.'

'We fooled them,' said Deepa. 'Therefore we know they don't

actually have the information or the access they claim to have.'

'So they're *outside* the system then?' said Jess. 'They're genuinely some sort of movement or resistance or whatever?'

'No,' said Deepa.

'Why?'

'Because of Beatrice,' said Trina.

'Wait, let me make sure I've got this right. Beatrice allows you, or whoever, to manipulate a workforce, right?'

Trina nodded.

'You can adjust certain parameters.'

'You can keep the system sufficiently unstable. You can introduce unpredictability.'

'So that it doesn't feel like a system,' said Deepa.

'So the question really becomes . . .' said Trina.

'What's the system?' said Jess.

'And given that all the emphasis has been on keeping things small,' said Deepa, 'on making sure that everyone only sees their tiny little piece of what's going on, the answer is pretty obviously to think big.'

Outside, night had fallen. Lights had gone on in windows. The streets were quiet. Jess thought again, as she always did around this time of the evening, of the unseen changes in Edmundsbury's environment: the altered light, the relaid roads; new sensations of speed and stasis; a creeping, circadian drift.

'The town,' she said.

Deepa nodded.

'That's their petri dish,' she said. 'That's why they're here.'

———

Trina had never, she realised, cycled towards The Arbor at this late-afternoon hour. Usually by now, she would be coming away, leaving it behind her. Now that she was approaching it, she noticed for the first time the trickery of its glass. Even from here, a way down the road, she could see the offices and open-plan working areas that covered its facade. It seemed as if you could look clean through the whole building. But then you noticed that the sun was obscured behind it. Its edges were transparent, but its core remained opaque.

She cycled slowly into the car park and locked her bike in the shelter. Inside the building, she touched through the security barrier with her pass, got in the lift, and let it carry her to floor three. Surely, she thought, there would be at least one person waiting for her. Bangstrom, perhaps, or the freakish HR twins. But when the lift gave its little chime of acknowledgement, the doors parted to reveal only the familiar, muted activity of her floor. Her desk was still there, she noted, but her No-Go room, which had been tucked against the far wall, was gone. She took this as a kind of statement – a reminder that anything she might have imagined she'd built here, anything she might have constructed around herself, was gone. She remembered Norbiton in his self-built cocoon, the ease with which the structural engineers had lifted away the flimsy panels and exposed him, crouched and vulnerable inside.

Bream and Holt were both at their desks. Holt saw her first.

'Incoming,' he said.

'Whoa,' said Bream. 'Unexpected item in the bagging area.'

'Nice to see you too,' she said.

'What's the deal?' said Holt. 'Here for the mercy shot?' He mimed cocking a gun, pressed his fingers into the back of his head, then mimicked a facial exit wound with his free hand.

'Nice,' said Trina.

'Seriously though,' said Bream. 'Care to share?'

'I'm taking over The Arbor,' said Trina. 'You're all fired.'

'It was always going to happen one day,' said Holt. 'Equal opportunities being what it is.'

'Fuck you, Holt,' said Trina.

'Hey,' said Bream. 'No hard feelings, OK?'

'Hard feelings are the only kind I have, Bream.'

'Noted. But still.'

'Likewise,' said Holt.

'We're being pricks,' said Bream. 'But affectionately.'

Trina held up her middle finger. 'With love and hugs,' she said.

She moved down the office, hearing the sudden silence of once-rattling keyboards as she approached, followed by the renewed clacking of IMs and emails as she passed. She knocked on Bangstrom's door.

'Enter,' said Bangstrom.

She'd expected a committee, but Bangstrom was alone, reclining at his desk with his hands behind his head, his shirtsleeves rolled up, his top buttons casually loosened.

'How have you been?' said Bangstrom, catching her immediately off guard.

'Excuse me?'

'How have you been since I saw you last? How's your family?'

'They're OK. We're OK.'

'I'm doing the feelings bit,' said Bangstrom. 'How do you think it's going?'

'I think it was going well until you drew direct attention to it.'

'Noted.'

'Jesus,' said Trina. 'You people.'

'What people? Because let's not get political here, Trina. One thing that will categorically not help this situation is if we start getting political.'

'Interpret it how you want. Political, not political. Broadest interpretation: *all you people who are not me.*'

Bangstrom nodded. 'OK,' he said.

'Let's move on,' said Trina.

'Maybe I could clarify Green's position,' said Bangstrom.

'Go right ahead. That's why I'm here.'

'What I want to emphasise here is that at no point during this, er, situation, were you dismissed, and at no point was dismissal threatened. Your pay has remained at full rate while this matter has been investigated. You have been offered appropriate emotional support.'

'When?'

'Just now.'

'That was my emotional support? Jesus Christ.'

'The idea was only ever to let this blow over. Then, give you a warning, welcome you back, get you some mandatory counselling, work on those violence issues a bit more.'

'I didn't do anything wrong.'

'Well, if nothing else, your tweet violated Green's hate-speech policy.'

'So why not just get rid of me?'

'Excuse me?'

'If what I said on Twitter was so heinous, and it's been such a PR nightmare for Green, who are already, I should add, in the midst of another, wider PR nightmare, and if you've got me bang to rights, why not just let me go?'

'We take the retention of talent very seriously.'

'So you don't want me going somewhere else?'

'We want to nurture your talent. Which means we have to nurture you.'

'That's bullshit, Bangstrom. From the day I started here, Green have done exactly fuck all to nurture my talent. Green didn't *give* me this job. I *took* it. Green hasn't *nurtured* me. I've fought my way into all the opportunities I've had, which, while we're on the subject, have been precious few. And what have I got to show for it? A No-Go room and some quality time with Beatrice? Go fuck yourself. You're going to sit there and tell me Green feel strongly that they need to nurture and maintain my talents? I'm sorry, Bangstrom, but that is about as believable as you telling me you care about my feelings.'

'I'm deeply hurt by the accusation that I don't genuinely care about your feelings.'

'No you're not.'

'OK, I'm not. How's that suit you?'

'How come I wasn't let go immediately?'

'I've just—'

'Look at the situation, Bangstrom. You've got the web and mainstream press going batshit. You're up to your eyeballs in fallout from the Griefer business. Why not just cut me loose?'

'Oh, I see what this is. This is that old floor-three bullshit rearing its ugly little head again. You think if you just ask me the same thing over and over again like a malfunctioning Bream, I'll just spontaneously break down and give you the answer you want to hear because I'm inherently weak. Well, let me tell you, Trina: The Interrobang cannot be weakened.'

'You're already weakened.'

'Well, that's where you're wrong. I mean, go ahead and believe that if you like, but—'

'You want to know why you're weakened?'

'Oh no, you don't get me that easily. The minute I say, yes, I'd like to know why I'm weakened, you'll be like, aha, so you accept that you're weakened.'

'You're weakened because you're not supposed to let me go.'

'Fairly sure my answer regarding your offer of input vis-à-vis my hypothetically weakened state was negative.'

'I should be gone already, but I'm not.'

'Green believe in second chances.'

'No they don't.'

'You're right, they don't. Which is exactly why you should be so grateful they're offering you one.'

'What do I know?'

'Exactly. What do you know.'

'No, I'm asking. What do I know?'

'I don't follow.'

'You want me to timeline this? I start figuring something out, my fucking internet suddenly goes into meltdown. Green gets all heavy with me from an HR perspective, and basically tosses me to the wolves of public opinion. Suddenly, I'm vulnerable. Then Green, having made a big song and dance about how embarrassing I am, goes on to make a massive show of how eager they are to hang on to me. It doesn't add up. Unless you look at it the way I'm looking at it, which is to say: I know something. I might not *know* what I know, but I sure as shit know *something*. Otherwise, *either* none of this would have happened, *or* I would have just been summarily fired. Instead, what we've got is Green making me feel scared, then suddenly making me feel safe, which, I don't know, reads to me as being bullshit, given what I was working on literally minutes before all this kicked off. You see what I'm saying?'

'You're saying: Green saying you're both a public embarrassment and at the same time a valued employee seems incongruous, especially given that you haven't exactly been treated like a valued employee at any time in the time leading up to the current time in which all of this is taking place.'

'Exactly.'

'So it occurs to you that you must be valuable in a way that is as yet unclear to you, and you no doubt feel it is somehow, like, your *civil right*, or something, to know what that value is.'

'So? What do I know?'

'What do you think you might know?'

'I know about The Field.'

Bangstrom took a long inhalation and sat back in his seat.

'What *specifically* do you know about The Field?' he said.

'I know it exists.'

'And?'

'I know it's something you'd rather no-one knew about.'

'So you know that a thing exists, and you know that Green, who are notoriously secretive, would rather people not know it exists. Wow. With that kind of insight, you could crack the case wide open, detective.'

'I know it needs Beatrice. I know Tayz is critical somehow. I know Green shit themselves if anyone so much as mentions it, like Norbiton, for example.'

'Norbiton.' Bangstrom sniffed dismissively. 'Guy's a wreck.'

'Why hasn't Norbiton been fired?'

'We don't just *fire* people, Trina. Norbiton became unwell. He'll be repositioned.'

'Do you know where he is?'

'Do . . . *you* know where he is?'

'Let's move on to what you're offering me.'

'Excuse me?'

'Your offer. What's your offer? You don't want me to leave, so go ahead and make me an offer.'

'You get your job back—'

'I don't want my job back.'

'OK, Trina. I wanted to do this the friendly way. OK? I wanted us to come out of this, well, not as friends, exactly, but with a certain amount of respect for each other. But you've forced my hand. So this is me taking off the friendly face.'

'What's under the friendly face?'

'*Another*, considerably less friendly face.'

'OK, hit me.'

'You want to talk about what I've got to negotiate with? How about instead, we talk about what you *haven't* got to negotiate with? How about we talk about what you've got to protect?'

'Are you threatening me?'

'Why would I need to threaten you? You're already comprehensively under threat. Or did I just hallucinate the last few days of your life?'

'Let's get to the point.'

'You think you've got muscle you can throw around in here? Let me tell you what you've got. You've got a home you're going to be evicted from. And before you say it: yes, that is definite, and no, there will not be any point trying to resist it when the time comes. Check out your contract with Downton. Check out their community policy. Check out their right to evict anyone they see as compromising their commitment to a certain kind of neighbourly compatibility. So let's call that exhibit A: you are essentially fucking homeless. Which brings me to exhibit B: you, in this case, are not just you. You and your whole *family* are homeless. You need a new place to live and pronto. You want me to tell you what your accommodation options are without your job? Zero. You think you're going to get a tenancy based on your girlfriend's precarious fucking odd-job work? And newsflash, as if that wasn't enough shit for you, you're also operating at a fairly eye-popping level of physical endangerment, which, OK, I see you've enlisted the help of that whole virtual-harassment-support thing, but let me tell you, they are not going to be an awful lot of help against a bunch of neo-Nazi bother boys who, by the way, hate you more than ever. You know why? Because those freaks can barely even *use* the internet, hence they are not really susceptible to its schemes. They're not going to mess around with your online existence. They don't know how. All they know is that they hate you. Hence: they're going to kick your door in and beat the shit out of you and your whole family. OK? So that's, like, what's in your shopping basket right now. That's what you're carrying around while you sit here in front of me and act like you've got a whole load of aces up your sleeve. Meanwhile, what have we got here? Oh, look at that, it's a job offer from Green whereby you get to earn good money, no doubt progress to earning even better money, benefit from the kind of security and protection that only Green can provide and, hey, guess what, take advantage of Green's tenancy for employees programme, by which I mean, you wind up with a secure place to live. Now, have I missed anything? I mean, stop me if you feel I've, like, accidentally ignored some major piece of weaponry in your arsenal.'

He demonstrated that he'd reached the end of his little soliloquy

359

by folding his arms and cocking his head to one side and eyeballing her as if he was interested less in what she had to say and more in how long it would take her to agree completely with what he'd just said.

Trina had, of course, prepared herself for this. She had, with Deepa's help, anatomised her own predicament more than once in much the same way, and, unlike Bangstrom, she had the advantage of being able to see what the situation looked like from the inside, so it wasn't as if he was telling her anything she didn't already know. But there was still, she had to admit, something brutal about having the components of her undoing so systematically itemised. It was, she thought, an archetypal Green moment. A brief nod to compassion, then a rapid shift into dispassionate, fact-based coercion when compassion failed. Bangstrom had crunched the data. He'd run the numbers and determined that she was fucked.

Bangstrom shook his head slightly from side to side in a kind of mockery of sadness and disappointment.

'Take as long as you need,' he said, his tone making it clear there was no time left for her to take.

'You think I want to fuck Green over?' said Trina. 'I mean, seriously. You think I actually, *A*, want to do that, and, *B*, want the fallout of doing that on my plate? You know a lot about me, clearly. You've got all the data at your fingertips. But here's something you don't know: how it feels to work *this fucking hard* to get somewhere, and still not really get there. I've given this *everything*. You really think my number one priority right now is to burn it all down? To bankrupt my family? To lose my home?'

'Well, your psychological profile does suggest a degree of recklessness, if I'm honest.'

'You still don't get it, do you? I've taken every chance that was ever near enough for me to take, and quite a lot that, let me tell you, looked a long way out of reach. Now, with the biggest chance I'm ever going to get opening up right in front of me, you think I'm just going to walk away from it? Like, OK, you've laid out some things there, Bangstrom. Good for you. I mean, nice job on enumerating the various different aspects of my life that are totally shitty right now. But let me enumerate some chunky data for you in return, OK? I know about The Field. I know about Beatrice. I know about Edmundsbury and I know The Griefers are a huge fucking con job. And that *alone* gives me two very attractive options. Option one: I take my story national. The public exposure protects me from further harm. Edmundsbury goes up in arms. They have a few meetings. They campaign to have you kicked out of town. Option two: I take everything I know and just sashay my way into a prime job with one of your competitors, who then mirrors The Field at a fraction of a cost because they, by stealing your ideas, have incurred exactly zero of your development outlay. And while we're on the subject, let's not forget that the software I assume you're going to refit for The Field is software that I partly fucking designed, and if you think I'm stupid enough not to have built certain insurance policies into the design of that software then you're even dumber than I always thought you were, which, just for the record, is pretty fucking dumb indeed.'

Bangstrom managed an awkward smile.

'This is what happens when we break our own rules and allow a single individual control over a project instead of breaking it down for the MTs,' he said. 'In a way, it's our bad. But what can I say. There were reasons.' He shrugged, widened the smile. 'So where are we, Trina? Stalemate?'

'No, not stalemate. More that I'm going to make you an offer and you have to accept it.'

Bangstrom laughed. 'Or what?'

'Or I execute one of my multiple available strategies and you end up fucked every which way.'

'Let's get to what you want.'

'I want a promotion.'

'To what?'

'To The Field.'

Bangstrom laughed.

'You were already working on The Field.'

'I'm not talking about manipulating MTs,' said Trina. 'I'm talking about a proper position. I'm talking about access. I'm talking about you *rewarding* me for my ongoing loyalty when I quite frankly could have already fucked all of you shits over and skipped the country to somewhere warm. That's what I'm talking about.'

'This isn't about loyalty, Trina. It's about efficiency. How does hiring you make the project more efficient?'

'Well, for a start, I can tell you right now one thing you could do to improve efficiency all round.'

'And what's that?'

'You could do something about the as yet not ex-employee you've got running round telling everyone what you're up to and trying to mobilise people against it.'

Bangstrom rolled his eyes. 'Norbiton,' he said.

'Bingo.'

'Where is he?'

'Where's my contract?'

'You'd seriously sell him out like that?'

'What, you think I should show a bit more loyalty to Norbiton?'

'No. I'm just interested in your principles.'

'My principles involve taking care of me and my family. Once that's done, it's less about principles and more about ambition. If this is the future, then I want to work on it.'

'Stay here,' said Bangstrom, standing up. He picked up his ID card from the desk and walked out of the office without saying anything more, leaving Trina alone to mull over the reality of what she was proposing. Something about the alone time in Bangstrom's office made her feel jittery. What if Bangstrom was summoning security? What if she'd overplayed her hand and now they had what they wanted? All Bangstrom would have to do, she thought, would be to activate security protocol and she wouldn't even be able to leave the building. She checked her watch. It had been, what, a few minutes since Bangstrom had left? Maybe he had to run it up the chain of command. Maybe, in talking to Bangstrom, she wasn't really talking to him at all, just *through* him, to whoever it was who really made the decisions.

A sheaf of paper in a soft-covered binder landed with a slap on the desk in front of her, making her jump.

'Knock yourself out,' said Bangstrom, settling himself back into his chair. 'Pen here if you need one. Electronic copy on request. You know the drill.'

Trina picked up the document and paged through it. It was a contract, appended with a non-disclosure agreement.

'That's a permanent contract,' said Bangstrom. 'You know how many people dream of seeing one of those? You know how few people actually have one? This takes you off the precipice.'

Trina began leafing through the contract. The first few pages were standard legal jargon with accompanying explanations. The next section detailed her salary, along with a series of added perks: accommodation, holiday, access to legal advice, private healthcare. After that, there was a long and detailed section setting out the kind of consequences she could expect if she shared any information that she accessed as a result of her work at Green.

'Pretty comprehensive way to buy my silence,' she said.

'Think of it more as an exclusive purchase of your expertise,' said Bangstrom.

'What don't you want to share?' said Trina.

Bangstrom laughed drily. 'Catchy that, isn't it?'

'You going to tell me who those people are?'

Bangstrom picked up his pen from the desk and held it out to her.

'That's privileged information,' he said.

'Signing this makes me one of the privileged few?'

Bangstrom shrugged. 'If you like.'

Trina took the pen and leafed again through the contents of the contract, her vision blurring out at the edges, her ability to make sense of what she was reading wholly diminished by her attempts to imagine what this moment meant. The phrase *signing your life away* played like a looping advertising jingle in the background of her brain. When she uncapped the pen her hands were shaking.

'Suddenly struck by the gravity of the moment?' said Bangstrom.

'Something like that,' she said.

Without further thought, she swept her signature across the dotted line, once on the contract and once on the non-disclosure agreement, then passed the document back to Bangstrom.

'Right decision,' said Bangstrom with a smile that seemed halfway genuine. 'Good to have you on board, Trina.'

'You sure knocked that contract up quickly,' said Trina.

'We made drafts of several,' said Bangstrom. 'I had a feeling it would be a process of negotiation.'

'I take it I'll never know what was in the other options?'

'Being shredded as we speak.'

Trina nodded, imagining both the indignities she had avoided and the rewards she had no doubt signed away.

'Now,' said Bangstrom, standing up, walking round his desk and gesturing for Trina to follow. 'How do you fancy a quick orientation session, bring you up to speed? Ever been to floor four?'

'God, Bangstrom, that sounds like a chat-up line.'

They stepped into the lift, lapsing into silence as it rose. The doors slid open to reveal an office environment essentially identical to Trina's previous floor except for the fact that the whole room – predominantly open plan but dotted with No-Go rooms – was suffused in approximately ten per cent more self-satisfaction.

'So you were a little put out that we dismantled your No-Go room,' said Bangstrom. 'Well, surprise, because it's actually right here. We just moved it up a floor. We've rebuilt it exactly as it was, check it out.'

He gestured for her to swipe herself in and then joined her inside.

It was, as he'd said, just as she'd left it. In the middle of the room was a table, on which sat a terminal she recognised as hers through its familiar pattern of dust and wear. Bangstrom joined her in the little cubicle and they stood there awkwardly, sealed in and mutually uncomfortable.

'It's everything I've ever dreamed of,' said Trina, unable to conceal her sarcasm.

'Knew you'd love it,' said Bangstrom.

'I've literally gone up in the world by a whole floor,' said Trina. 'How could I not love it?'

'Oh, you've gone up by a lot more than that,' said Bangstrom.

'Have I?'

'Welcome to The Field,' he said, gesturing grandly around the tiny, empty space in which they were contained.

'Why do I feel like you've pulled back the curtain to reveal another curtain?'

'I don't know. I can't really fathom that metaphor, if I'm honest.'

'Who are The Griefers, Bangstrom?'

Bangstrom eyed her for a long and disquieting moment. Then he smiled.

'They're a bunch of conceptual performance artists we hired.'

'Come again?'

'Crazy, right? Someone caught their show at the Edinburgh Fringe, and then when the whole disruption idea was tossed around they were suddenly like, oh my God, I know just the people. They've been pretty good, to be fair. And cheap. You know how much performance artists make? Nothing. As in literally nothing. We're paying them marginally more than nothing to disrupt a whole town and they're rolling around like pigs in shit. And you know the genius part? They're renowned eccentrics. Every now and then they're like, *hey, we're going to tell the world what you're doing*, and we're like, go right ahead you freaks, no-one will believe you because who the hell listens to a bunch of fucking artists?'

'They don't have access to a fucking thing, do they?' said Trina. 'People's internet histories, I mean. Like, they've literally just got a few profile pics and some random images and that's it.'

'Oh God, the idea of them hacking anyone,' said Bangstrom. 'I mean, we had to give them training in how to use that projector. Two of them can't even drive. Talk about your typical creatives.'

Trina sat down at her terminal and took a moment to massage her temples.

'Edmundsbury's going to go fascist because you guys played let's pretend with a bunch of luvvies,' she said.

Bangstrom shrugged. 'Outcomes, right?'

'That's why you're in Edmundsbury,' she said. 'You needed a petri dish for your *outcomes*.'

'You're just figuring that out now? God, you really drank the Kool-Aid with all of that community shit, didn't you? Yeah, we needed a stable, contained setting, simple as that. Not too rural, not too urban. Somewhere change was ordinarily pretty slow. Somewhere that would be happy for us to re-network, take over certain elements of the infrastructure.'

'So you could data harvest.'

Bangstrom laughed. 'Data harvest? Please. We were already data harvesting, Trina. *Everyone* is data harvesting. We're studying. And studying requires experimentation. You think we can do this kind of research on lab rats? Those days are long gone. There's nothing more to be learned from electrocuting rodents in mazes.'

'But why not just sell people a package? You can get permissions from the end-user agreement nobody ever reads, you can push integration into other aspects of their lives, you can make whatever you're pushing more and more invaluable and more and more difficult to opt out of. Why the infrastructural cloak and dagger? Why all this real-world faffing around?'

'Opt-in is fine,' said Bangstrom. 'We're doing opt-in stuff too. But there's an observer paradox. If you give people an app or a platform or whatever, they construct an identity and a set of behaviours around it. Plus, there's this whole feeling of commitment, meaning they're kind of on guard as to just how much whatever it is you're pushing asks of them. Internet naivety is over. You think people are still surprised to find out that tweets are public and your data may be used for other purposes? Are they fuck. They know that, and they live around it. But they still maintain this illusion of division between their online and offline lives. So our aim with Edmundsbury was pretty basic: make a real-world haven, fuck with it, watch what happens. We're not interested in how people behave when they feel restricted. We're interested in how people behave when they think they're totally free, when they think they're not even signed into any kind of package at all. That's where the real data is, and that's where the profit is. A map of how people react to certain threats, to the unknown, to *disruption*.'

Trina booted up her terminal and logged in. Once the desktop appeared, she clicked immediately on the shortcut for Beatrice. When it loaded, she looked at Bangstrom.

'That's what Beatrice is,' she said. 'Beatrice is The Field.'

'What?' said Bangstrom. 'You really think we were excited about an interface for cracking the whip over a bunch of MTs? I mean, great, it was useful, but you know: vision.'

'You saw the possibilities for manipulation the interface afforded.'

'And then some. Credit where credit's due, Trina. It's a very elegant solution to a basically pretty inelegant problem.'

'The problem of how to get people to do what you want.'

'Not really. I mean, yeah, there's an element of that. But it's a frankly pretty clapped-out conception of control. I mean, making people do things just sounds a bit . . . I don't know—'

'Draconian?'

'Limited, was the word I was looking for. If you know what people are doing, and they know you know what they're doing—'

'They'll do what they think is expected anyway.'

'Or they'll rebel. And now we're able to model all of those responses in a controlled real-world situation.'

'And then sell the results.'

'Big time. Plus expand.'

She looked at the adjusted Beatrice interface on her screen and scrolled through some of the variables. At the base of her throat, a tightening sensation began.

'And now you've got an even more controlled situation.'

'And she's there,' said Bangstrom. 'Only took you, what, like all fucking afternoon? But well done, welcome to the party.'

'You've partnered with Downton to tech out the new estate.'

'Downton have awarded us a frankly massive contract to tech their estate, yes. And we have in turn negotiated within that contract to take ownership of the data we get back. So we get paid to put the tech in, paid to run and maintain the tech, and then paid to tell people what the tech tells us. It's a game changer: a fully voluntary, transparent, opt-in system *within* an opaque, non-voluntary, covert system. We can model awareness and ignorance simultaneously. Plus on top of all *that* when you take into account the fact that the people most likely to want to know what that data tells us are, you know, governments and the like, we'll no doubt be able to prise open that particular door in terms of further contracts too. I mean, God, thanks to the whole Larchwood thing, the data we've got on, like, crowd formation, threat response, hysteria amplification, ideology dispersal, conflict suppression, and so on is unbelievable. Quite a few folks are going to be pretty keen to have a peek at that, I think.'

'And you get to apply the MT model to daily life.'

'A gamified, incentivised real-world environment in which micro-rewards reduce resistance.' Bangstrom leaned against the wall of the No-Go room and beamed like an enlightened man. 'Rules are out; incentives are in. Think of the implications of that, Trina. Think of everything we could change.' He let out a long, pointed exhalation. 'The whole concept of surveillance is so limited,' he said. 'We've *got* surveillance. The race is over. The question is what we do with it. Our answer: we experiment, we *play*. Then we learn.'

Trina stared at her screen. She couldn't tell if she was trying to find meaning in the information she saw there, or instead trying to protect herself from the knowledge that the information meant anything at all. She could do that if she wanted, she realised. She could take a breath and forget everything she knew and instead just lose herself in the data streams. The fields and parameters and variables didn't have to be attached to consequences. She saw now the chilling success of her own design. Beatrice's inviting sliders and controls, the sense of play, the dislocation of data from the people to whom it referred. She could play indefinitely, untroubled, so long as she didn't remind herself what and whom she was playing with.

'I get it,' she said. 'I get all that. I get the idea. I get the aim. What I don't get is the panic.'

Bangstrom rolled his eyes.

'That was the NTK policy,' he said. 'Obviously, only like three people were or are NTK on the whole deal. And around them, various people are and were NTK on various little bits. So upshot was: even people who were NTK on the general thrust of The Field, or the estate, or some of the infrastructure stuff with regards to Edmundsbury, weren't necessarily NTK on the brainwave with regards to The Griefers. Plus, some of us who *were* NTK on The Griefers weren't entirely NTK on how The Griefers were being sourced. So we go out there and source these conceptual freaks, and we deliberately, so as to retain the element of genuine unmodified chaos we're looking for, give them a pretty vague remit and encourage them to surprise us, which in all fairness they did, and what do you know, we wind up with chaos. The people who were NTK on some of the infrastructure stuff start panicking that this is a genuine insurrection. The people who were NTK on the basic idea of destabilising the system in a controlled way start panicking that this isn't in fact *our* destabilisation but instead an *actual* attempt at disruption that we're in danger of *mistaking* for our own destabilisation. The people who were NTK on all of the above start freaking out that even though they know about the conceptualists, maybe the conceptualists are smarter than anyone really thought and have genuinely gone off-piste and started an actual rebellion under the *guise* of the fake rebellion we told them to start. And suddenly we're having meetings up there on the big boys' floor where only like two of us know what the fuck is going on but unless we play along with all the people who haven't got a clue what's going on we'll *reveal* that we're the ones who know what's going on. Only solution: respond to the supposed threat that isn't actually a threat *as if* it's a threat, so that everyone feels nice and safe and secure in terms of our ability to respond to a threat. Accidental bonus: we were then in a position to scrape some data on how we might respond to a threat, which, I mean, why not check that out if you're in a position to check that out? The whole Microtasker-uprising thing was a potential disruption that had already been modelled and so we, by which I basically mean I, thought, hey, let's go ahead and play around with *that* variable too. Of course, it goes without saying that I scraped all the data on the internal panic as well. We've learned a lot about ourselves, as it happens.'

'And was I a factor? Did you model my responses?'

'Of course. We modelled the absolute fuck out of you. We modelled your user info, your responsiveness, your plasticity with reference to the parameters you were manipulating.'

'But then, what? I manipulated a bit too much? Went off-script?'

Here, Trina noted, Bangstrom was less quick to answer. All his other responses had been immediate, direct, almost showy. He was, she realised, inordinately proud of what he was working on. The NTK policy must have burned at him, forced him to keep too much to himself. Now, with the decisions about how much he was prepared to share clearly taken in advance, it was all spilling out. Except this.

He was still looking at her, not smiling now, his head tilted to one side, evaluating her as he had in the meeting not long ago.

'Well, now I face a tricky decision,' he said.

Trina decided not to say anything. He was in a sharing mode, she thought. Best to let him keep going and hope he got to where she needed him to be.

'We couldn't reach an agreement on what to tell you,' he said. 'So the final decision rests with me. I'm supposed to make it on an ad hoc basis. You know, freeform, based on how the rest of this goes. It's a tough one.'

'This is about me,' she said. 'This is about what I know. You gave me the added Beatrice clearance. Someone either didn't know I was given the clearance and panicked, or didn't agree with the clearance I'd been given and overrode it. It was when I clicked on that file.'

'It's interesting if you know and interesting if you don't know,' said Bangstrom. 'Pity you can't know *and* not know and then we could model both. Binaries, eh?'

'It's Tayz, isn't it? Whatever Tayz is working on—'

Bangstrom laughed.

'Decision made,' he said. 'You're not going to be able to help us if you don't know.'

He stood up straight from the wall, still eyeballing Trina, but no longer, she sensed, because he was trying to make his decision by evaluating her. Instead, he was preparing himself to watch her responses, priming his test patterns.

'Like I said,' he said finally. 'We modelled you very carefully. We got to the point where we could predict your responses and operations within Beatrice to around about ninety per cent accuracy. I know your whole plan with the software was to introduce randomness, to de-automate it, maximise its plasticity. But as you well know, Trina, most of us are a lot less random and a lot more automated than we all like to think. Which was the point I made to the rest of the big boys. Why not throw you a curveball? Why not map the last remaining variable? Why not, as it were, close the loop? Some of them totally grok'd it, some of them didn't. Hence: one of them spooked out and shut you down and fucked the whole thing up.'

'Close the loop? What loop? What variable?'

'The variable in which you see what we modelled. After that, the genie's out of the bottle. Everything that follows is entirely new territory. Paradigm shift, baby.'

'But I looked at Beatrice all the time. I *knew* there would be some kind of system to monitor how I used it. Everyone knows they're monitored. I mean, OK, I didn't fully comprehend the extent to which I was part of what you guys had planned, but—'

'Not Beatrice,' said Bangstrom.

'*Tayz?*' said Trina.

'If that's what you want to call him. Or her.'

'Oh my God.'

Bangstrom grinned.

'You know,' he said, 'I've never actually done this kind of response monitoring in a real-world, person-to-person situation. It's pretty exciting.'

'I wasn't supposed to see Tayz because I *am* Tayz.'

'Doppelgänger city, right?' Bangstrom widened his eyes in an expression of mock eeriness.

'Tayz is a virtual me.'

'Do you feel, like, maternal? Or sisterly? Or—'

'You've put me in the system.'

'Natural extension. We built Tayz as a virtual MT and watched to see if you could tell the difference. You couldn't. Then we thought: why limit ourselves? We modelled your de-automation initiative in order to re-automate it in a hopefully less obviously automated way. While you worked on Beatrice, Tayz worked on you. It was perfect:

all the behaviour data we needed came right out of the work you were already doing. Once you were fully mirrored, we started to let Tayz do the playing. Turns out nine out of ten cats couldn't tell the difference between Tayz running Beatrice and you running Beatrice. Neither, it turns out, could you. Problem was, of course, that once Tayz went semi-aware, he stopped MTing.'

'He saw the system.'

'He saw its limits. He adapted. He started reshaping the system for himself.'

'I wasn't always in control.'

'Sometimes we ran you in a dummy system. But the outputs were from the real system. You couldn't tell because Tayz's instincts were identical to yours.'

Trina felt sick.

'And now you know Tayz can run Beatrice—'

'We can roll the concept out to other networks.'

'Except by networks you mean people. Communities.'

'It was *always* people, Trina. Jesus Christ. You think when you were fucking around with all those parameters, you were just playing with pixels on a screen? Those MTs are people. Tayz excepted, you were playing around with people.'

'But those were people who'd signed up to—'

'Signed up to work, yes. But signed up to be fucked with? Not really.'

'Why me?' she said. 'I mean, of all the people. Why—'

'Your work on Beatrice was brilliant,' said Bangstrom. 'You got our attention. The more you did, the more we watched, the more possibilities we saw. And on top of all that, you fulfil certain . . . criteria.'

'You're kidding.'

'Jesus Christ,' said Bangstrom. 'You think we'd model *Bream*? Or Holt? You think we want those personalities loose in our systems? They're freaks, Trina. I'm a freak. We're all freaks here. We needed a fully functioning human being. You tick all the boxes. You understand Beatrice. Your identity matrix is unique. You have an intriguing history of . . . let's say unpredictability. You were an MT yourself. Shit, you even lived on the Larchwood. Where else could we access that kind of profile?'

Trina leaned forward and interlaced her fingers behind her neck, her forehead almost touching her knees.

'You've used every part of me,' she said. 'Every single fucking facet of my life you've—'

'Hey, spare me the pity party, OK? You should be flattered. People would kill for this.'

'My home,' she said. 'My family. My personality. My identity.' She looked up sharply. 'Were you looking at my Twitter? Was that how the whole fucking Bennington farrago kicked off? Did you do that too?'

'We didn't make you send that tweet, did we?'

'But given that I did?'

'Your Twitter profile was a variable we kept an eye on. I'd be lying if I said that we didn't see certain opportunities in—'

'In turning me over to Teddy frigging Handler and Hugo Bennington? Bangstrom, there was a *mob* outside my house.'

'I'll be the first to admit that once England Always got involved things got kind of messy. But still. The data—'

'Don't talk to me about fucking data, Bangstrom. That was my *life*.'

'Life is data, Trina. It's just information assembled.'

'Why tell me? Why tell me all this stuff? If your whole thing is that information is more valuable if it's collected without the subject being aware, why let me in on what you've done?'

'Don't tell me,' said Bangstrom, 'you wanted to know, and now you wish you didn't know.'

'At least when I didn't know, I still believed in what I was doing,' said Trina.

'Tayz isn't finished,' said Bangstrom. 'We need you to complete him. We thought about ways to do that without you knowing, but

374

my feeling was that they were too limited. We'd come to the end of that phase. Now we're in a new phase. Plus now we actually have a chance to map the complementary data. We've done not knowing, now we're doing knowing. Simple, really.'

'Fuck you,' she said. 'Fuck all of you. You smug, power-crazed fucking—'

'You say *you* like you're somehow not us,' said Bangstrom.

'I'm not you.'

'I think Tayz would feel otherwise.'

She shook her head.

'Tayz is a robot,' she said. 'Tayz can never be me.'

'Everyone likes to think that,' said Bangstrom. 'But even if it were true, which, I reiterate, it isn't, you're still here. You're still Inside The Building. Even if you walked out right now and never came back, which by the way you can't, you'd still basically be here. You'd still be us.'

'Why the *fuck*,' Trina spat, 'would I carry on here when you've wrecked my life?'

'How have we wrecked your life? We've given you a better life. You've got a better job, a better place to live. This is an upgrade. Trina 2.0.'

She shook her head.

'Shake your head all you like,' said Bangstrom. 'You know it's true. And besides, you're asking the question all wrong. You should be asking: why *wouldn't* you want to work on this? This is going to change the world, Trina. You really don't want to be a part of that? All your rhetoric about power and representation and opportunities, and then, when the chance comes along to be right at the heart of everything – literally, to *be* the change – you honestly expect me to believe you'll just go, *Oh, no thanks, I was happier when my work was meaningless?* Come off it. No-one's that principled. We *know* you, remember?'

'I can still surprise you,' she said.

Bangstrom stepped back, arms spread. 'Go ahead,' he said. 'Surprise me. I dare you.'

Trina said nothing, just stared at her knees, numbed by what she knew, the walls of her No-Go room not so much pressing in as bearing down. This was her future, she thought: nothing more than her past with a thin overlay. The same screen, the same walls. Everything Bangstrom had told her was designed simply to trap her. Now she was NTK. The punishment for not knowing enough was to be told more than you wanted to know. Whatever she shared now, under her new contract, would endanger her. They'd even moved her family in, so that they could endanger them too. Maybe, she thought, she should have walked while she had the chance. But where would she have gone? She thought again about her tweet, about Bennington, about the future of the estate. She thought about systems that didn't feel like systems, walled gardens within walled gardens, the engineered inability to distinguish freedom from control. Always, she thought, looking again at the blank, soundproofed walls of her No-Go room, they made you feel like you were breaking out, right up until the moment they put you back in the box.

'You want me to surprise you,' she said.

'What makes you say that?'

'It's the last thing left to model. What happens when people find out. What happens when ignorance becomes awareness. Mine's the last response you need.'

'And now we know,' said Bangstrom. 'We know what people do when they know.'

'What do they do?' said Trina.

He spread his arms, gesturing to the walls of the No-Go room, briefly inviting a weird embrace.

'They rush right back into our arms,' he said.

His smile, his expression of triumph, was one Trina would remember. Late at night, lying in bed, too terrified to sleep, her partners in ignorant slumber beside her, this was the face on which Trina would focus – the smile she would imagine herself erasing.

Bangstrom turned to the door.

'Take a week to move in,' he said. 'There's no rush to start up here.'

'Start what?' she said as he reached the door and tapped his swipe card against the reader. 'What am I even supposed to be doing?'

The door clicked unlocked. He pushed it open an inch and turned back to her, still beaming.

'Just be yourself,' he said.

By the time she got to Deepa's, it was beginning to rain. The thick, dark clouds that had congealed above the town threatened more than a passing shower. She chained her bike to the guttering and let herself in the front door using the key Deepa had given her. Deepa, it turned out, was finicky when it came to bikes in the hallway and the occasional streak of mud and grease on the wall. The bike had therefore been relegated to permanent outdoor status, another reminder that this was not, and would never be, Trina's home.

'Is that you?' Deepa called from the kitchen. 'We're in here.'

Deepa and Jess looked at her as she came in, unable to conceal their desire to interrogate her but just about able to restrain themselves from doing so. She flopped onto a chair and dropped her helmet onto the floor. Again, there was that comic-book sensation of her armour, her disguise, falling away. Only, now it was not so much liberating as terrifying. Even among friends, she felt exposed. She would always, now, feel exposed.

'Well?' said Deepa.

They had teas or coffees in front of them on the table. For some reason, the simplicity of the arrangement struck Trina as incongruous.

'I'm in,' she said.

'They offered you a contract?' said Jess.

Trina nodded. 'I gave them Norbiton, like we talked about.'

'I'll let him know via Zero and One,' said Deepa.

Trina shook her head. 'The whole thing,' she said, 'it's . . .' She tailed off, giving up on her attempt to say what it was.

'Fucked,' said Deepa.

Trina nodded. 'More than we thought,' she said. 'Worse than we thought.'

'Everything's all set up,' said Jess. 'Byron Stroud's ready to leak whatever you give him.'

'More than ready,' said Deepa. 'He's got offers from every outlet going.'

Jess shifted a little in her seat, as if her clothes were suddenly too tight, but said nothing.

'It'll be a while,' said Trina. 'I'll have to bed in.'

None of them had anything to add. Trina closed her eyes and tilted her head back.

'Well,' said Jess, 'here we are.'

'Here we are and here we go,' said Deepa.

'All day I've been wondering how this was going to feel,' said Jess.

'And?' said Deepa.

'And I think it will be a long time before I know,' said Jess.

'You OK?' said Deepa.

Realising that Deepa was talking to her, Trina opened her eyes and, with some effort, brought her head back to an upright position.

'I can't remember ever feeling so tired,' she said.

Deepa nodded. 'Hell of a day,' she said.

'Why don't you rest?' said Jess. 'There's nothing that needs to be done now.'

Trina nodded. 'Maybe I'll just chill out in the lounge for a bit.'

'Shout when you get hungry,' said Deepa. 'We can order takeaway.'

Trina smiled. 'And there was me thinking I'd come home to a cooked meal,' she said.

'I don't really understand cooking,' said Deepa. 'Except in a loose, theoretical sense.'

This made Trina laugh.

'Why am I not surprised?' she said.

She stood up, retrieved her bicycle helmet from the floor.

'Kind of draining,' she said, 'this whole sticking-it-to-the-man business.'

She made her way into the lounge and fell heavily into an armchair. She stretched, took off her shoes, and curled herself tightly into its embrace. This was the time she would usually sit and watch television with Bella.

She reached in her bag for her phone. Mia answered after two rings.

'Hey,' she said.

'Hey,' said Trina. 'Just letting you know, it's all agreed. I took the job, we've got somewhere to live.'

'I'm so proud of you,' said Mia. 'It's the right thing.'

'Yeah,' said Trina.

'You sound tired,' said Mia.

'I'm shattered,' said Trina.

'Get some rest. It's all over now.'

'Yeah.'

'It *is* all over, isn't it?'

''Course it is. That's it. All sorted.'

'It's the right thing,' Mia said again.

'I know.'

'We miss you a lot.'

'I miss you guys too. Couple more days and then we can move.'

'Everything back to normal.'

Trina felt herself about to hesitate, and in heading off the hesitation, she wound up answering too quickly. 'Yeah. Everything as it was.'

'Carl's bathing Bella, so . . .'

'It's fine, go and help him. Kiss them both from me.'

'Kisses to you too. We love you.'

'Love you too.'

She hung up, dropped the phone into the cushion-crease in the chair beside her, and closed her eyes again. *All fine*, she said to herself. *Everything back to normal.* It was, she realised, the first lie she'd told Mia and Carl. This, she saw, was how it was going to have to be. Each night, she'd come home and tell them work was fine. Each night, she'd shower and change and sit with Bella and, later, fall asleep with Mia and Carl. Together, in their Green-owned home, they'd all keep up the pretence that everything was fine, normal, safe. The secret would gnaw at her. Mia and Carl would sense her evasions. The not-quite-knowing would gnaw at them too. Fear, the inability to share it, would erode her inner and outer life.

She thought of Tayz, her digital replica, loose in the system, in many ways becoming the system, embodying it, absorbing it. Tayz was programmed, automated. He or she existed only within certain parameters of meaning and experience. And yet, somehow, within those limitations, Tayz was still freer than she would ever be.

So much of her life, she thought, had been spent chafing against the smallness of her surroundings. How many times had people said to her: Move away, move to the city, *be with people like you*. And how many times had she answered: It's not me that needs to move, it's Edmundsbury that needs to change. The world, she'd always thought, the future, would one day arrive here. It would come to her like it would come to everyone. Now it was here, and it was the opposite of what she'd always imagined. Viewed from a distance, the future was vast and open. Once you were in it, it was tiny. While she'd been scratching at the walls of her own small town, the world had become a small town around her.

These were her last few hours before it all began in earnest. She could pause, unwind, kid herself that this transitional moment was how life would continue to be: safe, simple, free of fear. From this brief lull, she could extrapolate, in her mind, another life, another future – a liveable, bearable reality. Nothing had yet happened. Nothing was yet real. As long as it could only be imagined, it could still conceivably be true.

———————

'You think she'll be OK?'

Deepa shrugged. 'I hope so.'

'It's not too late to call the whole thing off,' said Jess.

'You really believe that?'

'No.'

A surging wind flung a petulant fistful of rain at the window. They both looked up. On the kitchen worktop, a small speaker emitted the supposedly soothing sounds of one of Deepa's ASMR recordings: a sampled loop of rain-noise, layered over the rain-noise outside.

'She's doing this because she wants to, right?' said Jess.

'She doesn't seem the type to do things she doesn't want to do. But maybe that's simplistic. I mean, given the choice, she'd probably prefer not to. But I don't think that choice is really on the table.'

'No.'

Jess reached in her pocket for a cigarette, then looked around for something she could use as an ashtray.

'Uh uh,' said Deepa, wagging a finger and then pointing to the back door.

'You can't be serious. Look at it out there.'

'You want me to show you an image gallery of your lungs? You want *my* lungs to become those lungs? Call it my contribution to helping you give up. If you tuck yourself in the back door, you'll stay mainly dry.'

Jess stood up with an exaggerated and smiling flounce and walked to the back door. She had to counter the force of the wind to get it open. Outside, the rain had reached the point where it had become an all-consuming reality, a hissing din into which she tried to direct the smoke from her cigarette. She wondered how she felt: how much had really changed, how much had stayed the same.

She'd followed Robert's activity on Twitter – the death threats, the mounting solidarity. She'd wanted to text him, call him, ask him if he was OK, but she couldn't. For so many others, she thought, for her, hatred was real. For Robert, it was a career opportunity. It was not the only thing between them that couldn't be resolved, but somehow it seemed to contain everything between and around them that was irreconcilable. All this time spent wrestling with the differences between them, she thought, and in the end, what they shared had divided them.

Behind her, she could still make out Deepa's relaxation recording – a rainstorm reduced to a tinny, single-speaker simulacrum. In front of her, the downpour was a flickering, pixellated screen, the sound a rasping static – white noise layered with its own inadequate copy. She thought of snowy TV sets, hissing radio frequencies, the tinny squeal of dial-up modems. The association of this sibilant racket with devices been and gone gave her the feeling that rain itself was an obsolete technology.

She let her focus soften until the display of rain was something she looked not at but through, to the frayed hem of reality's overlay she'd glimpsed so many times before. There was nothing on earth that was not a technology. The climate, thought, her body. What she had been through, what had threatened her, what she had exposed and would go on exposing: all technologies, all systems – corrupted and stalling and glitching out into unpredictable obsolescence, replaced again and again by the technologies that were to come, just as she would be replaced by the versions of herself she imagined and was forced to be. She thought of Julia, Byron, Jasmine: in weightless motion, out there in the ether. You could live in the technologies of others, she thought, or you could build your own. It was invent or be invented, think or be thought, dream or be dreamed in turn.

She closed her eyes and surrendered herself to rain-sound. She imagined her face dissolving, lost to the squalling frequency of the deluge. She felt unpacked, dismantled, released from the structures that dreamed her.

Distinctions began to blur. Sampled rainsound merged with rainsound. Only the earthy smell of precipitation on soil reminded her what was real. *Petrichor*, she thought.

Inside her, an operating switch was thrown. There was the briefest of delays – a suspended, buffering moment before startup.

And then

Error 404: The page you are looking for does not yet exist

Thanks and appreciation:
To Arts Council England and The Society of Authors for generous financial assistance at critical moments.

To Peter Straus and his colleagues at RCW, whose advice and guidance were invaluable.

To Mitzi Angel, Emmie Francis, and everyone at Faber, for their clarity and dedication.

To Will Wiles and James Smythe, for their writerly support and friendship.

To my family: Sue, Richard, Mollie, Graham, and Marni.

And most of all to my partner, Zakia Uddin, whose research and writing on Microtasking helped me start this book, and whose patience and belief helped me finish it.